A Heron Books Collection

CROME YELLOW
ANTIC HAY

ALDOUS HUXLEY

CROME YELLOW
A NOVEL

ANTIC HAY
A NOVEL

Original Illustrations by Pauline Ellison

HERON BOOKS, LONDON

Published by arrangement with
Chatto & Windus Ltd., London

© *1968, Illustrations, Edito-Service S.A.*
Geneva, Switzerland

CONTENTS

CROME YELLOW

CHAPTER I

ALONG this particular stretch of line no express had ever passed. All the trains—the few that there were —stopped at all the stations. Denis knew the names of those stations by heart. Bole, Tritton, Spavin Delawarr, Knipswich for Timpany, West Bowlby, and, finally, Camlet-on-the-Water. Camlet was where he always got out, leaving the train to creep indolently onward, goodness only knew whither, into the green heart of England.

They were snorting out of West Bowlby now. It was the next station, thank Heaven. Denis took his chattels off the rack and piled them neatly in the corner opposite his own. A futile proceeding. But one must have something to do. When he had finished, he sank back into his seat and closed his eyes. It was extremely hot.

Oh, this journey! It was two hours cut clean out of his life; two hours in which he might have done so much, so much—written the perfect poem, for example, or read the one illuminating book. Instead of which—his gorge rose at the smell of the dusty cushions against which he was leaning.

Two hours. One hundred and twenty minutes. Anything might be done in that time. Anything. Nothing. Oh, he had had hundreds of hours, and what had he done with them? Wasted them, spilt the precious minutes as though his reservoir were inexhaustible. Denis groaned in the spirit, condemned himself utterly with all his works. What right had he to sit in the sunshine, to

occupy corner seats in third-class carriages, to be alive?
None, none, none.

Misery and a nameless nostalgic distress possessed
him. He was twenty-three, and oh! so agonizingly
conscious of the fact.

The train came bumpingly to a halt. Here was Camlet
at last. Denis jumped up, crammed his hat over his eyes,
deranged his pile of baggage, leaned out of the window
and shouted for a porter, seized a bag in either hand, and
had to put them down again in order to open the door.
When at last he had safely bundled himself and his
baggage on to the platform, he ran up the train towards
the van.

"A bicycle, a bicycle!" he said breathlessly to the
guard. He felt himself a man of action. The guard paid
no attention, but continued methodically to hand out,
one by one, the packages labelled to Camlet. "A bicycle!"
Denis repeated. "A green machine, cross-framed, name
of Stone. S–T–O–N–E."

"All in good time, sir," said the guard soothingly. He
was a large, stately man with a naval beard. One pictured
him at home, drinking tea, surrounded by a numerous
family. It was in that tone that he must have spoken to
his children when they were tiresome. "All in good time,
sir." Denis's man of action collapsed, punctured.

He left his luggage to be called for later, and pushed
off on his bicycle. He always took his bicycle when he
went into the country. It was part of the theory of
exercise. One day one would get up at six o'clock and
pedal away to Kenilworth, or Stratford-on-Avon—anywhere. And within a radius of twenty miles there were
always Norman churches and Tudor mansions to be seen
in the course of an afternoon's excursion. Somehow they

never did get seen, but all the same it was nice to feel that the bicycle was there, and that one fine morning one really might get up at six.

Once at the top of the long hill which led up from Camlet station, he felt his spirits mounting. The world, he found, was good. The far-away blue hills, the harvests whitening on the slopes of the ridge along which his road led him, the treeless sky-lines that changed as he moved —yes, they were all good. He was overcome by the beauty of those deeply embayed combes, scooped in the flanks of the ridge beneath him. Curves, curves: he repeated the word slowly, trying as he did so to find some term in which to give expression to his appreciation. Curves—no, that was inadequate. He made a gesture with his hand, as though to scoop the achieved expression out of the air, and almost fell off his bicycle. What was the word to describe the curves of those little valleys? They were as fine as the lines of a human body, they were informed with the subtlety of art. . . .

Galbe. That was a good word; but it was French. *Le galbe évasé de ses hanches*: had one ever read a French novel in which that phrase didn't occur? Some day he would compile a dictionary for the use of novelists. *Galbe, gonflé, goulu: parfum, peau, pervers, potelé, pudeur: vertu, volupté*.

But he really must find that word. Curves, curves. . . . Those little valleys had the lines of a cup moulded round a woman's breast; they seemed the dinted imprints of some huge divine body that had rested on these hills. Cumbrous locutions, these; but through them he seemed to be getting nearer to what he wanted. Dinted, dimpled, wimpled—his mind wandered down echoing corridors of assonance and alliteration ever further and further

13

from the point. He was enamoured with the beauty of words.

Becoming once more aware of the outer world, he found himself on the crest of a descent. The road plunged down, steep and straight, into a considerable valley. There, on the opposite slope, a little higher up the valley, stood Crome, his destination. He put on his brakes; this view of Crome was pleasant to linger over. The façade with its three projecting towers rose precipitously from among the dark trees of the garden. The house basked in full sunlight; the old brick rosily glowed. How ripe and rich it was, how superbly mellow! And at the same time, how austere! The hill was becoming steeper and steeper; he was gaining speed in spite of his brakes. He loosed his grip of the levers, and in a moment was rushing headlong down. Five minutes later he was passing through the gate of the great courtyard. The front door stood hospitably open. He left his bicycle leaning against the wall and walked in. He would take them by surprise.

CHAPTER II

HE took nobody by surprise; there was nobody to take. All was quiet; Denis wandered from room to empty room, looking with pleasure at the familiar pictures and furniture, at all the little untidy signs of life that lay scattered here and there. He was rather glad that they were all out; it was amusing to wander through the house as though one were exploring a dead, deserted Pompeii. What sort of life would the excavator reconstruct from these remains; how would he people these empty chambers? There was the long gallery, with its rows of respectable and (though, of course, one couldn't publicly admit it) rather boring Italian primitives, its Chinese sculptures, its unobtrusive, dateless furniture. There was the panelled drawing-room, where the huge chintz-covered arm-chairs stood, oases of comfort among the austere flesh-mortifying antiques. There was the morning-room, with its pale lemon walls, its painted Venetian chairs and rococo tables, its mirrors, its modern pictures. There was the library, cool, spacious, and dark, book-lined from floor to ceiling, rich in portentous folios. There was the dining-room, solidly, portwinily English, with its great mahogany table, its eighteenth-century chairs and sideboard, its eighteenth-century pictures—family portraits, meticulous animal paintings. What could one reconstruct from such data? There was much of Henry Wimbush in the long gallery and the library, something of Anne, perhaps, in the morning-room. That was all. Among the accumulations of ten generations the living had left but few traces.

15

Lying on the table in the morning-room he saw his own book of poems. What tact! He picked it up and opened it. It was what the reviewers call "a slim volume." He read at hazard:

> ". . . But silence and the topless dark
> Vault in the lights of Luna Park
> And Blackpool from the nightly gloom
> Hollows a bright tumultuous tomb."

He put it down again, shook his head, and sighed. "What genius I had then!" he reflected, echoing the aged Swift. It was nearly six months since the book had been published; he was glad to think he would never write anything of the same sort again. Who could have been reading it, he wondered? Anne, perhaps; he liked to think so. Perhaps, too, she had at last recognized herself in the Hamadryad of the poplar sapling; the slim Hamadryad whose movements were like the swaying of a young tree in the wind. "The Woman who was a Tree" was what he had called the poem. He had given her the book when it came out, hoping that the poem would tell her what he hadn't dared to say. She had never referred to it.

He shut his eyes and saw a vision of her in a red velvet cloak, swaying into the little restaurant where they sometimes dined together in London—three quarters of an hour late, and he at his table, haggard with anxiety, irritation, hunger. Oh, she was damnable!

It occurred to him that perhaps his hostess might be in her boudoir. It was a possibility; he would go and see. Mrs. Wimbush's boudoir was in the central tower on the garden front. A little staircase corkscrewed up to it from the hall. Denis mounted, tapped at the door. "Come in."

Ah, she was there; he had rather hoped she wouldn't be. He opened the door.

Priscilla Wimbush was lying on the sofa. A blotting-pad rested on her knees and she was thoughtfully sucking the end of a silver pencil.

"Hullo," she said, looking up. "I'd forgotten you were coming."

"Well, here I am, I'm afraid," said Denis deprecatingly. "I'm awfully sorry."

Mrs. Wimbush laughed. Her voice, her laughter, were deep and masculine. Everything about her was manly. She had a large, square, middle-aged face, with a massive projecting nose and little greenish eyes, the whole surmounted by a lofty and elaborate coiffure of a curiously improbable shade of orange. Looking at her, Denis always thought of Wilkie Bard as the cantatrice.

> "That's why I'm going to
> Sing in op'ra, sing in op'ra,
> Sing in op-pop-pop-pop-popera."

To-day she was wearing a purple silk dress with a high collar and a row of pearls. The costume, so richly dowagerish, so suggestive of the Royal Family, made her look more than ever like something on the Halls.

"What have you been doing all this time?" she asked.

"Well," said Denis, and he hesitated, almost voluptuously. He had a tremendously amusing account of London and its doings all ripe and ready in his mind. It would be a pleasure to give it utterance. "To begin with," he said . . .

But he was too late. Mrs. Wimbush's question had been what the grammarians call rhetorical; it asked for

17

no answer. It was a little conversational flourish, a gambit in the polite game.

"You find me busy at my horoscopes," she said, without even being aware that she had interrupted him.

A little pained, Denis decided to reserve his story for more receptive ears. He contented himself, by way of revenge, with saying "Oh?" rather icily.

"Did I tell you how I won four hundred on the Grand National this year?"

"Yes," he replied, still frigid and monosyllabic. She must have told him at least six times.

"Wonderful, isn't it? Everything is in the Stars. In the Old Days, before I had the Stars to help me, I used to lose thousands. Now"—she paused an instant—"well, look at that four hundred on the Grand National. That's the Stars."

Denis would have liked to hear more about the Old Days. But he was too discreet and, still more, too shy to ask. There had been something of a bust up; that was all he knew. Old Priscilla—not so old then, of course, and sprightlier—had lost a great deal of money, dropped it in handfuls and hatfuls on every racecourse in the country. She had gambled too. The number of thousands varied in the different legends, but all put it high. Henry Wimbush was forced to sell some of his Primitives—a Taddeo da Poggibonsi, an Amico di Taddeo, and four or five nameless Sienese—to the Americans. There was a crisis. For the first time in his life Henry asserted himself, and with good effect, it seemed.

Priscilla's gay and gadding existence had come to an abrupt end. Nowadays she spent almost all her time at Crome, cultivating a rather ill-defined malady. For consolation she dallied with New Thought and the Occult.

Her passion for racing still possessed her, and Henry, who was a kind-hearted fellow at bottom, allowed her forty pounds a month betting money. Most of Priscilla's days were spent in casting the horoscopes of horses, and she invested her money scientifically, as the Stars dictated. She betted on football too, and had a large notebook in which she registered the horoscopes of all the players in all the teams of the League. The process of balancing the horoscopes of two elevens one against the other was a very delicate and difficult one. A match between the Spurs and the Villa entailed a conflict in the heavens so vast and so complicated that it was not to be wondered at if she sometimes made a mistake about the outcome.

"Such a pity you don't believe in these things, Denis, such a pity," said Mrs. Wimbush in her deep, distinct voice.

"I can't say I feel it so."

"Ah, that's because you don't know what it's like to have faith. You've no idea how amusing and exciting life becomes when you do believe. All that happens means something; nothing you do is ever insignificant. It makes life so jolly, you know. Here am I at Crome. Dull as ditchwater, you'd think; but no, I don't find it so. I don't regret the Old Days a bit. I have the Stars . . ." She picked up the sheet of paper that was lying on the blotting-pad. "Inman's horoscope," she explained. "(I thought I'd like to have a little fling on the billiards championship this autumn.) I have the Infinite to keep in tune with," she waved her hand. "And then there's the next world and all the spirits, and one's Aura, and Mrs. Eddy and saying you're not ill, and the Christian Mysteries and Mrs. Besant. It's all splendid. One's never dull for a moment. I can't think how I used to get on before—in the Old Days. Pleasure?—running about, that's all it was; just running about. Lunch, tea, dinner, theatre, supper, every day. It was fun, of course, while it lasted. But there wasn't much left of it afterwards. There's rather a good thing about that in Barbecue-Smith's new book. Where is it?"

She sat up and reached for a book that was lying on the little table by the head of the sofa.

"Do you know him, by the way?" she asked.

"Who?"

"Mr. Barbecue-Smith."

Denis knew of him vaguely. Barbecue-Smith was a name in the Sunday papers. He wrote about the Conduct of Life. He might even be the author of *What a Young Girl Ought to Know*.

"No, not personally," he said.

"I've invited him for next week-end." She turned over the pages of the book. "Here's the passage I was thinking of. I marked it. I always mark the things I like."

Holding the book almost at arm's length, for she was somewhat long-sighted, and making suitable gestures with her free hand, she began to read, slowly, dramatically.

"'What are thousand pound fur coats, what are quarter million incomes?'" She looked up from the page with a histrionic movement of the head; her orange coiffure nodded portentously. Denis looked at it, fascinated. Was it the Real Thing and henna, he wondered, or was it one of those Complete Transformations one sees in the advertisements?

"'What are Thrones and Sceptres?'"

The orange Transformation—yes, it must be a Transformation—bobbed up again.

"'What are the gaieties of the Rich, the splendours of

20

the Powerful, what is the pride of the Great, what are the gaudy pleasures of High Society?'"

The voice, which had risen in tone, questioningly, from sentence to sentence, dropped suddenly and boomed reply.

"'They are nothing. Vanity, fluff, dandelion seed in the wind, thin vapours of fever. The things that matter happen in the heart. Seen things are sweet, but those unseen are a thousand times more significant. It is the Unseen that counts in Life.'"

Mrs. Wimbush lowered the book. "Beautiful, isn't it?" she said.

Denis preferred not to hazard an opinion, but uttered a non-committal "H'm."

"Ah, it's a fine book this, a beautiful book," said Priscilla, as she let the pages flick back, one by one, from under her thumb. "And here's the passage about the Lotus Pool. He compares the Soul to a Lotus Pool, you know." She held up the book again and read. "'A Friend of mine has a Lotus Pool in his garden. It lies in a little dell embowered with wild roses and eglantine, among which the nightingale pours forth its amorous descant all the summer long. Within the pool the Lotuses blossom, and the birds of the air come to drink and bathe themselves in its crystal waters. . . .' Ah, and that reminds me," Priscilla exclaimed, shutting the book with a clap and uttering her big profound laugh—"that reminds me of the things that have been going on in our bathing-pool since you were here last. We gave the village people leave to come and bathe here in the evenings. You've no idea of the things that happened."

She leaned forward, speaking in a confidential whisper; every now and then she uttered a deep gurgle of laughter.

". . . mixed bathing . . . saw them out of my window
. . . sent for a pair of field-glasses to make sure . . . no
doubt of it. . . ." The laughter broke out again. Denis
laughed too. Barbecue-Smith was tossed on the floor.

"It's time we went to see if tea's ready," said Priscilla.
She hoisted herself up from the sofa and went swishing
off across the room, striding beneath the trailing silk.
Denis followed her, faintly humming to himself:

> "That's why I'm going to
> Sing in op'ra, sing in op'ra,
> Sing in op-pop-pop-pop-popera."

And then the little twiddly bit of accompaniment at the
end: "ra-ra."

CHAPTER III

THE terrace in front of the house was a long narrow
strip of turf, bounded along its outer edge by a
graceful stone balustrade. Two little summer-houses of
brick stood at either end. Below the house the ground
sloped very steeply away, and the terrace was a remark-
ably high one; from the balusters to the sloping lawn
beneath was a drop of thirty feet. Seen from below, the
high unbroken terrace wall, built like the house itself of
brick, had the almost menacing aspect of a fortification—
a castle bastion, from whose parapet one looked out
across airy depths to distances level with the eye. Below,
in the foreground, hedged in by solid masses of sculptured yew trees, lay the stone-brimmed swimming-pool.
Beyond it stretched the park, with its massive elms, its
green expanses of grass, and, at the bottom of the valley,
the gleam of the narrow river. On the farther side of the
stream the land rose again in a long slope, chequered
with cultivation. Looking up the valley, to the right, one
saw a line of blue, far-off hills.

The tea-table had been planted in the shade of one of
the little summer-houses, and the rest of the party was
already assembled about it when Denis and Priscilla made
their appearance. Henry Wimbush had begun to pour
out the tea. He was one of those ageless, unchanging
men on the farther side of fifty, who might be thirty,
who might be anything. Denis had known him almost as
long as he could remember. In all those years his pale,
rather handsome face had never grown any older; it was

23

like the pale grey bowler hat which he always wore, winter and summer—unageing, calm, serenely without expression.

Next him, but separated from him and from the rest of the world by the almost impenetrable barriers of·her deafness, sat Jenny Mullion. She was perhaps thirty, had a tilted nose and a pink-and-white complexion, and wore her brown hair plaited and coiled in two lateral buns over her ears. In the secret tower of her deafness she sat apart, looking down at the world through sharply piercing eyes. What did she think of men and women and things? That was something that Denis had never been able to discover. In her enigmatic remoteness Jenny was a little disquieting. Even now some interior joke seemed to be amusing her, for she was smiling to herself, and her brown eyes were like very bright round marbles.

On his other side the serious, moon-like innocence of Mary Bracegirdle's face shone pink and childish. She was nearly twenty-three, but one wouldn't have guessed it. Her short hair, clipped like a page's, hung in a bell of elastic gold about her cheeks. She had large blue china eyes, whose expression was one of ingenuous and often puzzled earnestness.

Next to Mary a small gaunt man was sitting, rigid and erect in his chair. In appearance Mr. Scogan was like one of those extinct bird-lizards of the Tertiary. His nose was beaked, his dark eye had the shining quickness of a robin's. But there was nothing soft or gracious or feathery about him. The skin of his wrinkled brown face had a dry and scaly look; his hands were the hands of a crocodile. His movements were marked by the lizard's disconcertingly abrupt clockwork speed; his speech was thin, fluty, and dry. Henry Wimbush's schoolfellow and exact contemporary, Mr. Scogan looked far older and, at the same time, far more youthfully alive than did that gentle aristocrat with the face like a grey bowler.

Mr. Scogan might look like an extinct saurian, but Gombauld was altogether and essentially human. In the old-fashioned natural histories of the 'thirties he might have figured in a steel engraving as a type of Homo Sapiens—an honour which at that time commonly fell to Lord Byron. Indeed, with more hair and less collar, Gombauld would have been completely Byronic—more than Byronic, even, for Gombauld was of Provençal descent, a black-haired young corsair of thirty, with flashing teeth and luminous large dark eyes. Denis looked at him enviously. He was jealous of his talent: if only he wrote verse as well as Gombauld painted pictures! Still more, at the moment, he envied Gombauld his looks, his vitality, his easy confidence of manner. Was it surprising that Anne should like him? Like him?—it might even be something worse, Denis reflected bitterly, as he walked at Priscilla's side down the long grass terrace.

Between Gombauld and Mr. Scogan a very much lowered deck-chair presented its back to the new arrivals as they advanced towards the tea-table. Gombauld was leaning over it; his face moved vivaciously; he smiled, he laughed, he made quick gestures with his hands. From the depths of the chair came up a sound of soft, lazy laughter. Denis started as he heard it. That laughter—how well he knew it! What emotions it evoked in him! He quickened his pace.

In her low deck-chair Anne was nearer to lying than to sitting. Her long, slender body reposed in an attitude of listless and indolent grace. Within its setting of light brown hair her face had a pretty regularity that was almost doll-like. And indeed there were moments when she seemed nothing more than a doll; when the oval face, with its long-lashed, pale blue eyes, expressed nothing; when it was no more than a lazy mask of wax. She was Henry Wimbush's own niece; that bowler-like countenance was one of the Wimbush heirlooms; it ran in the family, appearing in its female members as a blank doll-face. But across this dollish mask, like a gay melody dancing over an unchanging fundamental bass, passed Anne's other inheritance—quick laughter, light ironic amusement, and the changing expressions of many moods. She was smiling now as Denis looked down at her: her cat's smile, he called it, for no very good reason. The mouth was compressed, and on either side of it two tiny wrinkles had formed themselves in her cheeks. An infinity of slightly malicious amusement lurked in those little folds, in the puckers about the half-closed eyes, in the eyes themselves, bright and laughing between the narrowed lids.

The preliminary greetings spoken, Denis found an empty chair between Gombauld and Jenny and sat down.

"How are you, Jenny?" he shouted to her.

Jenny nodded and smiled in mysterious silence, as though the subject of her health were a secret that could not be publicly divulged.

"How's London been since I went away?" Anne inquired from the depth of her chair.

The moment had come; the tremendously amusing narrative was waiting for utterance. "Well," said Denis, smiling happily, "to begin with . . ."

"Has Priscilla told you of our great antiquarian find?" Henry Wimbush leaned forward; the most promising of buds was nipped.

26

"To begin with," said Denis desperately, "there was the Ballet . . ."

"Last week," Mr. Wimbush went on softly and implacably, "we dug up fifty yards of oaken drain-pipes; just tree trunks with a hole bored through the middle. Very interesting indeed. Whether they were laid down by the monks in the fifteenth century, or whether . . ."

Denis listened gloomily. "Extraordinary!" he said, when Mr. Wimbush had finished; "quite extraordinary!" He helped himself to another slice of cake. He didn't even want to tell his tale about London now; he was damped.

For some time past Mary's grave blue eyes had been fixed upon him. "What have you been writing lately?" she asked. It would be nice to have a little literary conversation.

"Oh, verse and prose," said Denis—"just verse and prose."

"Prose?" Mr. Scogan pounced alarmingly on the word. "You've been writing prose?"

"Yes."

"Not a novel?"

"Yes."

"My poor Denis!" exclaimed Mr. Scogan. "What about?"

Denis felt rather uncomfortable. "Oh, about the usual things, you know."

"Of course," Mr. Scogan groaned. "I'll describe the plot for you. Little Percy, the hero, was never good at games, but he was always clever. He passes through the usual public school and the usual university and comes to London, where he lives among the artists. He is bowed down with melancholy thought; he carries the

27

whole weight of the universe upon his shoulders. He writes a novel of dazzling brilliance; he dabbles delicately in Amour and disappears, at the end of the book, into the luminous Future."

Denis blushed scarlet. Mr. Scogan had described the plan of his novel with an accuracy that was appalling. He made an effort to laugh. "You're entirely wrong," he said. "My novel is not in the least like that." It was a heroic lie. Luckily, he reflected, only two chapters were written. He would tear them up that very evening when he unpacked.

Mr. Scogan paid no attention to his denial, but went on: "Why will you young men continue to write about things that are so entirely uninteresting as the mentality of adolescents and artists? Professional anthropologists might find it interesting to turn sometimes from the beliefs of the Blackfellow to the philosophical pre-occupations of the undergraduate. But you can't expect an ordinary adult man, like myself, to be much moved by the story of his spiritual troubles. And after all, even in England, even in Germany and Russia, there are more adults than adolescents. As for the artist, he is preoccupied with problems that are so utterly unlike those of the ordinary adult man—problems of pure æsthetics which don't so much as present themselves to people like myself —that a description of his mental processes is as boring to the ordinary reader as a piece of pure mathematics. A serious book about artists regarded as artists is unreadable; and a book about artists regarded as lovers, husbands, dipsomaniacs, heroes, and the like is really not worth writing again. Jean-Christophe is the stock artist of literature, just as Professor Radium of *Comic Cuts* is its stock man of science."

"I'm sorry to hear I'm as uninteresting as all that," said Gombauld.

"Not at all, my dear Gombauld," Mr. Scogan hastened to explain. "As a lover or a dipsomaniac, I've no doubt of your being a most fascinating specimen. But as a combiner of forms, you must honestly admit it, you're a bore."

"I entirely disagree with you," exclaimed Mary. She was somehow always out of breath when she talked, and her speech was punctuated by little gasps. "I've known a great many artists, and I've always found their mentality very interesting. Especially in Paris. Tschuplitski, for example—I saw a great deal of Tschuplitski in Paris this spring. . . ."

"Ah, but then you're an exception, Mary, you're an exception," said Mr. Scogan. "You are a *femme supérieure*."

A flush of pleasure turned Mary's face into a harvest moon.

CHAPTER IV

DENIS woke up next morning to find the sun shining, the sky serene. He decided to wear white flannel trousers—white flannel trousers and a black jacket, with a silk shirt and his new peach-coloured tie. And what shoes? White was the obvious choice, but there was something rather pleasing about the notion of black patent leather. He lay in bed for several minutes considering the problem.

Before he went down—patent leather was his final choice—he looked at himself critically in the glass. His hair might have been more golden, he reflected. As it was, its yellowness had the hint of a greenish tinge in it. But his forehead was good. His forehead made up in height what his chin lacked in prominence. His nose might have been longer, but it would pass. His eyes might have been blue and not green. But his coat was very well cut and, discreetly padded, made him seem robuster than he actually was. His legs, in their white casing, were long and elegant. Satisfied, he descended the stairs. Most of the party had already finished their breakfast. He found himself alone with Jenny.

"I hope you slept well," he said.

"Yes, isn't it lovely?" Jenny replied, giving two rapid little nods. "But we had such awful thunderstorms last week."

Parallel straight lines, Denis reflected, meet only at infinity. He might talk for ever of care-charmer sleep and she of meteorology till the end of time. Did one ever establish contact with anyone? We are all parallel straight lines. Jenny was only a little more parallel than most.

"They are very alarming, these thunderstorms," he said, helping himself to porridge. "Don't you think so? Or are you above being frightened?"

"No. I always go to bed in a storm. One is so much safer lying down."

"Why?"

"Because," said Jenny, making a descriptive gesture, "because lightning goes downwards and not flat ways. When you're lying down you're out of the current."

"That's very ingenious."

"It's true."

There was a silence. Denis finished his porridge and helped himself to bacon. For lack of anything better to say, and because Mr. Scogan's absurd phrase was for some reason running in his head, he turned to Jenny and asked:

"Do you consider yourself a *femme supérieure?*" He had to repeat the question several times before Jenny got the hang of it.

"No," she said, rather indignantly, when at last she heard what Denis was saying. "Certainly not. Has anyone been suggesting that I am?"

"No," said Denis. "Mr. Scogan told Mary she was one."

"Did he?" Jenny lowered her voice. "Shall I tell you what I think of that man? I think he's slightly sinister."

Having made this pronouncement, she entered the ivory tower of her deafness and closed the door. Denis could not induce her to say anything more, could not induce her even to listen. She just smiled at him, smiled and occasionally nodded.

Denis went out on to the terrace to smoke his after-breakfast pipe and to read his morning paper. An hour later, when Anne came down, she found him still reading. By this time he had got to the Court Circular and the Forthcoming Weddings. He got up to meet her as she approached, a Hamadryad in white muslin, across the grass.

"Why, Denis," she exclaimed, "you look perfectly sweet in your white trousers."

Denis was dreadfully taken aback. There was no possible retort. "You speak as though I were a child in a new frock," he said, with a show of irritation.

"But that's how I feel about you, Denis dear."

"Then you oughtn't to."

"But I can't help it. I'm so much older than you."

"I like that," he said. "Four years older."

"And if you do look perfectly sweet in your white trousers, why shouldn't I say so? And why did you put them on, if you didn't think you were going to look sweet in them?"

"Let's go into the garden," said Denis. He was put out; the conversation had taken such a preposterous and unexpected turn. He had planned a very different opening, in which he was to lead off with, "You look adorable this morning," or something of the kind, and she was to answer, "Do I?" and then there was to be a pregnant silence. And now she had got in first with the trousers. It was provoking; his pride was hurt.

That part of the garden that sloped down from the foot of the terrace to the pool had a beauty which did not depend on colour so much as on forms. It was as beautiful by moonlight as in the sun. The silver of water, the dark shapes of yew and ilex trees remained, at all hours and seasons, the dominant features of the scene. It was a landscape in black and white. For colour there was the flower-garden; it lay to one side of the pool, separated from it by a huge Babylonian wall of yews. You passed through a tunnel in the hedge, you opened a wicket in a wall, and you found yourself, startlingly and suddenly, in the world of colour. The July borders blazed and flared under the sun. Within its high brick walls the garden was like a great tank of warmth and perfume and colour.

Denis held open the little iron gate for his companion. "It's like passing from a cloister into an Oriental palace," he said, and took a deep breath of the warm, flower-scented air. "'In fragrant volleys they let fly . . .' How does it go?

> "'Well shot, ye firemen! O how sweet
> And round your equal fires do meet;
> Whose shrill report no ear can tell,
> But echoes to the eye and smell . . .'"

"You have a bad habit of quoting," said Anne. "As I never know the context or author, I find it humiliating."

Denis apologized. "It's the fault of one's education. Things somehow seem more real and vivid when one can apply somebody else's ready-made phrase about them. And then there are lots of lovely names and words— Monophysite, Iamblichus, Pomponazzi; you bring them out triumphantly, and feel you've clinched the argument with the mere magical sound of them. That's what comes of the higher education."

"You may regret your education," said Anne; "I'm ashamed of my lack of it. Look at those sunflowers! Aren't they magnificent?"

"Dark faces and golden crowns—they're kings in Ethiopia. And I like the way the tits cling to the flowers and pick out the seeds, while the other loutish birds, grubbing dirtily for their food, look up in envy from the ground. Do they look up in envy? That's the literary touch, I'm afraid. Education again. It always comes back to that." He was silent.

Anne had sat down on a bench that stood in the shade of an old apple tree. "I'm listening," she said.

He did not sit down, but walked backwards and forwards in front of the bench, gesticulating a little as he talked. "Books," he said—"books. One reads so many, and one sees so few people and so little of the world. Great thick books about the universe and the mind and ethics. You've no idea how many there are. I must have read twenty or thirty tons of them in the last five years. Twenty tons of ratiocination. Weighted with that, one's pushed out into the world."

He went on walking up and down. His voice rose, fell, was silent a moment, and then talked on. He moved his hands, sometimes he waved his arms. Anne looked and listened quietly, as though she were at a lecture. He was a nice boy, and to-day he looked charming—charming!

One entered the world, Denis pursued, having ready-made ideas about everything. One had a philosophy and tried to make life fit into it. One should have lived first and then made one's philosophy to fit life. . . . Life, facts, things were horribly complicated; ideas, even the most difficult of them, deceptively simple. In the world of ideas everything was clear; in life all was obscure, embroiled. Was it surprising that one was miserable, horribly unhappy? Denis came to a halt in front of the bench, and as he asked this last question he stretched out his arms and stood for an instant in an attitude of crucifixion, then let them fall again to his sides.

"My poor Denis!" Anne was touched. He was really too pathetic as he stood there in front of her in his white flannel trousers. "But does one suffer about these things? It seems very extraordinary."

"You're like Scogan," cried Denis bitterly. "You regard me as a specimen for an anthropologist. Well, I suppose I am."

"No, no," she protested, and drew in her skirt with a gesture that indicated that he was to sit down beside her. He sat down. "Why can't you just take things for granted and as they come?" she asked. "It's so much simpler."

"Of course it is," said Denis. "But it's a lesson to be learnt gradually. There are the twenty tons of ratiocination to be got rid of first."

"I've always taken things as they come," said Anne. "It seems so obvious. One enjoys the pleasant things, avoids the nasty ones. There's nothing more to be said."

"Nothing—for you. But, then, you were born a pagan; I am trying laboriously to make myself one. I can take nothing for granted, I can enjoy nothing as it comes along. Beauty, pleasure, art, women—I have to invent an excuse, a justification for everything that's delightful. Otherwise I can't enjoy it with an easy conscience. I make up a little story about beauty and pretend that it has something to do with truth and goodness. I have to say that art is the process by which one reconstructs the divine reality out of chaos. Pleasure is one of the mystical roads to union with the infinite—the ecstasies of drinking, dancing, love-making. As for women, I am perpetually assuring myself that they're the broad highway to divinity. And to think that I'm only just beginning to see through the silliness of the whole thing! It's incredible to me that anyone should have escaped these horrors."

"It's still more incredible to me," said Anne, "that anyone should have been a victim to them. I should like to see myself believing that men are the highway to divinity." The amused malice of her smile planted two little folds on either side of her mouth, and through their half-closed lids her eyes shone with laughter. "What you need, Denis, is a nice plump young wife, a fixed income, and a little congenial but regular work."

"What I need is you." That was what he ought to have retorted, that was what he wanted passionately to say. He could not say it. His desire fought against his shyness. "What I need is you." Mentally he shouted the words, but not a sound issued from his lips. He looked at her despairingly. Couldn't she see what was going on inside him? Couldn't she understand? "What I need is you." He would say it, he would—he would.

"I think I shall go and bathe," said Anne. "It's so hot." The opportunity had passed.

CHAPTER V

M R. WIMBUSH had taken them to see the sights of the Home Farm, and now they were standing, all six of them—Henry Wimbush, Mr. Scogan, Denis, Gombauld, Anne, and Mary—by the low wall of the piggery, looking into one of the styes.

"This is a good sow," said Henry Wimbush. "She had a litter of fourteen."

"Fourteen?" Mary echoed incredulously. She turned astonished blue eyes towards Mr. Wimbush, then let them fall on to the seething mass of *élan vital* that fermented in the sty.

An immense sow reposed on her side in the middle of the pen. Her round, black belly, fringed with a double line of dugs, presented itself to the assault of an army of small, brownish-black swine. With a frantic greed they tugged at their mother's flank. The old sow stirred sometimes uneasily or uttered a little grunt of pain. One small pig, the runt, the weakling of the litter, had been unable to secure a place at the banquet. Squealing shrilly, he ran backwards and forwards, trying to push in among his stronger brothers or even to climb over their tight little black backs towards the maternal reservoir.

"There *are* fourteen," said Mary. "You're quite right. I counted. It's extraordinary."

"The sow next door," Mr. Wimbush went on, "has done very badly. She only had five in her litter. I shall give her another chance. If she does no better next time, I shall fat her up and kill her. There's the boar," he pointed towards a farther sty. "Fine old beast, isn't he? But he's getting past his prime. He'll have to go too."

"How cruel!" Anne exclaimed.

"But how practical, how eminently realistic!" said Mr. Scogan. "In this farm we have a model of sound paternal government. Make them breed, make them work, and when they're past working or breeding or begetting, slaughter them."

"Farming seems to be mostly indecency and cruelty," said Anne.

With the ferrule of his walking-stick Denis began to scratch the boar's long bristly back. The animal moved a little so as to bring himself within easier range of the instrument that evoked in him such delicious sensations; then he stood stock still, softly grunting his contentment. The mud of years flaked off his sides in a grey powdery scurf.

"What a pleasure it is," said Denis, "to do somebody a kindness. I believe I enjoy scratching this pig quite as much as he enjoys being scratched. If only one could always be kind with so little expense of trouble. . . ."

A gate slammed; there was a sound of heavy footsteps.

"Morning, Rowley!" said Henry Wimbush.

"Morning, sir," old Rowley answered. He was the most venerable of the labourers on the farm—a tall, solid man, still unbent, with grey side-whiskers and a steep, dignified profile. Grave, weighty in his manner, splendidly respectable, Rowley had the air of a great English states-man of the mid-nineteenth century. He halted on the outskirts of the group, and for a moment they all looked at the pigs in a silence that was only broken by the sound of grunting or the squelch of a sharp hoof in the mire. Rowley turned at last, slowly and ponderously and nobly, as he did everything, and addressed himself to Henry Wimbush.

"Look at them, sir," he said, with a motion of his hand towards the wallowing swine. "Rightly is they called pigs."

"Rightly indeed," Mr. Wimbush agreed.

"I am abashed by that man," said Mr. Scogan, as old Rowley plodded off slowly and with dignity. "What wisdom, what judgment, what a sense of values! 'Rightly are they called swine.' Yes. And I wish I could, with as much justice, say, 'Rightly are we called men.'"

They walked on towards the cowsheds and the stables of the cart-horses. Five white geese, taking the air this fine morning, even as they were doing, met them in the way. They hesitated, cackled; then, converting their lifted necks into rigid, horizontal snakes, they rushed off in disorder, hissing horribly as they went. Red calves paddled in the dung and mud of a spacious yard. In another enclosure stood the bull, massive as a locomotive. He was a very calm bull, and his face wore an expression of melancholy stupidity. He gazed with reddish-brown eyes at his visitors, chewed thoughtfully at the tangible memories of an earlier meal, swallowed and regurgitated, chewed again. His tail lashed savagely from side to side; it seemed to have nothing to do with his impassive bulk. Between his short horns was a triangle of red curls, short and dense.

"Splendid animal," said Henry Wimbush. "Pedigree stock. But he's getting a little old, like the boar."

39

"Fat him up and slaughter him," Mr. Scogan pronounced, with a delicate old-maidish precision of utterance.

"Couldn't you give the animals a little holiday from producing children?" asked Anne. "I'm so sorry for the poor things."

Mr. Wimbush shook his head. "Personally," he said, "I rather like seeing fourteen pigs grow where only one grew before. The spectacle of so much crude life is refreshing."

"I'm glad to hear you say so," Gombauld broke in warmly. "Lots of life: that's what we want. I like pullulation; everything ought to increase and multiply as hard as it can."

Gombauld grew lyrical. Everybody ought to have children—Anne ought to have them, Mary ought to have them—dozens and dozens. He emphasized his point by thumping with his walking-stick on the bull's leather flanks. Mr. Scogan ought to pass on his intelligence to little Scogans, and Denis to little Denises. The bull turned his head to see what was happening, regarded the drumming stick for several seconds, then turned back again satisfied, it seemed, that nothing was happening. Sterility was odious, unnatural, a sin against life. Life, life, and still more life. The ribs of the placid bull resounded.

Standing with his back against the farmyard pump, a little apart, Denis examined the group. Gombauld, passionate and vivacious, was its centre. The others stood round, listening—Henry Wimbush, calm and polite beneath his grey bowler; Mary, with parted lips and eyes that shone with the indignation of a convinced birth-controller. Anne looked on through half-shut eyes, smiling; and beside her stood Mr. Scogan, bolt upright in an attitude of metallic rigidity that contrasted strangely with that fluid grace of hers which even in stillness suggested a soft movement.

Gombauld ceased talking, and Mary, flushed and outraged, opened her mouth to refute him. But she was too slow. Before she could utter a word Mr. Scogan's fluty voice had pronounced the opening phrases of a discourse. There was no hope of getting so much as a word in edgeways; Mary had perforce to resign herself.

"Even your eloquence, my dear Gombauld," he was saying—"even your eloquence must prove inadequate to reconvert the world to a belief in the delights of mere multiplication. With the gramophone, the cinema, and the automatic pistol, the goddess of Applied Science has presented the world with another gift, more precious even than these—the means of dissociating love from propagation. Eros, for those who wish it, is now an entirely free god; his deplorable associations with Lucina may be broken at will. In the course of the next few centuries, who knows? the world may see a more complete severance. I look forward to it optimistically. Where the great Erasmus Darwin and Miss Anna Seward, Swan of Lichfield, experimented—and, for all their scientific ardour, failed—our descendants will experiment and succeed. An impersonal generation will take the place of Nature's hideous system. In vast state incubators, rows upon rows of gravid bottles will supply the world with the population it requires. The family system will disappear; society, sapped at its very base, will have to find new foundations; and Eros, beautifully and irresponsibly free, will flit like a gay butterfly from flower to flower through a sunlit world."

"It sounds lovely," said Anne.

"The distant future always does."

Mary's china blue eyes, more serious and more aston-ished than ever, were fixed on Mr. Scogan. "Bottles?" she said. "Do you really think so? Bottles. . . ."

CHAPTER VI

MR. BARBECUE-SMITH arrived in time for tea on Saturday afternoon. He was a short and corpulent man, with a very large head and no neck. In his earlier middle age he had been distressed by this absence of neck, but was comforted by reading in Balzac's *Louis Lambert* that all the world's great men have been marked by the same peculiarity, and for a simple and obvious reason: Greatness is nothing more nor less than the harmonious functioning of the faculties of the head and heart; the shorter the neck, the more closely these two organs approach one another; *argal* . . . It was convincing.

Mr. Barbecue-Smith belonged to the old school of journalists. He sported a leonine head with a greyish-black mane of oddly unappetizing hair brushed back from a broad but low forehead. And somehow he always seemed slightly, ever so slightly, soiled. In younger days he had gaily called himself a Bohemian. He did so no longer. He was a teacher now, a kind of prophet. Some of his books of comfort and spiritual teaching were in their hundred and twentieth thousand.

Priscilla received him with every mark of esteem. He had never been to Crome before; she showed him round the house. Mr. Barbecue-Smith was full of admiration.

"So quaint, so old-world," he kept repeating. He had a rich, rather unctuous voice.

Priscilla praised his latest book. "Splendid, I thought it was," she said in her large, jolly way.

"I'm happy to think you found it a comfort," said Mr. Barbecue-Smith.

"Oh, tremendously! And the bit about the Lotus Pool—I thought that so beautiful."

"I knew you would like that. It came to me, you know, from without." He waved his hand to indicate the astral world.

They went out into the garden for tea. Mr. Barbecue-Smith was duly introduced.

"Mr. Stone is a writer too," said Priscilla, as she introduced Denis.

"Indeed!" Mr. Barbecue-Smith smiled benignly, and, looking up at Denis with an expression of Olympian condescension, "And what sort of things do you write?"

Denis was furious, and, to make matters worse, he felt himself blushing hotly. Had Priscilla no sense of proportion? She was putting them in the same category— Barbecue-Smith and himself. They were both writers, they both used pen and ink. To Mr. Barbecue-Smith's question he answered, "Oh, nothing much, nothing," and looked away.

"Mr. Stone is one of our younger poets." It was Anne's voice. He scowled at her, and she smiled back exasperatingly.

"Excellent, excellent," said Mr. Barbecue-Smith, and he squeezed Denis's arm encouragingly. "The Bard's is a noble calling."

As soon as tea was over Mr. Barbecue-Smith excused himself; he had to do some writing before dinner. Priscilla quite understood. The prophet retired to his chamber.

Mr. Barbecue-Smith came down to the drawing-room

at ten to eight. He was in a good humour, and, as he descended the stairs, he smiled to himself and rubbed his large white hands together. In the drawing-room some-one was playing softly and ramblingly on the piano. He wondered who it could be. One of the young ladies, perhaps. But no, it was only Denis, who got up hurriedly and with some embarrassment as he came into the room.

"Do go on, do go on," said Mr. Barbecue-Smith. "I am very fond of music."

"Then I couldn't possibly go on," Denis replied. "I only make noises."

There was a silence. Mr. Barbecue-Smith stood with his back to the hearth, warming himself at the memory of last winter's fires. He could not control his interior satisfaction, but still went on smiling to himself. At last he turned to Denis.

"You write," he asked, "don't you?"

"Well, yes—a little, you know."

"How many words do you find you can write in an hour?"

"I don't think I've ever counted."

"Oh, you ought to, you ought to. It's most im-portant."

Denis exercised his memory. "When I'm in good form," he said, "I fancy I do a twelve-hundred-word review in about four hours. But sometimes it takes me much longer."

Mr. Barbecue-Smith nodded. "Yes, three hundred words an hour at your best." He walked out into the middle of the room, turned round on his heels, and con-fronted Denis again. "Guess how many words I wrote this evening between five and half-past seven."

"I can't imagine."

"No, but you must guess. Between five and half-past seven—that's two and a half hours."

"Twelve hundred words," Denis hazarded.

"No, no, no." Mr. Barbecue-Smith's expanded face shone with gaiety. "Try again."

"Fifteen hundred."

"No."

"I give it up," said Denis. He found he couldn't summon up much interest in Mr. Barbecue-Smith's writing.

"Well, I'll tell you. Three thousand eight hundred."

Denis opened his eyes. "You must get a lot done in a day," he said.

Mr. Barbecue-Smith suddenly became extremely confidential. He pulled up a stool to the side of Denis's arm-chair, sat down in it, and began to talk softly and rapidly.

"Listen to me," he said, laying his hand on Denis's sleeve. "You want to make your living by writing; you're young, you're inexperienced. Let me give you a little sound advice."

What was the fellow going to do? Denis wondered: give him an introduction to the editor of *John o' London's Weekly*, or tell him where he could sell a light middle for seven guineas? Mr. Barbecue-Smith patted his arm several times and went on.

"The secret of writing," he said, breathing it into the young man's ear—"the secret of writing is Inspiration."

Denis looked at him in astonishment.

"Inspiration . . ." Mr. Barbecue-Smith repeated.

"You mean the native wood-note business?"

Mr. Barbecue-Smith nodded.

"Oh, then I entirely agree with you," said Denis. "But what if one hasn't got Inspiration?"

"That was precisely the question I was waiting for," said Mr. Barbecue-Smith. "You ask me what one should do if one hasn't got Inspiration. I answer: you have Inspiration; everyone has Inspiration. It's simply a question of getting it to function."

The clock struck eight. There was no sign of any of the other guests; everybody was always late at Crome. Mr. Barbecue-Smith went on.

"That's my secret," he said. "I give it you freely." (Denis made a suitably grateful murmur and grimace.) "I'll help you to find your Inspiration, because I don't like to see a nice, steady young man like you exhausting his vitality and wasting the best years of his life in a grinding intellectual labour that could be completely obviated by Inspiration. I did it myself, so I know what it's like. Up till the time I was thirty-eight I was a writer like you—a writer without Inspiration. All I wrote I squeezed out of myself by sheer hard work. Why, in those days I was never able to do more than six-fifty words an hour, and what's more, I often didn't sell what I wrote." He sighed. "We artists," he said parenthetically, "we intellectuals aren't much appreciated here in England." Denis wondered if there was any method, consistent, of course, with politeness, by which he could dissociate himself from Mr. Barbecue-Smith's "we." There was none; and besides, it was too late now, for Mr. Barbecue-Smith was once more pursuing the tenor of his discourse.

"At thirty-eight I was a poor, struggling, tired, over-worked, unknown journalist. Now, at fifty . . ." He paused modestly and made a little gesture, moving his fat hands outwards, away from one another, and expanding his fingers as though in demonstration. He was exhibiting himself. Denis thought of that advertisement of Nestlé's milk—the two cats on the wall, under the moon, one black and thin, the other white, sleek, and fat. Before Inspiration and after.

"Inspiration has made the difference," said Mr. Barbecue-Smith solemnly. "It came quite suddenly—like a gentle dew from heaven." He lifted his hand and let it fall back on to his knee to indicate the descent of the dew. "It was one evening. I was writing my first little book about the Conduct of Life—*Humble Heroisms*. You may have read it; it has been a comfort—at least I hope and think so—a comfort to many thousands. I was in the middle of the second chapter, and I was stuck. Fatigue, overwork—I had only written a hundred words in the last hour, and I could get no further. I sat biting the end of my pen and looking at the electric light, which hung above my table, a little above and in front of me." He indicated the position of the lamp with elaborate care. "Have you ever looked at a bright light intently for a long time?" he asked, turning to Denis. Denis didn't think he had. "You can hypnotize yourself that way," Mr. Barbecue-Smith went on.

The gong sounded in a terrific crescendo from the hall. Still no sign of the others. Denis was horribly hungry.

"That's what happened to me," said Mr. Barbecue-Smith. "I was hypnotized. I lost consciousness like that." He snapped his fingers. "When I came to, I found that it was past midnight, and I had written four thousand words. Four thousand," he repeated, opening his mouth very wide on the *ou* of thousand. "Inspiration had come to me."

"What a very extraordinary thing," said Denis.

"I was afraid of it at first. It didn't seem to me natural. I didn't feel, somehow, that it was quite right, quite fair, I might almost say, to produce a literary composition unconsciously. Besides, I was afraid I might have written nonsense."

"And had you written nonsense?" Denis asked.

"Certainly not," Mr. Barbecue-Smith replied, with a trace of annoyance. "Certainly not. It was admirable. Just a few spelling mistakes and slips, such as there generally are in automatic writing. But the style, the thought—all the essentials were admirable. After that, Inspiration came to me regularly. I wrote the whole of *Humble Heroisms* like that. It was a great success, and so has everything been that I have written since." He leaned forward and jabbed at Denis with his finger. "That's my secret," he said, "and that's how you could write too, if you tried—without effort, fluently, well."

"But how?" asked Denis, trying not to show how deeply he had been insulted by that final "well."

"By cultivating your Inspiration, by getting into touch with your Subconscious. Have you ever read my little book, *Pipe-Lines to the Infinite*?"

Denis had to confess that that was, precisely, one of the few, perhaps the only one, of Mr. Barbecue-Smith's works he had not read.

"Never mind, never mind," said Mr. Barbecue-Smith. "It's just a little book about the connection of the Subconscious with the Infinite. Get into touch with the Subconscious and you are in touch with the Universe. Inspiration, in fact. You follow me?"

"Perfectly, perfectly," said Denis. "But don't you find that the Universe sometimes sends you very irrelevant messages?"

"I don't allow it to," Mr. Barbecue-Smith replied. "I canalize it. I bring it down through pipes to work the turbines of my conscious mind."

"Like Niagara," Denis suggested. Some of Mr. Barbecue-Smith's remarks sounded strangely like quotations—quotations from his own works, no doubt.

"Precisely. Like Niagara. And this is how I do it." He leaned forward, and with a raised forefinger marked his points as he made them, beating time, as it were, to his discourse. "Before I go off into my trance, I concentrate on the subject I wish to be inspired about. Let us say I am writing about the humble heroisms; for ten minutes before I go into the trance I think of nothing but orphans supporting their little brothers and sisters, of dull work well and patiently done, and I focus my mind on such great philosophical truths as the purification and uplifting of the soul by suffering, and the alchemical transformation of leaden evil into golden good." (Denis again hung up his little festoon of quotation marks.) "Then I pop off. Two or three hours later I wake up again, and find that inspiration has done its work. Thousands of words, comforting, uplifting words, lie before me. I type them out neatly on my machine and they are ready for the printer."

"It all sounds wonderfully simple," said Denis.

"It is. All the great and splendid and divine things of life are wonderfully simple." (Quotation marks again.) "When I have to do my aphorisms," Mr. Barbecue-Smith continued, "I prelude my trance by turning over the pages of any Dictionary of Quotations or Shakespeare

50

Calendar that comes to hand. That sets the key, so to speak; that ensures that the Universe shall come flowing in, not in a continuous rush, but in aphorismic drops. You see the idea?"

Denis nodded. Mr. Barbecue-Smith put his hand in his pocket and pulled out a notebook. "I did a few in the train to-day," he said, turning over the pages. "Just dropped off into a trance in the corner of my carriage. I find the train very conducive to good work. Here they are." He cleared his throat and read:

"*The Mountain Road may be steep, but the air is pure up there, and it is from the Summit that one gets the view.*"

"*The Things that Really Matter happen in the Heart.*"

It was curious, Denis reflected, the way the Infinite sometimes repeated itself.

"*Seeing is Believing. Yes, but Believing is also Seeing. If I believe in God, I see God, even in the things that seem to be evil.*"

Mr. Barbecue-Smith looked up from his notebook. "That last one," he said, "is particularly subtle and beautiful, don't you think? Without Inspiration I could never have hit on that." He re-read the apophthegm with a slower and more solemn utterance. "Straight from the Infinite," he commented reflectively, then addressed himself to the next aphorism.

"*The flame of a candle gives Light, but it also Burns.*"

Puzzled wrinkles appeared on Mr. Barbecue-Smith's forehead. "I don't exactly know what that means," he said. "It's very gnomic. One could apply it, of course, to the Higher Education—illuminating, but provoking the Lower Classes to discontent and revolution. Yes, I suppose that's what it is. But it's gnomic, it's gnomic." He rubbed his chin thoughtfully. The gong sounded again, clamorously, it seemed imploringly: dinner was growing cold. It roused Mr. Barbecue-Smith from meditation. He turned to Denis.

"You understand me now when I advise you to cultivate your Inspiration. Let your Subconscious work for you; turn on the Niagara of the Infinite."

There was the sound of feet on the stairs. Mr. Barbecue-Smith got up, laid his hand for an instant on Denis's shoulder, and said:

"No more now. Another time. And remember, I rely absolutely on your discretion in this matter. There are intimate, sacred things that one doesn't wish to be generally known."

"Of course," said Denis. "I quite understand."

CHAPTER VII

AT Crome all the beds were ancient hereditary pieces of furniture. Huge beds, like four-masted ships, with furled sails of shining coloured stuff. Beds carved and inlaid, beds painted and gilded. Beds of walnut and oak, of rare exotic woods. Beds of every date and fashion from the time of Sir Ferdinando, who built the house, to the time of his namesake in the late eighteenth century, the last of the family, but all of them grandiose, magnificent.

The finest of all was now Anne's bed. Sir Julius, son to Sir Ferdinando, had had it made in Venice against his wife's first lying-in. Early *seicento* Venice had expended all its extravagant art in the making of it. The body of the bed was like a great square sarcophagus. Clustering roses were carved in high relief on its wooden panels, and luscious *putti* wallowed among the roses. On the black groundwork of the panels the carved reliefs were gilded and burnished. The golden roses twined in spirals up the four pillar-like posts, and cherubs, seated at the top of each column, supported a wooden canopy fretted with the same carved flowers.

Anne was reading in bed. Two candles stood on the little table beside her. In their rich light her face, her bare arm and shoulder took on warm hues and a sort of peach-like quality of surface. Here and there in the canopy above her carved golden petals shone brightly among profound shadows, and the soft light, falling on the sculptured panel of the bed, broke restlessly among the intricate roses, lingered in a broad caress on the blown

53

cheeks, the dimpled bellies, the tight, absurd little posteriors of the sprawling *putti*.

There was a discreet tap at the door. She looked up. "Come in, come in." A face, round and childish within its sleek bell of golden hair, peered round the opening door. More childish-looking still, a suit of mauve pyjamas made its entrance.

It was Mary. "I thought I'd just look in for a moment to say good-night," she said, and sat down on the edge of the bed.

Anne closed her book. "That was very sweet of you."

"What are you reading?" She looked at the book. "Rather second-rate, isn't it?" The tone in which Mary pronounced the word "second-rate" implied an almost infinite denigration. She was accustomed in London to associate only with first-rate people who liked first-rate things, and she knew that there were very, very few first-rate things in the world, and that those were mostly French.

"Well, I'm afraid I like it," said Anne. There was nothing more to be said. The silence that followed was a rather uncomfortable one. Mary fiddled uneasily with the bottom button of her pyjama jacket. Leaning back on her mound of heaped-up pillows, Anne waited and wondered what was coming.

"I'm so awfully afraid of repressions," said Mary at last, bursting suddenly and surprisingly into speech. She pronounced the words on the tail-end of an expiring breath, and had to gasp for new air almost before the phrase was finished.

"What's there to be depressed about?"

"I said repressions, not depressions."

"Oh, repressions; I see," said Anne. "But repressions of what?"

Mary had to explain. "The natural instincts of sex . . ." she began didactically. But Anne cut her short.

"Yes, yes. Perfectly. I understand. Repressions; old maids and all the rest. But what about them?"

"That's just it," said Mary. "I'm afraid of them. It's always dangerous to repress one's instincts. I'm beginning to detect in myself symptoms like the ones you read of in the books. I constantly dream that I'm falling down wells; and sometimes I even dream that I'm climbing up ladders. It's most disquieting. The symptoms are only too clear."

"Are they?"

"One may become a nymphomaniac if one's not careful. You've no idea how serious these repressions are if you don't get rid of them in time."

"It sounds too awful," said Anne. "But I don't see that I can do anything to help you."

"I thought I'd just like to talk it over with you."

"Why, of course; I'm only too happy, Mary darling."

Mary coughed and drew a deep breath. "I presume," she began sententiously, "I presume we may take for granted that an intelligent young woman of twenty-three who has lived in civilized society in the twentieth century has no prejudices."

"Well, I confess I still have a few."

"But not about repressions."

"No, not many about repressions; that's true."

"Or, rather, about getting rid of repressions."

"Exactly."

"So much for our fundamental postulate," said Mary. Solemnity was expressed in every feature of her round young face, radiated from her large blue eyes. "We come next to the desirability of possessing experience. I hope we are agreed that knowledge is desirable and that ignorance is undesirable."

Obedient as one of those complaisant disciples from whom Socrates could get whatever answer he chose, Anne gave her assent to this proposition.

"And we are equally agreed, I hope, that marriage is what it is."

"It is."

"Good!" said Mary. "And repressions being what they are . . ."

"Exactly."

"There would therefore seem to be only one conclusion."

"But I knew that," Anne exclaimed, "before you began."

"Yes, but now it's been proved," said Mary. "One must do things logically. The question is now . . ."

"But where does the question come in? You've reached your only possible conclusion—logically, which is more than I could have done. All that remains is to impart the information to someone you like—someone you like really rather a lot, someone you're in love with, if I may express myself so baldly."

"But that's just where the question comes in," Mary exclaimed. "I'm not in love with anybody."

"Then, if I were you, I should wait till you are."

"But I can't go on dreaming night after night that I'm falling down a well. It's too dangerous."

"Well, if it really is *too* dangerous, then of course you must do something about it; you must find somebody else."

"But who?" A thoughtful frown puckered Mary's brow. "It must be somebody intelligent, somebody with intellectual interests that I can share. And it must be somebody with a proper respect for women, somebody who's prepared to talk seriously about his work and his ideas and about my work and my ideas. It isn't, as you see, at all easy to find the right person."

"Well," said Anne, "there are three unattached and intelligent men in the house at the present time. There's Mr. Scogan, to begin with; but perhaps he's rather too much of a genuine antique. And there are Gombauld and Denis. Shall we say that the choice is limited to the last two?"

Mary nodded. "I think we had better," she said, and then hesitated, with a certain air of embarrassment.

"What is it?"

"I was wondering," said Mary, with a gasp, "whether they really were unattached. I thought that perhaps you might . . . you might . . ."

"It was very nice of you to think of me, Mary darling," said Anne, smiling the tight cat's smile. "But as far as I'm concerned, they are both entirely unattached."

"I'm very glad of that," said Mary, looking relieved. "We are now confronted with the question: Which of the two?"

"I can give no advice. It's a matter for your taste."

"It's not a matter of my taste," Mary pronounced, "but of their merits. We must weigh them and consider them carefully and dispassionately."

"You must do the weighing yourself," said Anne; there was still the trace of a smile at the corners of her mouth and round the half-closed eyes. "I won't run the risk of advising you wrongly."

57

"Gombauld has more talent," Mary began, "but he is less civilized than Denis." Mary's pronounciation of "civilized" gave the word a special and additional significance. She uttered it meticulously, in the very front of her mouth, hissing delicately on the opening sibilant. So few people were civilized, and they, like the first-rate works of art, were mostly French. "Civilization is most important, don't you think?"

Anne held up her hand. "I won't advise," she said. "You must make the decision."

"Gombauld's family," Mary went on reflectively, "comes from Marseilles. Rather a dangerous heredity, when one thinks of the Latin attitude towards women. But then, I sometimes wonder whether Denis is altogether serious-minded, whether he isn't rather a dilettante. It's very difficult. What do you think?"

"I'm not listening," said Anne. "I refuse to take any responsibility."

Mary sighed. "Well," she said, "I think I had better go to bed and think about it."

"Carefully and dispassionately," said Anne.

At the door Mary turned round. "Good-night," she said, and wondered as she said the words why Anne was smiling in that curious way. It was probably nothing, she reflected. Anne often smiled for no apparent reason; it was probably just a habit. "I hope I shan't dream of falling down wells again to-night," she added.

"Ladders are worse," said Anne.

Mary nodded. "Yes, ladders are much graver."

CHAPTER VIII

BREAKFAST on Sunday morning was an hour later than on week-days, and Priscilla, who usually made no public appearance before luncheon, honoured it by her presence. Dressed in black silk, with a ruby cross as well as her customary string of pearls round her neck, she presided. An enormous Sunday paper concealed all but the extreme pinnacle of her coiffure from the outer world.

"I see Surrey has won," she said, with her mouth full, "by four wickets. The sun is in Leo: that would account for it!"

"Splendid game, cricket," remarked Mr. Barbecue-Smith heartily to no one in particular; "so thoroughly English."

Jenny, who was sitting next to him, woke up suddenly with a start. "What?" she said. "What?"

"So English," repeated Mr. Barbecue-Smith.

Jenny looked at him, surprised. "English? Of course I am."

He was beginning to explain, when Mrs. Wimbush vailed her Sunday paper, and appeared, a square, mauve-powdered face in the midst of orange splendours. "I see there's a new series of articles on the next world just beginning," she said to Mr. Barbecue-Smith. "This one's called 'Summer Land and Gehenna.'"

"Summer Land," echoed Mr. Barbecue-Smith, closing his eyes. "Summer Land. A beautiful name. Beautiful—beautiful."

Mary had taken the seat next to Denis's. After a night of careful consideration she had decided on Denis. He might have less talent than Gombauld, he might be a little lacking in seriousness, but somehow he was safer.

"Are you writing much poetry here in the country?" she asked, with a bright gravity.

"None," said Denis curtly. "I haven't brought my typewriter."

"But do you mean to say you can't write without a typewriter?"

Denis shook his head. He hated talking at breakfast, and, besides, he wanted to hear what Mr. Scogan was saying at the other end of the table.

". . . My scheme for dealing with the Church," Mr. Scogan was saying, is beautifully simple. At the present time the Anglican clergy wear their collars the wrong way round. I would compel them to wear, not only their collars, but all their clothes, turned back to front—coat, waistcoat, trousers, boots—so that every clergyman should present to the world a smooth façade, unbroken by stud, button, or lace. The enforcement of such a livery would act as a wholesome deterrent to those intending to enter the Church. At the same time it would enormously enhance, what Archbishop Laud so rightly insisted on, the 'beauty of holiness' in the few incorrigibles who could not be deterred."

"In hell, it seems," said Priscilla, reading in her Sunday paper, "the children amuse themselves by flaying lambs alive."

"Ah, but, dear lady, that's only a symbol," exclaimed Mr. Barbecue-Smith, "a material symbol of a h-piritual truth. Lambs signify . . ."

"Then there are military uniforms," Mr. Scogan went

60

on. "When scarlet and pipeclay were abandoned for khaki, there were some who trembled for the future of war. But then, finding how elegant the new tunic was, how closely it clipped the waist, how voluptuously, with the lateral bustles of the pockets, it exaggerated the hips; when they realized the brilliant potentialities of breeches and top-boots, they were reassured. Abolish these military elegances, standarize a uniform of sack-cloth and mackintosh, you will very soon find that . . ."

"Is anyone coming to church with me this morning?" asked Henry Wimbush. No one responded. He baited his bare invitation. "I read the lessons, you know. And there's Mr. Bodiham. His sermons are sometimes worth hearing."

"Thank you, thank you," said Mr. Barbecue-Smith. "I for one prefer to worship in the infinite church of Nature. How does our Shakespeare put it? 'Sermons in books, stones in the running brooks.'" He waved his arm in a fine gesture towards the window, and even as he did so he became vaguely, but none the less insistently, none the less uncomfortably aware that something had gone wrong with the quotation. Something—what could it be? Sermons? Stones? Books?

CHAPTER IX

MR. BODIHAM was sitting in his study at the Rectory. The nineteenth-century Gothic windows, narrow and pointed, admitted the light grudgingly; in spite of the brilliant July weather, the room was sombre. Brown varnished bookshelves lined the walls, filled with row upon row of those thick, heavy theological works which the second-hand booksellers generally sell by weight. The mantelpiece, the overmantel, a towering structure of spindly pillars and little shelves, were brown and varnished. The writing-desk was brown and varnished. So were the chairs, so was the door. A dark red-brown carpet with patterns covered the floor. Everything was brown in the room, and there was a curious brownish smell.

In the midst of this brown gloom Mr. Bodiham sat at his desk. He was the man in the Iron Mask. A grey metallic face with iron cheek-bones and a narrow iron brow; iron folds, hard and unchanging, ran perpendicularly down his cheeks; his nose was the iron beak of some thin, delicate bird of rapine. He had brown eyes, set in sockets rimmed with iron; round them the skin was dark, as though it had been charred. Dense wiry hair covered his skull; it had been black, it was turning grey. His ears were very small and fine. His jaws, his chin, his upper lip were dark, iron-dark, where he had shaved. His voice, when he spoke and especially when he raised it in preaching, was harsh, like the grating of iron hinges when a seldom-used door is opened.

It was nearly half-past twelve. He had just come back from church, hoarse and weary with preaching. He preached with fury, with passion, an iron man beating with a flail upon the souls of his congregation. But the souls of the faithful at Crome were made of india-rubber, solid rubber; the flail rebounded. They were used to Mr. Bodiham at Crome. The flail thumped on india-rubber, and as often as not the rubber slept.

That morning he had preached, as he had often preached before, on the nature of God. He had tried to make them understand about God, what a fearful thing it is to fall into His hands. God—they thought of something soft and merciful. They blinded themselves to facts; still more, they blinded themselves to the Bible. The passengers on the *Titanic* sang "Nearer my God to Thee" as the ship was going down. Did they realize what they were asking to be brought nearer to? A white fire of righteousness, an angry fire. . . .

When Savonarola preached, men sobbed and groaned aloud. Nothing broke the polite silence with which Crome listened to Mr. Bodiham—only an occasional cough and sometimes the sound of heavy breathing. In the front pew sat Henry Wimbush, calm, well-bred, beautifully dressed. There were times when Mr. Bodiham wanted to jump down from the pulpit and shake him into life,—times when he would have liked to beat and kill his whole congregation.

He sat at his desk dejectedly. Outside the Gothic windows the earth was warm and marvellously calm. Everything was as it had always been. And yet, and yet . . . It was nearly four years now since he had preached that sermon on Matthew xxiv. 7: "For nation shall rise up against nation, and kingdom against kingdom: and there shall be famines, and pestilences, and earthquakes, in divers places." It was nearly four years. He had had the sermon printed; it was so terribly, so vitally important that all the world should know what he had to say. A copy of the little pamphlet lay on his desk—eight small grey pages, printed by a fount of type that had grown blunt, like an old dog's teeth, by the endless champing and champing of the press. He opened it and began to read it yet once again.

"'For nation shall rise up against nation, and kingdom against kingdom: and there shall be famines, and pestilences, and earthquakes, in divers places.'

"Nineteen centuries have elapsed since Our Lord gave utterance to those words, and not a single one of them has been without wars, plagues, famines, and earthquakes. Mighty empires have crashed in ruin to the ground, diseases have unpeopled half the globe, there have been vast natural cataclysms in which thousands have been overwhelmed by flood and fire and whirlwind. Time and again, in the course of these nineteen centuries, such things have happened, but they have not brought Christ back to earth. They were 'signs of the times' inasmuch as they were signs of God's wrath against the chronic wickedness of mankind, but they were not signs of the times in connection with the Second Coming.

"If earnest Christians have regarded the present war as a true sign of the Lord's approaching return, it is not merely because it happens to be a great war involving the lives of millions of people, not merely because famine is tightening its grip on every country in Europe, not merely because disease of every kind, from syphilis to spotted fever, is rife among the warring nations; no, it is not for these reasons that we regard this war as a true

Sign of the Times, but because in its origin and its progress it is marked by certain characteristics which seem to connect it almost beyond a doubt with the predictions in Christian Prophecy relating to the Second Coming of the Lord.

"Let me enumerate the features of the present war which most clearly suggest that it is a Sign foretelling the near approach of the Second Advent. Our Lord said that 'this Gospel of the Kingdom shall be preached in all the world for a witness unto all nations; and then shall the end come.' Although it would be presumptuous for us to say what degree of evangelization will be regarded by God as sufficient, we may at least confidently hope that a century of unflagging missionary work has brought the fulfilment of this condition at any rate near. True, the larger number of the world's inhabitants have remained deaf to the preaching of the true religion; but that does not vitiate the fact that the Gospel *has* been preached 'for a witness' to all unbelievers from the Papist to the Zulu. The responsibility for the continued prevalence of unbelief lies, not with the preachers, but with those preached to.

"Again, it has been generally recognized that 'the drying up of the waters of the great river Euphrates,' mentioned in the sixteenth chapter of Revelations, refers to the decay and extinction of Turkish power, and is a sign of the near approaching end of the world as we know it. The capture of Jerusalem and the successes in Mesopotamia are great strides forward in the destruction of the Ottoman Empire; though it must be admitted that the Gallipoli episode proved that the Turk still possesses a 'notable horn' of strength. Historically speaking, this drying up of Ottoman power has been going on for the past century; the last two years have witnessed a great acceleration of the process, and there can be no doubt that complete desiccation is within sight.

"Closely following on the words concerning the drying up of Euphrates comes the prophecy of Armageddon, that world war with which the Second Coming is to be so closely associated. Once begun, the world war can end only with the return of Christ, and His coming will be sudden and unexpected, like that of a thief in the night.

"Let us examine the facts. In history, exactly as in St. John's Gospel, the world war is immediately preceded by the drying up of Euphrates, or the decay of Turkish power. This fact alone would be enough to connect the present conflict with the Armageddon of Revelations and therefore to point to the near approach of the Second Advent. But further evidence of an even more solid and convincing nature can be adduced.

"Armageddon is brought about by the activities of three unclean spirits, as it were toads, which come out of the mouths of the Dragon, the Beast, and the False Prophet. If we can identify these three powers of evil much light will clearly be thrown on the whole question.

"The Dragon, the Beast, and the False Prophet can all be identified in history. Satan, who can only work through human agency, has used these three powers in the long war against Christ which has filled the last nineteen centuries with religious strife. The Dragon, it has been sufficiently established, is pagan Rome, and the spirit issuing from its mouth is the spirit of Infidelity. The Beast, alternatively symbolized as a Woman, is undoubtedly the Papal power, and Popery is the spirit which it spews forth. There is only one power which answers to the description of the False Prophet, the wolf in sheep's clothing, the agent of the devil working in the guise of the Lamb, and that power is the so-called 'Society of Jesus.' The spirit that issues from the mouth of the False Prophet is the spirit of False Morality.

"We may assume, then, that the three evil spirits are Infidelity, Popery, and False Morality. Have these three influences been the real cause of the present conflict? The answer is clear.

"The spirit of Infidelity is the very spirit of German criticism. The Higher Criticism, as it is mockingly called, denies the possibility of miracles, prediction, and real inspiration, and attempts to account for the Bible as a natural development. Slowly but surely, during the last eighty years, the spirit of Infidelity has been robbing the Germans of their Bible and their faith, so that Germany is to-day a nation of unbelievers. Higher Criticism has thus made the war possible; for it would be absolutely impossible for any Christian nation to wage war as Germany is waging it.

"We come next to the spirit of Popery, whose influence in causing the war was quite as great as that of Infidelity, though not, perhaps, so immediately obvious. Since the Franco-Prussian War the Papal power has steadily declined in France, while in Germany it has steadily increased. To-day France is an anti-papal state, while Germany possesses a powerful Roman Catholic minority. Two papally controlled states, Germany and Austria, are at war with six anti-papal states—England, France, Italy, Russia, Serbia, and Portugal. Belgium is, of course, a thoroughly papal state, and there can be little doubt that the presence on the Allies' side of an element so essentially hostile has done much to hamper the righteous cause and is responsible for our comparative ill-success. That the spirit of Popery is behind the war is thus seen clearly enough in the grouping of the opposed powers, while the rebellion in the Roman Catholic parts of Ireland has merely confirmed a conclusion already obvious to any unbiased mind.

"The spirit of False Morality has played as great a part in this war as the two other evil spirits. The Scrap of Paper incident is the nearest and most obvious example of Germany's adherence to this essentially unchristian or Jesuitical morality. The end is German world-power, and in the attainment of this end, any means are justifiable. It is the true principle of Jesuitry applied to international politics.

"The identification is now complete. As was predicted in Revelations, the three evil spirits have gone forth just as the decay of the Ottoman power was nearing completion, and have joined together to make the world war. The warning, 'Behold, I come as a thief,' is therefore meant for the present period—for you and me and all the world. This war will lead on inevitably to the war of Armageddon, and will only be brought to an end by the Lord's personal return.

"And when He returns, what will happen? Those who are in Christ, St. John tells us, will be called to the Supper of the Lamb. Those who are found fighting against Him will be called to the Supper of the Great God—that grim banquet where they shall not feast, but be feasted on. 'For,' as St. John says, 'I saw an angel standing in the sun; and he cried in a loud voice, saying to all the fowls that fly in the midst of heaven, Come and gather yourselves together unto the supper of the Great God; that ye may eat the flesh of kings, and the flesh of captains, and the flesh of mighty men, and the flesh of horses, and

68

of them that sit on them, and the flesh of all men, both free and bond, both small and great.' All the enemies of Christ will be slain with the sword of him that sits upon the horse, 'and all the fowls will be filled with their flesh.' That is the Supper of the Great God.

"It may be soon or it may, as men reckon time, be long; but sooner or later, inevitably, the Lord will come and deliver the world from its present troubles. And woe unto them who are called, not to the Supper of the Lamb, but to the Supper of the Great God. They will realize then, but too late, that God is a God of Wrath as well as a God of Forgiveness. The God who sent bears to devour the mockers of Elisha, the God who smote the Egyptians for their stubborn wickedness, will assuredly smite them too, unless they make haste to repent. But perhaps it is already too late. Who knows but that to-morrow, in a moment even, Christ may be upon us unawares, like a thief? In a little while, who knows? the angel standing in the sun may be summoning the ravens and vultures from their crannies in the rocks to feed upon the putre-fying flesh of the millions of unrighteous whom God's wrath has destroyed. Be ready, then; the coming of the Lord is at hand. May it be for all of you an object of hope, not a moment to be looked forward to with terror and trembling."

Mr. Bodiham closed the little pamphlet and leaned back in his chair. The argument was sound, absolutely compelling; and yet—it was four years since he had preached that sermon; four years, and England was at peace, the sun shone, the people of Crome were as wicked and indifferent as ever—more so, indeed, if that were possible. If only he could understand, if the heavens would but make a sign! But his questionings remained unanswered. Seated there in his brown varnished chair under the Ruskinian window, he could have screamed aloud. He gripped the arms of his chair—gripping, gripping for control. The knuckles of his hands whitened; he bit his lip. In a few seconds he was able to relax the tension; he began to rebuke himself for his rebellious impatience.

Four years, he reflected; what were four years, after all? It must inevitably take a long time for Armageddon to ripen, to yeast itself up. The episode of 1914 had been a preliminary skirmish. And as for the war having come to an end—why, that, of course, was illusory. It was still going on, smouldering away in Silesia, in Ireland, in Anatolia; the discontent in Egypt and India was preparing the way, perhaps, for a great extension of the slaughter among the heathen peoples. The Chinese boycott of Japan, and the rivalries of that country and America in the Pacific, might be breeding a great new war in the East. The prospect, Mr. Bodiham tried to assure himself, was hopeful; the real, the genuine Armageddon might soon begin, and then, like a thief in the night . . . But, in spite of all his comfortable reasoning, he remained unhappy, dissatisfied. Four years ago he had been so confident; God's intention seemed then so plain. And now? Now, he did well to be angry. And now he suffered too.

Sudden and silent as a phantom Mrs. Bodiham appeared, gliding noiselessly across the room. Above her black dress her face was pale with an opaque whiteness, her eyes were pale as water in a glass, and her strawy hair was almost colourless. She held a large envelope in her hand.

"This came for you by the post," she said softly.

The envelope was unsealed. Mechanically Mr. Bodiham tore it open. It contained a pamphlet, larger than his own and more elegant in appearance. "The House of Sheeny, Clerical Outfitters, Birmingham." He turned over the pages. The catalogue was tastefully and ecclesiastically printed in antique characters with illuminated Gothic initials. Red marginal lines, crossed at the corners after the manner of an Oxford picture frame, enclosed each page of type; little red crosses took the place of full stops. Mr. Bodiham turned the pages.

Soutane in best black merino. Ready to wear; in all sizes.

Clerical frock-coats. From nine guineas. A dressy garment, tailored by our own experienced ecclesiastical cutters.

Half-tone illustrations represented young curates, some dapper, some Rugbeian and muscular, some with ascetic faces and large ecstatic eyes, dressed in jackets, in frock-coats, in surplices, in clerical evening dress, in black Norfolk suitings.

A large assortment of chasubles.

Rope girdles.

Sheeny's Special Skirt Cassocks. Tied by a string about the waist. . . . When worn under a surplice presents an appearance indistinguishable from that of a complete cassock. . . . Recommended for summer wear and hot climates.

With a gesture of horror and disgust Mr. Bodiham threw the catalogue into the waste-paper basket. Mrs. Bodiham looked at him; her pale, glaucous eyes reflected his action without comment.

"The village," she said in her quiet voice, "the village grows worse and worse every day."

"What has happened now?" asked Mr. Bodiham, feeling suddenly very weary.

"I'll tell you." She pulled up a brown varnished chair and sat down. In the village of Crome, it seemed, Sodom and Gomorrah had come to a second birth.

The sermon attributed to "*Mr. Bodiham*" in Chapter IX is a reproduction of the substance of an Address, given by the Rev. E. H. Horne, in A.D. 1916, to a meeting of clergy, and then published. It is now reprinted as an Appendix in a small book by him, entitled *The Significance of Air War* (Marshall, Morgan & Scott).

CHAPTER X

D ENIS did not dance, but when ragtime came
squirting out of the pianola in gushes of treacle
and hot perfume, in jets of Bengal light, then things
began to dance inside him. Little black nigger corpuscles
jigged and drummed in his arteries. He became a cage of
movement, a walking *palais de danse*. It was very uncomfortable, like the preliminary symptoms of a disease.
He sat in one of the window-seats, glumly pretending
to read.

At the pianola, Henry Wimbush, smoking a long cigar
through a tunnelled pillar of amber, trod out the shattering dance music with serene patience. Locked together,
Gombauld and Anne moved with a harmoniousness that
made them seem a single creature, two-headed and four-
legged. Mr. Scogan, solemnly buffoonish, shuffled round
the room with Mary. Jenny sat in the shadow behind the
piano, scribbling, so it seemed, in a big red notebook. In
arm-chairs by the fireplace, Priscilla and Mr. Barbecue-
Smith discussed higher things, without, apparently, being
disturbed by the noise of the Lower Plane.

"Optimism," said Mr. Barbecue-Smith, with a tone
of finality, speaking through strains of the "Wild, Wild
Women"—"optimism is the opening out of the soul
towards the light; it is an expansion towards and into
God, it is a h-piritual self-unification with the Infinite."

"How true!" sighed Priscilla, nodding the baleful
splendours of her coiffure.

"Pessimism, on the other hand, is the contraction of

73

the soul towards darkness; it is a focusing of the self upon a point in the Lower Plane; it is a h-piritual slavery to mere facts, to gross physical phenomena."

"They're making a wild man of me." The refrain sang itself over in Denis's mind. Yes, they were; damn them! A wild man, but not wild enough; that was the trouble. Wild inside; raging, writhing—yes, "writhing" was the word, writhing with desire. But outwardly he was hopelessly tame; outwardly—baa, baa, baa.

There they were, Anne and Gombauld, moving together as though they were a single supple creature. The beast with two backs. And he sat in a corner, pretending to read, pretending he didn't want to dance, pretending he rather despised dancing. Why? It was the baa-baa business again.

Why was he born with a different face? Why *was* he? Gombauld had a face of brass—one of those old, brazen rams that thumped against the walls of cities till they fell. He was born with a different face—a woolly face.

The music stopped. The single harmonious creature broke in two. Flushed, a little breathless, Anne swayed across the room to the pianola, laid her hand on Mr. Wimbush's shoulder.

"A waltz this time, please, Uncle Henry," she said.

"A waltz," he repeated, and turned to the cabinet where the rolls were kept. He trod off the old roll and trod on the new, a slave at the mill, uncomplaining and beautifully well bred. "Rum; Tum; Rum-ti-ti; Tum-ti-ti. . . ." The melody wallowed oozily along, like a ship moving forward over a sleek and oily swell. The four-legged creature, more graceful, more harmonious in its movements than ever, slid across the floor. Oh, why was he born with a different face?

"What are you reading?"

He looked up, startled. It was Mary. She had broken from the uncomfortable embrace of Mr. Scogan, who had now seized on Jenny for his victim.

"What are you reading?"

"I don't know," said Denis truthfully. He looked at the title page; the book was called *The Stock Breeder's Vade Mecum*.

"I think you are so sensible to sit and read quietly," said Mary, fixing him with her china eyes. "I don't know why one dances. It's so boring."

Denis made no reply; she exacerbated him. From the arm-chair by the fireplace he heard Priscilla's deep voice.

"Tell me, Mr. Barbecue-Smith—you know all about science, I know——" A deprecating noise came from Mr. Barbecue-Smith's chair. "This Einstein theory. It seems to upset the whole starry universe. It makes me so worried about my horoscopes. You see . . ."

Mary renewed her attack. "Which of the contemporary poets do you like best?" she asked. Denis was filled with fury. Why couldn't this pest of a girl leave him alone? He wanted to listen to the horrible music, to watch them dancing—oh, with what grace, as though they had been made for one another!—to savour his misery in peace. And she came and put him through this absurd catechism! She was like "Mangold's Questions": "What are the three diseases of wheat?"—"Which of the contemporary poets do you like best?"

"Blight, Mildew, and Smut," he replied, with the laconism of one who is absolutely certain of his own mind.

It was several hours before Denis managed to go to sleep that night. Vague but agonizing miseries possessed his mind. It was not only Anne who made him miserable; he was wretched about himself, the future, life in general, the universe. "This adolescence business," he repeated to himself every now and then, "is horribly boring." But the fact that he knew his disease did not help him to cure it.

After kicking all the clothes off the bed, he got up and sought relief in composition. He wanted to imprison his nameless misery in words. At the end of an hour, nine more or less complete lines emerged from among the blots and scratchings.

> "I do not know what I desire
>   When summer nights are dark and still,
>   When the wind's many-voicéd quire
>   Sleeps among the muffled branches.
>   I long and know not what I will:
>   And not a sound of life or laughter stanches
>   Time's black and silent flow.
>   I do not know what I desire,
>   I do not know."

He read it through aloud; then threw the scribbled sheet into the waste-paper basket and got into bed again. In a very few minutes he was asleep.

CHAPTER XI

M R. BARBECUE-SMITH was gone. The motor had whirled him away to the station; a faint smell of burning oil commemorated his recent departure. A considerable detachment had come into the courtyard to speed him on his way; and now they were walking back, round the side of the house, towards the terrace and the garden. They walked in silence; nobody had yet ventured to comment on the departed guest.

"Well?" said Anne, at last, turning with raised inquiring eyebrows to Denis. "Well?" It was time for someone to begin.

Denis declined the invitation; he passed it on to Mr. Scogan. "Well?" he said.

Mr. Scogan did not respond; he only repeated the question, "Well?"

It was left for Henry Wimbush to make a pronouncement. "A very agreeable adjunct to the week-end," he said. His tone was obituary.

They had descended, without paying much attention where they were going, the steep yew-walk that went down, under the flank of the terrace, to the pool. The house towered above them, immensely tall, with the whole height of the built-up terrace added to its own seventy feet of brick façade. The perpendicular lines of the three towers soared up, uninterrupted, enhancing the impression of height until it became overwhelming. They paused at the edge of the pool to look back.

"The man who built this house knew his business," said Denis. "He was an architect."

"Was he?" said Henry Wimbush reflectively. "I doubt it. The builder of this house was Sir Ferdinando Lapith, who flourished during the reign of Elizabeth. He inherited the estate from his father, to whom it had been granted at the time of the dissolution of the monasteries; for Crome was originally a cloister of monks and this swimming-pool their fish-pond. Sir Ferdinando was not content merely to adapt the old monastic buildings to his own purposes; but using them as a stone quarry for his barns and byres and outhouses, he built for himself a grand new house of brick—the house you see now."

He waved his hand in the direction of the house and was silent. Severe, imposing, almost menacing, Crome loomed down on them.

"The great thing about Crome," said Mr. Scogan, seizing the opportunity to speak, "is the fact that it's so unmistakably and aggressively a work of art. It makes no compromise with nature, but affronts it and rebels against it. It has no likeness to Shelley's tower, in the 'Epipsychidion,' which, if I remember rightly—

"'Seems not now a work of human art,
    But as it were titanic, in the heart
    Of earth having assumed its form and grown
    Out of the mountain, from the living stone,
    Lifting itself in caverns light and high.'

No, no; there isn't any nonsense of that sort about Crome. That the hovels of the peasantry should look as though they had grown out of the earth, to which their inmates are attached, is right, no doubt, and suitable. But the house of an intelligent, civilized, and sophisticated

78

man should never seem to have sprouted from the clods. It should rather be an expression of his grand unnatural remoteness from the cloddish life. Since the days of William Morris that's a fact which we in England have been unable to comprehend. Civilized and sophisticated men have solemnly played at being peasants. Hence quaintness, arts and crafts, cottage architecture, and all the rest of it. In the suburbs of our cities you may see, reduplicated in endless rows, studiedly quaint imitations and adaptations of the village hovel. Poverty, ignorance, and a limited range of materials produced the hovel, which possesses undoubtedly, in suitable surroundings, its own 'as it were titanic' charm. We now employ our wealth, our technical knowledge, our rich variety of materials for the purpose of building millions of imitation hovels in totally unsuitable surroundings. Could imbecility go further?"

Henry Wimbush took up the thread of his interrupted discourse. "All that you say, my dear Scogan," he began, "is certainly very just, very true. But whether Sir Ferdinando shared your views about architecture or if, indeed, he had any views about architecture at all, I very much doubt. In building this house, Sir Ferdinando was, as a matter of fact, preoccupied by only one thought—the proper placing of his privies. Sanitation was the one great interest of his life. In 1573 he even published, on this subject, a little book—now extremely scarce—called, *Certaine Priuy Counsels* by *One of Her Maiestie's Most Honourable Priuy Counsel, F. L. Knight,* in which the whole matter is treated with great learning and elegance. His guiding principle in arranging the sanitation of a house was to secure that the greatest possible distance should separate the privy from the sewage arrangements.

Hence it followed inevitably that the privies were to be placed at the top of the house, being connected by vertical shafts with pits or channels in the ground. It must not be thought that Sir Ferdinando was moved only by material and merely sanitary considerations; for the placing of his privies in an exalted position he had also certain excellent spiritual reasons. For, he argues in the third chapter of his *Privy Counsels*, the necessities of nature are so base and brutish that in obeying them we are apt to forget that we are the noblest creatures of the universe. To counteract these degrading effects he advised that the privy should be in every house the room nearest to heaven, that it should be well provided with windows commanding an extensive and noble prospect, and that the walls of the chamber should be lined with bookshelves containing all the ripest products of human wisdom, such as the Proverbs of Solomon, Boëthius's *Consolations of Philosophy*, the apophthegms of Epictetus and Marcus Aurelius, the *Enchiridion* of Erasmus, and all other works, ancient or modern, which testify to the nobility of the human soul. In Crome he was able to put his theories into practice. At the top of each of the three projecting towers he placed a privy. From these a shaft went down the whole height of the house, that is to say, more than seventy feet, through the cellars, and into a series of conduits provided with flowing water tunnelled in the ground on a level with the base of the raised terrace. These conduits emptied themselves into the stream several hundred yards below the fish-pond. The total depth of the shafts from the top of the towers to their subterranean conduits was a hundred and two feet. The eighteenth century, with its passion for modernization, swept away these monuments of sanitary ingenuity.

Were it not for tradition and the explicit account of them left by Sir Ferdinando, we should be unaware that these noble privies had ever existed. We should even suppose that Sir Ferdinando built his house after this strange and splendid model for merely æsthetic reasons."

The contemplation of the glories of the past always evoked in Henry Wimbush a certain enthusiasm. Under the grey bowler his face worked and glowed as he spoke. The thought of these vanished privies moved him profoundly. He ceased to speak; the light gradually died out of his face, and it became once more the replica of the grave, polite hat which shaded it. There was a long silence; the same gently melancholy thoughts seemed to possess the mind of each of them. Permanence, transience —Sir Ferdinando and his privies were gone, Crome still stood. How brightly the sun shone and how inevitable was death! The ways of God were strange; the ways of man were stranger still. . . .

"It does one's heart good," exclaimed Mr. Scogan at last, "to hear of these fantastic English aristocrats. To have a theory about privies and to build an immense and splendid house in order to put it into practice—it's magnificent, beautiful! I like to think of them all: the eccentric milords rolling across Europe in ponderous carriages, bound on extraordinary errands. One is going to Venice to buy La Bianchi's larynx; he won't get it till she's dead, of course, but no matter; he's prepared to wait; he has a collection, pickled in glass bottles, of the throats of famous opera singers. And the instruments of renowned virtuosi—he goes in for them too; he will try to bribe Paganini to part with his little Guarnerio, but he has small hope of success. Paganini won't sell his fiddle; but perhaps he might sacrifice one of his guitars.

Others are bound on crusades—one to die miserably among the savage Greeks, another, in his white top hat, to lead Italians against their oppressors. Others have no business at all; they are just giving their oddity a continental airing. At home they cultivate themselves at leisure and with greater elaboration. Beckford builds towers, Portland digs holes in the ground, Cavendish, the millionaire, lives in a stable, eats nothing but mutton, and amuses himself—oh, solely for his private delectation —by anticipating the electrical discoveries of half a century. Glorious eccentrics! Every age is enlivened by their presence. Some day, my dear Denis," said Mr. Scogan, turning a beady bright regard in his direction— "some day you must become their biographer—'The Lives of Queer Men.' What a subject! I should like to undertake it myself."

Mr. Scogan paused, looked up once more at the towering house, then murmured the word, "Eccentricity," two or three times.

"Eccentricity. . . . It's the justification of all aristocracies. It justifies leisured classes and inherited wealth and privilege and endowments and all the other injustices of that sort. If you're to do anything reasonable in this world, you must have a class of people who are secure, safe from public opinion, safe from poverty, leisured, not compelled to waste their time in the imbecile routines that go by the name of Honest Work. You must have a class of which the members can think and, within the obvious limits, do what they please. You must have a class in which people who have eccentricities can indulge them and in which eccentricity in general will be tolerated and understood. That's the important thing about an aristocracy. Not only is it eccentric itself—often grandiosely so; it also tolerates and even encourages eccentricity in others. The eccentricities of the artist and the new-fangled thinker don't inspire it with that fear, loathing, and disgust which the burgesses instinctively feel towards them. It is a sort of Red Indian Reservation planted in the midst of a vast horde of Poor Whites—colonials at that. Within its boundaries wild men disport themselves —often, it must be admitted, a little grossly, a little too flamboyantly; and when kindred spirits are born outside the pale it offers them some sort of refuge from the hatred which the Poor Whites, *en bons bourgeois*, lavish on anything that is wild or out of the ordinary. After the social revolution there will be no Reservations; the Redskins will be drowned in the great sea of Poor Whites. What then? Will they suffer you to go on writing villanelles, my good Denis? Will you, unhappy Henry, be allowed to live in this house of the splendid privies, to continue your quiet delving in the mines of futile knowledge? Will Anne . . ."

"And you," said Anne, interrupting him, "will you be allowed to go on talking?"

"You may rest assured," Mr. Scogan replied, "that I shall not. I shall have some Honest Work to do."

"BLIGHT, Mildew, and Smut. . . ." Mary was puzzled and distressed. Perhaps her ears had played her false. Perhaps what he had really said was, "Squire, Binyon, and Shanks," or "Childe, Blunden, and Earp," or even "Abercrombie, Drinkwater, and Rabindranath Tagore." Perhaps. But then her ears never did play her false. "Blight, Mildew, and Smut." The impression was distinct and ineffaceable. "Blight, Mildew . . ." she was forced to the conclusion, reluctantly, that Denis had indeed pronounced those improbable words. He had deliberately repelled her attempt to open a serious discussion. That was horrible. A man who would not talk seriously to a woman just because she was a woman—oh, impossible! Egeria or nothing. Perhaps Gombauld would be more satisfactory. True, his meridional heredity was a little disquieting; but at least he was a serious worker, and it was with his work that she would associate herself. And Denis? After all, what *was* Denis? A dilettante, an amateur. . . .

Gombauld had annexed for his painting-room a little disused granary that stood by itself in a green close beyond the farmyard. It was a square brick building with a peaked roof and little windows set high up in each of its walls. A ladder of four rungs led up to the door; for the granary was perched above the ground, and out of reach of the rats, on four massive toadstools of grey stone. Within, there lingered a faint smell of dust and cobwebs; and the narrow shaft of sunlight that came slanting in at every hour of the day through one of the little windows was always alive with silvery motes. Here Gombauld worked, with a kind of concentrated ferocity, during six or seven hours of each day. He was pursuing something new, something terrific, if only he could catch it.

During the last eight years, nearly half of which had been spent in the process of winning the war, he had worked his way industriously through cubism. Now he had come out on the other side. He had begun by painting a formalized nature; then, little by little, he had risen from nature into the world of pure form, till in the end he was painting nothing but his own thoughts, externalized in the abstract geometrical forms of the mind's devising. He found the process arduous and exhilarating. And then, quite suddenly, he grew dissatisfied; he felt himself cramped and confined within intolerably narrow limitations. He was humiliated to find how few and crude and uninteresting were the forms he could invent; the inventions of nature were without number, inconceivably subtle and elaborate. He had done with cubism. He was out on the other side. But the cubist discipline preserved him from falling into excesses of nature worship. He took from nature its rich, subtle, elaborate forms, but his aim was always to work them into a whole that should have the thrilling simplicity and formality of an idea; to combine prodigious realism with prodigious simplification. Memories of Caravaggio's portentous achievements haunted him. Forms of a breathing, living reality emerged from darkness, built themselves up into compositions as luminously simple and single as a mathematical idea. He thought of the "Call of Matthew," of "Peter Crucified," of the "Lute Players," of "Magdalen." He had the secret, that astonishing ruffian, he had the secret! And now Gombauld was after it, in hot pursuit. Yes, it would be something terrific, if only he could catch it.

For a long time an idea had been stirring and spreading, yeastily, in his mind. He had made a portfolio full of studies, he had drawn a cartoon; and now the idea was taking shape on canvas. A man fallen from a horse. The huge animal, a gaunt white cart-horse, filled the upper half of the picture with its great body. Its head, lowered towards the ground, was in shadow; the immense bony body was what arrested the eye, the body and the legs, which came down on either side of the picture like the pillars of an arch. On the ground, between the legs of the towering beast, lay the foreshortened figure of a man, the head in the extreme foreground, the arms flung wide to right and left. A white, relentless light poured down from a point in the right foreground. The beast, the fallen man, were sharply illuminated; round them, beyond and behind them, was the night. They were alone in the darkness, a universe in themselves. The horse's body filled the upper part of the picture; the legs, the great hoofs, frozen to stillness in the midst of their trampling, limited it on either side. And beneath lay the man, his foreshortened face at the focal point in the centre, his arms outstretched towards the sides of the picture. Under the arch of the horse's belly, between his legs, the eye looked through into an intense darkness; below, the space was closed in by the figure of the prostrate man. A central gulf of darkness surrounded by luminous forms. . . .

The picture was more than half finished. Gombauld had been at work all the morning on the figure of the man, and now he was taking a rest—the time to smoke a cigarette. Tilting back his chair till it touched the wall, he looked thoughtfully at his canvas. He was pleased, and at the same time he was desolated. In itself, the thing was good; he knew it. But that something he was after, that something that would be so terrific if only he could catch it—had he caught it? Would he ever catch it?

Three little taps—rat, tat, tat! Surprised, Gombauld turned his eyes towards the door. Nobody ever disturbed him while he was at work; it was one of the unwritten laws. "Come in!" he called. The door, which was ajar, swung open, revealing, from the waist upwards, the form of Mary. She had only dared to mount half-way up the ladder. If he didn't want her, retreat would be easier and more dignified than if she climbed to the top.

"May I come in?" she asked.

"Certainly."

She skipped up the remaining two rungs and was over the threshold in an instant. "A letter came for you by the second post," she said. "I thought it might be important, so I brought it out to you." Her eyes, her childish face were luminously candid as she handed him the letter. There had never been a flimsier pretext.

Gombauld looked at the envelope and put it in his pocket unopened. "Luckily," he said, "it isn't at all important. Thanks very much all the same."

There was a silence; Mary felt a little uncomfortable. "May I have a look at what you've been painting?" she had the courage to say at last.

Gombauld had only half smoked his cigarette; in any case he wouldn't begin work again till he had finished. He would give her the five minutes that separated him from the bitter end. "This is the best place to see it from," he said.

Mary looked at the picture for some time without saying anything. Indeed, she didn't know what to say; she was taken aback, she was at a loss. She had expected a cubist masterpiece, and here was a picture of a man and a horse, not only recognizable as such, but even aggressively in drawing. *Trompe-l'œil*—there was no other word to describe the delineation of that foreshortened figure under the trampling feet of the horse. What was she to think, what was she to say? Her orientations were gone. One could admire representationalism in the Old Masters. Obviously. But in a modern . . .? At eighteen she might have done so. But now, after five years of schooling among the best judges, her instinctive reaction to a contemporary piece of representation was contempt —an outburst of laughing disparagement. What could Gombauld be up to? She had felt so safe in admiring his work before. But now—she didn't know what to think. It was very difficult, very difficult.

"There's rather a lot of chiaroscuro, isn't there?" she ventured at last, and inwardly congratulated herself on having found a critical formula so gentle and at the same time so penetrating.

"There is," Gombauld agreed.

Mary was pleased; he accepted her criticism; it was a serious discussion. She put her head on one side and screwed up her eyes. "I think it's awfully fine," she said. "But of course it's a little too . . . too . . . *trompe-l'œil* for my taste." She looked at Gombauld, who made no response, but continued to smoke, gazing meditatively all the time at his picture. Mary went on gaspingly. "When I was in Paris this spring I saw a lot of Tschuplitski. I admire his work so tremendously. Of course, it's frightfully abstract now—frightfully abstract and frightfully intellectual. He just throws a few oblongs on to his canvas—quite flat, you know, and painted in pure primary colours. But his design is wonderful. He's getting more and more abstract every day. He'd quite given up the third dimension when I was there and was just thinking of giving up the second. Soon, he says, there'll be just the blank canvas. That's the logical conclusion. Complete abstraction. Painting's finished; he's finishing it. When he's reached pure abstraction he's going to take up architecture. He says it's more intellectual than painting. Do you agree?" she asked, with a final gasp.

Gombauld dropped his cigarette end and trod on it. "Tschuplitski's finished painting," he said. "I've finished my cigarette. But I'm going on painting." And, advancing towards her, he put his arm round her shoulders and turned her round, away from the picture.

Mary looked up at him; her hair swung back, a soundless bell of gold. Her eyes were serene; she smiled. So the moment had come. His arm was round her. He moved slowly, almost imperceptibly, and she moved with him. It was a peripatetic embracement. "Do you agree with him?" she repeated. The moment might have come, but she would not cease to be intellectual, serious.

"I don't know. I shall have to think about it." Gombauld loosened his embrace, his hand dropped from her shoulder. "Be careful going down the ladder," he added solicitously.

Mary looked round, startled. They were in front of the open door. She remained standing there for a moment in bewilderment. The hand that had rested on her shoulder made itself felt lower down her back; it administered three or four kindly little smacks. Replying automatically to its stimulus, she moved forward.

"Be careful going down the ladder," said Gombauld once more.

She was careful. The door closed behind her and she was alone in the little green close. She walked slowly back through the farmyard; she was pensive.

CHAPTER XIII

HENRY WIMBUSH brought down with him to dinner a budget of printed sheets loosely bound together in a cardboard portfolio.

"To-day," he said, exhibiting it with a certain solemnity, "to-day I have finished the printing of my *History of Crome*. I helped to set up the type of the last page this evening."

"The famous History?" cried Anne. The writing and the printing of this *Magnum Opus* had been going on as long as she could remember. All her childhood long Uncle Henry's History had been a vague and fabulous thing, often heard of and never seen.

"It has taken me nearly thirty years," said Mr. Wimbush. "Twenty-five years of writing and nearly four of printing. And now it's finished—the whole chronicle, from Sir Ferdinando Lapith's birth to the death of my father William Wimbush—more than three centuries and a half: a history of Crome, written at Crome, and printed at Crome by my own press."

"Shall we be allowed to read it now it's finished?" asked Denis.

Mr. Wimbush nodded. "Certainly," he said. "And I hope you will not find it uninteresting," he added modestly. "Our muniment room is particularly rich in ancient records, and I have some genuinely new light to throw on the introduction of the three-pronged fork."

"And the people?" asked Gombauld. "Sir Ferdinando

and the rest of them—were they amusing? Were there any crimes or tragedies in the family?"

"Let me see," Henry Wimbush rubbed his chin thoughtfully. "I can only think of two suicides, one violent death, four or perhaps five broken hearts, and half a dozen little blots on the scutcheon in the way of misalliances, seductions, natural children, and the like. No, on the whole, it's a placid and uneventful record."

"The Wimbushes and the Lapiths were always an unadventurous, respectable crew," said Priscilla, with a note of scorn in her voice. "If I were to write my family history now! Why, it would be one long continuous blot from beginning to end." She laughed jovially, and helped herself to another glass of wine.

"If I were to write mine," Mr. Scogan remarked, "it wouldn't exist. After the second generation we Scogans are lost in the mists of antiquity."

"After dinner," said Henry Wimbush, a little piqued by his wife's disparaging comment on the masters of Crome, "I'll read you an episode from my History that will make you admit that even the Lapiths, in their own respectable way, had their tragedies and strange adventures."

"I'm glad to hear it," said Priscilla.

"Glad to hear what?" asked Jenny, emerging suddenly from her private interior world like a cuckoo from a clock. She received an explanation, smiled, nodded, cuckooed a last "I see," and popped back, clapping shut the door behind her.

Dinner was eaten; the party had adjourned to the drawing-room.

"Now," said Henry Wimbush, pulling up a chair to the lamp. He put on his round pince-nez, rimmed with

92

tortoise-shell, and began cautiously to turn over the pages of his loose and still fragmentary book. He found his place at last. "Shall I begin?" he asked, looking up.

"Do," said Priscilla, yawning.

In the midst of an attentive silence Mr. Wimbush gave a little preliminary cough and started to read.

"The infant who was destined to become the fourth baronet of the name of Lapith was born in the year 1740. He was a very small baby, weighing not more than three pounds at birth, but from the first he was sturdy and healthy. In honour of his maternal grandfather, Sir Hercules Occam of Bishop's Occam, he was christened Hercules. His mother, like many other mothers, kept a notebook, in which his progress from month to month was recorded. He walked at ten months, and before his second year was out he had learnt to speak a number of words. At three years he weighed but twenty-four pounds, and at six, though he could read and write perfectly and showed a remarkable aptitude for music, he was no larger and heavier than a well-grown child of two. Meanwhile, his mother had borne two other children, a boy and a girl, one of whom died of croup during infancy, while the other was carried off by smallpox before it reached the age of five. Hercules remained the only surviving child.

"On his twelfth birthday Hercules was still only three feet and two inches in height. His head, which was very handsome and nobly shaped, was too big for his body, but otherwise he was exquisitely proportioned and, for his size, of great strength and agility. His parents, in the hope of making him grow, consulted all the most eminent physicians of the time. Their various prescriptions were followed to the letter, but in vain. One ordered

93

a very plentiful meat diet; another exercise; a third constructed a little rack, modelled on those employed by the Holy Inquisition, on which young Hercules was stretched, with excruciating torments, for half an hour every morning and evening. In the course of the next three years Hercules gained perhaps two inches. After that his growth stopped completely, and he remained for the rest of his life a pigmy of three feet and four inches. His father, who had built the most extravagant hopes upon his son, planning for him in his imagination a military career equal to that of Marlborough, found himself a disappointed man. 'I have brought an abortion into the world,' he would say, and he took so violent a dislike to his son that the boy dared scarcely come into his presence. His temper, which had been serene, was turned by disappointment to moroseness and savagery. He avoided all company (being, as he said, ashamed to show himself, the father of a *lusus naturæ*, among normal, healthy human beings), and took to solitary drinking, which carried him very rapidly to his grave; for the year before Hercules came of age his father was taken off by an apoplexy. His mother, whose love for him had increased with the growth of his father's unkindness, did not long survive, but little more than a year after her husband's death succumbed, after eating two dozen of oysters, to an attack of typhoid fever.

"Hercules thus found himself at the age of twenty-one alone in the world, and master of a considerable fortune, including the estate and mansion of Crome. The beauty and intelligence of his childhood had survived into his manly age, and, but for his dwarfish stature, he would have taken his place among the handsomest and most accomplished young men of his time. He was well read in Greek and Latin authors, as well as in all the moderns of any merit who had written in English, French, or Italian. He had a good ear for music, and was no indifferent performer on the violin, which he used to play like a bass viol, seated on a chair with the instrument between his legs. To the music of the harpsichord and clavichord he was extremely partial, but the smallness of his hands made it impossible for him ever to perform upon these instruments. He had a small ivory flute made for him, on which, whenever he was melancholy, he used to play a simple country air or jig, affirming that this rustic music had more power to clear and raise the spirits than the most artificial productions of the masters. From an early age he practised the composition of poetry, but, though conscious of his great powers in this art, he would never publish any specimen of his writing. 'My stature,' he would say, 'is reflected in my verses; if the public were to read them it would not be because I am a poet, but because I am a dwarf.' Several MS. books of Sir Hercules's poems survive. A single specimen will suffice to illustrate his qualities as a poet.

"In ancient days, while yet the world was young,
Ere Abram fed his flocks or Homer sung;
When blacksmith Tubal tamed creative fire,
And Jabal dwelt in tents and Jubal struck the lyre;
Flesh grown corrupt brought forth a monstrous birth
And obscene giants trod the shrinking earth,
Till God, impatient of their sinful brood,
Gave rein to wrath and drown'd them in the Flood.
Teeming again, repeopled Tellus bore
The lubber Hero and the Man of War;
Huge towers of Brawn, topp'd with an empty Skull,
Witlessly bold, heroically dull.

Long ages pass'd and Man grown more refin'd,
Slighter in muscle but of vaster Mind,
Smiled at his grandsire's broadsword, bow and bill,
And learn'd to wield the Pencil and the Quill.
The glowing canvas and the written page
Immortaliz'd his name from age to age,
His name emblazon'd on Fame's temple wall;
For Art grew great as Humankind grew small.
Thus man's long progress step by step we trace;
The Giant dies, the hero takes his place;
The Giant vile, the dull heroic Block:
At one we shudder and at one we mock.
Man last appears. In him the Soul's pure flame
Burns brightlier in a not inord'nate frame.
Of old when Heroes fought and Giants swarmed,
Men were huge mounds of matter scarce inform'd;
Wearied by leavening so vast a mass,
The spirit slept and all the mind was crass.
The smaller carcase of these later days
Is soon inform'd; the Soul unwearied plays
And like a Pharos darts abroad her mental rays.
But can we think that Providence will stay
Man's footsteps here upon the upward way?
Mankind in understanding and in grace
Advanc'd so far beyond the Giants' race?
Hence impious thought! Still led by GOD's own Hand,
Mankind proceeds towards the Promised Land.
A time will come (prophetic, I descry
Remoter dawns along the gloomy sky),
When happy mortals of a Golden Age
Will backward turn the dark historic page,
And in our vaunted race of Men behold
A form as gross, a Mind as dead and cold,
As we in Giants see, in warriors of old.
A time will come, wherein the soul shall be
From all superfluous matter wholly free:

When the light body, agile as a fawn's,
Shall sport with grace along the velvet lawns.
Nature's most delicate and final birth,
Mankind perfected shall possess the earth.
But ah, not yet! For still the Giants' race,
Huge, though diminish'd, tramps the Earth's fair face;
Gross and repulsive, yet perversely proud,
Men of their imperfections boast aloud.
Vain of their bulk, of all they still retain
Of giant ugliness absurdly vain;
At all that's small they point their stupid scorn
And, monsters, think themselves divinely born.
Sad is the Fate of those, ah, sad indeed,
The rare precursors of the nobler breed!
Who come man's golden glory to foretell,
But pointing Heav'nwards live themselves in Hell.

"As soon as he came into the estate, Sir Hercules set about remodelling his household. For though by no means ashamed of his deformity—indeed, if we may judge from the poem quoted above, he regarded himself as being in many ways superior to the ordinary race of man—he found the presence of full-grown men and women embarrassing. Realizing, too, that he must abandon all ambitions in the great world, he determined to retire absolutely from it and to create, as it were, at Crome a private world of his own, in which all should be proportionable to himself. Accordingly, he discharged all the old servants of the house and replaced them gradually, as he was able to find suitable successors, by others of dwarfish stature. In the course of a few years he had assembled about himself a numerous household, no member of which was above four feet high and the smallest among them scarcely two feet and six inches. His father's dogs, such as setters, mastiffs, greyhounds, and a pack of beagles, he sold or gave away as too large and too boisterous for his house, replacing them by pugs and King Charles spaniels and whatever other breeds of dog were the smallest. His father's stable was also sold. For his own use, whether riding or driving, he had six black Shetland ponies, with four very choice piebald animals of New Forest breed.

"Having thus settled his household entirely to his own satisfaction, it only remained for him to find some suitable companion with whom to share this paradise. Sir Hercules had a susceptible heart, and had more than once, between the ages of sixteen and twenty, felt what it was to love. But here his deformity had been a source of the most bitter humiliation, for, having once dared to declare himself to a young lady of his choice, he had been received with laughter. On his persisting, she had picked him up and shaken him like an importunate child, telling him to run away and plague her no more. The story soon got about—indeed, the young lady herself used to tell it as a particularly pleasant anecdote—and the taunts and mockery it occasioned were a source of the most acute distress to Hercules. From the poems written at this period we gather that he meditated taking his own life. In course of time, however, he lived down this humiliation; but never again, though he often fell in love, and that very passionately, did he dare to make any advances to those in whom he was interested. After coming to the estate and finding that he was in a position to create his own world as he desired it, he saw that, if he was to have a wife—which he very much desired, being of an affectionate and, indeed, amorous temper—he must choose her as he had chosen his servants—from among the race of dwarfs. But to find a suitable wife was, he found, a matter of some difficulty; for he would marry none who was not distinguished by beauty and gentle birth. The dwarfish daughter of Lord Bemboro he refused on the ground that besides being a pigmy she was hunchbacked; while another young lady, an orphan belonging to a very good family in Hampshire, was rejected by him because her face, like that of so many dwarfs, was wizened and repulsive. Finally, when he was almost despairing of success, he heard from a reliable source that Count Titimalo, a Venetian nobleman, possessed a daughter of exquisite beauty and great accomplishments, who was but three feet in height. Setting out at once for Venice, he went immediately on his arrival to pay his respects to the count, whom he found living with his wife and five children in a very mean apartment in one of the poorer quarters of the town. Indeed, the count was so far reduced in his circumstances that he was even then negotiating (so it was rumoured) with a travelling company of clowns and acrobats, who had had the misfortune to lose their performing dwarf, for the sale of his diminutive daughter Filomena. Sir Hercules arrived in time to save her from this untoward fate, for he was so much charmed by Filomena's grace and beauty, that at the end of three days' courtship he made her a formal offer of marriage, which was accepted by her no less joyfully than by her father, who perceived in an English son-in-law a rich and unfailing source of revenue. After an unostentatious marriage, at which the English ambassador acted as one of the witnesses, Sir Hercules and his bride returned by sea to England, where they settled down, as it proved, to a life of uneventful happiness.

"Crome and its household of dwarfs delighted Filomena, who felt herself now for the first time to be a free woman living among her equals in a friendly world. She had many tastes in common with her husband, especially that of music. She had a beautiful voice, of a power surprising in one so small, and could touch A in alt without effort. Accompanied by her husband on his fine Cremona fiddle, which he played, as we have noted before, as one plays a bass viol, she would sing all the liveliest and tenderest airs from the operas and cantatas of her native country. Seated together at the harpsichord, they found that they could with their four hands play all the music written for two hands of ordinary size, a circumstance which gave Sir Hercules unfailing pleasure.

"When they were not making music or reading together, which they often did, both in English and Italian, they spent their time in healthful outdoor exercises, sometimes rowing in a little boat on the lake, but more often riding or driving, occupations in which, because they were entirely new to her, Filomena especially delighted. When she had become a perfectly proficient rider, Filomena and her husband used often to go hunting in the park, at that time very much more extensive than it is now. They hunted not foxes nor hares, but rabbits, using a pack of about thirty black and fawn-coloured pugs, a kind of dog which, when not overfed, can course a rabbit as well as any of the smaller breeds. Four dwarf grooms, dressed in scarlet liveries and mounted on white Exmoor ponies, hunted the pack, while their master and mistress, in green habits, followed either on the black Shetlands or on the piebald New Forest ponies. A picture of the whole hunt—dogs, horses, grooms, and masters— was painted by William Stubbs, whose work Sir Hercules admired so much that he invited him, though a man of ordinary stature, to come and stay at the mansion for the purpose of executing this picture. Stubbs likewise painted a portrait of Sir Hercules and his lady driving in their green enamelled calash drawn by four black Shetlands. Sir Hercules wears a plum-coloured velvet coat and white breeches; Filomena is dressed in flowered muslin and a very large hat with pink feathers. The two figures in their gay carriage stand out sharply against a dark background of trees; but to the left of the picture the trees fall away and disappear, so that the four black ponies are seen against a pale and strangely lurid sky that has the golden-brown colour of thunder-clouds lighted up by the sun.

"In this way four years passed happily by. At the end of that time Filomena found herself great with child. Sir Hercules was overjoyed. 'If God is good,' he wrote in his day-book, 'the name of Lapith will be preserved and our rarer and more delicate race transmitted through the generations until in the fullness of time the world shall recognize the superiority of those beings whom now it uses to make mock of.' On his wife's being brought to bed of a son he wrote a poem to the same effect. The child was christened Ferdinando in memory of the builder of the house.

"With the passage of the months a certain sense of disquiet began to invade the minds of Sir Hercules and his lady. For the child was growing with an extraordinary rapidity. At a year he weighed as much as Hercules had weighed when he was three. 'Ferdinando goes *crescendo*,' wrote Filomena in her diary. 'It seems not natural.' At eighteen months the baby was almost as tall as their smallest jockey, who was a man of thirty-six. Could it be that Ferdinando was destined to become a man of the normal, gigantic dimensions? It was a thought to which neither of his parents dared yet give open utterance, but in the secrecy of their respective diaries they brooded over it in terror and dismay.

"On his third birthday Ferdinando was taller than his mother and not more than a couple of inches short of his father's height. 'To-day for the first time,' wrote Sir Hercules, 'we discussed the situation. The hideous truth can be concealed no longer: Ferdinando is not one of us. On this, his third birthday, a day when we should have been rejoicing at the health, the strength, and beauty of our child, we wept together over the ruin of our happiness. God give us strength to bear this cross.'

"At the age of eight Ferdinando was so large and so exuberantly healthy that his parents decided, though reluctantly, to send him to school. He was packed off to Eton at the beginning of the next half. A profound peace settled upon the house. Ferdinando returned for the summer holidays larger and stronger than ever. One day he knocked down the butler and broke his arm. 'He is rough, inconsiderate, unamenable to persuasion,' wrote his father. 'The only thing that will teach him manners is corporal chastisement.' Ferdinando, who at this age was already seventeen inches taller than his father, received no corporal chastisement.

"One summer holidays about three years later Ferdinando returned to Crome accompanied by a very large mastiff dog. He had bought it from an old man at Windsor who found the beast too expensive to feed. It was a savage, unreliable animal; hardly had it entered the house when it attacked one of Sir Hercules's favourite pugs, seizing the creature in its jaws and shaking it till it was nearly dead. Extremely put out by this occurrence, Sir Hercules ordered that the beast should be chained up

in the stable-yard. Ferdinando sullenly answered that the dog was his, and he would keep it where he pleased. His father, growing angry, bade him take the animal out of the house at once, on pain of his utmost displeasure. Ferdinando refused to move. His mother at this moment coming into the room, the dog flew at her, knocked her down, and in a twinkling had very severely mauled her arm and shoulder; in another instant it must infallibly have had her by the throat, had not Sir Hercules drawn his sword and stabbed the animal to the heart. Turning on his son, he ordered him to leave the room immediately, as being unfit to remain in the same place with the mother whom he had nearly murdered. So awe-inspiring was the spectacle of Sir Hercules standing with one foot on the carcase of the gigantic dog, his sword drawn and still bloody, so commanding were his voice, his gestures, and the expression of his face, that Ferdinando slunk out of the room in terror and behaved himself for all the rest of the vacation in an entirely exemplary fashion. His mother soon recovered from the bites of the mastiff, but the effect on her mind of this adventure was ineradicable; from that time forth she lived always among imaginary terrors.

"The two years which Ferdinando spent on the Continent, making the Grand Tour, were a period of happy repose for his parents. But even now the thought of the future haunted them; nor were they able to solace themselves with all the diversions of their younger days. The Lady Filomena had lost her voice and Sir Hercules was grown too rheumatical to play the violin. He, it is true, still rode after his pugs, but his wife felt herself too old and, since the episode of the mastiff, too nervous for such sports. At most, to please her husband, she would follow the hunt at a distance in a little gig drawn by the safest and oldest of the Shetlands.

"The day fixed for Ferdinando's return came round. Filomena, sick with vague dreads and presentiments, retired to her chamber and her bed. Sir Hercules received his son alone. A giant in a brown travelling-suit entered the room. 'Welcome home, my son,' said Sir Hercules in a voice that trembled a little.

"'I hope I see you well, sir.' Ferdinando bent down to shake hands, then straightened himself up again. The top of his father's head reached to the level of his hip.

"Ferdinando had not come alone. Two friends of his own age accompanied him, and each of the young men had brought a servant. Not for thirty years had Crome been desecrated by the presence of so many members of the common race of men. Sir Hercules was appalled and indignant, but the laws of hospitality had to be obeyed. He received the young gentlemen with grave politeness and sent the servants to the kitchen, with orders that they should be well cared for.

"The old family dining-table was dragged out into the light and dusted (Sir Hercules and his lady were accustomed to dine at a small table twenty inches high). Simon, the aged butler, who could only just look over the edge of the big table, was helped at supper by the three servants brought by Ferdinando and his guests.

"Sir Hercules presided, and with his usual grace supported a conversation on the pleasures of foreign travel, the beauties of art and nature to be met with abroad, the opera at Venice, the singing of the orphans in the churches of the same city, and on other topics of a similar nature. The young men were not particularly attentive to his discourses; they were occupied in watching the efforts of the butler to change the plates and replenish the glasses. They covered their laughter by violent and repeated fits of coughing or choking. Sir Hercules affected not to notice, but changed the subject of the conversation to sport. Upon this one of the young men asked whether it was true, as he had heard, that he used to hunt the rabbit with a pack of pug dogs. Sir Hercules replied that it was, and proceeded to describe the chase in some detail. The young men roared with laughter.

"When supper was over, Sir Hercules climbed down from his chair and, giving as his excuse that he must see how his lady did, bade them good-night. The sound of laughter followed him up the stairs. Filomena was not asleep; she had been lying on her bed listening to the sound of enormous laughter and the tread of strangely heavy feet on the stairs and along the corridors. Sir Hercules drew a chair to her bedside and sat there for a long time in silence, holding his wife's hand and sometimes gently squeezing it. At about ten o'clock they were startled by a violent noise. There was a breaking of glass, a stamping of feet, with an outburst of shouts and laughter. The uproar continuing for several minutes, Sir Hercules rose to his feet and, in spite of his wife's entreaties, prepared to go and see what was happening. There was no light on the staircase, and Sir Hercules groped his way down cautiously, lowering himself from stair to stair and standing for a moment on each tread before adventuring on a new step. The noise was louder here; the shouting articulated itself into recognizable words and phrases. A line of light was visible under the dining-room door. Sir Hercules tiptoed across the hall towards it. Just as he approached the door there was another terrific crash of breaking glass and jangled metal.

What could they be doing? Standing on tiptoe he managed to look through the keyhole. In the middle of the ravaged table old Simon, the butler, so primed with drink that he could scarcely keep his balance, was dancing a jig. His feet crunched and tinkled among the broken glass, and his shoes were wet with spilt wine. The three young men sat round, thumping the table with their hands or with the empty wine bottles, shouting and laughing encouragement. The three servants leaning against the wall laughed too. Ferdinando suddenly threw a handful of walnuts at the dancer's head, which so dazed and surprised the little man that he staggered and fell down on his back, upsetting a decanter and several glasses. They raised him up, gave him some brandy to drink, thumped him on the back. The old man smiled and hiccoughed, 'To-morrow,' said Ferdinando, 'we'll have a concerted ballet of the whole household.' With father Hercules wearing his club and lion-skin,' added one of his companions, and all three roared with laughter.

"Sir Hercules would look and listen no further. He crossed the hall once more and began to climb the stairs, lifting his knees painfully high at each degree. This was the end; there was no place for him now in the world, no place for him and Ferdinando together.

"His wife was still awake; to her questioning glance he answered, 'They are making mock of old Simon. To-morrow it will be our turn.' They were silent for a time.

"At last Filomena said, 'I do not want to see to-morrow.'

"'It is better not,' said Sir Hercules. Going into his closet he wrote in his day-book a full and particular account of all the events of the evening. While he was still engaged in this task he rang for a servant and ordered hot water and a bath to be made ready for him at eleven o'clock. When he had finished writing he went into his wife's room, and preparing a dose of opium twenty times as strong as that which she was accustomed to take when she could not sleep, he brought it to her, saying, 'Here is your sleeping-draught.'

"Filomena took the glass and lay for a little time, but did not drink immediately. The tears came into her eyes. 'Do you remember the songs we used to sing, sitting out there *sulla terrazza* in summer-time?' She began singing softly in her ghost of a cracked voice a few bars from Stradella's '*Amor, amor, non dormir piu.*' 'And you playing on the violin. It seems such a short time ago, and yet so long, long, long. *Addio, amore. A rivederti.*' She drank off the draught and, lying back on the pillow, closed her eyes. Sir Hercules kissed her hand and tiptoed away, as though he were afraid of waking her. He returned to his closet, and having recorded his wife's last words to him, he poured into his bath the water that had been brought up in accordance with his orders. The water being too hot for him to get into the bath at once, he took down from the shelf his copy of Suetonius. He wished to read how Seneca had died. He opened the book at random. 'But dwarfs,' he read, 'he held in abhorrence as being *lusus naturæ* and of evil omen.' He winced as though he had been struck. This same Augustus, he remembered, had exhibited in the amphitheatre a young man called Lucius, of good family, who was not quite two feet in height and weighed seventeen pounds, but had a sten-torian voice. He turned over the pages. Tiberius, Caligula, Claudius, Nero : it was a tale of growing horror. 'Seneca his preceptor, he forced to kill himself.' And there was

Petronius, who had called his friends about him at the last, bidding them talk to him, not of the consolations of philosophy, but of love and gallantry, while the life was ebbing away through his opened veins. Dipping his pen once more in the ink he wrote on the last page of his diary: 'He died a Roman death.' Then, putting the toes of one foot into the water and finding that it was not too hot, he threw off his dressing-gown and, taking a razor in his hand, sat down in the bath. With one deep cut he severed the artery in his left wrist, then lay back and composed his mind to meditation. The blood oozed out, floating through the water in dissolving wreaths and spirals. In a little while the whole bath was tinged with pink. The colour deepened; Sir Hercules felt himself mastered by an invincible drowsiness; he was sinking from vague dream to dream. Soon he was sound asleep. There was not much blood in his small body."

CHAPTER XIV

FOR their after-luncheon coffee the party generally adjourned to the library. Its windows looked east, and at this hour of the day it was the coolest place in the whole house. It was a large room, fitted, during the eighteenth century, with white painted shelves of an elegant design. In the middle of one wall a door, ingeniously upholstered with rows of dummy books, gave access to a deep cupboard, where, among a pile of letter-files and old newspapers, the mummy-case of an Egyptian lady, brought back by the second Sir Ferdinando on his return from the Grand Tour, mouldered in the darkness. From ten yards away and at a first glance, one might almost have mistaken this secret door for a section of shelving filled with genuine books. Coffee-cup in hand, Mr. Scogan was standing in front of the dummy book-shelf. Between the sips he discoursed.

"The bottom shelf," he was saying, "is taken up by an Encyclopædia in fourteen volumes. Useful, but a little dull, as is also Caprimulge's *Dictionary of the Finnish Language*. The *Biographical Dictionary* looks much more promising. *Biography of Men who were Born Great, Biography of Men who Achieved Greatness, Biography of Men who had Greatness Thrust upon Them*, and *Biography of Men who were Never Great at All*. Then there are ten volumes of *Thom's Works and Wanderings*, while the *Wild Goose Chase, a Novel*, by an anonymous author, fills no less than six. But what's this, what's this?" Mr. Scogan stood on tiptoe and peered up. "Seven volumes

of the *Tales of Knockespotch*. The *Tales of Knockespotch*,"
he repeated. "Ah, my dear Henry," he said, turning
round, "these are your best books. I would willingly
give all the rest of your library for them."

The happy possessor of a multitude of first editions,
Mr. Wimbush could afford to smile indulgently.

"Is it possible," Mr. Scogan went on, "that they
possess nothing more than a back and a title?" He opened
the cupboard door and peeped inside, as though he hoped
to find the rest of the books behind it. "Phooh!" he
said, and shut the door again. "It smells of dust and
mildew. How symbolical! One comes to the great
masterpieces of the past, expecting some miraculous
illumination, and one finds, on opening them, only darkness and dust and a faint smell of decay. After all, what
is reading but a vice, like drink or venery or any other
form of excessive self-indulgence? One reads to tickle
and amuse one's mind; one reads, above all, to prevent
oneself thinking. Still—the *Tales of Knockespotch* . . ."

He paused, and thoughtfully drummed with his fingers
on the backs of the non-existent, unattainable books.

"But I disagree with you about reading," said Mary.
"About serious reading, I mean."

"Quite right, Mary, quite right," Mr. Scogan answered.
"I had forgotten there were any serious people in the
room."

"I like the idea of the Biographies," said Denis.
"There's room for us all within the scheme; it's comprehensive."

"Yes, the Biographies are good, the Biographies are
excellent," Mr. Scogan agreed. "I imagine them written
in a very elegant Regency style—Brighton Pavilion in
words—perhaps by the great Dr. Lemprière himself.

You know his classical dictionary? Ah!" Mr. Scogan raised his hand and let it limply fall again in a gesture which implied that words failed him. "Read his biography of Helen; read how Jupiter, disguised as a swan, was 'enabled to avail himself of his situation' *vis-à-vis* to Leda. And to think that he may have, must have written these biographies of the Great! What a work, Henry! And, owing to the idiotic arrangement of your library, it can't be read."

"I prefer the *Wild Goose Chase*," said Anne. "A novel in six volumes—it must be restful."

"Restful," Mr. Scogan repeated. "You've hit on the right word. A *Wild Goose Chase* is sound, but a bit old-fashioned—pictures of clerical life in the fifties, you know; specimens of the landed gentry; peasants for pathos and comedy; and in the background, always the picturesque beauties of nature soberly described. All very good and solid, but, like certain puddings, just a little dull. Personally, I like much better the notion of *Thom's Works and Wanderings*. The eccentric Mr. Thom of Thom's Hill. Old Tom Thom, as his intimates used to call him. He spent ten years in Tibet organizing the clarified butter industry on modern European lines, and was able to retire at thirty-six with a handsome fortune. The rest of his life he devoted to travel and ratiocination; here is the result." Mr. Scogan tapped the dummy books. "And now we come to the *Tales of Knockespotch*. What a masterpiece and what a great man! Knockespotch knew how to write fiction. Ah, Denis, if you could only read Knockespotch you wouldn't be writing a novel about the wearisome development of a young man's character, you wouldn't be describing in endless, fastidious detail, cultured life in Chelsea and Bloomsbury and Hampstead.

You would be trying to write a readable book. But then, alas! owing to the peculiar arrangement of our host's library, you never will read Knockespotch."

"Nobody could regret the fact more than I do," said Denis.

"It was Knockespotch," Mr. Scogan continued, "the great Knockespotch, who delivered us from the dreary tyranny of the realistic novel. My life, Knockespotch said, is not so long that I can afford to spend precious hours writing or reading descriptions of middle-class interiors. He said again, 'I am tired of seeing the human mind bogged in a social plenum; I prefer to paint it in a vacuum, freely and sportively bombinating.'"

"I say," said Gombauld, "Knockespotch was a little obscure sometimes, wasn't he?"

"He was," Mr. Scogan replied, "and with intention. It made him seem even profounder than he actually was. But it was only in his aphorisms that he was so dark and oracular. In his Tales he was always luminous. Oh, those Tales—those Tales! How shall I describe them? Fabulous characters shoot across his pages like gaily dressed performers on the trapeze. There are extraordinary adventures and still more extraordinary speculations. Intelligences and emotions, relieved of all the imbecile preoccupations of civilized life, move in intricate and subtle dances, crossing and recrossing, advancing, retreating, impinging. An immense erudition and an immense fancy go hand in hand. All the ideas of the present and of the past, on every possible subject, bob up among the Tales, smile gravely or grimace a caricature of themselves, then disappear to make place for something new. The verbal surface of his writing is rich and fantastically diversified. The wit is incessant. The . . ."

"But couldn't you give us a specimen," Denis broke in—"a concrete example?"

"Alas!" Mr. Scogan replied, "Knockespotch's great book is like the sword Excalibur. It remains stuck fast in this door, awaiting the coming of a writer with genius enough to draw it forth. I am not even a writer, I am not so much as qualified to attempt the task. The extraction of Knockespotch from his wooden prison I leave, my dear Denis, to you."

"Thank you," said Denis.

CHAPTER XV

"IN the time of the amiable Brantôme," Mr. Scogan was saying, "every debutante at the French Court was invited to dine at the King's table, where she was served with wine in a handsome silver cup of Italian workmanship. It was no ordinary cup, this goblet of the debutantes; for, inside, it had been most curiously and ingeniously engraved with a series of very lively amorous scenes. With each draught that the young lady swallowed these engravings became increasingly visible, and the Court looked on with interest, every time she put her nose in the cup, to see whether she blushed at what the ebbing wine revealed. If the debutante blushed, they laughed at her for her innocence; if she did not, she was laughed at for being too knowing."

"Do you propose," asked Anne, "that the custom should be revived at Buckingham Palace?"

"I do not," said Mr. Scogan. "I merely quoted the anecdote as an illustration of the customs, so genially frank, of the sixteenth century. I might have quoted other anecdotes to show that the customs of the seventeenth and eighteenth, of the fifteenth and fourteenth centuries, and indeed of every other century, from the time of Hammurabi onward, were equally genial and equally frank. The only century in which customs were not characterized by the same cheerful openness was the nineteenth, of blessed memory. It was the astonishing exception. And yet, with what one must suppose was a deliberate disregard of history, it looked upon its horribly

114

pregnant silences as normal and natural and right; the frankness of the previous fifteen or twenty thousand years was considered abnormal and perverse. It was a curious phenomenon."

"I entirely agree." Mary panted with excitement in her effort to bring out what she had to say. "Havelock Ellis says . . ."

Mr. Scogan, like a policeman arresting the flow of traffic, held up his hand. "He does; I know. And that brings me to my next point: the nature of the reaction."

"Havelock Ellis . . ."

"The reaction, when it came—and we may say roughly that it set in a little before the beginning of this century—the reaction was to openness, but not to the same openness as had reigned in the earlier ages. It was to a scientific openness, not to the jovial frankness of the past, that we returned. The whole question of Amour became a terribly serious one. Earnest young men wrote in the public prints that from this time forth it would be impossible ever again to make a joke of any sexual matter. Professors wrote thick books in which sex was sterilized and dissected. It has become customary for serious young women, like Mary, to discuss, with philosophic calm, matters of which the merest hint would have sufficed to throw the youth of the sixties into a delirium of amorous excitement. It is all very estimable, no doubt. But still"—Mr. Scogan sighed— "I for one should like to see, mingled with this scientific ardour, a little more of the jovial spirit of Rabelais and Chaucer."

"I entirely disagree with you," said Mary. "Sex isn't a laughing matter; it's serious."

115

"Perhaps," answered Mr. Scogan, "perhaps I'm an obscene old man, for I must confess that I cannot always regard it as wholly serious."

"But I tell you . . ." began Mary furiously. Her face had flushed with excitement. Her cheeks were the cheeks of a great ripe peach.

"Indeed," Mr. Scogan continued, "it seems to me one of the few permanently and everlastingly amusing subjects that exist. Amour is the one human activity of any importance in which laughter and pleasure preponderate, if ever so slightly, over misery and pain."

"I entirely disagree," said Mary. There was a silence.

Anne looked at her watch. "Nearly a quarter to eight," she said. "I wonder when Ivor will turn up." She got up from her deck-chair and, leaning her elbows on the balustrade of the terrace, looked out over the valley and towards the farther hills. Under the level evening light the architecture of the land revealed itself. The deep shadows, the bright contrasting lights gave the hills a new solidity. Irregularities of the surface, unsuspected before, were picked out with light and shade. The grass, the corn, the foliage of trees were stippled with intricate shadows. The surface of things had taken on a marvellous enrichment.

"Look!" said Anne suddenly, and pointed. On the opposite side of the valley, at the crest of the ridge, a cloud of dust flushed by the sunlight to rosy gold was moving rapidly along the sky-line. "It's Ivor. One can tell by the speed."

The dust cloud descended into the valley and was lost. A horn with the voice of a sea-lion made itself heard, approaching. A minute later Ivor came leaping round the corner of the house. His hair waved in the wind of his own speed; he laughed as he saw them.

"Anne darling," he cried, and embraced her, embraced Mary, very nearly embraced Mr. Scogan. "Well, here I am. I've come with incredulous speed." Ivor's vocabulary was rich, but a little erratic. "I'm not late for dinner, am I?" He hoisted himself up on to the balustrade, and sat there, kicking his heels. With one arm he embraced a large stone flower-pot, leaning his head sideways against its hard and lichenous flanks in an attitude of trustful affection. He had brown, wavy hair, and his eyes were of a very brilliant, pale, improbable blue. His head was narrow, his face thin and rather long, his nose aquiline. In old age—though it was difficult to imagine Ivor old—he might grow to have an Iron Ducal grimness. But now, at twenty-six, it was not the structure of his face that impressed one; it was its expression. That was charming and vivacious, and his smile was an irradiation. He was for ever moving, restlessly and rapidly, but with an engaging gracefulness. His frail and slender body seemed to be fed by a spring of inexhaustible energy.

"No, you're not late."

"You're in time to answer a question," said Mr. Scogan. "We were arguing whether Amour were a serious matter or no. What do you think? Is it serious?"

"Serious?" echoed Ivor. "Most certainly."

"I told you so," cried Mary triumphantly.

"But in what sense serious?" Mr. Scogan asked.

"I mean as an occupation. One can go on with it without ever getting bored."

"I see," said Mr. Scogan. "Perfectly."

"One can occupy oneself with it," Ivor continued, "always and everywhere. Women are always wonderfully the same. Shapes vary a little, that's all. In Spain"—with his free hand he described a series of ample curves—"one can't pass them on the stairs. In England"—he put the tip of his forefinger against the tip of his thumb and, lowering his hand, drew out this circle into an imaginary cylinder—"in England they're tubular. But their sentiments are always the same. At least, I've always found it so."

"I'm delighted to hear it," said Mr. Scogan.

THE ladies had left the room and the port was circulating. Mr. Scogan filled his glass, passed on the decanter, and, leaning back in his chair, looked about him for a moment in silence. The conversation rippled idly round him, but he disregarded it; he was smiling at some private joke. Gombauld noticed his smile.

"What's amusing you?" he asked.

"I was just looking at you all, sitting round this table," said Mr. Scogan.

"Are we as comic as all that?"

"Not at all," Mr. Scogan answered politely. "I was merely amused by my own speculations."

"And what were they?"

"The idlest, the most academic of speculations. I was looking at you one by one and trying to imagine which of the first six Cæsars you would each resemble, if you were given the opportunity of behaving like a Cæsar. The Cæsars are one of my touchstones," Mr. Scogan explained. "They are characters functioning, so to speak, in the void. They are human beings developed to their logical conclusions. Hence their unequalled value as a touchstone, a standard. When I meet someone for the first time, I ask myself this question: Given the Cæsarean environment, which of the Cæsars would this person resemble—Julius, Augustus, Tiberius, Caligula, Claudius, Nero? I take each trait of character, each mental and emotional bias, each little oddity, and magnify them a

119

thousand times. The resulting image gives me his Cæsarean formula."

"And which of the Cæsars do you resemble?" asked Gombauld.

"I am potentially all of them," Mr. Scogan replied, "all—with the possible exception of Claudius, who was much too stupid to be a development of anything in my character. The seeds of Julius's courage and compelling energy, of Augustus's prudence, of the libidinousness and cruelty of Tiberius, of Caligula's folly, of Nero's artistic genius and enormous vanity, are all within me. Given the opportunities, I might have been something fabulous. But circumstances were against me. I was born and brought up in a country rectory; I passed my youth doing a great deal of utterly senseless hard work for a very little money. The result is that now, in middle age, I am the poor thing that I am. But perhaps it is as well. Perhaps, too, it's as well that Denis hasn't been permitted to flower into a little Nero, and that Ivor remains only potentially a Caligula. Yes, it's better so, no doubt. But it would have been more amusing, as a spectacle, if they had had the chance to develop, untrammelled, the full horror of their potentialities. It would have been pleasant and interesting to watch their tics and foibles and little vices swelling and burgeoning and blossoming into enormous and fantastic flowers of cruelty and pride and lewdness and avarice. The Cæsarean environment makes the Cæsar, as the special food and the queenly cell make the queen bee. We differ from the bees in so far that, given the proper food, they can be sure of making a queen every time. With us there is no such certainty; out of every ten men placed in the Cæsarean environment one will be temperamentally good, or intelligent, or great.

The rest will blossom into Cæsars; he will not. Seventy and eighty years ago simple-minded people, reading of the exploits of the Bourbons in South Italy, cried out in amazement: To think that such things should be happening in the nineteenth century! And a few years since we too were astonished to find that in our still more astonishing twentieth century, unhappy blackamoors on the Congo and the Amazon were being treated as English serfs were treated in the time of Stephen. To-day we are no longer surprised at these things. The Black and Tans harry Ireland, the Poles maltreat the Silesians, the bold Fascisti slaughter their poorer countrymen: we take it all for granted. Since the war we wonder at nothing. We have created a Cæsarean environment and a host of little Cæsars has sprung up. What could be more natural?"

Mr. Scogan drank off what was left of his port and refilled the glass.

"At this very moment," he went on, "the most frightful horrors are taking place in every corner of the world. People are being crushed, slashed, disembowelled, mangled; their dead bodies rot and their eyes decay with the rest. Screams of pain and fear go pulsing through the air at the rate of eleven hundred feet per second. After travelling for three seconds they are perfectly inaudible. These are distressing facts; but do we enjoy life any the less because of them? Most certainly we do not. We feel sympathy, no doubt; we represent to ourselves imaginatively the sufferings of nations and individuals and we deplore them. But, after all, what are sympathy and imagination? Precious little, unless the person for whom we feel sympathy happens to be closely involved in our affections; and even then they don't go very far. And a good thing too; for if one had an imagination vivid enough and a sympathy sufficiently sensitive really to comprehend and to feel the sufferings of other people, one would never have a moment's peace of mind. A really sympathetic race would not so much as know the meaning of happiness. But luckily, as I've already said, we aren't a sympathetic race. At the beginning of the war I used to think I really suffered, through imagination and sympathy, with those who physically suffered. But after a month or two I had to admit that, honestly, I didn't. And yet I think I have a more vivid imagination than most. One is always alone in suffering; the fact is depressing when one happens to be the sufferer, but it makes pleasure possible for the rest of the world."

There was a pause. Henry Wimbush pushed back his chair.

"I think perhaps we ought to go and join the ladies," he said.

"So do I," said Ivor, jumping up with alacrity. He turned to Mr. Scogan. "Fortunately," he said, "we can share our pleasures. We are not always condemned to be happy alone."

CHAPTER XVII

IVOR brought his hands down with a bang on to the final chord of his rhapsody. There was just a hint in that triumphant harmony that the seventh had been struck along with the octave by the thumb of the left hand; but the general effect of splendid noise emerged clearly enough. Small details matter little so long as the general effect is good. And, besides, that hint of the seventh was decidedly modern. He turned round in his seat and tossed the hair back out of his eyes.

"There," he said. "That's the best I can do for you, I'm afraid."

Murmurs of applause and gratitude were heard, and Mary, her large china eyes fixed on the performer, cried out aloud, "Wonderful!" and gasped for new breath as though she were suffocating.

Nature and fortune had vied with one another in heaping on Ivor Lombard all their choicest gifts. He had wealth and he was perfectly independent. He was good looking, possessed an irresistible charm of manner, and was the hero of more amorous successes than he could well remember. His accomplishments were extraordinary for their number and variety. He had a beautiful untrained tenor voice; he could improvise, with a startling brilliance, rapidly and loudly, on the piano. He was a good amateur medium and telepathist, and had a considerable first-hand knowledge of the next world. He could write rhymed verses with an extraordinary rapidity. For painting symbolical pictures he had a dashing style, and if the drawing

123

was sometimes a little weak, the colour was always pyrotechnical. He excelled in amateur theatricals and, when occasion offered, he could cook with genius. He resembled Shakespeare in knowing little Latin and less Greek. For a mind like his, education seemed supererogatory. Training would only have destroyed his natural aptitudes.

"Let's go out into the garden," Ivor suggested. "It's a wonderful night."

"Thank you," said Mr. Scogan, "but I for one prefer these still more wonderful arm-chairs." His pipe had begun to bubble oozily every time he pulled at it. He was perfectly happy.

Henry Wimbush was also happy. He looked for a moment over his pince-nez in Ivor's direction and then, without saying anything, returned to the grimy little sixteenth-century account books which were now his favourite reading. He knew more about Sir Ferdinando's household expenses than about his own.

The outdoor party, enrolled under Ivor's banner, consisted of Anne, Mary, Denis, and, rather unexpectedly, Jenny. Outside it was warm and dark; there was no moon. They walked up and down the terrace, and Ivor sang a Neapolitan song: "Stretti, stretti"—close, close —with something about the little Spanish girl to follow. The atmosphere began to palpitate. Ivor put his arm round Anne's waist, dropped his head sideways on to her shoulder, and in that position walked on, singing as he walked. It seemed the easiest, the most natural, thing in the world. Denis wondered why he had never done it. He hated Ivor.

"Let's go down to the pool," said Ivor. He disengaged his embrace and turned round to shepherd his little flock.

They made their way along the side of the house to the entrance of the yew-tree walk that led down to the lower garden. Between the blank precipitous wall of the house and the tall yew trees the path was a chasm of impenetrable gloom. Somewhere there were steps down to the right, a gap in the yew hedge. Denis, who headed the party, groped his way cautiously; in this darkness, one had an irrational fear of yawning precipices, of horrible spiked obstructions. Suddenly from behind him he heard a shrill, startled, "Oh!" and then a sharp, dry concussion that might have been the sound of a slap. After that, Jenny's voice was heard pronouncing, "I am going back to the house." Her tone was decided, and even as she pronounced the words she was melting away into the darkness. The incident, whatever it had been, was closed. Denis resumed his forward groping. From somewhere behind Ivor began to sing again, softly:

> "Phillis plus avare que tendre,
> Ne gagnant rien à refuser,
> Un jour exigea à Silvandre
> Trente moutons pour un baiser."

The melody drooped and climbed again with a kind of easy languor; the warm darkness seemed to pulse like blood about them.

> "Le lendemain, nouvelle affaire:
> Pour le berger, le troc fut bon . . ."

"Here are the steps," cried Denis. He guided his companions over the danger, and in a moment they had the turf of the yew-tree walk under their feet. It was lighter here, or at least it was just perceptibly less dark; for the yew walk was wider than the path that had led them under the lea of the house. Looking up, they could see between the high black hedges a strip of sky and a few stars.

"Car il obtint de la bergère . . ."

went on Ivor, and then interrupted himself to shout, "I'm going to run down," and he was off, full speed, down the invisible slope, singing unevenly as he went:

"Trente baisers pour un mouton."

The others followed. Denis shambled in the rear, vainly exhorting everyone to caution: the slope was steep, one might break one's neck. What was wrong with these people, he wondered? They had become like young kittens after a dose of cat-nip. He himself felt a certain kittenishness sporting within him; but it was, like all his emotions, rather a theoretical feeling; it did not over-masteringly seek to express itself in a practical demonstration of kittenishness.

"Be careful," he shouted once more, and hardly were the words out of his mouth when, thump! there was the sound of a heavy fall in front of him, followed by the long "F-f-f-f-f" of a breath indrawn with pain and afterwards by a very sincere, "Oo-ooh!" Denis was almost pleased; he had told them so, the idiots, and they wouldn't listen. He trotted down the slope towards the unseen sufferer.

Mary came down the hill like a runaway steam-engine. It was tremendously exciting, this blind rush through the dark; she felt she would never stop. But the ground grew level beneath her feet, her speed insensibly slackened, and suddenly she was caught by an extended arm and brought to an abrupt halt.

"Well," said Ivor as he tightened his embrace, "you're caught now, Anne."

126

She made an effort to release herself. "It's not Anne. It's Mary."

Ivor burst into a peal of amused laughter. "So it is!" he exclaimed. "I seem to be making nothing but floaters this evening. I've already made one with Jenny." He laughed again, and there was something so jolly about his laughter that Mary could not help laughing too. He did not remove his encircling arm, and somehow it was all so amusing and natural that Mary made no further attempt to escape from it. They walked along by the side of the pool, interlaced. Mary was too short for him to be able, with any comfort, to lay his head on her shoulder. He rubbed his cheek, caressed and caressing, against the thick, sleek mass of her hair. In a little while he began to sing again; the night trembled amorously to the sound of his voice. When he had finished he kissed her. Anne or Mary: Mary or Anne. It didn't seem to make much difference which it was. There were differences in detail, of course; but the general effect was the same; and, after all, the general effect was the important thing.

Denis made his way down the hill.

"Any damage done?" he called out.

"Is that you, Denis? I've hurt my ankle so—and my knee, and my hand. I'm all in pieces."

"My poor Anne," he said. "But then," he couldn't help adding, "it was silly to start running downhill in the dark."

"Ass!" she retorted in a tone of tearful irritation; "of course it was."

He sat down beside her on the grass, and found himself breathing the faint, delicious atmosphere of perfume that she carried always with her.

"Light a match," she commanded. "I want to look at my wounds."

He felt in his pockets for the match-box. The light spurted and then grew steady. Magically, a little universe had been created, a world of colours and forms—Anne's face, the shimmering orange of her dress, her white, bare arms, a patch of green turf—and round about a darkness that had become solid and utterly blind. Anne held out her hands; both were green and earthy with her fall, and the left exhibited two or three red abrasions.

"Not so bad," she said. But Denis was terribly distressed, and his emotion was intensified when, looking up at her face, he saw that the trace of tears, involuntary tears of pain, lingered on her eyelashes. He pulled out his handkerchief and began to wipe away the dirt from the wounded hand. The match went out; it was not worth while to light another. Anne allowed herself to be attended to, meekly and gratefully. "Thank you," she said, when he had finished cleaning and bandaging her hand; and there was something in her tone that made him feel that she had lost her superiority over him, that she was younger than he, had become, suddenly, almost a child. He felt tremendously large and protective. The feeling was so strong that instinctively he put his arm about her. She drew closer, leaned against him, and so they sat in silence. Then, from below, soft but wonderfully clear through the still darkness, they heard the sound of Ivor's singing. He was going on with his half-finished song:

> "Le lendemain Phillis plus tendre,
> Ne voulant déplaire au berger,
> Fut trop heureuse de lui rendre
> Trente moutons pour un baiser."

There was a rather prolonged pause. It was as though time were being allowed for the giving and receiving of a few of those thirty kisses. Then the voice sang on:

> "Le lendemain Phillis peu sage
> Aurait donné moutons et chien
> Pour un baiser que le volage
> A Lisette donnait pour rien."

The last note died away into an uninterrupted silence.

"Are you better?" Denis whispered. "Are you comfortable like this?"

She nodded a Yes to both questions.

"Trente moutons pour un baiser." The sheep, the woolly mutton—baa, baa, baa . . .? Or the shepherd? Yes, decidedly, he felt himself to be the shepherd now. He was the master, the protector. A wave of courage swelled through him, warm as wine. He turned his head, and began to kiss her face, at first rather randomly, then, with more precision, on the mouth.

Anne averted her head; he kissed the ear, the smooth nape that this movement presented him. "No," she protested; "no, Denis."

"Why not?"

"It spoils our friendship, and that was so jolly."

"Bosh!" said Denis.

She tried to explain. "Can't you see," she said, "it isn't . . . it isn't our stunt at all." It was true. Somehow she had never thought of Denis in the light of a man who might make love; she had never so much as conceived the possibilities of an amorous relationship with him. He was so absurdly young, so . . . so . . . she couldn't find the adjective, but she knew what she meant.

"Why isn't it our stunt?" asked Denis. "And, by the way, that's a horrible and inappropriate expression."

"Because it isn't."

"But if I say it is?"

"It makes no difference. I say it isn't."

"I shall make you say it is."

"All right, Denis. But you must do it another time. I must go in and get my ankle into hot water. It's beginning to swell."

Reasons of health could not be gainsaid. Denis got up reluctantly, and helped his companion to her feet. She took a cautious step. "Ooh!" She halted and leaned heavily on his arm.

"I'll carry you," Denis offered. He had never tried to carry a woman, but on the cinema it always looked an easy piece of heroism.

"You couldn't," said Anne.

"Of course I can." He felt larger and more protective than ever. "Put your arms round my neck," he ordered. She did so and, stooping, he picked her up under the knees and lifted her from the ground. Good heavens, what a weight! He took five staggering steps up the slope, then almost lost his equilibrium, and had to deposit his burden suddenly, with something of a bump.

Anne was shaking with laughter. "I said you couldn't, my poor Denis."

"I can," said Denis, without conviction. "I'll try again."

"It's perfectly sweet of you to offer, but I'd rather walk, thanks." She laid her hand on his shoulder and, thus supported, began to limp slowly up the hill.

"My poor Denis!" she repeated, and laughed again. Humiliated, he was silent. It seemed incredible that, only two minutes ago, he should have been holding her in his embrace, kissing her. Incredible. She was helpless then, a child. Now she had regained all her superiority; she was once more the far-off being, desired and unassailable. Why had he been such a fool as to suggest that carrying stunt? He reached the house in a state of the profoundest depression.

He helped Anne upstairs, left her in the hands of a maid, and came down again to the drawing-room. He was surprised to find them all sitting just where he had left them. He had expected that, somehow, everything would be quite different—it seemed such a prodigious time since he went away. All silent and all damned, he reflected, as he looked at them. Mr. Scogan's pipe still wheezed; that was the only sound. Henry Wimbush was still deep in his account books; he had just made the discovery that Sir Ferdinando was in the habit of eating oysters the whole summer through, regardless of the absence of the justifying R. Gombauld, in horn-rimmed spectacles, was reading. Jenny was mysteriously scribbling in her red notebook. And, seated in her favourite arm-chair at the corner of the hearth, Priscilla was looking through a pile of drawings. One by one she held them out at arm's length and, throwing back her mountainous orange head, looked long and attentively through half-closed eyelids. She wore a pale sea-green dress; on the slope of her mauve-powdered décolletage diamonds twinkled. An immensely long cigarette-holder projected at an angle from her face. Diamonds were embedded in her high-piled coiffure; they glittered every time she moved. It was a batch of Ivor's drawings—sketches of Spirit Life, made in the course of tranced tours through the other world. On the back of each sheet descriptive titles were written: "Portrait of an Angel, 15th March

131

'20"; "Astral Beings at Play, 3rd December '19"; "A Party of Souls on their Way to a Higher Sphere, 21st May '21." Before examining the drawing on the obverse of each sheet, she turned it over to read the title. Try as she could—and she tried hard—Priscilla had never seen a vision or succeeded in establishing any communication with the Spirit World. She had to be content with the reported experiences of others.

"What have you done with the rest of your party?" she asked, looking up as Denis entered the room.

He explained. Anne had gone to bed, Ivor and Mary were still in the garden. He selected a book and a comfortable chair, and tried, as far as the disturbed state of his mind would permit him, to compose himself for an evening's reading. The lamplight was utterly serene; there was no movement save the stir of Priscilla among her papers. All silent and all damned, Denis repeated to himself, all silent and all damned. . . .

It was nearly an hour later when Ivor and Mary made their appearance.

"We waited to see the moon rise," said Ivor.

"It was gibbous, you know," Mary explained, very technical and scientific.

"It was so beautiful down in the garden! The trees, the scent of the flowers, the stars . . ." Ivor waved his arms. "And when the moon came up, it was really too much. It made me burst into tears." He sat down at the piano and opened the lid.

"There were a great many meteorites," said Mary to anyone who would listen. "The earth must just be coming into the summer shower of them. In July and August . . ."

But Ivor had already begun to strike the keys. He played the garden, the stars, the scent of flowers, the rising moon. He even put in a nightingale that was not there. Mary looked on and listened with parted lips. The others pursued their occupations, without appearing to be seriously disturbed. On this very July day, exactly three hundred and fifty years ago, Sir Ferdinando had eaten seven dozen oysters. The discovery of this fact gave Henry Wimbush a peculiar pleasure. He had a natural piety which made him delight in the celebration of memorial feasts. The three hundred and fiftieth anniversary of the seven dozen oysters. . . . He wished he had known before dinner; he would have ordered champagne.

On her way to bed Mary paid a call. The light was out in Anne's room, but she was not yet asleep.

"Why didn't you come down to the garden with us?" Mary asked.

"I fell down and twisted my ankle. Denis helped me home."

Mary was full of sympathy. Inwardly, too, she was relieved to find Anne's non-appearance so simply accounted for. She had been vaguely suspicious, down there in the garden—suspicious of what, she hardly knew; but there had seemed to be something a little *louche* in the way she had suddenly found herself alone with Ivor. Not that she minded, of course; far from it. But she didn't like the idea that perhaps she was the victim of a put-up job.

"I do hope you'll be better to-morrow," she said, and she commiserated with Anne on all she had missed—the garden, the stars, the scent of flowers, the meteorites through whose summer shower the earth was now passing, the rising moon and its gibbosity. And then they had had such interesting conversation. What about? About almost everything. Nature, art, science, poetry, the stars, spiritualism, the relations of the sexes, music, religion. Ivor, she thought, had an interesting mind.

The two young ladies parted affectionately.

CHAPTER XVIII

THE nearest Roman Catholic church was upwards of twenty miles away. Ivor, who was punctilious in his devotions, came down early to breakfast and had his car at the door, ready to start, by a quarter to ten. It was a smart, expensive-looking machine, enamelled a pure lemon yellow and upholstered in emerald green leather. There were two seats—three if you squeezed tightly enough—and their occupants were protected from wind, dust, and weather by a glazed sedan that rose, an elegant eighteenth-century hump, from the midst of the body of the car.

Mary had never been to a Roman Catholic service, thought it would be an interesting experience, and, when the car moved off through the great gates of the court-yard, she was occupying the spare seat in the sedan. The sea-lion horn roared, faintlier, faintlier, and they were gone.

In the parish church of Crome Mr. Bodiham preached on 1 Kings vi. 18: "And the cedar of the house within was carved with knops"—a sermon of immediate local interest. For the past two years the problem of the War Memorial had exercised the minds of all those in Crome who had enough leisure, or mental energy, or party spirit to think of such things. Henry Wimbush was all for a library—a library of local literature, stocked with county histories, old maps of the district, monographs on the local antiquities, dialect dictionaries, handbooks of the local geology and natural history. He liked to think of the villagers, inspired by such reading, making up parties of a Sunday afternoon to look for fossils and flint arrow-heads. The villagers themselves favoured the idea of a memorial reservoir and water supply. But the busiest and most articulate party followed Mr. Bodiham in demanding something religious in character—a second lich-gate, for example, a stained-glass window, a monument of marble, or, if possible, all three. So far, however, nothing had been done, partly because the memorial committee had never been able to agree, partly for the more cogent reason that too little money had been subscribed to carry out any of the proposed schemes. Every three or four months Mr. Bodiham preached a sermon on the subject. His last had been delivered in March; it was high time that his congregation had a fresh reminder.

"And the cedar of the house within was carved with knops."

Mr. Bodiham touched lightly on Solomon's temple. From thence he passed to temples and churches in general. What were the characteristics of these buildings dedicated to God? Obviously, the fact of their, from a human point of view, complete uselessness. They were unpractical buildings "carved with knops." Solomon might have built a library—indeed, what could be more to the taste of the world's wisest man? He might have dug a reservoir—what more useful in a parched city like Jerusalem? He did neither; he built a house all carved with knops, useless and unpractical. Why? Because he was dedicating the work to God. There had been much talk in Crome about the proposed War Memorial. A War Memorial was, in its very nature, a work dedicated to God. It was a token of thankfulness that the first stage in the culminating world-war had been crowned by the triumph

of righteousness; it was at the same time a visibly em-
bodied supplication that God might not long delay the
Advent which alone could bring the final peace. A library,
a reservoir? Mr. Bodiham scornfully and indignantly
condemned the idea. These were works dedicated to man,
not to God. As a War Memorial they were totally unsuitable. A lich-gate had been suggested. This was an
object which answered perfectly to the definition of a
War Memorial: a useless work dedicated to God and
carved with knops. One lich-gate, it was true, already
existed. But nothing would be easier than to make a
second entrance into the churchyard; and a second
entrance would need a second gate. Other suggestions
had been made. Stained-glass windows, a monument of
marble. Both these were admirable, especially the latter.
It was high time that the War Memorial was erected. It
might soon be too late. At any moment, like a thief in
the night, God might come. Meanwhile a difficulty stood
in the way. Funds were inadequate. All should subscribe
according to their means. Those who had lost relations
in the war might reasonably be expected to subscribe a
sum equal to that which they would have had to pay in
funeral expenses if the relative had died while at home.
Further delay was disastrous. The War Memorial must
be built at once. He appealed to the patriotism and the
Christian sentiments of all his hearers.

Henry Wimbush walked home thinking of the books
he would present to the War Memorial Library, if ever
it came into existence. He took the path through the
fields; it was pleasanter than the road. At the first stile
a group of village boys, loutish young fellows all dressed
in the hideous ill-fitting black which makes a funeral of
every English Sunday and holiday, were assembled,

drearily guffawing as they smoked their cigarettes. They made way for Henry Wimbush, touching their caps as he passed. He returned their salute; his bowler and face were one in their unruffled gravity.

In Sir Ferdinando's time, he reflected, in the time of his son, Sir Julius, these young men would have had their Sunday diversions even at Crome, remote and rustic Crome. There would have been archery, skittles, dancing —social amusements in which they would have partaken as members of a conscious community. Now they had nothing, nothing except Mr. Bodiham's forbidding Boys' Club and the rare dances and concerts organized by himself. Boredom or the urban pleasures of the county metropolis were the alternatives that presented themselves to these poor youths. Country pleasures were no more; they had been stamped out by the Puritans.

In Manningham's Diary for 1600 there was a queer passage, he remembered, a very queer passage. Certain magistrates in Berkshire, Puritan magistrates, had had wind of a scandal. One moonlit summer night they had ridden out with their *posse* and there, among the hills, they had come upon a company of men and women, dancing, stark naked, among the sheep-cotes. The magistrates and their men had ridden their horses into the crowd. How self-conscious the poor people must suddenly have felt, how helpless without their clothes against armed and booted horsemen! The dancers are arrested, whipped, gaoled, set in the stocks; the moonlight dance is never danced again. What old, earthy, Panic rite came to extinction here? he wondered. Who knows?—perhaps their ancestors had danced like this in the moonlight ages before Adam and Eve were so much as thought of. He liked to think so. And now it was no more. These weary young men, if they wanted to dance, would have to bicycle six miles to the town. The country was desolate, without life of its own, without indigenous pleasures. The pious magistrates had snuffed out for ever a little happy flame that had burned from the beginning of time.

"And as on Tullia's tomb one lamp burned clear,
    Unchanged for fifteen hundred year . . ."

He repeated the lines to himself, and was desolated to think of all the murdered past.

CHAPTER XIX

HENRY WIMBUSH'S long cigar burned aromatically. The *History of Crome* lay on his knee; slowly he turned over the pages.

"I can't decide what episode to read you to-night," he said thoughtfully. "Sir Ferdinando's voyages are not without interest. Then, of course, there's his son, Sir Julius. It was he who suffered from the delusion that his perspiration engendered flies; it drove him finally to suicide. Or there's Sir Cyprian." He turned the pages more rapidly. "Or Sir Henry. Or Sir George. . . . No, I'm inclined to think I won't read about any of these."

"But you must read something," insisted Mr. Scogan, taking his pipe out of his mouth.

"I think I shall read about my grandfather," said Henry Wimbush, "and the events that led up to his marriage with the eldest daughter of the last Sir Ferdinando."

"Good," said Mr. Scogan. "We are listening."

"Before I begin reading," said Henry Wimbush, looking up from the book and taking off the pince-nez which he had just fitted to his nose—"before I begin, I must say a few preliminary words about Sir Ferdinando, the last of the Lapiths. At the death of the virtuous and unfortunate Sir Hercules, Ferdinando found himself in possession of the family fortune, not a little increased by his father's temperance and thrift; he applied himself forthwith to the task of spending it, which he did in an ample and jovial fashion. By the time he was forty he had eaten and, above all, drunk and loved away about half his capital, and would infallibly have soon got rid of the rest in the same manner, if he had not had the good fortune to become so madly enamoured of the Rector's daughter as to make a proposal of marriage. The young lady accepted him, and in less than a year had become the absolute mistress of Crome and her husband. An extraordinary reformation made itself apparent in Sir Ferdinando's character. He grew regular and economical in his habits; he even became temperate, rarely drinking more than a bottle and a half of port at a sitting. The waning fortune of the Lapiths began once more to wax, and that in despite of the hard times (for Sir Ferdinando married in 1809 in the height of the Napoleonic Wars). A prosperous and dignified old age, cheered by the spectacle of his children's growth and happiness—for Lady Lapith had already borne him three daughters, and there seemed no good reason why she should not bear many more of them, and sons as well—a patriarchal decline into the family vault, seemed now to be Sir Ferdinando's enviable destiny. But Providence willed otherwise. To Napoleon, cause already of such infinite mischief, was due, though perhaps indirectly, the untimely and violent death which put a period to this reformed existence.

"Sir Ferdinando, who was above all things a patriot, had adopted, from the earliest days of the conflict with the French, his own peculiar method of celebrating our victories. When the happy news reached London, it was his custom to purchase immediately a large store of liquor and, taking a place on whichever of the outgoing coaches he happened to light on first, to drive through the country proclaiming the good news to all he met on

141

the road and dispensing it, along with the liquor, at every stopping-place to all who cared to listen or drink. Thus, after the Nile, he had driven as far as Edinburgh; and later, when the coaches, wreathed with laurel for triumph, with cypress for mourning, were setting out with the news of Nelson's victory and death, he sat through all a chilly October night on the box of the Norwich *Meteor* with a nautical keg of rum on his knees and two cases of old brandy under the seat. This genial custom was one of the many habits which he abandoned on his marriage. The victories in the Peninsula, the retreat from Moscow, Leipzig, and the abdication of the tyrant all went un-celebrated. It so happened, however, that in the summer of 1815 Sir Ferdinando was staying for a few weeks in the capital. There had been a succession of anxious, doubtful days; then came the glorious news of Waterloo. It was too much for Sir Ferdinando; his joyous youth awoke again within him. He hurried to his wine merchant and bought a dozen bottles of 1760 brandy. The Bath coach was on the point of starting; he bribed his way on to the box and, seated in glory beside the driver, pro-claimed aloud the downfall of the Corsican bandit and passed about the warm liquid joy. They clattered through Uxbridge, Slough, Maidenhead. Sleeping Reading was awakened by the great news. At Didcot one of the ostlers was so much overcome by patriotic emotions and the 1760 brandy that he found it impossible to do up the buckles of the harness. The night began to grow chilly, and Sir Ferdinando found that it was not enough to take a nip at every stage: to keep up his vital warmth he was compelled to drink between the stages as well. They were approaching Swindon. The coach was travelling at a dizzy speed—six miles in the last half-hour—when, without having manifested the slightest premonitory symptom of unsteadiness, Sir Ferdinando suddenly toppled sideways off his seat and fell, head foremost, into the road. An unpleasant jolt awakened the slumbering passengers. The coach was brought to a standstill; the guard ran back with a light. He found Sir Ferdinando still alive, but unconscious; blood was oozing from his mouth. The back wheels of the coach had passed over his body, breaking most of his ribs and both arms. His skull was fractured in two places. They picked him up, but he was dead before they reached the next stage. So perished Sir Ferdinando, a victim to his own patriotism. Lady Lapith did not marry again, but determined to devote the rest of her life to the well-being of her three children—Georgiana, now five years old, and Emmeline and Caroline, twins of two."

Henry Wimbush paused, and once more put on his pince-nez. "So much by way of introduction," he said. "Now I can begin to read about my grandfather."

"One moment," said Mr. Scogan, "till I've refilled my pipe."

Mr. Wimbush waited. Seated apart in a corner of the room, Ivor was showing Mary his sketches of Spirit Life. They spoke together in whispers.

Mr. Scogan had lighted his pipe again. "Fire away," he said.

Henry Wimbush fired away.

"It was in the spring of 1833 that my grandfather, George Wimbush, first made the acquaintance of the 'three lovely Lapiths,' as they were always called. He was then a young man of twenty-two, with curly yellow hair and a smooth pink face that was the mirror of his youthful and ingenuous mind. He had been educated at

Harrow and Christ Church, he enjoyed hunting and all other field sports, and, though his circumstances were comfortable to the verge of affluence, his pleasures were temperate and innocent. His father, an East Indian merchant, had destined him for a political career, and had gone to considerable expense in acquiring a pleasant little Cornish borough as a twenty-first birthday gift for his son. He was justly indignant when, on the very eve of George's majority, the Reform Bill of 1832 swept the borough out of existence. The inauguration of George's political career had to be postponed. At the time he got to know the lovely Lapiths he was waiting; he was not at all impatient.

"The lovely Lapiths did not fail to impress him. Georgiana, the eldest, with her black ringlets, her flashing eyes, her noble aquiline profile, her swan-like neck, and sloping shoulders, was orientally dazzling; and the twins, with their delicately turned-up noses, their blue eyes, and chestnut hair, were an identical pair of ravishingly English charmers.

"Their conversation at this first meeting proved, however, to be so forbidding that, but for the invincible attraction exercised by their beauty, George would never have had the courage to follow up the acquaintance. The twins, looking up their noses at him with an air of languid superiority, asked him what he thought of the latest French poetry and whether he liked the *Indiana* of George Sand. But what was almost worse was the question with which Georgiana opened her conversation with him. 'In music,' she asked, leaning forward and fixing him with her large dark eyes, 'are you a classicist or a transcendentalist?' George did not lose his presence of mind. He had enough appreciation of music to know that he hated anything classical, and so, with a promptitude which did him credit, he replied, 'I am a transcendentalist.' Georgiana smiled bewitchingly. 'I am glad,' she said; 'so am I. You went to hear Paganini last week, of course. "The Prayer of Moses"—ah!' She closed her eyes. 'Do you know anything more transcendental than that?' 'No,' said George, 'I don't.' He hesitated, was about to go on speaking, and then decided that after all it would be wiser not to say—what was in fact true—that he had enjoyed above all Paganini's Farmyard Imitations. The man had made his fiddle bray like an ass, cluck like a hen, grunt, squeal, bark, neigh, quack, bellow, and growl; that last item, in George's estimation, had almost compensated for the tediousness of the rest of the concert. He smiled with pleasure at the thought of it. Yes, decidedly, he was no classicist in music; he was a thoroughgoing transcendentalist.

"George followed up this first introduction by paying a call on the young ladies and their mother, who occupied, during the season, a small but elegant house in the neighbourhood of Berkeley Square. Lady Lapith made a few discreet inquiries, and having found that George's financial position, character, and family were all passably good, she asked him to dine. She hoped and expected that her daughters would all marry into the peerage; but, being a prudent woman, she knew it was advisable to prepare for all contingencies. George Wimbush, she thought, would make an excellent second string for one of the twins.

"At this first dinner, George's partner was Emmeline. They talked of Nature. Emmeline protested that to her high mountains were a feeling and the hum of human cities torture. George agreed that the country was very agreeable, but held that London during the season also had its charms. He noticed with surprise and a certain solicitous distress that Miss Emmeline's appetite was poor, that it didn't, in fact exist. Two spoonfuls of soup, a morsel of fish, no bird, no meat, and three grapes—that was her whole dinner. He looked from time to time at her two sisters; Georgiana and Caroline seemed to be quite as abstemious. They waved away whatever was offered them with an expression of delicate disgust, shutting their eyes and averting their faces from the proffered dish, as though the lemon sole, the duck, the loin of veal, the trifle, were objects revolting to the sight and smell. George, who thought the dinner capital, ventured to comment on the sisters' lack of appetite.

"'Pray, don't talk to me of eating,' said Emmeline, drooping like a sensitive plant. 'We find it so coarse, so unspiritual, my sisters and I. One can't think of one's soul while one is eating.'

"George agreed; one couldn't. 'But one must live,' he said.

"'Alas!' Emmeline sighed. 'One must. Death is very beautiful, don't you think?' She broke a corner off a piece of toast and began to nibble at it languidly. 'But since, as you say, one must live . . .' She made a little gesture of resignation. 'Luckily a very little suffices to keep one alive.' She put down her corner of toast half eaten.

"George regarded her with some surprise. She was pale, but she looked extraordinarily healthy, he thought; so did her sisters. Perhaps if you were really spiritual you needed less food. He, clearly, was not spiritual.

"After this he saw them frequently. They all liked him, from Lady Lapith downwards. True, he was not very romantic or poetical; but he was such a pleasant, unpretentious, kind-hearted young man, that one couldn't help liking him. For his part, he thought them wonderful, wonderful, especially Georgiana. He enveloped them all in a warm, protective affection. For they needed protection; they were altogether too frail, too spiritual for this world. They never ate, they were always pale, they often complained of fever, they talked much and lovingly of death, they frequently swooned. Georgiana was the most ethereal of all; of the three she ate least, swooned most often, talked most of death, and was the palest— with a pallor that was so startling as to appear positively artificial. At any moment, it seemed, she might loose her precarious hold on this material world and become all spirit. To George the thought was a continual agony. If she were to die . . .

"She contrived, however, to live through the season, and that in spite of the numerous balls, routs, and other parties of pleasure which, in company with the rest of the lovely trio, she never failed to attend. In the middle of July the whole household moved down to the country. George was invited to spend the month of August at Crome.

"The house-party was distinguished; in the list of visitors figured the names of two marriageable young men of title. George had hoped that country air, repose, and natural surroundings might have restored to the three sisters their appetites and the roses of their cheeks. He was mistaken. For dinner, the first evening, Georgiana ate only an olive, two or three salted almonds, and half a peach. She was as pale as ever. During the meal she spoke of love.

"'True love,' she said, 'being infinite and eternal, can

only be consummated in eternity. Indiana and Sir Rodolphe celebrated the mystic wedding of their souls by jumping into Niagara. Love is incompatible with life. The wish of two people who truly love one another is not to live together but to die together.'

"'Come, come, my dear,' said Lady Lapith, stout and practical. 'What would become of the next generation, pray, if all the world acted on your principles?'

"'Mamma! . . .' Georgiana protested, and dropped her eyes.

"'In my young days,' Lady Lapith went on, 'I should have been laughed out of countenance if I'd said a thing like that. But then in my young days souls weren't as fashionable as they are now and we didn't think death was at all poetical. It was just unpleasant.'

"'Mamma! . . .' Emmeline and Caroline implored in unison.

"'In my young days——' Lady Lapith was launched into her subject; nothing, it seemed, could stop her now. 'In my young days, if you didn't eat, people told you you needed a dose of rhubarb. Nowadays . . .'

"There was a cry; Georgiana had swooned sideways on to Lord Timpany's shoulder. It was a desperate expedient; but it was successful. Lady Lapith was stopped.

"The days passed in an uneventful round of pleasures. Of all the gay party George alone was unhappy. Lord Timpany was paying his court to Georgiana, and it was clear that he was not unfavourably received. George looked on, and his soul was a hell of jealousy and despair. The boisterous company of the young men became intolerable to him; he shrank from them, seeking gloom and solitude. One morning, having broken away from them on some vague pretext, he returned to the house alone. The young men were bathing in the pool below; their cries and laughter·floated up to him, making the quiet house seem lonelier and more silent. The lovely sisters and their mamma still kept their chambers; they did not customarily make their appearance till luncheon, so that the male guests had the morning to themselves. George sat down in the hall and abandoned himself to thought.

"At any moment she might die; at any moment she might become Lady Timpany. It was terrible, terrible. If she died, then he would die too; he would go to seek her beyond the grave. If she became Lady Timpany . . . ah, then! The solution of the problem would not be so simple. If she became Lady Timpany: it was a horrible thought. But then suppose she were in love with Timpany—though it seemed incredible that anyone could be in love with Timpany—suppose her life depended on Timpany, suppose she couldn't live without him? He was fumbling his way along this clueless labyrinth of suppositions when the clock struck twelve. On the last stroke, like an automaton released by the turning clockwork, a little maid, holding a large covered tray, popped out of the door that led from the kitchen regions into the hall. From his deep arm-chair George watched her (himself, it was evident, unobserved) with an idle curiosity. She pattered across the room and came to a halt in front of what seemed a blank expanse of panelling. She reached out her hand and, to George's extreme astonishment, a little door swung open, revealing the foot of a winding staircase. Turning sideways in order to get her tray through the narrow opening, the little maid darted in with a rapid crablike motion. The door closed behind her with a click. A minute later it opened again and the maid, without her tray, hurried back across the hall and disappeared in the direction of the kitchen. George tried to recompose his thoughts, but an invincible curiosity drew his mind towards the hidden door, the staircase, the little maid. It was in vain he told himself that the matter was none of his business, that to explore the secrets of that surprising door, that mysterious staircase within, would be a piece of unforgivable rudeness and indiscretion. It was in vain; for five minutes he struggled heroically with his curiosity, but at the end of that time he found himself standing in front of the innocent sheet of panelling through which the little maid had disappeared. A glance sufficed to show him the position of the secret door—secret, he perceived, only to those who looked with a careless eye. It was just an ordinary door let in flush with the panelling. No latch nor handle betrayed its position, but an unobtrusive catch sunk in the wood invited the thumb. George was astonished that he had not noticed it before; now he had seen it, it was so obvious, almost as obvious as the cupboard door in the library with its lines of imitation shelves and its dummy books. He pulled back the catch and peeped inside. The staircase, of which the degrees were made not of stone but of blocks of ancient oak, wound up and out of sight. A slit-like window admitted the daylight; he was at the foot of the central tower, and the little window looked out over the terrace; they were still shouting and splashing in the pool below.

"George closed the door and went back to his seat. But his curiosity was not satisfied. Indeed, this partial satisfaction had but whetted its appetite. Where did the staircase lead? What was the errand of the little maid?

It was no business of his, he kept repeating—no business of his. He tried to read, but his attention wandered. A quarter-past twelve sounded on the harmonious clock. Suddenly determined, George rose, crossed the room, opened the hidden door, and began to ascend the stairs. He passed the first window, corkscrewed round, and came to another. He paused for a moment to look out; his heart beat uncomfortably, as though he were affronting some unknown danger. What he was doing, he told himself, was extremely ungentlemanly, horribly underbred. He tiptoed onward and upward. One turn more, then half a turn, and a door confronted him. He halted before it, listened; he could hear no sound. Putting his eye to the keyhole, he saw nothing but a stretch of white sunlit wall. Emboldened, he turned the handle and stepped across the threshold. There he halted, petrified by what he saw, mutely gaping.

"In the middle of a pleasantly sunny little room—'it is now Priscilla's boudoir,' Mr. Wimbush remarked parenthetically—stood a small circular table of mahogany. Crystal, porcelain, and silver,—all the shining apparatus of an elegant meal—were mirrored in its polished depths. The carcase of a cold chicken, a bowl of fruit, a great ham, deeply gashed to its heart of tenderest white and pink, the brown cannon ball of a cold plum-pudding, a slender Hock bottle, and a decanter of claret jostled one another for a place on this festive board. And round the table sat the three sisters, the three lovely Lapiths—eating!

"At George's sudden entrance they had all looked towards the door, and now they sat, petrified by the same astonishment which kept George fixed and staring. Georgiana, who sat immediately facing the door, gazed at him with dark, enormous eyes. Between the thumb and forefinger of her right hand she was holding a drumstick of the dismembered chicken; her little finger, elegantly crooked, stood apart from the rest of her hand. Her mouth was open, but the drumstick had never reached its destination; it remained, suspended, frozen, in mid-air. The other two sisters had turned round to look at the intruder. Caroline still grasped her knife and fork; Emmeline's fingers were round the stem of her claret glass. For what seemed a very long time, George and the three sisters stared at one another in silence. They were a group of statues. Then suddenly there was movement. Georgiana dropped her chicken bone, Caroline's knife and fork clattered on her plate. The movement propagated itself, grew more decisive; Emmeline sprang to her feet, uttering a cry. The wave of panic reached George; he turned and, mumbling something unintelligible as he went, rushed out of the room and down the winding stairs. He came to a standstill in the hall, and there, all by himself in the quiet house, he began to laugh.

"At luncheon it was noticed that the sisters ate a little more than usual. Georgiana toyed with some French beans and a spoonful of calves'-foot jelly. 'I feel a little stronger to-day,' she said to Lord Timpany, when he congratulated her on this increase of appetite; 'a little more material,' she added, with a nervous laugh. Looking up, she caught George's eye; a blush suffused her cheeks and she looked hastily away.

"In the garden that afternoon they found themselves for a moment alone.

"'You won't tell anyone, George? Promise you won't tell anyone,' she implored. 'It would make us look so

152

ridiculous. And besides, eating *is* unspiritual, isn't it? Say you won't tell anyone.'

"'I will,' said George brutally. 'I'll tell everyone, unless . . .'

"'It's blackmail.'

"'I don't care,' said George. 'I'll give you twenty-four hours to decide.'

"Lady Lapith was disappointed, of course; she had hoped for better things—for Timpany and a coronet. But George, after all, wasn't so bad. They were married at the New Year.

"My poor grandfather!" Mr. Wimbush added, as he closed his book and put away his pince-nez. "Whenever I read in the papers about oppressed nationalities, I think of him." He relighted his cigar. "It was a maternal government, highly centralized, and there were no representative institutions."

Henry Wimbush ceased speaking. In the silence that ensued Ivor's whispered commentary on the spirit sketches once more became audible. Priscilla, who had been dozing, suddenly woke up.

"What?" she said in the startled tones of one newly returned to consciousness; "what?"

Jenny caught the words. She looked up, smiled, nodded reassuringly. "It's about a ham," she said.

"What's about a ham?"

"What Henry has been reading." She closed the red notebook lying on her knees and slipped a rubber band round it. "I'm going to bed," she announced, and got up.

"So am I," said Anne, yawning. But she lacked the energy to rise from her arm-chair.

The night was hot and oppressive. Round the open windows the curtains hung unmoving. Ivor, fanning

153

himself with the portrait of an Astral Being, looked out into the darkness and drew a breath.

"The air's like wool," he declared.

"It will get cooler after midnight," said Henry Wimbush, and cautiously added, "perhaps."

"I shan't sleep, I know."

Priscilla turned her head in his direction; the monumental coiffure nodded exorbitantly at her slightest movement. "You must make an effort," she said. "When I can't sleep, I concentrate my will: I say, 'I will sleep, I am asleep!' And pop! off I go. That's the power of thought."

"But does it work on stuffy nights?" Ivor inquired. "I simply cannot sleep on a stuffy night."

"Nor can I," said Mary, "except out of doors."

"Out of doors! What a wonderful idea!" In the end they decided to sleep on the towers—Mary on the western tower, Ivor on the eastern. There was a flat expanse of leads on each of the towers, and you could get a mattress through the trap doors that opened on to them. Under the stars, under the gibbous moon, assuredly they would sleep. The mattresses were hauled up, sheets and blankets were spread, and an hour later the two insomniasts, each on his separate tower, were crying their good-nights across the dividing gulf.

On Mary the sleep-compelling charm of the open air did not work with its expected magic. Even through the mattress one could not fail to be aware that the leads were extremely hard. Then there were noises: the owls screeched tirelessly, and once, roused by some unknown terror, all the geese of the farmyard burst into a sudden frenzy of cackling. The stars and the gibbous moon demanded to be looked at, and when one meteorite had streaked across the sky, you could not help waiting, open-eyed and alert, for the next. Time passed; the moon climbed higher and higher in the sky. Mary felt less sleepy than she had when she first came out. She sat up and looked over the parapet. Had Ivor been able to sleep? she wondered. And as though in answer to her mental question, from behind the chimney-stack at the farther end of the roof a white form noiselessly emerged—a form that, in the moonlight, was recognizably Ivor's. Spreading his arms to right and left, like a tight-rope dancer, he began to walk forward along the roof-tree of the house. He swayed terrifyingly as he advanced. Mary looked on speechlessly; perhaps he was walking in his sleep! Suppose he were to wake up suddenly, now! If she spoke or moved it might mean his death. She dared look no more, but sank back on her pillows. She listened intently. For what seemed an immensely long time there was no sound. Then there was a patter of feet on the tiles, followed by a scrabbling noise and a whispered "Damn!" And suddenly Ivor's head and shoulders appeared above the parapet. One leg followed, then the other. He was on the leads. Mary pretended to wake up with a start.

"Oh!" she said. "What are you doing here?"

"I couldn't sleep," he explained, "so I came along to see if you couldn't. One gets bored by oneself on a tower. Don't you find it so?"

It was light before five. Long, narrow clouds barred the east, their edges bright with orange fire. The sky was pale and watery. With the mournful scream of a soul in pain, a monstrous peacock, flying heavily up from below, alighted on the parapet of the tower. Ivor and Mary started broad awake.

"Catch him!" cried Ivor, jumping up. "We'll have a feather." The frightened peacock ran up and down the parapet in an absurd distress, curtseying and bobbing and clucking; his long tail swung ponderously back and forth as he turned and turned again. Then with a flap and swish he launched himself upon the air and sailed magnificently earthward, with a recovered dignity. But he had left a trophy. Ivor had his feather, a long-lashed eye of purple and green, of blue and gold. He handed it to his companion.

"An angel's feather," he said.

Mary looked at it for a moment, gravely and intently. Her purple pyjamas clothed her with an ampleness that hid the lines of her body; she looked like some large, comfortable, unjointed toy, a sort of Teddy bear—but a Teddy bear with an angel's head, pink cheeks, and hair like a bell of gold. An angel's face, the feather of an angel's wing. . . . Somehow the whole atmosphere of this sunrise was rather angelic.

"It's extraordinary to think of sexual selection," she said at last, looking up from her contemplation of the miraculous feather.

"Extraordinary!" Ivor echoed. "I select you, you select me. What luck!"

He put his arm round her shoulders and they stood looking eastward. The first sunlight had begun to warm and colour the pale light of the dawn. Mauve pyjamas and white pyjamas; they were a young and charming couple. The rising sun touched their faces. It was all extremely symbolic; but then, if you choose to think so, nothing in this world is not symbolical. Profound and beautiful truth!

"I must be getting back to my tower," said Ivor at last.

"Already?"

"I'm afraid so. The varletry will soon be up and about."

"Ivor...." There was a prolonged and silent farewell.

"And now," said Ivor, "I repeat my tight-rope stunt."

Mary threw her arms round his neck. "You mustn't, Ivor. It's dangerous. Please."

He had to yield at last to her entreaties. "All right," he said, "I'll go down through the house and up at the other end."

He vanished through the trap door into the darkness that still lurked within the shuttered house. A minute later he had reappeared on the farther tower; he waved his hand, and then sank down, out of sight, behind the parapet. From below, in the house, came the thin wasp-like buzzing of an alarum-clock. He had gone back just in time.

IVOR was gone. Lounging behind the wind-screen in his yellow sedan he was whirling across rural England. Social and amorous engagements of the most urgent character called him from hall to baronial hall, from castle to castle, from Elizabethan manor-house to Georgian mansion, over the whole expanse of the kingdom. To-day in Somerset, to-morrow in Warwickshire, on Saturday in the West Riding, by Tuesday morning in Argyll—Ivor never rested. The whole summer through, from the beginning of July till the end of September, he devoted himself to his engagements; he was a martyr to them. In the autumn he went back to London for a holiday. Crome had been a little incident, an evanescent bubble on the stream of his life; it belonged already to the past. By tea-time he would be at Gobley, and there would be Zenobia's welcoming smile. And on Thursday morning —but that was a long, long way ahead. He would think of Thursday morning when Thursday morning arrived. Meanwhile there was Gobley, meanwhile Zenobia.

In the visitors' book at Crome Ivor had left, according to his invariable custom in these cases, a poem. He had improvised it magisterially in the ten minutes preceding his departure. Denis and Mr. Scogan strolled back together from the gates of the courtyard, whence they had bidden their last farewells; on the writing-table in the hall they found the visitors' book, open, and Ivor's composition scarcely dry. Mr. Scogan read it aloud:

"The magic of those immemorial kings,
 Who webbed enchantment on the bowls of night,
 Sleeps in the soul of all created things;
 In the blue sea, th' Acroceraunian height,
 In the eyed butterfly's auricular wings
 And orgied visions of the anchorite;
 In all that singing flies and flying sings,
 In rain, in pain, in delicate delight.
 But much more magic, much more cogent spells
 Weave here their wizardries about my soul.
 Crome calls me like the voice of vesperal bells,
 Haunts like a ghostly-peopled necropole.
   Fate tears me hence. Hard fate! since far from Crome
   My soul must weep, remembering its Home."

"Very nice and tasteful and tactful," said Mr. Scogan, when he had finished. "I am only troubled by the butterfly's auricular wings. You have a first-hand knowledge of the workings of a poet's mind, Denis; perhaps you can explain."

"What could be simpler," said Denis. "It's a beautiful word, and Ivor wanted to say that the wings were golden."

"You make it luminously clear."

"One suffers so much," Denis went on, "from the fact that beautiful words don't always mean what they ought to mean. Recently, for example, I had a whole poem ruined, just because the word 'carminative' didn't mean what it ought to have meant. Carminative—it's admirable, isn't it?"

"Admirable," Mr. Scogan agreed. "And what does it mean?"

"It's a word I've treasured from my earliest infancy," said Denis, "treasured and loved. They used to give me cinnamon when I had a cold—quite useless, but not disagreeable. One poured it drop by drop out of narrow bottles, a golden liquor, fierce and fiery. On the label was a list of its virtues, and among other things it was described as being in the highest degree carminative. I adored the word. 'Isn't it carminative?' I used to say to myself when I'd taken my dose. It seemed so wonderfully to describe that sensation of internal warmth, that glow, that—what shall I call it?—physical self-satisfaction which followed the drinking of cinnamon. Later, when I discovered alcohol, 'carminative' described for me that similar, but nobler, more spiritual glow which wine evokes not only in the body but in the soul as well. The carminative virtues of burgundy, of rum, of old brandy, of Lacryma Christi, of Marsala, of Aleatico, of stout, of gin, of champagne, of claret, of the raw new wine of this year's Tuscan vintage—I compared them, I classified them. Marsala is rosily, downily carminative; gin pricks and refreshes while it warms. I had a whole table of carmination values. And now"—Denis spread out his hands, palm upwards, despairingly–"now I know what carminative really means."

"Well, what *does* it mean?" asked Mr. Scogan, a little impatiently.

"Carminative," said Denis, lingering lovingly over the syllables, "carminative. I imagined vaguely that it had something to do with *carmen-carminis*, still more vaguely with *caro-carnis*, and its derivatives, like carnival and carnation. Carminative—there was the idea of singing and the idea of flesh, rose-coloured and warm, with a suggestion of the jollities of mi-Carême and the masked holidays of Venice. Carminative—the warmth, the glow, the interior ripeness were all in the word. Instead of which . . ."

"Do come to the point, my dear Denis," protested Mr. Scogan. "Do come to the point."

"Well, I wrote a poem the other day," said Denis; "I wrote a poem about the effects of love."

"Others have done the same before you," said Mr. Scogan. "There is no need to be ashamed."

"I was putting forward the notion," Denis went on, "that the effects of love were often similar to the effects of wine, that Eros could intoxicate as well as Bacchus. Love, for example, is essentially carminative. It gives one the sense of warmth, the glow.

' And passion carminative as wine . . .'

was what I wrote. Not only was the line elegantly sonorous; it was also, I flattered myself, very aptly and compendiously expressive. Everything was in the word carminative—a detailed, exact foreground, an immense, indefinite hinterland of suggestion.

' And passion carminative as wine . . .'

I was not ill-pleased. And then suddenly it occurred to me that I had never actually looked up the word in a dictionary. Carminative had grown up with me from the days of the cinnamon bottle. It had always been taken for granted. Carminative: for me the word was as rich in content as some tremendous, elaborate work of art; it was a complete landscape with figures.

' And passion carminative as wine . . .'

It was the first time I had ever committed the word to writing, and all at once I felt I would like lexicographical authority for it. A small English-German dictionary was all I had at hand. I turned up C, ca, car, carm. There it was: 'Carminative: *windtreibend.*' *Windtreibend!*" he repeated. Mr. Scogan laughed. Denis shook his head. "Ah," he said, "for me it was no laughing matter. For me it marked the end of a chapter, the death of something young and precious. There were the years—years of childhood and innocence—when I had believed that carminative meant—well, carminative. And now, before me lies the rest of my life—a day, perhaps, ten years, half a century, when I shall know that carminative means *windtreibend.*

> 'Plus ne suis ce que j'ai été
> Et ne le saurai jamais être.'

It is a realization that makes one rather melancholy."

"Carminative," said Mr. Scogan thoughtfully.

"Carminative," Denis repeated, and they were silent for a time. "Words," said Denis at last, "words—I wonder if you can realize how much I love them. You are too much preoccupied with mere things and ideas and people to understand the full beauty of words. Your mind is not a literary mind. The spectacle of Mr. Gladstone finding thirty-four rhymes to the name 'Margot' seems to you rather pathetic than anything else. Mallarmé's envelopes with their versified addresses leave you cold, unless they leave you pitiful; you can't see that

> 'Apte à ne point te cabrer, hue!
> Poste, et j'ajouterai, dia!
> Si tu ne fuis onze-bis Rue
> Balzac, chez cet Heredia,'

is a little miracle."

"You're right," said Mr. Scogan. "I can't."

"You don't feel it to be magical?"

"No."

162

"That's the test for the literary mind," said Denis; "the feeling of magic, the sense that words have power. The technical, verbal part of literature is simply a development of magic. Words are man's first and most grandiose invention. With language, he created a whole new universe; what wonder if he loved words and attributed power to them! With fitted, harmonious words the magicians summoned rabbits out of empty hats and spirits from the elements. Their descendants, the literary men, still go on with the process, morticing their verbal formulas together and, before the power of the finished spell, trembling with delight and awe. Rabbits out of empty hats? No, their spells are more subtly powerful, for they evoke emotions out of empty minds. Formulated by their art, the most insipid statements become enormously significant. For example, I proffer the constatation, 'Black ladders lack bladders.' A self-evident truth, one on which it would not have been worth while to insist, had I chosen to formulate it in such words as 'Black fire-escapes have no bladders,' or, 'Les échelles noires manquent de vessie.' But since I put it as I do, 'Black ladders lack bladders,' it becomes, for all its self-evidence, significant, unforgettable, moving. The creation by word-power of something out of nothing—what is that but magic? And, I may add, what is that but literature? Half the world's greatest poetry is simply 'Les échelles noires manquent de vessie,' translated into magic significance as, 'Black ladders lack bladders.' And you can't appreciate words. I'm sorry for you."

"A mental carminative," said Mr. Scogan reflectively. "That's what you need."

CHAPTER XXI

PERCHED on its four stone mushrooms, the little granary stood two or three feet above the grass of the green close. Beneath it there was a perpetual shade and a damp growth of long, luxuriant grasses. Here, in the shadow, in the green dampness, a family of white ducks had sought shelter from the afternoon sun. Some stood, preening themselves, some reposed with their long bellies pressed to the ground, as though the cool grass were water. Little social noises burst fitfully forth, and from time to time some pointed tail would execute a brilliant Lisztian tremolo. Suddenly their jovial repose was shattered. A prodigious thump shook the wooden flooring above their heads; the whole granary trembled, little fragments of dirt and crumbled wood rained down among them. With a loud, continuous quacking the ducks rushed out from beneath this nameless menace, and did not stay their flight till they were safely in the farmyard.

"Don't lose your temper," Anne was saying. "Listen! You've frightened the ducks. Poor dears! no wonder." She was sitting sideways in a low, wooden chair. Her right elbow rested on the back of the chair and she supported her cheek on her hand. Her long, slender body drooped into curves of a lazy grace. She was smiling, and she looked at Gombauld through half-closed eyes.

"Damn you!" Gombauld repeated, and stamped his foot again. He glared at her round the half-finished portrait on the easel.

"Poor ducks!" Anne repeated. The sound of their quacking was faint in the distance; it was inaudible.

"Can't you see you make me lose my time?" he asked. "I can't work with you dangling about distractingly like this."

"You'd lose less time if you stopped talking and stamping your feet and did a little painting for a change. After all, what am I dangling about for, except to be painted?"

Gombauld made a noise like a growl. "You're awful," he said, with conviction. "Why do you ask me to come and stay here? Why do you tell me you'd like me to paint your portrait?"

"For the simple reasons that I like you—at least, when you're in a good temper—and that I think you're a good painter."

"For the simple reason"—Gombauld mimicked her voice—"that you want me to make love to you and, when I do, to have the amusement of running away."

Anne threw back her head and laughed. "So you think it amuses me to have to evade your advances! So like a man! If you only knew how gross and awful and boring men are when they try to make love and you don't want them to make love! If you could only see yourselves through our eyes!"

Gombauld picked up his palette and brushes and attacked his canvas with the ardour of irritation. "I suppose you'll be saying next that you didn't start the game, that it was I who made the first advances, and that you were the innocent victim who sat still and never did anything that could invite or allure me on."

"So like a man again!" said Anne. "It's always the same old story about the woman tempting the man. The woman lures, fascinates, invites; and man—noble man, innocent man—falls a victim. My poor Gombauld! Surely you're not going to sing that old song again. It's so unintelligent, and I always thought you were a man of sense."

"Thanks," said Gombauld.

"Be a little objective," Anne went on. "Can't you see that you're simply externalizing your own emotions? That's what you men are always doing; it's so barbarously naïve. You feel one of your loose desires for some woman, and because you desire her strongly you immediately accuse her of luring you on, of deliberately provoking and inviting the desire. You have the mentality of savages. You might just as well say that a plate of strawberries and cream deliberately lures you on to feel greedy. In ninety-nine cases out of a hundred women are as passive and innocent as the strawberries and cream."

"Well, all I can say is that this must be the hundredth case," said Gombauld, without looking up.

Anne shrugged her shoulders and gave vent to a sigh. "I'm at a loss to know whether you're more silly or more rude."

After painting for a little time in silence Gombauld began to speak again. "And then there's Denis," he said, renewing the conversation as though it had only just been broken off. "You're playing the same game with him. Why can't you leave that wretched young man in peace?"

Anne flushed with a sudden and uncontrollable anger. "It's perfectly untrue about Denis," she said indignantly. "I never dreamt of playing what you beautifully call the same game with him." Recovering her calm, she added in her ordinary cooing voice and with her exacerbating smile, "You've become very protective towards poor Denis all of a sudden."

"I have," Gombauld replied, with a gravity that was somehow a little too solemn. "I don't like to see a young man . . ."

". . . being whirled along the road to ruin," said Anne, continuing his sentence for him. "I admire your sentiments and, believe me, I share them."

She was curiously irritated at what Gombauld had said about Denis. It happened to be so completely untrue. Gombauld might have some slight ground for his reproaches. But Denis—no, she had never flirted with Denis. Poor boy! He was very sweet. She became somewhat pensive.

Gombauld painted on with fury. The restlessness of an unsatisfied desire, which, before, had distracted his mind, making work impossible, seemed now to have converted itself into a kind of feverish energy. When it was finished, he told himself, the portrait would be diabolic. He was painting her in the pose she had naturally adopted at the first sitting. Seated sideways, her elbow on the back of the chair, her head and shoulders turned at an angle from the rest of her body, towards the front, she had fallen into an attitude of indolent abandonment. He had emphasized the lazy curves of her body; the lines sagged as they crossed the canvas, the grace of the painted figure seemed to be melting into a kind of soft decay. The hand that lay along the knee was as limp as a glove. He was at work on the face now; it had begun to emerge on the canvas, doll-like in its regularity and listlessness. It was Anne's face—but her face as it would be, utterly unillumined by the inward lights of thought and emotion. It was the lazy, expressionless mask which was sometimes her face. The portrait was terribly like; and at the same time it was the most malicious of lies. Yes, it would be diabolic when it was finished, Gombauld decided; he wondered what she would think of it.

CHAPTER XXII

FOR the sake of peace and quiet Denis had retired earlier on this same afternoon to his bedroom. He wanted to work, but the hour was a drowsy one, and lunch, so recently eaten, weighed heavily on body and mind. The meridian demon was upon him; he was possessed by that bored and hopeless post-prandial melancholy which the cœnobites of old knew and feared under the name of "accidie." He felt, like Ernest Dowson, "a little weary." He was in the mood to write something rather exquisite and gentle and quietist in tone; something a little droopy and at the same time—how should he put it?—a little infinite. He thought of Anne, of love hopeless and unattainable. Perhaps that was the ideal kind of love, the hopeless kind—the quiet, theoretical kind of love. In this sad mood of repletion he could well believe it. He began to write. One elegant quatrain had flowed from beneath his pen:

> "A brooding love which is at most
>   The stealth of moonbeams when they slide,
> Evoking colour's bloodless ghost,
>   O'er some scarce-breathing breast or side . . ."

when his attention was attracted by a sound from outside. He looked down from his window; there they were, Anne and Gombauld, talking, laughing together. They crossed the courtyard in front, and passed out of sight through the gate in the right-hand wall. That was the way to the green close and the granary; she was going to sit for him again.

His pleasantly depressing melancholy was dissipated by a puff of violent emotion; angrily he threw his quatrain into the waste-paper basket and ran downstairs. "The stealth of moonbeams," indeed!

In the hall he saw Mr. Scogan; the man seemed to be lying in wait. Denis tried to escape, but in vain. Mr. Scogan's eye glittered like the eye of the Ancient Mariner.

"Not so fast," he said, stretching out a small saurian hand with pointed nails—"not so fast. I was just going down to the flower garden to take the sun. We'll go together."

Denis abandoned himself; Mr. Scogan put on his hat and they went out arm in arm. On the shaven turf of the terrace Henry Wimbush and Mary were playing a solemn game of bowls. They descended by the yew-tree walk. It was here, thought Denis, here that Anne had fallen, here that he had kissed her, here—and he blushed with retrospective shame at the memory—here that he had tried to carry her and failed. Life was awful!

"Sanity!" said Mr. Scogan, suddenly breaking a long silence. "Sanity—that's what's wrong with me and that's what will be wrong with you, my dear Denis, when you're old enough to be sane or insane. In a sane world I should be a great man; as things are, in this curious establishment, I am nothing at all; to all intents and purposes I don't exist. I am just *Vox et præterea nihil.*"

Denis made no response; he was thinking of other things. "After all," he said to himself—"after all, Gombauld is better looking than I, more entertaining, more confident; and, besides, he's already somebody and I'm still only potential. . . ."

"Everything that ever gets done in this world is done

170

by madmen," Mr. Scogan went on. Denis tried not to listen, but the tireless insistence of Mr. Scogan's discourse gradually compelled his attention. "Men such as I am, such as you may possibly become, have never achieved anything. We're too sane; we're merely reasonable. We lack the human touch, the compelling enthusiastic mania. People are quite ready to listen to the philosophers for a little amusement, just as they would listen to a fiddler or a mountebank. But as to acting on the advice of the men of reason—never. Wherever the choice has had to be made between the man of reason and the madman, the world has unhesitatingly followed the madman. For the madman appeals to what is fundamental, to passion and the instincts; the philosophers to what is superficial and supererogatory—reason."

They entered the garden; at the head of one of the alleys stood a green wooden bench, embayed in the midst of a fragrant continent of lavender bushes. It was here, though the place was shadeless and one breathed hot, dry perfume instead of air—it was here that Mr. Scogan elected to sit. He thrived on untempered sunlight.

"Consider, for example, the case of Luther and Erasmus." He took out his pipe and began to fill it as he talked. "There was Erasmus, a man of reason if ever there was one. People listened to him at first—a new virtuoso performing on that elegant and resourceful instrument, the intellect; they even admired and venerated him. But did he move them to behave as he wanted them to behave —reasonably, decently, or at least a little less porkishly than usual? He did not. And then Luther appears, violent, passionate, a madman insanely convinced about matters in which there can be no conviction. He shouted, and men rushed to follow him. Erasmus was no longer listened

171

to; he was reviled for his reasonableness. Luther was serious, Luther was reality—like the Great War. Erasmus was only reason and decency; he lacked the power, being a sage, to move men to action. Europe followed Luther and embarked on a century and a half of war and bloody persecution. It's a melancholy story." Mr. Scogan lighted a match. In the intense light the flame was all but invisible. The smell of burning tobacco began to mingle with the sweetly acrid smell of the lavender.

"If you want to get men to act reasonably, you must set about persuading them in a maniacal manner. The very sane precepts of the founders of religions are only made infectious by means of enthusiasms which to a sane man must appear deplorable. It is humiliating to find how impotent unadulterated sanity is. Sanity, for example, informs us that the only way in which we can preserve civilization is by behaving decently and intelligently. Sanity appeals and argues; our rulers persevere in their customary porkishness, while we acquiesce and obey. The only hope is a maniacal crusade; I am ready, when it comes, to beat a tambourine with the loudest, but at the same time I shall feel a little ashamed of myself. However"—Mr. Scogan shrugged his shoulders and, pipe in hand, made a gesture of resignation—"it's futile to complain that things are as they are. The fact remains that sanity unassisted is useless. What we want, then, is a sane and reasonable exploitation of the forces of insanity. We sane men will have the power yet." Mr. Scogan's eyes shone with a more than ordinary brightness, and, taking his pipe out of his mouth, he gave vent to his loud, dry, and somehow rather fiendish laugh.

"But I don't want power," said Denis. He was sitting in limp discomfort at one end of the bench, shading his eyes from the intolerable light. Mr. Scogan, bolt upright at the other end, laughed again.

"Everybody wants power," he said. "Power in some form or other. The sort of power you hanker for is literary power. Some people want power to persecute other human beings; you expend your lust for power in persecuting words, twisting them, moulding them, torturing them to obey you. But I divagate."

"Do you?" asked Denis faintly.

"Yes," Mr. Scogan continued, unheeding, "the time will come. We men of intelligence will learn to harness the insanities to the service of reason. We can't leave the world any longer to the direction of chance. We can't allow dangerous maniacs like Luther, mad about dogma, like Napoleon, mad about himself, to go on casually appearing and turning everything upside-down. In the past it didn't so much matter; but our modern machine is too delicate. A few more knocks like the Great War, another Luther or two, and the whole concern will go to pieces. In future, the men of reason must see that the madness of the world's maniacs is canalized into proper channels, is made to do useful work, like a mountain torrent driving a dynamo. . . ."

"Making electricity to light a Swiss hotel," said Denis. "You ought to complete the simile."

Mr. Scogan waved away the interruption. "There's only one thing to be done," he said. "The men of intelligence must combine, must conspire, and seize power from the imbeciles and maniacs who now direct us. They must found the Rational State."

The heat that was slowly paralysing all Denis's mental and bodily faculties seemed to bring to Mr. Scogan additional vitality. He talked with an ever-increasing energy, his hands moved in sharp, quick, precise gestures, his eyes shone. Hard, dry, and continuous, his voice went on sounding and sounding in Denis's ears with the insistence of a mechanical noise.

"In the Rational State," he heard Mr. Scogan saying, "human beings will be separated out into distinct species, not according to the colour of their eyes or the shape of their skulls, but according to the qualities of their mind and temperament. Examining psychologists, trained to what would now seem an almost superhuman clair-voyance, will test each child that is born and assign it to its proper species. Duly labelled and docketed, the child will be given the education suitable to members of its species, and will be set, in adult life, to perform those functions which human beings of his variety are capable of performing."

"How many species will there be?" asked Denis.

"A great many, no doubt," Mr. Scogan answered; "the classification will be subtle and elaborate. But it is not in the power of a prophet to go into details, nor is it his business. I will do no more than indicate the three main species into which the subjects of the Rational State will be divided."

He paused, cleared his throat, and coughed once or twice, evoking in Denis's mind the vision of a table with a glass and water-bottle, and, lying across one corner, a long white pointer for the lantern pictures.

"The three main species," Mr. Scogan went on, "will be these: the Directing Intelligences, the Men of Faith, and the Herd. Among the Intelligences will be found all those capable of thought, those who know how to attain to a certain degree of freedom—and, alas, how limited, even among the most intelligent, that freedom is!—from the mental bondage of their time. A select body of Intelligences, drawn from among those who have turned their attention to the problems of practical life, will be the governors of the Rational State. They will employ as their instruments of power the second great species of humanity—the men of Faith, the Madmen, as I have been calling them, who believe in things unreasonably, with passion, and are ready to die for their beliefs and their desires. These wild men, with their fearful potentialities for good or for mischief, will no longer be allowed to react casually to a casual environment. There will be no more Cæsar Borgias, no more Luthers and Mohammeds, no more Joanna Southcotts, no more Comstocks. The old-fashioned Man of Faith and Desire, that haphazard creature of brute circumstance, who might drive men to tears and repentance, or who might equally well set them on to cutting one another's throats, will be replaced by a new sort of madman, still externally the same, still bubbling with a seemingly spontaneous enthusiasm, but, ah, how very different from the madman of the past! For the new Man of Faith will be expending his passion, his desire, and his enthusiasm in the propagation of some reasonable idea. He will be, all unawares, the tool of some superior intelligence."

Mr. Scogan chuckled maliciously; it was as though he were taking a revenge, in the name of reason, on the enthusiasts. "From their earliest years, as soon, that is, as the examining psychologists have assigned them their place in the classified scheme, the Men of Faith will have had their special education under the eye of the Intelligences. Moulded by a long process of suggestion, they will go out into the world, preaching and practising with a generous mania the coldly reasonable projects of the

Directors from above. When these projects are accomplished, or when the ideas that were useful a decade ago have ceased to be useful, the Intelligences will inspire a new generation of madmen with a new eternal truth. The principal function of the Men of Faith will be to move and direct the Multitude, that third great species consisting of those countless millions who lack intelligence and are without valuable enthusiasm. When any particular effort is required of the Herd, when it is thought necessary, for the sake of solidarity, that humanity shall be kindled and united by some single enthusiastic desire or idea, the Men of Faith, primed with some simple and satisfying creed, will be sent out on a mission of evangelization. At ordinary times, when the high spiritual temperature of a Crusade would be unhealthy, the Men of Faith will be quietly and earnestly busy with the great work of education. In the upbringing of the Herd, humanity's almost boundless suggestibility will be scientifically exploited. Systematically, from earliest infancy, its members will be assured that there is no happiness to be found except in work and obedience; they will be made to believe that they are happy, that they are tremendously important beings, and that everything they do is noble and significant. For the lower species the earth will be restored to the centre of the universe and man to pre-eminence on the earth. Oh, I envy the lot of the commonalty in the Rational State! Working their eight hours a day, obeying their betters, convinced of their own grandeur and significance and immortality, they will be marvellously happy, happier than any race of men has ever been. They will go through life in a rosy state of intoxication, from which they will never awake. The Men of Faith will play the cup-bearers at this lifelong bacchanal, filling and ever filling again with the warm liquor that the Intelligences, in sad and sober privacy behind the scenes, will brew for the intoxication of their subjects."

"And what will be my place in the Rational State?" Denis drowsily inquired from under his shading hand.

Mr. Scogan looked at him for a moment in silence. "It's difficult to see where you would fit in," he said at last. "You couldn't do manual work; you're too independent and unsuggestible to belong to the larger Herd; you have none of the characteristics required in a Man of Faith. As for the Directing Intelligences, they will have to be marvellously clear and merciless and penetrating." He paused and shook his head. "No, I can see no place for you; only the lethal chamber."

Deeply hurt, Denis emitted the imitation of a loud Homeric laugh. "I'm getting sunstroke here," he said, and got up.

Mr. Scogan followed his example, and they walked slowly away down the narrow path, brushing the blue lavender flowers in their passage. Denis pulled a sprig of lavender and sniffed at it; then some dark leaves of rosemary that smelt like incense in a cavernous church. They passed a bed of opium poppies, dispetaled now; the round, ripe seed-heads were brown and dry—like Polynesian trophies, Denis thought; severed heads stuck on poles. He liked the fancy enough to impart it to Mr. Scogan.

"Like Polynesian trophies. . . ." Uttered aloud, the fancy seemed less charming and significant than it did when it first occurred to him.

There was a silence, and in a growing wave of sound the whir of the reaping machines swelled up from the fields beyond the garden and then receded into a remoter hum.

177

"It is satisfactory to think," said Mr. Scogan, as they strolled slowly onward, "that a multitude of people are toiling in the harvest fields in order that we may talk of Polynesia. Like every other good thing in this world, leisure and culture have to be paid for. Fortunately, however, it is not the leisured and the cultured who have to pay. Let us be duly thankful for that, my dear Denis— duly thankful," he repeated, and knocked the ashes out of his pipe.

Denis was not listening. He had suddenly remembered Anne. She was with Gombauld—alone with him in his studio. It was an intolerable thought.

"Shall we go and pay a call on Gombauld?" he suggested carelessly. "It would be amusing to see what he's doing now."

He laughed inwardly to think how furious Gombauld would be when he saw them arriving.

CHAPTER XXIII

GOMBAULD was by no means so furious at their apparition as Denis had hoped and expected he would be. Indeed, he was rather pleased than annoyed when the two faces, one brown and pointed, the other round and pale, appeared in the frame of the open door. The energy born of his restless irritation was dying within him, returning to its emotional elements. A moment more and he would have been losing his temper again—and Anne would be keeping hers, infuriatingly. Yes, he was positively glad to see them.

"Come in, come in," he called out hospitably.

Followed by Mr. Scogan, Denis climbed the little ladder and stepped over the threshold. He looked suspiciously from Gombauld to his sitter, and could learn nothing from the expression of their faces except that they both seemed pleased to see the visitors. Were they really glad, or were they cunningly simulating gladness? He wondered.

Mr. Scogan, meanwhile, was looking at the portrait.

"Excellent," he said approvingly, "excellent. Almost too true to character, if that is possible; yes, positively too true. But I'm surprised to find you putting in all this psychology business." He pointed to the face, and with his extended finger followed the slack curves of the painted figure. "I thought you were one of the fellows who went in exclusively for balanced masses and impinging planes."

Gombauld laughed. "This is a little infidelity," he said.

179

"I'm sorry," said Mr. Scogan. "I for one, without ever having had the slightest appreciation of painting, have always taken particular pleasure in Cubismus. I like to see pictures from which nature has been completely banished, pictures which are exclusively the product of the human mind. They give me the same pleasure as I derive from a good piece of reasoning or a mathematical problem or an achievement of engineering. Nature, or anything that reminds me of nature, disturbs me; it is too large, too complicated, above all too utterly pointless and incomprehensible. I am at home with the works of man; if I choose to set my mind to it, I can understand anything that any man has made or thought. That is why I always travel by Tube, never by bus if I can possibly help it. For, travelling by bus, one can't avoid seeing, even in London, a few stray works of God—the sky, for example, an occasional tree, the flowers in the window-boxes. But travel by Tube and you see nothing but the works of man—iron riveted into geometrical forms, straight lines of concrete, patterned expanses of tiles. All is human and the product of friendly and comprehensible minds. All philosophies and all religions—what are they but spiritual Tubes bored through the universe! Through these narrow tunnels, where all is recognizably human, one travels comfortable and secure, contriving to forget that all round and below and above them stretches the blind mass of earth, endless and unexplored. Yes, give me the Tube and Cubismus every time; give me ideas, so snug and neat and simple and well made. And preserve me from nature, preserve me from all that's inhumanly large and complicated and obscure. I haven't the courage, and, above all, I haven't the time to start wandering in that labyrinth."

While Mr. Scogan was discoursing, Denis had crossed

over to the farther side of the little square chamber, where Anne was sitting, still in her graceful, lazy pose, on the low chair.

"Well?" he demanded, looking at her almost fiercely. What was he asking of her? He hardly knew himself.

Anne looked up at him, and for answer echoed his "Well?" in another, a laughing key.

Denis had nothing more, at the moment, to say. Two or three canvases stood in the corner behind Anne's chair, their faces turned to the wall. He pulled them out and began to look at the paintings.

"May I see too?" Anne requested.

He stood them in a row against the wall. Anne had to turn round in her chair to look at them. There was the big canvas of the man fallen from the horse, there was a painting of flowers, there was a small landscape. His hands on the back of the chair, Denis leaned over her. From behind the easel at the other side of the room Mr. Scogan was talking away. For a long time they looked at the pictures, saying nothing; or, rather, Anne looked at the pictures, while Denis, for the most part, looked at Anne.

"I like the man and the horse; don't you?" she said at last, looking up with an inquiring smile.

Denis nodded, and then in a queer, strangled voice, as though it had cost him a great effort to utter the words, he said, "I love you."

It was a remark which Anne had heard a good many times before and mostly heard with equanimity. But on this occasion—perhaps because they had come so unexpectedly, perhaps for some other reason—the words provoked in her a certain surprised commotion.

"My poor Denis," she managed to say, with a laugh; but she was blushing as she spoke.

181

IT was noon. Denis, descending from his chamber, where he had been making an unsuccessful effort to write something about nothing in particular, found the drawing-room deserted. He was about to go out into the garden when his eye fell on a familiar but mysterious object—the large red notebook in which he had so often seen Jenny quietly and busily scribbling. She had left it lying on the window-seat. The temptation was great. He picked up the book and slipped off the elastic band that kept it discreetly closed.

"Private. Not to be opened," was written in capital letters on the cover. He raised his eyebrows. It was the sort of thing one wrote in one's Latin Grammar while one was still at one's preparatory school.

> "Black is the raven, black is the rook,
> But blacker the thief who steals this book!"

It was curiously childish, he thought, and he smiled to himself. He opened the book. What he saw made him wince as though he had been struck.

Denis was his own severest critic; so, at least, he had always believed. He liked to think of himself as a merciless vivisector probing into the palpitating entrails of his own soul; he was Brown Dog to himself. His weaknesses, his absurdities—no one knew them better than he did. Indeed, in a vague way he imagined that nobody beside himself was aware of them at all. It seemed, somehow, inconceivable that he should appear to other people as

they appeared to him, inconceivable that they ever spoke
of him among themselves in that same freely critical and,
to be quite honest, mildly malicious tone in which he was
accustomed to talk of them. In his own eyes he had defects, but to see them was a privilege reserved to him
alone. For the rest of the world he was surely an image
of flawless crystal. It was almost axiomatic.

On opening the red notebook that crystal image of
himself crashed to the ground, and was irreparably
shattered. He was not his own severest critic after all.
The discovery was a painful one.

The fruit of Jenny's unobtrusive scribbling lay before
him. A caricature of himself, reading (the book was
upside-down). In the background a dancing couple,
recognizable as Gombauld and Anne. Beneath, the
legend: "Fable of the Wallflower and the Sour Grapes."
Fascinated and horrified, Denis pored over the drawing.
It was masterful. A mute, inglorious Rouveyre appeared
in every one of those cruelly clear lines. The expression
of the face, an assumed aloofness and superiority tempered by a feeble envy; the attitude of the body and
limbs, an attitude of studious and scholarly dignity, given
away by the fidgety pose of the turned-in feet—these
things were terrible. And, more terrible still, was the likeness, was the magisterial certainty with which his physical
peculiarities were all recorded and subtly exaggerated.

Denis looked deeper into the book. There were caricatures of other people: of Priscilla and Mr. Barbecue-
Smith; of Henry Wimbush, of Anne and Gombauld; of
Mr. Scogan, whom Jenny had represented in a light that
was more than slightly sinister, that was, indeed, diabolic;
of Mary and Ivor. He scarcely glanced at them. A fearful
desire to know the worst about himself possessed him.

183

He turned over the leaves, lingering at nothing that was not his own image. Seven full pages were devoted to him. "Private. Not to be opened." He had disobeyed the injunction; he had only got what he deserved. Thoughtfully he closed the book, and slid the rubber band once more into its place. Sadder and wiser, he went out on to the terrace. And so this, he reflected, this was how Jenny employed the leisure hours in her ivory tower apart. And he had thought her a simple-minded, uncritical creature! It was he, it seemed, who was the fool. He felt no resentment towards Jenny. No, the distressing thing wasn't Jenny herself; it was what she and the phenomenon of her red book represented, what they stood for and concretely symbolized. They represented all the vast conscious world of men outside himself; they symbolized something that in his studious solitariness he was apt not to believe in. He could stand at Piccadilly Circus, could watch the crowds shuffle past, and still imagine himself the one fully conscious, intelligent, individual being among all those thousands. It seemed, somehow, impossible that other people should be in their way as elaborate and complete as he in his. Impossible; and yet, periodically he would make some painful discovery about the external world and the horrible reality of its consciousness and its intelligence. The red notebook was one of these discoveries, a footprint in the sand. It put beyond a doubt the fact that the outer world really existed.

Sitting on the balustrade of the terrace, he ruminated this unpleasant truth for some time. Still chewing on it, he strolled pensively down towards the swimming-pool. A peacock and his hen trailed their shabby finery across the turf of the lower lawn. Odious birds! Their necks, thick and greedily fleshy at the roots, tapered up to the

184

cruel inanity of their brainless heads, their flat eyes and piercing beaks. The fabulists were right, he reflected, when they took beasts to illustrate their tractates of human morality. Animals resemble men with all the truthfulness of a caricature. (Oh, the red notebook!) He threw a piece of stick at the slowly pacing birds. They rushed towards it, thinking it was something to eat.

He walked on. The profound shade of a giant ilex tree engulfed him. Like a great wooden octopus, it spread its long arms abroad.

"Under the spreading ilex tree . . ."

He tried to remember who the poem was by, but couldn't.

"The smith, a brawny man is he,
With arms like rubber bands."

Just like his; he would have to try and do his Muller exercises more regularly.

He emerged once more into the sunshine. The pool lay before him, reflecting in its bronze mirror the blue and various green of the summer day. Looking at it, he thought of Anne's bare arms and seal-sleek bathing-dress, her moving knees and feet.

"And little Luce with the white legs,
And bouncing Barbary . . ."

Oh, these rags and tags of other people's making! Would he ever be able to call his brain his own? Was there, indeed, anything in it that was truly his own, or was it simply an education?

He walked slowly round the water's edge. In an embayed recess among the surrounding yew trees, leaning her back against the pedestal of a pleasantly comic version of the Medici Venus, executed by some nameless mason of the *seicento*, he saw Mary pensively sitting.

"Hullo!" he said, for he was passing so close to her that he had to say something.

Mary looked up. "Hullo!" she answered in a melancholy, uninterested tone.

In this alcove, hewed out of the dark trees, the atmosphere seemed to Denis agreeably elegiac. He sat down beside her under the shadow of the pubic goddess. There was a prolonged silence.

At breakfast that morning Mary had found on her plate a picture postcard of Gobley Great Park. A stately Georgian pile, with a façade sixteen windows wide; parterres in the foreground; huge, smooth lawns receding out of the picture to right and left. Ten years more of the hard times and Gobley, with all its peers, will be deserted and decaying. Fifty years, and the countryside will know the old landmarks no more. They will have vanished as the monasteries vanished before them. At the moment, however, Mary's mind was not moved by these considerations.

On the back of the postcard, next to the address, was written, in Ivor's bold, large hand, a single quatrain.

"Hail, maid of moonlight! Bride of the sun, farewell!
    Like bright plumes moulted in an angel's flight,
There sleep within my heart's most mystic cell
    Memories of morning, memories of the night."

There followed a postscript of three lines: "Would you mind asking one of the housemaids to forward the packet of safety-razor blades I left in the drawer of my washstand. Thanks.—IVOR."

186

Seated under the Venus's immemorial gesture, Mary considered life and love. The abolition of her repressions, so far from bringing the expected peace of mind, had brought nothing but disquiet, a new and hitherto unexperienced misery. Ivor, Ivor ... She couldn't do without him now. It was eviden on the other hand, from the poem on the back of the picture postcard, that Ivor could very well do without her. He was at Gobley now; so was Zenobia. Mary knew Zenobia. She thought of the last verse of the song he had sung that night in the garden.

> "Le lendemain, Phillis peu sage
> Aurait donné moutons et chien
> Pour un baiser que le volage
> A Lisette donnait pour rien."

Mary shed tears at the memory; she had never been so unhappy in all her life before.

It was Denis who first broke the silence. "The individual," he began in a soft and sadly philosophical tone, "is not a self-supporting universe. There are times when he comes into contact with other individuals, when he is forced to take cognizance of the existence of other universes beside himself."

He had contrived this highly abstract generalization as a preliminary to a personal confidence. It was the first gambit in a conversation that was to lead up to Jenny's caricatures.

"True," said Mary; and, generalizing for herself, she added, "When one individual comes into intimate contact with another, she—or he, of course, as the case may be—must almost inevitably receive or inflict suffering."

"One is apt," Denis went on, "to be so spellbound by the spectacle of one's own personality that one forgets that the spectacle presents itself to other people as well as to oneself."

Mary was not listening. "The difficulty," she said, "makes itself acutely felt in matters of sex. If one individual seeks intimate contact with another individual in the natural way, she is certain to receive or inflict suffering. If, on the other hand, she avoids contacts, she risks the equally grave sufferings that follow on unnatural repressions. As you see, it's a dilemma."

"When I think of my own case," said Denis, making a more decided move in the desired direction, "I am amazed how ignorant I am of other people's mentality in general and, above all and in particular, of their opinions about myself. Our minds are sealed books only occasionally opened to the outside world." He made a gesture that was faintly suggestive of the drawing off of a rubber band.

"It's an awful problem," said Mary thoughtfully. "One has to have had personal experience to realize quite how awful it is."

"Exactly." Denis nodded. "One has to have had first-hand experience." He leaned towards her and slightly lowered his voice. "This very morning, for example . . ." he began, but his confidences were cut short. The deep voice of the gong, tempered by distance to a pleasant booming, floated down from the house. It was lunchtime. Mechanically Mary rose to her feet, and Denis, a little hurt that she should exhibit such a desperate anxiety for her food and so slight an interest in his spiritual experiences, followed her. They made their way up to the house without speaking.

CHAPTER XXV

"I HOPE you all realize," said Henry Wimbush during dinner, "that next Monday is Bank Holiday, and that you will all be expected to help in the Fair."

"Heavens!" cried Anne. "The Fair—I had forgotten all about it. What a nightmare! Couldn't you put a stop to it, Uncle Henry?"

Mr. Wimbush sighed and shook his head. "Alas," he said, "I fear I cannot. I should have liked to put an end to it years ago; but the claims of Charity are strong."

"It's not charity we want," Anne murmured rebelliously; "it's justice."

"Besides," Mr. Wimbush went on, "the Fair has become an institution. Let me see, it must be twenty-two years since we started it. It was a modest affair then. Now . . ." he made a sweeping movement with his hand and was silent.

It spoke highly for Mr. Wimbush's public spirit that he still continued to tolerate the Fair. Beginning as a sort of glorified church bazaar, Crome's yearly Charity Fair had grown into a noisy thing of merry-go-rounds, cocoa-nut shies, and miscellaneous side shows—a real genuine fair on the grand scale. It was the local St. Bartholomew, and the people of all the neighbouring villages, with even a contingent from the county town, flocked into the park for their Bank Holiday amusement. The local hospital profited handsomely, and it was this fact alone which prevented Mr. Wimbush, to whom the Fair was a cause of recurrent and never-diminishing agony, from putting a stop to the nuisance which yearly desecrated his park and garden.

"I've made all the arrangements already," Henry Wimbush went on. "Some of the larger marquees will be put up to-morrow. The swings and the merry-go-round arrive on Sunday."

"So there's no escape," said Anne, turning to the rest of the party. "You'll all have to do something. As a special favour you're allowed to choose your slavery. My job is the tea tent, as usual, Aunt Priscilla . . ."

"My dear," said Mrs. Wimbush, interrupting her, "I have more important things to think about than the Fair. But you need have no doubt that I shall do my best when Monday comes to encourage the villagers."

"That's splendid," said Anne. "Aunt Priscilla will encourage the villagers. What will you do, Mary?"

"I won't do anything where I have to stand by and watch other people eat."

"Then you'll look after the children's sports."

"All right," Mary agreed. "I'll look after the children's sports."

"And Mr. Scogan?"

Mr. Scogan reflected. "May I be allowed to tell fortunes?" he asked at last. "I think I should be good at telling fortunes."

"But you can't tell fortunes in that costume!"

"Can't I?" Mr. Scogan surveyed himself.

"You'll have to be dressed up. Do you still persist?"

"I'm ready to suffer all indignities."

"Good!" said Anne; and turning to Gombauld, "You must be our lightning artist," she said. "'Your portrait for a shilling in five minutes.'"

"It's a pity I'm not Ivor," said Gombauld, with a

laugh. "I could throw in a picture of their Auras for an extra sixpence."

Mary flushed. "Nothing is to be gained," she said severely, "by speaking with levity of serious subjects. And, after all, whatever your personal views may be, psychical research is a perfectly serious subject."

"And what about Denis?"

Denis made a deprecating gesture. "I have no accomplishments," he said. "I'll just be one of those men who wear a thing in their buttonholes and go about telling people which is the way to tea and not to walk on the grass."

"No, no," said Anne. "That won't do. You must do something more than that."

"But what? All the good jobs are taken, and I can do nothing but lisp in numbers."

"Well, then, you must lisp," concluded Anne. "You must write a poem for the occasion—an 'Ode on Bank Holiday.' We'll print it on Uncle Henry's press and sell it at twopence a copy."

"Sixpence," Denis protested. "It'll be worth sixpence."

Anne shook her head. "Twopence," she repeated firmly. "Nobody will pay more than twopence."

"And now there's Jenny," said Mr. Wimbush. "Jenny," he said, raising his voice, "what will you do?"

Denis thought of suggesting that she might draw caricatures at sixpence an execution, but decided it would be wiser to go on feigning ignorance of her talent. His mind reverted to the red notebook. Could it really be true that he looked like that?

"What will I do," Jenny echoed, "what will I do?" She frowned thoughtfully for a moment; then her face brightened and she smiled. "When I was young," she said, "I learnt to play the drums."

"The drums?"

Jenny nodded, and, in proof of her assertion, agitated her knife and fork, like a pair of drumsticks, over her plate. "If there's any opportunity of playing the drums . . ." she began.

"But of course," said Anne, "there's any amount of opportunity. We'll put you down definitely for the drums. That's the lot," she added.

"And a very good lot too," said Gombauld. "I look forward to my Bank Holiday. It ought to be gay."

"It ought indeed," Mr. Scogan assented. "But you may rest assured that it won't be. No holiday is ever anything but a disappointment."

"Come, come," protested Gombauld. "My holiday at Crome isn't being a disappointment."

"Isn't it?" Anne turned an ingenuous mask towards him.

"No, it isn't," he answered.

"I'm delighted to hear it."

"It's in the very nature of things," Mr. Scogan went on; "our holidays can't help being disappointments. Reflect for a moment. What is a holiday? The ideal, the Platonic Holiday of Holidays is surely a complete and absolute change. You agree with me in my definition?" Mr. Scogan glanced from face to face round the table; his sharp nose moved in a series of rapid jerks through all the points of the compass. There was no sign of dissent; he continued: "A complete and absolute change; very well. But isn't a complete and absolute change precisely the thing we can never have—never, in the very nature of things?" Mr. Scogan once more looked rapidly about him. "Of course it is. As ourselves, as specimens of Homo Sapiens, as members of a society, how can we hope to have anything like an absolute change? We are tied down by the frightful limitation of our human faculties, by the notions which society imposes on us through our fatal suggestibility, by our own personalities. For us, a complete holiday is out of the question. Some of us struggle manfully to take one, but we never succeed, if I may be allowed to express myself metaphorically, we never succeed in getting farther than Southend."

"You're depressing," said Anne.

"I mean to be," Mr. Scogan replied, and, expanding the fingers of his right hand, he went on: "Look at me, for example. What sort of a holiday can I take? In endowing me with passions and faculties Nature has been horribly niggardly. The full range of human potentialities is in any case distressingly limited; my range is a limitation within a limitation. Out of the ten octaves that make up the human instrument, I can compass perhaps two. Thus, while I may have a certain amount of intelligence, I have no æsthetic sense; while I possess the mathematical faculty, I am wholly without the religious emotions; while I am naturally addicted to venery, I have little ambition and am not at all avaricious. Education has further limited my scope. Having been brought up in society, I am impregnated with its laws; not only should I be afraid of taking a holiday from them, I should also feel it painful to try to do so. In a word, I have a conscience as well as a fear of gaol. Yes, I know it by experience. How often have I tried to take holidays, to get away from myself, my own boring nature, my insufferable mental surroundings!" Mr. Scogan sighed. "But always without success," he added, "always without success. In

193

my youth I was always striving—how hard!—to feel
religiously and æsthetically. Here, said I to myself, are
two tremendously important and exciting emotions. Life
would be richer, warmer, brighter, altogether more amusing, if I could feel them. I tried to feel them. I read the
works of the mystics. They seemed to me nothing but the
most deplorable claptrap—as indeed they always must to
anyone who does not feel the same emotion as the authors
felt when they were writing. For it is the emotion that
matters. The written work is simply an attempt to express
emotion, which is in itself inexpressible, in terms of
intellect and logic. The mystic objectifies a rich feeling
in the pit of the stomach into a cosmology. For other
mystics that cosmology is a symbol of the rich feeling.
For the unreligious it is a symbol of nothing, and so
appears merely grotesque. A melancholy fact! But I
divagate." Mr. Scogan checked himself. "So much for
the religious emotion. As for the æsthetic—I was at even
greater pains to cultivate that. I have looked at all the
right works of art in every part of Europe. There was a
time when, I venture to believe, I knew more about
Taddeo da Poggibonsi, more about the cryptic Amico di
Taddeo, even than Henry does. To-day, I am happy to
say, I have forgotten most of the knowledge I then so
laboriously acquired; but without vanity I can assert that
it was prodigious. I don't pretend, of course, to know
anything about nigger sculpture or the later seventeenth
century in Italy; but about all the periods that were
fashionable before 1900 I am, or was, omniscient. Yes, I
repeat it, omniscient. But did that fact make me any more
appreciative of art in general? It did not. Confronted by
a picture, of which I could tell you all the known and
presumed history—the date when it was painted, the

character of the painter, the influences that had gone to make it what it was—I felt none of that strange excitement and exaltation which is, as I am informed by those who do feel it, the true æsthetic emotion. I felt nothing but a certain interest in the subject of the picture; or more often, when the subject was hackneyed and religious, I felt nothing but a great weariness of spirit. Nevertheless, I must have gone on looking at pictures for ten years before I would honestly admit to myself that they merely bored me. Since then I have given up all attempts to take a holiday. I go on cultivating my old stale daily self in the resigned spirit with which a bank clerk performs from ten till six his daily task. A holiday, indeed! I'm sorry for you, Gombauld, if you still look forward to having a holiday."

Gombauld shrugged his shoulders. "Perhaps," he said, "my standards aren't as elevated as yours. But personally I found the war quite as thorough a holiday from all the ordinary decencies and sanities, all the common emotions and preoccupations, as I ever want to have."

"Yes," Mr. Scogan thoughtfully agreed. "Yes, the war was certainly something of a holiday. It was a step beyond Southend; it was Weston-super-Mare; it was almost Ilfracombe."

CHAPTER XXVI

A LITTLE canvas village of tents and booths had sprung up, just beyond the boundaries of the garden, in the green expanse of the park. A crowd thronged its streets, the men dressed mostly in black—holiday best, funeral best—the women in pale muslins. Here and there tricolour bunting hung inert. In the midst of the canvas town, scarlet and gold and crystal, the merry-go-round glittered in the sun. The balloon-man walked among the crowd, and above his head, like a huge, inverted bunch of many-coloured grapes, the balloons strained upwards. With a scythe-like motion the boat-swings reaped the air, and from the funnel of the engine which worked the roundabout rose a thin, scarcely wavering column of black smoke.

Denis had climbed to the top of one of Sir Ferdinando's towers, and there, standing on the sun-baked leads, his elbows resting on the parapet, he surveyed the scene. The steam-organ sent up prodigious music. The clashing of automatic cymbals beat out with inexorable precision the rhythm of piercingly sounded melodies. The harmonies were like a musical shattering of glass and brass. Far down in the bass the Last Trump was hugely blowing, and with such persistence, such resonance, that its alternate tonic and dominant detached themselves from the rest of the music and made a tune of their own, a loud, monotonous see-saw.

Denis leaned over the gulf of swirling noise. If he threw himself over the parapet, the noise would surely

buoy him up, keep him suspended, bobbing, as a fountain balances a ball on its breaking crest. Another fancy came to him, this time in metrical form.

"My soul is a thin white sheet of parchment stretched
    Over a bubbling cauldron."

Bad, bad. But he liked the idea of something thin and distended being blown up from underneath.

"My soul is a thin tent of gut. . . ."

or better—

"My soul is a pale, tenuous membrane. . . ."

That was pleasing: a thin, tenuous membrane. It had the right anatomical quality. Tight blown, quivering in the blast of noisy life. It was time for him to descend from the serene empyrean of words into the actual vortex. He went down slowly. "My soul is a thin, tenuous membrane. . . ."

On the terrace stood a knot of distinguished visitors. There was old Lord Moleyn, like a caricature of an English milord in a French comic paper: a long man, with a long nose and long, drooping moustaches and long teeth of old ivory, and lower down, absurdly, a short covert coat, and below that long, long legs cased in pearl-grey trousers—legs that bent unsteadily at the knee and gave a kind of sideways wobble as he walked. Beside him, short and thick-set, stood Mr. Callamay, the venerable conservative statesman, with a face like a Roman bust, and short white hair. Young girls didn't much like going for motor drives alone with Mr. Callamay; and of old Lord Moleyn one wondered why he wasn't living in gilded exile on the island of Capri among the other distinguished persons who, for one reason or another, find it impossible to live in England. They were talking to Anne, laughing, the one profoundly, the other hootingly.

A black silk balloon towing a black-and-white striped parachute proved to be old Mrs. Budge from the big house on the other side of the valley. She stood low on the ground, and the spikes of her black-and-white sunshade menaced the eyes of Priscilla Wimbush, who towered over her—a massive figure dressed in purple and topped with a queenly toque on which the nodding black plumes recalled the splendours of a first-class Parisian funeral.

Denis peeped at them discreetly from the window of the morning-room. His eyes were suddenly become innocent, childlike, unprejudiced. They seemed, these people, inconceivably fantastic. And yet they really existed, they functioned by themselves, they were conscious, they had minds. Moreover, he was like them. Could one believe it? But the evidence of the red notebook was conclusive.

It would have been polite to go and say, "How d'you do?" But at the moment Denis did not want to talk, could not have talked. His soul was a tenuous, tremulous, pale membrane. He would keep its sensibility intact and virgin as long as he could. Cautiously he crept out by a side door and made his way down towards the park. His soul fluttered as he approached the noise and movement of the fair. He paused for a moment on the brink, then stepped in and was engulfed.

Hundreds of people, each with his own private face and all of them real, separate, alive: the thought was disquieting. He paid twopence and saw the Tattooed Woman; twopence more, the Largest Rat in the World.

198

From the home of the Rat he emerged just in time to see a hydrogen-filled balloon break loose for home. A child howled up after it; but calmly, a perfect sphere of flushed opal, it mounted, mounted. Denis followed it with his eyes until it became lost in the blinding sunlight. If he could but send his soul to follow it! . . .

He sighed, stuck his steward's rosette in his button-hole, and started to push his way, aimlessly but officially, through the crowd.

CHAPTER XXVII

MR. SCOGAN had been accommodated in a little canvas hut. Dressed in a black skirt and a red bodice, with a yellow-and-red bandana handkerchief tied round his black wig, he looked—sharp-nosed, brown, and wrinkled—like the Bohemian hag of Frith's Derby Day. A placard pinned to the curtain of the doorway announced the presence within the tent of "Sesostris, the Sorceress of Ecbatana." Seated at a table, Mr. Scogan received his clients in mysterious silence, indicating with a movement of the finger that they were to sit down opposite him and to extend their hands for his inspection. He then examined the palm that was presented him, using a magnifying glass and a pair of horn spectacles. He had a terrifying way of shaking his head, frowning and clicking with his tongue as he looked at the lines. Sometimes he would whisper, as though to himself, "Terrible, terrible!" or "God preserve us!" sketching out the sign of the cross as he uttered the words. The clients who came in laughing grew suddenly grave; they began to take the witch seriously. She was a formidable-looking woman; could it be, was it possible, that there was something in this sort of thing after all? After all, they thought, as the hag shook her head over their hands, after all . . . And they waited, with an uncomfortably beating heart, for the oracle to speak. After a long and silent inspection, Mr. Scogan would suddenly look up and ask, in a hoarse whisper, some horrifying question, such as, "Have you ever been hit on the head with a hammer by a young man with red hair?" When the answer was in the negative, which it could hardly fail to be, Mr. Scogan would nod several times, saying, "I was afraid so. Everything is still to come, still to come, though it can't be very far off now." Sometimes, after a long examination, he would just whisper, "Where ignorance is bliss, 'tis folly to be wise," and refuse to divulge any details of a future too appalling to be envisaged without despair. Sesostris had a success of horror. People stood in a queue outside the witch's booth waiting for the privilege of hearing sentence pronounced upon them.

Denis, in the course of his round, looked with curiosity at this crowd of suppliants before the shrine of the oracle. He had a great desire to see how Mr. Scogan played his part. The canvas booth was a rickety, ill-made structure. Between its walls and its sagging roof were long gaping chinks and crannies. Denis went to the tea-tent and borrowed a wooden bench and a small Union Jack. With these he hurried back to the booth of Sesostris. Setting down the bench at the back of the booth, he climbed up, and with a great air of busy efficiency began to tie the Union Jack to the top of one of the tent-poles. Through the crannies in the canvas he could see almost the whole of the interior of the tent. Mr. Scogan's bandana-covered head was just below him; his terrifying whispers came clearly up. Denis looked and listened while the witch prophesied financial losses, death by apoplexy, destruction by air-raids in the next war.

"Is there going to be another war?" asked the old lady to whom he had predicted this end.

"Very soon," said Mr. Scogan, with an air of quiet confidence.

The old lady was succeeded by a girl dressed in white

muslin, garnished with pink ribbons, She was wearing a broad hat, so that Denis could not see her face; but from her figure and the roundness of her bare arms he judged her young and pleasing. Mr. Scogan looked at her hand then, whispered, "You are still virtuous."

The young lady giggled and exclaimed, "Oh, lor'!"

"But you will not remain so for long," added Mr. Scogan sepulchrally. The young lady giggled again. "Destiny, which interests itself in small things no less than in great, has announced the fact upon your hand." Mr. Scogan took up the magnifying-glass and began once more to examine the white palm. "Very interesting," he said, as though to himself—"very interesting. It's as clear as day." He was silent.

"What's clear?" asked the girl.

"I don't think I ought to tell you." Mr. Scogan shook his head; the pendulous brass ear-rings which he had screwed on to his ears tinkled.

"Please, please!" she implored.

The witch seemed to ignore her remark. "Afterwards, it's not at all clear. The fates don't say whether you will settle down to married life and have four children or whether you will try to go on the cinema and have none. They are only specific about this one rather crucial incident."

"What is it? What is it? Oh, do tell me!"

The white muslin figure leant eagerly forward.

Mr. Scogan sighed. "Very well," he said, "if you must know, you must know. But if anything untoward happens you must blame your own curiosity. Listen. Listen." He lifted up a sharp, claw-nailed forefinger. "This is what the fates have written. Next Sunday afternoon at six o'clock you will be sitting on the second stile on the footpath that leads from the church to the lower road. At that moment a man will appear walking along the footpath." Mr. Scogan looked at her hand again as though to refresh his memory of the details of the scene. "A man," he repeated—"a small man with a sharp nose, not exactly good looking nor precisely young, but fascinating." He lingered hissingly over the word. "He will ask you, 'Can you tell me the way to Paradise?' and you will answer, 'Yes, I'll show you,' and walk with him down towards the little hazel copse. I cannot read what will happen after that." There was a silence.

"Is it really true?" asked white muslin.

The witch gave a shrug of the shoulders. "I merely tell you what I read in your hand. Good afternoon. That will be sixpence. Yes, I have change. Thank you. Good afternoon."

Denis stepped down from the bench; tied insecurely and crookedly to the tent-pole, the Union Jack hung limp on the windless air. "If only I could do things like that!" he thought, as he carried the bench back to the tea-tent.

Anne was sitting behind a long table filling thick white cups from an urn. A neat pile of printed sheets lay before her on the table. Denis took one of them and looked at it affectionately. It was his poem. They had printed five hundred copies, and very nice the quarto broad-sheets looked.

"Have you sold many?" he asked in a casual tone.

Anne put her head on one side deprecatingly. "Only three so far, I'm afraid. But I'm giving a free copy to everyone who spends more than a shilling on his tea. So in any case it's having a circulation."

Denis made no reply, but walked slowly away. He

looked at the broadsheet in his hand and read the lines
to himself relishingly as he walked along:

"This day of roundabouts and swings,
   Struck weights, shied cocoa-nuts, tossed rings,
   Switchbacks, Aunt Sallies, and all such small
   High jinks—you call it ferial?
   A holiday? But paper noses
   Sniffed the artificial roses
   Of round Venetian cheeks through half
   Each carnival year, and masks might laugh
   At things the naked face for shame
   Would blush at—laugh and think no blame.
   A holiday? But Galba showed
   Elephants on an airy road;
   Jumbo trod the tightrope then,
   And in the circus arméd men
   Stabbed home for sport and died to break
   Those dull imperatives that make
   A prison of every working day,
   Where all must drudge and all obey.
   Sing Holiday! You do not know
   How to be free. The Russian snow
   Flowered with bright blood whose roses spread
   Petals of fading, fading red
   That died into the snow again,
   fnto the virgin snow; and men
   From all the ancient bonds were freed
   Old law, old custom, and old creed,
   Old right and wrong there bled to death:
   The frozen air received their breath,
   A little smoke that died away;
   And round about them where they lay
   The snow bloomed roses. Blood was there
   A red gay flower and only fair.
   Sing Holiday! Beneath the Tree

Of Innocence and Liberty,
Paper Nose and Red Cockade
Dance within the magic shade
That makes them drunken, merry, and strong
To laugh and sing their ferial song:
'Free, free . . .!'
　　　　　　But Echo answers
Faintly to the laughing dancers,
'Free'—and faintly laughs, and still,
Within the hollows of the hill,
Faintlier laughs and whispers, 'Free,'
Fadingly, diminishingly:
'Free,' and laughter faints away . . .
Sing Holiday! Sing Holiday!"

He folded the sheet carefully and put it in his pocket. The thing had its merits. Oh, decidedly, decidedly! But how unpleasant the crowd smelt! He lit a cigarette. The smell of cows was preferable. He passed through the gate in the park wall into the garden. The swimming-pool was a centre of noise and activity.

"Second Heat in the Young Ladies' Championship." It was the polite voice of Henry Wimbush. A crowd of sleek, seal-like figures in black bathing-dresses surrounded him. His grey bowler hat, smooth, round, and motionless in the midst of a moving sea, was an island of aristocratic calm.

Holding his tortoise-shell-rimmed pince-nez an inch or two in front of his eyes, he read out names from a list.

"Miss Dolly Miles, Miss Rebecca Balister, Miss Doris Gabell . . ."

Five young persons ranged themselves on the brink. From their seats of honour at the other end of the pool, old Lord Moleyn and Mr. Callamay looked on with eager interest.

Henry Wimbush raised his hand. There was an expectant silence. "When I say 'Go,' go. Go!" he said. There was an almost simultaneous splash.

Denis pushed his way through the spectators. Somebody plucked him by the sleeve; he looked down. It was old Mrs. Budge.

"Delighted to see you again, Mr. Stone," she said in her rich, husky voice. She panted a little as she spoke, like a short-winded lap-dog. It was Mrs. Budge who, having read in the *Daily Mirror* that the Government needed peach stones—what they needed them for she never knew—had made the collection of peach stones her peculiar "bit" of war work. She had thirty-six peach trees in her walled garden, as well as four hot-houses in which trees could be forced, so that she was able to eat peaches practically the whole year round. In 1916 she ate 4200 peaches, and sent the stones to the Government. In 1917 the military authorities called up three of her gardeners, and what with this and the fact that it was a bad year for wall fruit, she only managed to eat 2900 peaches during that crucial period of the national destinies. In 1918 she did rather better, for between January 1st and the date of the Armistice she ate 3300 peaches. Since the Armistice she had relaxed her efforts; now she did not eat more than two or three peaches a day. Her constitution, she complained, had suffered; but it had suffered for a good cause.

Denis answered her greeting by a vague and polite noise.

"So nice to see the young people enjoying themselves," Mrs. Budge went on. "And the old people too, for that matter. Look at old Lord Moleyn and dear Mr. Callamay. Isn't it delightful to see the way they enjoy themselves?"

Denis looked. He wasn't sure whether it was so very delightful after all. Why didn't they go and watch the sack races? The two old gentlemen were engaged at the moment in congratulating the winner of the race; it seemed an act of supererogatory graciousness; for, after all, she had only won a heat.

"Pretty little thing, isn't she?" said Mrs. Budge huskily, and panted two or three times.

"Yes," Denis nodded agreement. Sixteen, slender, but nubile, he said to himself, and laid up the phrase in his memory as a happy one. Old Mr. Callamay had put on his spectacles to congratulate the victor, and Lord Moleyn, leaning forward over his walking-stick, showed his long ivory teeth, hungrily smiling.

"Capital performance, capital," Mr. Callamay was saying in his deep voice.

The victor wriggled with embarrassment. She stood with her hands behind her back, rubbing one foot nervously on the other. Her wet bathing-dress shone, a torso of black polished marble.

"Very good indeed," said Lord Moleyn. His voice seemed to come from just behind his teeth, a toothy voice. It was as though a dog should suddenly begin to speak. He smiled again, Mr. Callamay readjusted his spectacles.

"When I say 'Go,' go. Go!"

Splash! The third heat had started.

"Do you know, I never could learn to swim," said Mrs. Budge.

"Really?"

"But I used to be able to float."

Denis imagined her floating—up and down, up and down on a great green swell. A blown black bladder; no, that wasn't good, that wasn't good at all. A new winner was being congratulated. She was atrociously stubby and fat. The last one, long and harmoniously, continuously curved from knee to breast, had been an Eve by Cranach; but this, this one was a bad Rugens.

". . . go—go—go!" Henry Wimbush's polite level voice once more pronounced the formula. Another batch of young ladies dived in.

Grown a little weary of sustaining a conversation with Mrs. Budge, Denis conveniently remembered that his duties as a steward called him elsewhere. He pushed out through the lines of spectators and made his way along the path left clear behind them. He was thinking again that his soul was a pale, tenuous membrane, when he was startled by hearing a thin, sibilant voice, speaking apparently from just above his head, pronounce the single word "Disgusting!"

He looked up sharply. The path along which he was walking passed under the lee of a wall of clipped yew. Behind the hedge the ground sloped steeply up towards the foot of the terrace and the house; for one standing on the higher ground it was easy to look over the dark barrier. Looking up, Denis saw two heads overtopping the hedge immediately above him. He recognized the iron mask of Mr. Bodiham and the pale, colourless face of his wife. They were looking over his head, over the heads of the spectators, at the swimmers in the pond.

"Disgusting!" Mrs. Bodiham repeated, hissing softly.

The rector turned up his iron mask towards the solid cobalt of the sky. "How long?" he said, as though to himself; "how long?" He lowered his eyes again, and they fell on Denis's upturned curious face. There was an abrupt movement, and Mr. and Mrs. Bodiham popped out of sight behind the hedge.

Denis continued his promenade. He wandered past the merry-go-round, through the thronged streets of the canvas village; the membrane of his soul flapped tumultuously in the noise and laughter. In a roped-off space beyond, Mary was directing the children's sports. Little creatures seethed round about her, making a shrill, tinny clamour; others clustered about the skirts and trousers of their parents. Mary's face was shining in the heat; with an immense output of energy she started a three-legged race. Denis looked on in admiration.

"You're wonderful," he said, coming up behind her and touching her on the arm.

"I've never seen such energy."

She turned towards him a face, round, red, and honest as the setting sun; the golden bell of her hair swung silently as she moved her head and quivered to rest.

"Do you know, Denis," she said, in a low, serious voice, gasping a little as she spoke—"do you know that there's a woman here who has had three children in thirty-one months?"

"Really," said Denis, making rapid mental calculations.

"It's appalling. I've been telling her about the Malthusian League. One really ought . . ."

But a sudden violent renewal of the metallic yelling announced the fact that somebody had won the race. Mary became once more the centre of a dangerous vortex. It was time, Denis thought, to move on; he might be asked to do something if he stayed too long.

He turned back towards the canvas village. The thought of tea was making itself insistent in his mind.

Tea, tea, tea. But the tea-tent was horribly thronged. Anne, with an unusual expression of grimness on her flushed face, was furiously working the handle of the urn; the brown liquid spurted incessantly into the proffered cups. Portentous, in the farther corner of the tent, Priscilla, in her royal toque, was encouraging the villagers. In a momentary lull Denis could hear her deep, jovial laughter and her manly voice. Clearly, he told himself, this was no place for one who wanted tea. He stood irresolute at the entrance to the tent. A beautiful thought suddenly came to him: if he went back to the house, went unobtrusively, without being observed, if he tiptoed into the dining-room and noiselessly opened the little doors of the side-board—ah, then! In the cool recess within he would find bottles and a siphon; a bottle of crystal gin and a quart of soda water, and then for the cups that inebriate as well as cheer. . . .

A minute later he was walking briskly up the shady yew-tree walk. Within the house it was deliciously quiet and cool. Carrying his well-filled tumbler with care, he went into the library. There, the glass on the corner of the table beside him, he settled into a chair with a volume of Sainte-Beuve. There was nothing, he found, like a Causerie du Lundi for settling and soothing the troubled spirits. That tenuous membrane of his had been too rudely buffeted by the afternoon's emotions; it required a rest.

CHAPTER XXVIII

TOWARDS sunset the fair itself became quiescent. It was the hour for the dancing to begin. At one side of the village of tents a space had been roped off. Acetylene lamps, hung round it on posts, cast a piercing white light. In one corner sat the band, and, obedient to its scraping and blowing, two or three hundred dancers trampled across the dry ground, wearing away the grass with their booted feet. Round this patch of all but daylight, alive with motion and noise, the night seemed preternaturally dark. Bars of light reached out into it, and every now and then a lonely figure or a couple of lovers, interlaced, would cross the bright shaft, flashing for a moment into visible existence, to disappear again as quickly and surprisingly as they had come.

Denis stood by the entrance of the enclosure, watching the swaying, shuffling crowd. The slow vortex brought the couples round and round again before him, as though he were passing them in review. There was Priscilla, still wearing her queenly toque, still encouraging the villagers —this time by dancing with one of the tenant farmers. There was Lord Moleyn, who had stayed on to the dis-organized, passoverish meal that took the place of dinner on this festal day; he one-stepped shamblingly, his bent knees more precariously wobbly than ever, with a terrified village beauty. Mr. Scogan trotted round with another. Mary was in the embrace of a young farmer of heroic proportions; she was looking up at him, talking, as Denis could see, very seriously. What about? he wondered.

The Malthusian League, perhaps. Seated in the corner among the band, Jenny was performing wonders of virtuosity upon the drums. Her eyes shone, she smiled to herself. A whole subterranean life seemed to be expressing itself in those loud rat-tats, those long rolls and flourishes of drumming. Looking at her, Denis ruefully remembered the red notebook; he wondered what sort of a figure he was cutting now. But the sight of Anne and Gombauld swimming past—Anne with her eyes almost shut and sleeping, as it were, on the sustaining wings of movement and music—dissipated these pre-occupations. Male and female created He them. . . . There they were, Anne and Gombauld, and a hundred couples more—all stepping harmoniously together to the old tune of Male and Female created He them. But Denis sat apart; he alone lacked his complementary opposite. They were all coupled but he; all but he. . . .

Somebody touched him on the shoulder and he looked up. It was Henry Wimbush.

"I never showed you our oaken drain-pipes," he said. "Some of the ones we dug up are lying quite close to here. Would you like to come and see them?"

Denis got up, and they walked off together into the darkness. The music grew fainter behind them. Some of the higher notes faded out altogether. Jenny's drumming and the steady sawing of the bass throbbed on, tuneless and meaningless in their ears. Henry Wimbush halted.

"Here we are," he said, and, taking an electric torch out of his pocket, he cast a dim beam over two or three blackened sections of tree trunk, scooped out into the semblance of pipes, which were lying forlornly in a little depression in the ground.

"Very interesting," said Denis, with a rather tepid enthusiasm.

They sat down on the grass. A faint white glare, rising from behind a belt of trees, indicated the position of the dancing-floor. The music was nothing but a muffled rhythmic pulse.

"I shall be glad," said Henry Wimbush, "when this function comes at last to an end."

"I can believe it."

"I do not know how it is," Mr. Wimbush continued, "but the spectacle of numbers of my fellow-creatures in a state of agitation moves in me a certain weariness, rather than any gaiety or excitement. That fact is, they don't very much interest me. They aren't in my line. You follow me? I could never take much interest, for example, in a collection of postage stamps. Primitives or seventeenth-century books—yes. They are my line. But stamps, no. I don't know anything about them; they're not my line. They don't interest me, they give me no emotion. It's rather the same with people, I'm afraid. I'm more at home with these pipes." He jerked his head sideways towards the hollowed logs. "The trouble with the people and events of the present is that you never know anything about them. What do I know of contemporary politics? Nothing. What do I know of the people I see round about me? Nothing. What they think of me or of anything else in the world, what they will do in five minutes' time, are things I can't guess at. For all I know, you may suddenly jump up and try to murder me in a moment's time."

"Come, come," said Denis.

"True," Mr. Wimbush continued, "the little I know about your past is certainly reassuring. But I know nothing of your present, and neither you nor I know anything of your future. It's appalling; in living people, one is dealing with unknown and unknowable quantities. One can only hope to find out anything about them by a long series of the most disagreeable and boring human contacts, involving a terrible expense of time. It's the same with current events; how can I find out anything about them except by devoting years to the most exhausting first-hand study, involving once more an endless number of the most unpleasant contacts? No, give me the past. It doesn't change; it's all there in black and white, and you can get to know about it comfortably and decorously and, above all, privately—by reading. By reading I know a great deal of Cæsar Borgia, of St. Francis, of Dr. Johnson; a few weeks have made me thoroughly acquainted with these interesting characters, and I have been spared the tedious and revolting process of getting to know them by personal contact, which I should have to do it they were living now. How gay and delightful life would be if one could get rid of all the human contacts! Perhaps, in the future, when machines have attained to a state of perfection—for I confess that I am, like Godwin and Shelley, a believer in perfectibility, the perfectibility of machinery—then, perhaps, it will be possible for those who, like myself, desire it, to live in a dignified seclusion, surrounded by the delicate attentions of silent and graceful machines, and entirely secure from any human intrusion. It is a beautiful thought."

"Beautiful," Denis agreed. "But what about the desirable human contacts, like love and friendship?"

The black silhouette against the darkness shook its head. "The pleasures even of these contacts are much exaggerated," said the polite level voice. "It seems to me doubtful whether they are equal to the pleasures of private reading and contemplation. Human contacts have been so highly valued in the past only because reading was not a common accomplishment and because books were scarce and difficult to reproduce. The world, you must remember, is only just becoming literate. As reading becomes more and more habitual and widespread, an ever-increasing number of people will discover that books will give them all the pleasures of social life and none of its intolerable tedium. At present people in search of pleasure naturally tend to congregate in large herds and to make a noise; in future their natural tendency will be to seek solitude and quiet. The proper study of mankind is books."

"I sometimes think that it may be," said Denis; he was wondering if Anne and Gombauld were still dancing together.

"Instead of which," said Mr. Wimbush, with a sigh, "I must go and see if all is well on the dancing-floor." They got up and began to walk slowly towards the white glare. "If all these people were dead," Henry Wimbush went on, "this festivity would be extremely agreeable. Nothing would be pleasanter than to read in a well-written book of an open-air ball that took place a century ago. How charming! one would say; how pretty and how amusing! But when the ball takes place to-day, when one finds oneself involved in it, then one sees the thing in its true light. It turns out to be merely this." He waved his hand in the direction of the acetylene flares. "In my youth," he went on after a pause, "I found myself, quite fortuitously, involved in a series of the most phantasmagorical amorous intrigues. A novelist could have made his fortune out of them, and even if I were to tell you, in my bald style, the details of these adventures, you would be amazed at the romantic tale. But I assure you, while they were happening—these romantic adventures—they seemed to me no more and no less exciting than any other incident of actual life. To climb by night up a rope-ladder to a second-floor window in an old house in Toledo seemed to me, while I was actually performing this rather dangerous feat, an action as obvious, as much to be taken for granted, as—how shall I put it?—as quotidian as catching the 8.52 from Surbiton to go to business on a Monday morning. Adventures and romance only take on their adventurous and romantic qualities at second-hand. Live them, and they are just a slice of life like the rest. In literature they become as charming as this dismal ball would be if we were celebrating its tercentenary." They had come to the entrance of the enclosure and stood there, blinking in the dazzling light. "Ah, if only we were!" Henry Wimbush added.

Anne and Gombauld were still dancing together.

CHAPTER XXIX

IT was after ten o'clock. The dancers had already dispersed and the last lights were being put out. To-morrow the tents would be struck, the dismantled merry-go-round would be packed into waggons and carted away. An expanse of worn grass, a shabby brown patch in the wide green of the park, would be all that remained. Crome Fair was over.

By the edge of the pool two figures lingered.

"No, no, no," Anne was saying in a breathless whisper, leaning backwards, turning her head from side to side in an effort to escape Gombauld's kisses. "No, please. No." Her raised voice had become imperative.

Gombauld relaxed his embrace a little. "Why not?" he said. "I will."

With a sudden effort Anne freed herself. "You won't," she retorted. "You've tried to take the most unfair advantage of me."

"Unfair advantage?" echoed Gombauld in genuine surprise.

"Yes, unfair advantage. You attack me after I've been dancing for two hours, while I'm still reeling drunk with the movement, when I've lost my head, when I've got no mind left but only a rhythmical body! It's as bad as making love to someone you've drugged or intoxicated."

Gombauld laughed angrily. "Call me a White Slaver and have done with it."

"Luckily," said Anne, "I am now completely sobered,

and if you try and kiss me again I shall box your ears. Shall we take a few turns round the pool?" she added. "The night is delicious."

For answer Gombauld made an irritated noise. They paced off slowly, side by side.

"What I like about the painting of Degas . . ." Anne began in her most detached and conversational tone.

"Oh, damn Degas!" Gombauld was almost shouting.

From where he stood, leaning in an attitude of despair against the parapet of the terrace, Denis had seen them, the two pale figures in a patch of moonlight, far down by the pool's edge. He had seen the beginning of what promised to be an endlessly passionate embracement, and at the sight he had fled. It was too much; he couldn't stand it. In another moment, he felt, he would have burst into irrepressible tears.

Dashing blindly into the house, he almost ran into Mr. Scogan, who was walking up and down the hall smoking a final pipe.

"Hullo!" said Mr. Scogan, catching him by the arm; dazed and hardly conscious of what he was doing or where he was, Denis stood there for a moment like a somnambulist. "What's the matter?" Mr. Scogan went on. "You look disturbed, distressed, depressed."

Denis shook his head without replying.

"Worried about the cosmos, eh?" Mr. Scogan patted him on the arm. "I know the feeling," he said. "It's a most distressing symptom. 'What's the point of it all? All is vanity. What's the good of continuing to function if one's doomed to be snuffed out at last along with everything else?' Yes, yes. I know exactly how you feel. It's most distressing if one allows oneself to be distressed.

But then why allow oneself to be distressed? After all, we all know that there's no ultimate point. But what difference does that make?"

At this point the somnambulist suddenly woke up. "What?" he said, blinking and frowning at his interlocutor. "What?" Then breaking away he dashed up the stairs, two steps at a time.

Mr. Scogan ran to the foot of the stairs and called up after him. "It makes no difference, none whatever. Life is gay all the same, always, under whatever circumstances—under whatever circumstances," he added, raising his voice to a shout. But Denis was already far out of hearing, and even if he had not been, his mind to-night was proof against all the consolations of philosophy. Mr. Scogan replaced his pipe between his teeth and resumed his meditative pacing. "Under any circumstances," he repeated to himself. It was ungrammatical to begin with; was it true? And is life really its own reward? He wondered. When his pipe had burned itself to its stinking conclusion he took a drink of gin and went to bed. In ten minutes he was deeply, innocently asleep.

Denis had mechanically undressed and, clad in those flowered silk pyjamas of which he was so justly proud, was lying face downwards on his bed. Time passed. When at last he looked up, the candle which he had left alight at his bedside had burned down almost to the socket. He looked at his watch; it was nearly half-past one. His head ached, his dry, sleepless eyes felt as though they had been bruised from behind, and the blood was beating within his ears a loud arterial drum. He got up, opened the door, tiptoed noiselessly along the passage, and began to mount the stairs towards the higher floors.

Arrived at the servants' quarters under the roof, he hesitated, then turning to the right he opened a little door at the end of the corridor. Within was a pitch-dark cupboard-like boxroom, hot, stuffy, and smelling of dust and old leather. He advanced cautiously into the blackness, groping with his hands. It was from this den that the ladder went up to the leads of the western tower. He found the ladder, and set his feet on the rungs; noiselessly, he lifted the trapdoor above his head; the moonlit sky was over him, he breathed the fresh, cool air of the night. In a moment he was standing on the leads, gazing out over the dim, colourless landscape, looking perpendicularly down at the terrace seventy feet below.

Why had he climbed up to this high, desolate place? Was it to look at the moon? Was it to commit suicide? As yet he hardly knew. Death—the tears came into his eyes when he thought of it. His misery assumed a certain solemnity; he was lifted up on the wings of a kind of exaltation. It was a mood in which he might have done almost anything, however foolish. He advanced towards the farther parapet; the drop was sheer there and uninterrupted. A good leap, and perhaps one might clear the narrow terrace and so crash down yet another thirty feet to the sun-baked ground below. He paused at the corner of the tower, looking now down into the shadowy gulf below, now up towards the rare stars and the waning moon. He made a gesture with his hand, muttered something, he could not afterwards remember what; but the fact that he had said it aloud gave the utterance a peculiarly terrible significance. Then he looked down once more into the depths.

"What *are* you doing, Denis?" questioned a voice from somewhere very close behind him.

Denis uttered a cry of frightened surprise, and very nearly went over the parapet in good earnest. His heart was beating terribly, and he was pale when, recovering himself, he turned round in the direction from which the voice had come.

"Are you ill?"

In the profound shadow that slept under the eastern parapet of the tower, he saw something he had not previously noticed—an oblong shape. It was a mattress, and someone was lying on it. Since that first memorable night on the tower, Mary had slept out every evening; it was a sort of manifestation of fidelity.

"It gave me a fright," she went on, "to wake up and see you waving your arms and gibbering there. What on earth were you doing?"

Denis laughed melodramatically. "What, indeed!" he said. If she hadn't woken up as she did, he would be lying in pieces at the bottom of the tower; he was certain of that, now.

"You hadn't got designs on me, I hope?" Mary inquired, jumping too rapidly to conclusions.

"I didn't know you were here," said Denis, laughing more bitterly and artificially than before.

"What *is* the matter, Denis?"

He sat down on the edge of the mattress, and for all reply went on laughing in the same frightful and improbable tone.

An hour later he was reposing with his head on Mary's knees, and she, with an affectionate solicitude that was wholly maternal, was running her fingers through his tangled hair. He had told her everything, everything: his hopeless love, his jealousy, his despair, his suicide—as it were providentially averted by her interposition. He had solemnly promised never to think of self-destruction again. And now his soul was floating in a sad serenity. It was embalmed in the sympathy that Mary so generously poured. And it was not only in receiving sympathy that Denis found serenity and even a kind of happiness; it was also in giving it. For if he had told Mary everything about his miseries, Mary, reacting to these confidences, had told him in return everything, or very nearly everything, about her own.

"Poor Mary!" He was very sorry for her. Still, she might have guessed that Ivor wasn't precisely a monument of constancy.

"Well," she concluded, "one must put a good face on it." She wanted to cry, but she wouldn't allow herself to be weak. There was a silence.

"Do you think," asked Denis hesitatingly—"do you really think that she . . . that Gombauld . . ."

"I'm sure of it," Mary answered decisively. There was another long pause.

"I don't know what to do about it," he said at last, utterly dejected.

"You'd better go away," advised Mary. "It's the safest thing, and the most sensible."

"But I've arranged to stay here three weeks more."

"You must concoct an excuse."

"I suppose you're right."

"I know I am," said Mary, who was recovering all her firm self-possession. "You can't go on like this, can you?"

"No, I can't go on like this," he echoed.

Immensely practical, Mary invented a plan of action. Startlingly, in the darkness, the church clock struck three.

"You must go to bed at once," she said. "I'd no idea it was so late."

Denis clambered down the ladder, cautiously descended the creaking stairs. His room was dark; the candle had long ago guttered to extinction. He got into bed and fell asleep almost at once.

CHAPTER XXX

DENIS had been called, but in spite of the parted curtains he had dropped off again into that drowsy, dozy state when sleep becomes a sensual pleasure almost consciously savoured. In this condition he might have remained for another hour if he had not been disturbed by a violent rapping at the door.

"Come in," he mumbled, without opening his eyes. The latch clicked, a hand seized him by the shoulder and he was rudely shaken.

"Get up, get up!"

His eyelids blinked painfully apart, and he saw Mary standing over him, bright-faced and earnest.

"Get up!" she repeated. "You must go and send the telegram. Don't you remember?"

"O Lord!" He threw off the bed-clothes; his tormentor retired.

Denis dressed as quickly as he could and ran up the road to the village post office. Satisfaction glowed within him as he returned. He had sent a long telegram, which would in a few hours evoke an answer ordering him back to town at once—on urgent business. It was an act performed, a decisive step taken—and he so rarely took decisive steps; he felt pleased with himself. It was with a whetted appetite that he came in to breakfast.

"Good morning," said Mr. Scogan. "I hope you're better."

"Better?"

"You were rather worried about the cosmos last night."

Denis tried to laugh away the impeachment. "Was I?" he lightly asked.

"I wish," said Mr. Scogan, "that I had nothing worse to prey on my mind. I should be a happy man."

"One is only happy in action," Denis enunciated, thinking of the telegram.

He looked out of the window. Great florid baroque clouds floated high in the blue heaven. A wind stirred among the trees, and their shaken foliage twinkled and glittered like metal in the sun. Everything seemed marvellously beautiful. At the thought that he would soon be leaving all this beauty he felt a momentary pang; but he comforted himself by recollecting how decisively he was acting.

"Action," he repeated aloud, and going over to the sideboard he helped himself to an agreeable mixture of bacon and fish.

Breakfast over, Denis repaired to the terrace, and, sitting there, raised the enormous bulwark of the *Times* against the possible assaults of Mr. Scogan, who showed an unappeased desire to go on talking about the Universe. Secure behind the crackling pages, he meditated. In the light of this brilliant morning the emotions of last night seemed somehow rather remote. And what if he had seen them ambracing in the moonlight? Perhaps it didn't mean much after all. And even if it did, why shouldn't he stay? He felt strong enough to stay, strong enough to be aloof, disinterested, a mere friendly acquaintance. And even if he weren't strong enough . . .

"What time do you think the telegram will arrive?" asked Mary suddenly, thrusting in upon him over the top of the paper.

Denis started guiltily. "I don't know at all," he said.

"I was only wondering," said Mary, "because there's a very good train at 3.27, and it would be nice if you could catch it, wouldn't it?"

"Awfully nice," he agreed weakly. He felt as though he were making arrangements for his own funeral. Train leaves Waterloo 3.27. No flowers. . . . Mary was gone. No, he was blowed if he'd let himself be hurried down to the Necropolis like this. He was blowed. The sight of Mr. Scogan looking out, with a hungry expression, from the drawing-room window made him precipitately hoist the *Times* once more. For a long while he kept it hoisted. Lowering it at last to take another cautious peep at his surroundings, he found himself, with what astonishment! confronted by Anne's faint, amused, malicious smile. She was standing before him,—the woman who was a tree, —the swaying grace of her movement arrested in a pose that seemed itself a movement.

"How long have you been standing there?" he asked, when he had done gaping at her.

"Oh, about half an hour, I suppose," she said airily. "You were so very deep in your paper—head over ears —I didn't like to disturb you."

"You look lovely this morning," Denis exclaimed. It was the first time he had ever had the courage to utter a personal remark of the kind.

Anne held up her hand as though to ward off a blow. "Don't bludgeon me, please." She sat down on the bench beside him. He was a nice boy, she thought, quite charming; and Gombauld's violent insistences were really becoming rather tiresome. "Why don't you wear white trousers?" she asked. "I like you so much in white trousers."

"They're at the wash," Denis replied rather curtly.

226

This white-trouser business was all in the wrong spirit. He was just preparing a scheme to manœuvre the conversation back to the proper path, when Mr. Scogan suddenly darted out of the house, crossed the terrace with clockwork rapidity, and came to a halt in front of the bench on which they were seated.

"To go on with our interesting conversation about the cosmos," he began. "I become more and more convinced that the various parts of the concern are fundamentally discrete. . . . But would you mind, Denis, moving a shade to your right?" He wedged himself between them on the bench. "And if you would shift a few inches to the left, my dear Anne. . . . Thank you. Discrete, I think, was what I was saying."

"You were," said Anne. Denis was speechless.

They were taking their after-luncheon coffee in the library when the telegram arrived. Denis blushed guiltily as he took the orange envelope from the salver and tore it open. "Return at once. Urgent family business." It was too ridiculous. As if he had any family business! Wouldn't it be best just to crumple the thing up and put it in his pocket without saying anything about it? He looked up; Mary's large blue china eyes were fixed upon him, seriously, penetratingly. He blushed more deeply than ever, hesitated in a horrible uncertainty.

"What's your telegram about?" Mary asked significantly.

He lost his head. "I'm afraid," he mumbled, "I'm afraid this means I shall have to go back to town at once." He frowned at the telegram ferociously.

"But that's absurd, impossible," cried Anne. She had been standing by the window talking to Gombauld; but

227

at Denis's words she came swaying across the room towards him.

"It's urgent," he repeated desperately.

"But you've only been here such a short time," Anne protested.

"I know," he said, utterly miserable. Oh, if only she could understand! Women were supposed to have intuition.

"If he must go, he must," put in Mary firmly.

"Yes, I must." He looked at the telegram again for inspiration. "You see, it's urgent family business," he explained.

Priscilla got up from her chair in some excitement. "I had a distinct presentiment of this last night," she said. "A distinct presentiment."

"A mere coincidence, no doubt," said Mary, brushing Mrs. Wimbush out of the conversation. "There's a very good train at 3.27." She looked at the clock on the mantelpiece. "You'll have nice time to pack."

"I'll order the motor at once." Henry Wimbush rang the bell. The funeral was well under way. It was awful, awful.

"I'm wretched you should be going," said Anne.

Denis turned towards her; she really did look wretched. He abandoned himself hopelessly, fatalistically to his destiny. This was what came of action, of doing something decisive. If only he'd just let things drift! If only . . .

"I shall miss your conversation," said Mr. Scogan.

Mary looked at the clock again. "I think perhaps you ought to go and pack," she said.

Obediently Denis left the room. Never again, he said to himself, never again would he do anything decisive.

Camlet, West Bowlby, Knipswich for Timpany, Spavin Delawarr; and then all the other stations; and then, finally, London. The thought of the journey appalled him. And what on earth was he going to do in London when he got there? He climbed wearily up the stairs. It was time for him to lay himself in his coffin.

The car was at the door—the hearse. The whole party had assembled to see him go. Good-bye, good-bye. Mechanically he tapped the barometer that hung in the porch; the needle stirred perceptibly to the left. A sudden smile lighted up his lugubrious face.

"'It sinks, and I am ready to depart,'" he said, quoting Landor with an exquisite aptness. He looked quickly round from face to face. Nobody had noticed. He climbed into the hearse.

ANTIC HAY

ANTIGUAY

MY MEN LIKE SATYRS GRAZING ON THE LAWNS

SHALL WITH THEIR GOAT-FEET DANCE THE ANTIC HAY

Marlowe

CHAPTER I

GUMBRIL, Theodore Gumbril Junior, B.A.Oxon., sat in his oaken stall on the north side of the School Chapel and wondered, as he listened through the uneasy silence of half a thousand schoolboys to the First Lesson, pondered, as he looked up at the vast window opposite, all blue and jaundiced and bloody with nineteenth-century glass, speculated in his rapid and rambling way about the existence and the nature of God.

Standing in front of the spread brass eagle and fortified in his convictions by the sixth chapter of Deuteronomy (for this first Sunday of term was the Fifth after Easter), the Reverend Pelvey could speak of these things with an enviable certainty. 'Hear, O Israel,' he was booming out over the top of the portentous Book: 'the Lord our God is one Lord.'

One Lord; Mr Pelvey knew; he had studied theology. But if theology and theosophy, then why not theography and theometry, why not theognomy, theotrophy, theotomy, theogamy? Why not theophysics and theo-chemistry? Why not that ingenious toy, the theotrope or wheel of gods? Why not a monumental theodrome?

In the great window opposite, young David stood like a cock, crowing on the dunghill of a tumbled giant. From the middle of Goliath's forehead there issued, like a narwhal's budding horn, a curious excrescence. Was it the embedded pebble? Or perhaps the giant's married life?

'... with all thine heart,' declaimed the Reverend Pelvey, 'and with all thy soul, and with all thy might.'

No, but seriously, Gumbril reminded himself, the problem was very troublesome indeed. God as a sense of warmth about the heart, God as exultation, God as tears in the eyes, God as a rush of power or thought – that was all right. But God as truth, God as $2+2=4$ – that wasn't so clearly all right. Was there any chance of their being the same? Were there bridges to join the two worlds? And could it be that the Reverend Pelvey, M.A., foghorning away from behind the imperial bird, could it be that he had an answer and a clue? That was hardly believable. Particularly if one knew Mr Pelvey personally. And Gumbril did.

'And these words which I command thee this day,' retorted Mr Pelvey, 'shall be in thine heart.'

Or in the heart, or in the head? Reply, Mr Pelvey, reply. Gumbril jumped between the horns of the dilemma and voted for other organs.

'And thou shalt teach them diligently unto thy children, and shalt talk of them when thou sittest in thine house, and when thou walkest by the way, and when thou liest down, and when thou risest up.'

Diligently unto thy children. ... Gumbril remembered his own childhood; they had not been very diligently taught to him. 'Beetles, black beetles' – his father had a really passionate feeling about the clergy. Mumbo-jumbery was another of his favourite words. An atheist and an anti-clerical of the strict old school he was. Not that, in any case, he gave himself much time to think about these things; he was too busy being an unsuccessful architect. As for Gumbril's mother, her diligence had not been dogmatic. She had just been diligently good, that was all. Good; good? It was a word people only used nowadays with a kind of deprecating humorousness. Good. Beyond good and evil? We are all that nowadays. Or merely below them, like earwigs? I glory in the name of earwig. Gumbril made a mental gesture and inwardly declaimed. But good in any case, there was no getting out of that, good she had been. Not nice, not merely *molto simpatica* – how charmingly and effectively these foreign tags assist one in the great task of calling a spade by some other name! – but good. You felt the active radiance of her goodness when you were near her. ... And that feeling, was that less real and valid than two plus two?

The Reverend Pelvey had nothing to reply. He was reading with a holy gusto of 'houses full of all good things, which thou filledst not, and wells digged, which thou diggedst not, vineyards and olive trees, which thou plantedst not.'

She had been good and she had died when he was still a boy; died – but he hadn't been told that till much later – of creeping and devouring pain. Malignant disease – oh, *caro nome*!

'Thou shalt fear the Lord thy God,' said Mr Pelvey.

Even when the ulcers are benign; thou shalt fear. He had travelled up from school to see her, just before she died. He hadn't known that she was going to die, but when he entered her room, when he saw her lying so weakly in the bed, he had suddenly begun to cry, uncontrollably. All the fortitude, the laughter even, had been hers. And she had spoken to him. A few words only; but they had contained all the wisdom he needed to live by. She had told him what he was, and what he should try to be, and how to be it. And crying, still crying, he had promised that he would try.

'And the Lord commanded us to do all these statutes,' said Mr Pelvey, 'for our good always, that he might preserve us alive, as it is at this day.'

And had he kept his promise, Gumbril wondered, had he preserved himself alive?

'Here endeth the First Lesson.' Mr Pelvey retreated from the eagle, and the organ presaged the coming *Te Deum*.

Gumbril hoisted himself to his feet; the folds of his B.A. gown billowed nobly about him as he rose. He sighed and shook his head with the gesture of one who tries to shake off a fly or an importunate thought. When the time came for singing, he sang. On the opposite side of the chapel two boys were grinning and whispering to one another behind their lifted Prayer Books. Gumbril frowned at them ferociously. The two boys caught his eye and their faces at once took on an expression of sickly piety; they began to sing with unction. They were two ugly, stupid-looking louts, who ought to have been apprenticed years ago to some useful trade. Instead of which they were wasting their own and their teacher's and their more intelligent comrades' time in trying, quite vainly, to acquire an elegant literary education. The minds of dogs, Gumbril reflected, do not benefit by being treated as though they were the minds of men.

'O Lord, have mercy upon us: have mercy upon us.'

Gumbril shrugged his shoulders and looked round the chapel

at the faces of the boys. Lord, indeed, have mercy upon us! He was disturbed to find the sentiment echoed on a somewhat different note in the Second Lesson, which was drawn from the twenty-third chapter of St Luke. 'Father, forgive them,' said Mr Pelvey in his unvaryingly juicy voice; 'for they know not what they do.' Ah, but suppose one did know what one was doing? suppose one knew only too well? And of course one always did know. One was not a fool.

But this was all nonsense, all nonsense. One must think of something better than this. What a comfort it would be, for example, if one could bring air cushions into chapel! These polished oaken stalls were devilishly hard; they were meant for stout and lusty pedagogues, not for bony starvelings like himself. An air cushion, a delicious pneu.

'Here endeth,' boomed Mr Pelvey, closing his book on the back of the German eagle.

As if by magic, Dr Jolly was ready at the organ with the *Benedictus*. It was positively a relief to stand again; this oak was adamantine. But air cushions, alas, would be too bad an example for the boys. Hardy young Spartans! it was an essential part of their education that they should listen to the word of revelation without pneumatic easement. No, air cushions wouldn't do. The real remedy, it suddenly flashed across his mind, would be trousers with pneumatic seats. For all occasions; not merely for church-going.

The organ blew a thin Puritan-preacher's note through one of its hundred nostrils. 'I believe ...' With a noise like the breaking of a wave, five hundred turned towards the East. The view of David and Goliath was exchanged for a Crucifixion in the grand manner of eighteen hundred and sixty. 'Father, forgive them; for they know not what they do.' No, no, Gumbril preferred to look at the grooved stonework rushing smoothly up on either side of the great east window towards the vaulted roof; preferred to reflect, like the dutiful son of an architect he was, that Perpendicular at its best— and its best is its largest— is the finest sort of English Gothic. At its worst and smallest, as in most of the colleges of Oxford, it is mean, petty, and, but for a certain picturesqueness, almost wholly disgusting. He felt like a lecturer:

next slide, please. 'And the life everlasting. Amen.' Like an oboe, Mr Pelvey intoned: 'The Lord be with you.'

For prayer, Gumbril reflected, there would be Dunlop knees. Still, in the days when he had made a habit of praying, they hadn't been necessary. 'Our Father ...' The words were the same as they were in the old days; but Mr Pelvey's method of reciting them made them sound rather different. Her dresses, when he had leaned his forehead against her knee to say those words – those words, good Lord! that Mr Pelvey was oboeing out of existence – were always black in the evenings, and of silk, and smelt of orris root. And when she was dying, she had said to him: 'Remember the Parable of the Sower, and the seeds that fell in shallow ground.' No, no. Amen, decidedly. 'O Lord, show thy mercy upon us,' chanted oboe Pelvey, and Gumbril trombone responded, profoundly and grotesquely: 'And grant us thy salvation.' No, the knees were obviously less important, except for people like revivalists and housemaids, than the seat. Sedentary are commoner than genuflectory professions. One would introduce little flat rubber bladders between two layers of cloth. At the upper end, hidden when one wore a coat, would be a tube with a valve: like a hollow tail. Blow it up – and there would be perfect comfort even for the boniest, even on rock. How did the Greeks stand marble benches in their theatres?

The moment had now come for the Hymn. This being the first Sunday of the Summer term, they sang that special hymn, written by the Headmaster, with music by Dr Jolly, on purpose to be sung on the first Sundays of terms. The organ quietly sketched out the tune. Simple it was, uplifting and manly.

One, two, three, four; one, two THREE – 4.
One, two-and three-and four-and; One, two THREE – 4.
ONE – 2, THREE – 4; ONE – 2 – 3 – 4,
and-ONE – 2, THREE – 4; ONE – 2 – 3 – 4.
One, two-and three, four; One, two THREE – 4.

Five hundred flawed adolescent voices took it up. For good example's sake, Gumbril opened and closed his mouth; noiselessly, however. It was only at the third verse that he gave rein to his uncertain baritone. He particularly liked the third verse; it

239

marked, in his opinion, the Headmaster's highest poetical achievement.

> (*f*) For slack hands and (*dim.*) idle minds
> (*mf*) Mischief still the Tempter finds.
> (*ff*) Keep him captive in his lair.

At this point Dr Jolly enriched his tune with a thick accompaniment in the lower registers, artfully designed to symbolize the depth, the gloom and general repulsiveness of the Tempter's home.

> (*ff*) Keep him captive in his lair.
> (*f*) Work will bind him. (*dim.*) Work is (*pp*) prayer.

Work, thought Gumbril, work. Lord, how passionately he disliked work! Let Austin have his swink to him reserved! Ah, if only one had work of one's own, proper work, decent work – not forced upon one by the griping of one's belly! Amen! Dr Jolly blew the two sumptuous jets of reverence into the air; Gumbril accompanied them with all his heart. Amen, indeed.

Gumbril sat down again. It might be convenient, he thought, to have the tail so long that one could blow up one's trousers while one actually had them on. In which case, it would have to be coiled round the waist like a belt; or looped up, perhaps, and fastened to a clip on one's braces.

'The nineteenth chapter of the Acts of the Apostles, part of the thirty-fourth verse.' The Headmaster's loud, harsh voice broke violently out from the pulpit. 'All with one voice about the space of two hours cried out, Great is Diana of the Ephesians.'

Gumbril composed himself as comfortably as he could on his oaken seat. It was going to be one of the Headmaster's real swingeing sermons. Great is Diana. And Venus? Ah, these seats, these seats!

Gumbril did not attend evening chapel. He stayed at home in his lodgings to correct the sixty-three Holiday Task Papers which had fallen to his share. They lay, thick piles of them, on the floor beside his chair: sixty-three answers to ten questions about the Italian Risorgimento. The Risorgimento, of all subjects! It had been one of the Headmaster's caprices. He had called a special masters' meeting at the end of last term to tell them all about the Risorgimento. It was his latest discovery.

'The Risorgimento, gentlemen, is the most important event in modern European history.' And he had banged the table; he had looked defiantly round the room in search of contradictors.

But nobody had contradicted him. Nobody ever did; they all knew better. For the Headmaster was as fierce as he was capricious. He was for ever discovering something new. Two terms ago it had been singeing; after the hair-cut and before the shampoo, there must be singeing.

'The hair, gentlemen, is a tube. If you cut it and leave the end unsealed, the water will get in and rot the tube. Hence the importance of singeing, gentlemen. Singeing seals the tube. I shall address the boys about it after chapel to-morrow morning; and I trust that all house-masters' – and he had glared around him from under his savage eyebrows – 'will see that their boys get themselves regularly singed after cutting.'

For weeks afterwards every boy trailed behind him a faint and nauseating whiff of burning, as though he were fresh from hell. And now it was the Risorgimento. One of these days, Gumbril reflected, it would be birth control, or the decimal system, or rational dress.

He picked up the nearest batch of papers. The printed questions were pinned to the topmost of them.

'Give a brief account of the character and career of Pope Pius IX, *with dates wherever possible.*'

Gumbril leaned back in his chair and thought of his own character, with dates. 1896: the first serious and conscious and deliberate lie. Did you break that vase, Theodore? No, mother. It lay on his conscience for nearly a month, eating deeper and deeper. Then he had confessed the truth. Or rather he had not confessed; that was too difficult. He led the conversation, very subtly, as he thought, round through the non-malleability of glass, through breakages in general, to this particular broken vase; he practically forced his mother to repeat her question. And then, with a burst of tears, he had answered, yes. It had always been difficult for him to say things directly, point-blank. His mother had told him, when she was dying. ... No, no; not that.

In 1898 or 1899 – oh, these dates! – he had made a pact with his little cousin, Molly, that she should let him see her with no clothes on, if he would do the same by her. She had fulfilled her part of the bargain; but he, overwhelmed at the last moment by a passion of modesty, had broken his promise.

Then, when he was about twelve and still at his preparatory school, in 1902 or 1903 he had done badly in his exams, on purpose; he had been frightened of Sadler, who was in the same form, and wanted to get the prize. Sadler was stronger than he was, and had a genius for persecution. He had done so badly that his mother was unhappy; and it was impossible for him to explain.

In 1906 he had fallen in love for the first time – ah, much more violently than ever since – with a boy of his own age. Platonic it had been and profound. He had done badly that term, too; not on purpose, but because he had spent so much time helping young Vickers with his work. Vickers was really very stupid. The next term he had 'come out' – *Staphylococcus pyogenes* is a lover of growing adolescence – with spots and boils all over his face and neck. Gumbril's affection ceased as suddenly as it had begun. He finished that term, he remembered, with a second prize.

But it was time to be thinking seriously of Pio Nono. With a sigh of disgusted weariness, Gumbril looked at his papers. What had Falarope Major to say of the Pontiff? 'Pius IX was called Ferretti. He was a liberal before he was a Pope. A kindly man of less than average intelligence, he thought that all difficulties could be settled by a little goodwill, a few reforms and a political amnesty. He wrote several encyclicals and a syllabus.' Gumbril admired the phrase about less than average intelligence; Falarope Major should have at least one mark for having learnt it so well by heart. He turned to the next paper. Higgs was of opinion that 'Pius the Ninth was a good but stupid man, who thought he could settle the Risorgimento with a few reforms and a political armistice.' Beddoes was severer. 'Pius IX was a bad man, who said that he was infallible, which showed he had a less than average intelligence.' Sopwith Minor shared the general opinion about Pio's intelligence, and displayed a great familiarity with

242

the wrong dates. Clegg-Weller was voluminous and informative.
' Pius IX was not so clever as his prime minister, Cardinal Anto-
nelli. When he came to the tiara he was a liberal, and Metternich
said he had never reckoned on a liberal pope. He then became a
conservative. He was kindly, but not intelligent, and he thought
Garibaldi and Cavour would be content with a few reforms and
an amnesty.' At the top of Garstang's paper was written: 'I have
had measles all the holidays, so have been unable to read more
than the first thirty pages of the book. Pope Pius IX does not
come into these pages, of the contents of which I will proceed to
give the following précis.' And the précis duly followed. Gumbril would have liked to give him full marks. But the business-
like answer of Appleyard called him back to a better sense of his
duty. 'Pius IX became Pope in 1846 and died in 1878. He was a
kindly man, but his intelligence was below the ...'

Gumbril laid the paper down and shut his eyes. No, this was
really impossible. Definitely, it couldn't go on, it could not go
on. There were thirteen weeks in the summer term, there would
be thirteen in the autumn and eleven or twelve in the spring; and
then another summer of thirteen, and so it would go on for ever.
For ever. It wouldn't do. He would go away and live uncomfortably on his three hundred. Or, no, he would go away and he
would make money – that was more like it – money on a large
scale, easily; he would be free and he would live. For the first
time, he would live. Behind his closed eyes, he saw himself living.

Over the plushy floors of some vast and ignoble Ritz slowly
he walked, at ease, with confidence: over the plushy floors and
there, at the end of a long vista, there was Myra Viveash, waiting,
this time, for him; coming forward impatiently to meet him, his
abject lover now, not the cool, free, laughing mistress who had
lent herself contemptuously once to his pathetic and silent importunity and then, after a day, withdrawn the gift again. Over
the plushy floors to dine. Not that he was in love with Myra any
longer: but revenge is sweet.

He sat in his own house. The Chinese statues looked out from
the niches; the Maillols passionately meditated, slept, and were
more than alive. The Goyas hung on the walls, there was a
Boucher in the bathroom; and when he entered with his guests,

243

what a Piazzetta exploded above the dining-room mantelpiece! Over the ancient wine they talked together, and he knew everything they knew and more; he gave, he inspired, it was the others who assimilated and were enriched. After dinner there were Mozart quartets; he opened his portfolios and showed his Daumiers, his Tiepolos, his Canaletto sketches, his drawings by Picasso and Lewis, and the purity of his naked Ingres. And later, talking of Odalisques, there were orgies without fatigue or disgust, and the women were pictures and lust in action, art.

Over the empty plains forty horses impelled him towards Mantua: rubadub – adubadub, with the silencer out. Towards the most romantic city in all the world.

When he spoke to women – how easily and insolently he spoke now! – they listened and laughed and looked at him sideways and dropped their eyelids over the admission, the invitation, of their glance. With Phyllis once he had sat, for how long? in a warm and moonless darkness, saying nothing, risking no gesture. And in the end they had parted, reluctantly and still in silence. Phyllis now was with him once again in the summer night; but this time he spoke, now softly, now in the angry breathless whisper of desire, he reached out and took her, and she was naked in his arms. All chance encounters, all plotted opportunities recurred; he knew, now, how to live, how to take advantage of them.

Over the empty plains towards Mantua, towards Mantua, he slid along at ease, free and alone. He explored the horrors of Roman society; visited Athens and Seville. To Unamuno and Papini he conversed familiarly in their own tongues. He understood perfectly and without effort the quantum theory. To his friend Shearwater he gave half a million for physiological research. He visited Schoenberg and persuaded him to write still better music. He exhibited to the politicians the full extent of their stupidity and their wickedness; he set them working for the salvation, not the destruction, of humanity. Once in the past when he had been called upon to make a public speech, he had felt so nervous that he was sick; the thousands who listened to him now bent like wheat under the wind of his eloquence. But it was only by the way and occasionally that he troubled himself to move them. He found it easy now to come to terms with every-one he met, to understand all points of view, to identify himself with even the most unfamiliar spirit. And he knew how every-body lived, and what it was like to be a mill-girl, a dustman, an engine-driver, a Jew, an Anglican bishop, a confidence-trickster. Accustomed as he was to being swindled and imposed upon without protest, he now knew the art of being brutal. He was just dressing down that insolent porter at the Continental, who had complained that ten francs wasn't enough (and had got, as a matter of historic fact, another five in addition), when his land-lady gave a knock, opened the door and said: 'Dinner's ready, Mr Gumbril.'

Feeling a little ashamed at having been interrupted in what was, after all, one of the ignobler and more trivial occupations of his new life, Gumbril went down to his fatty chop and green peas. It was the first meal to be eaten under the new dispensa-tion; he ate it, for all that it was unhappily indistinguishable from the meals of the past, with elation and a certain solemnity, as though he were partaking of a sacrament. He felt buoyant with the thought that at last, at last, he was doing something about life.

When the chop was eaten, he went upstairs and, after filling two suit-cases and a Gladstone bag with the most valued of his possessions, addressed himself to the task of writing to the Headmaster. He might have gone away, of course, without writing. But it would be nobler, more in keeping, he felt, with his new life, to leave a justification behind — or rather not a justification, a denouncement. He picked up his pen and denounced.

CHAPTER II

GUMBRIL SENIOR occupied a tall, narrow-shouldered and rachitic house in a little obscure square not far from Paddington. There were five floors, and a basement with beetles, and nearly a hundred stairs, which shook when any one ran too rudely down them. It was a prematurely old and decaying house in a decaying quarter. The square in which it stood was steadily coming down in the world. The houses, which a few years ago had all been occupied by respectable families, were now split up into squalid little maisonnettes, and from the neighbouring slums, which along with most other unpleasant things the old bourgeois families had been able to ignore, invading bands of children came to sport on the once-sacred pavements.

Mr Gumbril was almost the last survivor of the old inhabitants. He liked his house, and he liked his square. Social decadence had not affected the fourteen plane-trees which adorned its little garden, and the gambols of the dirty children did not disturb the starlings who came, evening by evening in summertime, to roost in their branches.

On fine evenings he used to sit out on his balcony waiting for the coming of the birds. And just at sunset, when the sky was most golden, there would be a twittering overhead, and the black, innumerable flocks of starlings would come sweeping across on the way from their daily haunts to their roosting-places, chosen so capriciously among the tree-planted squares and gardens of the city and so tenaciously retained, year after year, to the exclusion of every other place. Why his fourteen plane-trees should have been chosen, Mr Gumbril could never imagine. There were plenty of larger and more umbrageous gardens all round; but they remained birdless, while every evening, from the larger flocks, a faithful legion detached itself to settle clamorously among his trees. They sat and chattered till the sun went down and twilight was past, with intervals every now and then of silence that fell suddenly and inexplicably on all the birds

246

at once, lasted through a few seconds of thrilling suspense, to end as suddenly and senselessly in an outburst of the same loud and simultaneous conversation.

The starlings were Mr Gumbril's most affectionately cherished friends; sitting out on his balcony to watch and listen to them, he had caught at the shut of treacherous evenings many colds and chills on the liver, he had laid up for himself many painful hours of rheumatism. These little accidents did nothing, however, to damp his affection for the birds; and still on every evening that could possibly be called fine, he was always to be seen in the twilight, sitting on the balcony, gazing up, round-spectacled and rapt, at the fourteen plane-trees. The breezes stirred in his grey hair, tossing it up in long, light wisps that fell across his forehead and over his spectacles; and then he would shake his head impatiently, and the bony hand would be freed for a moment from its unceasing combing and clutching of the sparse grey beard to push back the strayed tendrils, to smooth and reduce to order the whole ruffled head. The birds chattered on, the hand went back to its clutching and combing; once more the wind blew, darkness came down, and the gas-lamps round the square lit up the outer leaves of the plane-trees, touched the privet bushes inside the railings with an emerald light; behind them was impenetrable night; instead of shorn grass and bedded geraniums there was mystery, there were endless depths. And the birds at last were silent.

Mr Gumbril would get up from his iron chair, stretch his arms and his stiff cold legs and go in through the french window to work. The birds were his diversion; when they were silent, it was time to think of serious matters.

To-night, however, he was not working; for always on Sunday evenings his old friend Porteous came to dine and talk. Breaking in unexpectedly at midnight, Gumbril Junior found them sitting in front of the gas fire in his father's study.

'My dear fellow, what on earth are you doing here?' Gumbril Senior jumped up excitedly at his son's entrance. The light silky hair floated up with the movement, turned for a moment into a silver aureole, then subsided again. Mr Porteous stayed where he was, calm, solid and undishevelled as a seated pillar-box. He

247

wore a monocle on a black ribbon, a black stock tie that revealed above its double folds a quarter of an inch of stiff white collar, a double-breasted black coat, a pair of pale checked trousers and patent-leather boots with cloth tops. Mr Porteous was very particular about his appearance. Meeting him casually for the first time, one would not have guessed that Mr Porteous was an expert on Late Latin poetry; and he did not mean that you should guess. Thin-limbed, bent and agile in his loose, crumpled clothes, Gumbril Senior had the air, beside Mr Porteous, of a strangely animated scarecrow.

'What on earth?' the old gentleman repeated his question.

Gumbril Junior shrugged his shoulders. 'I was bored, I decided to cease being a schoolmaster.' He spoke with a fine airy assumption of carelessness. 'How are you, Mr Porteous?'

'Thank you, invariably well.'

'Well, well,' said Gumbril Senior, sitting down again, 'I must say I'm not surprised. I'm only surprised that you stood it, not being a born pedagogue, for as long as you did. What ever induced you to think of turning usher, I can't imagine.' He looked at his son first through his spectacles, then over the top of them; the motives of the boy's conduct revealed themselves to neither vision.

'What else was there for me to do?' asked Gumbril Junior, pulling up a chair towards the fire. 'You gave me a pedagogue's education and washed your hands of me. No opportunities, no openings. I had no alternative. And now you reproach me.'

Mr Gumbril made an impatient gesture. 'You're talking nonsense,' he said. 'The only point of the kind of education you had is this, it gives a young man leisure to find out what he's interested in. You apparently weren't sufficiently interested in anything –'

'I am interested in everything,' interrupted Gumbril Junior.

'Which comes to the same thing,' said his father parenthetically, 'as being interested in nothing.' And he went on from the point at which he had been interrupted. 'You weren't sufficiently interested in anything to want to devote yourself to it. That was why you sought the last refuge of feeble minds with classical educations, you became a schoolmaster.'

'Come, come,' said Mr Porteous. 'I do a little teaching myself; I must stand up for the profession.'

Gumbril Senior let go his beard and brushed back the hair that the wind of his own vehemence had brought tumbling into his eyes. 'I don't denigrate the profession,' he said. 'Not at all. It would be an excellent profession if every one who went into it were as much interested in teaching as you are in your job, Porteous, or I in mine. It's these undecided creatures like Theodore, who ruin it by drifting in. Until all teachers are geniuses and enthusiasts, nobody will learn anything, except what they teach themselves.'

'Still,' said Mr Porteous, 'I wish I hadn't had to learn so much by myself. I wasted a lot of time finding out how to set to work and where to discover what I wanted.'

Gumbril Junior was lighting his pipe. 'I have come to the conclusion,' he said, speaking in little jerks between each suck of the flame into the bowl, 'that most people ... ought never ... to be taught anything at all.' He threw away the match. 'Lord have mercy upon us, they're dogs. What's the use of teaching them anything except to behave well, to work and obey? Facts, theories, the truth about the universe – what good are those to them? Teach them to understand – why, it only confuses them; makes them lose hold of the simple real appearance. Not more than one in a hundred can get any good out of a scientific or literary education.'

'And you're one of the ones?' asked his father.

'That goes without saying,' Gumbril Junior replied.

'I think you mayn't be so far wrong,' said Mr Porteous. 'When I think of my own children, for example ...' he sighed, 'I thought they'd be interested in the things that interested me; they don't seem to be interested in anything but behaving like little apes – not very anthropoid ones either, for that matter. At my eldest boy's age I used to sit up most of the night reading Latin texts. He sits up – or rather stands, reels, trots up – dancing and drinking. Do you remember St Bernard? "Vigilet tota nocte luxuriosus non solum patienter" (the ascetic and the scholar only watch patiently); "sed et libenter, ut suam expleat voluptatem." What the wise man does out of a sense of duty,

249

the fool does for fun. And I've tried very hard to make him like Latin.'

'Well, in any case,' said Gumbril Junior, 'you didn't try to feed him on history. That's the real unforgivable sin. And that's what I've been doing, up till this evening – encouraging boys of fifteen and sixteen to specialize in history, hours and hours a week, making them read bad writers' generalizations about subjects on which only our ignorance allows us to generalize; teaching them to reproduce these generalizations in horrid little "Essays" of their own; rotting their minds, in fact, with a diet of soft vagueness; scandalous it was. If these creatures are to be taught anything, it should be something hard and definite. Latin – that's excellent. Mathematics, physical science. Let them read history for amusement, certainly. But for Heaven's sake don't make it the staple of education!' Gumbril Junior spoke with the greatest earnestness, as though he were an inspector of schools, making a report. It was a subject on which, at the moment, he felt very profoundly; he felt profoundly on all subjects while he was talking about them. 'I wrote a long letter to the Headmaster about the teaching of history this evening,' he added. 'It's most important.' He shook his head thoughtfully, 'Most important.'

'Hora novissima, tempora pessima sunt, vigilemus,' said Mr Porteous, in the words of St Peter Damianus.

'Very true,' Gumbril Senior applauded. 'And talking about bad times, Theodore, what do you propose to do now, may I ask?'

'I mean to begin by making some money.'

Gumbril Senior put his hands on his knees, bent forward and laughed, 'Ha, ha, ha!' He had a profound bell-like laugh that was like the croaking of a very large and melodious frog. 'You won't,' he said, and shook his head till the hair fell into his eyes. 'You won't,' and he laughed again.

'To make money,' said Mr Porteous, 'one must be really interested in money.'

'And he's not,' said Gumbril Senior. 'None of us are.'

'When I was still uncommonly hard up,' Mr Porteous continued, 'we used to lodge in the same house with a Russian Jew, who was a furrier. That man was interested in money, if you like. It was a passion, an enthusiasm, an ideal. He could have led

250

a comfortable, easy life, and still have made enough to put by something for his old age. But for his high abstract ideal of money he suffered more than Michelangelo ever suffered for his art. He used to work nineteen hours a day, and the other five he slept, lying under his bench, in the dirt, breathing into his lungs the stink and the broken hairs. He is now very rich indeed and does nothing with his money, doesn't want to do anything, doesn't know what one does do with it. He desires neither power nor pleasure. His desire for lucre is purely disinterested. He reminds me of Browning's "Grammarian". I have a great admiration for him.'

Mr Porteous's own passion had been for the poems of Notker Balbulus and St Bernard. It had taken him nearly twenty years to get himself and his family out of the house where the Russian furrier used to lodge. But Notker was worth it, he used to say; Notker was worth even the weariness and the pallor of a wife who worked beyond her strength, even the shabbiness of ill-dressed and none too well-fed children. He had readjusted his monocle and gone on. But there had been occasions when it needed more than the monocle and the careful, distinguished clothes to keep up his morale. Still, those times were over now; Notker had brought him at last a kind of fame – even, indirectly, a certain small prosperity.

Gumbril Senior turned once more towards his son. 'And how do you propose,' he asked, 'to make this money?'

Gumbril Junior explained. He had thought it all out in the cab on the way from the station. 'It came to me this morning,' he said, 'in chapel, during service.'

'Monstrous,' put in Gumbril Senior, with a genuine indignation, 'monstrous these medieval survivals in schools! Chapel, indeed!'

'It came,' Gumbril Junior went on, 'like an apocalypse, suddenly, like a divine inspiration. A grand and luminous idea came to me – the idea of Gumbril's Patent Small-Clothes.'

'And what are Gumbril's Patent Small-Clothes?'

'A boon to those whose occupation is sedentary'; Gumbril Junior had already composed his prospectus and his first advertisements: 'a comfort to all travellers, civilization's substitute for

251

steatopygism, indispensable to first-nighters, the concert-goers'
friend, the ...'

'Lectulus Dei floridus,' intoned Mr Porteous.

'Gazophylacium Ecclesiæ,
Cithara benesonans Dei,
Cymbalum jubilationis Christi,
Promptuarium mysteriorum fidei, ora pro nobis.

Your Small-Clothes sound to me very like one of my old litanies,
Theodore.'

'We want scientific descriptions, not litanies,' said Gumbril
Senior. 'What *are* Gumbril's Patent Small-Clothes?'

'Scientifically, then,' said Gumbril Junior, 'my Patent Small-
Clothes may be described as trousers with a pneumatic seat,
inflateable by means of a tube fitted with a valve; the whole constructed of stout seamless red rubber, enclosed between two
layers of cloth.'

'I must say,' said Gumbril Senior in a tone of somewhat
grudging approbation, 'I have heard of worse inventions. You
are too stout, Porteous, to be able to appreciate the idea. We
Gumbrils are all a bony lot.'

'When I have taken out a patent for my invention,' his son
went on, very business-like and cool, 'I shall either sell it to
some capitalist, or I shall exploit it commercially myself. In
either case, I shall make money, which is more, I may say, than
you or any other Gumbril have ever done.'

'Quite right,' said Gumbril Senior, 'quite right'; and he
laughed very cheerfully. 'And nor will you. You can be grateful
to your intolerable Aunt Flo for having left you that three
hundred a year. You'll need it. But if you really want a capitalist,' he went on, 'I have exactly the man for you. He's a man
who has a mania for buying Tudor houses and making them
more Tudor than they are. I've pulled half a dozen of the
wretched things to pieces and put them together again differently
for him.'

'He doesn't sound much good to me,' said his son.

'Ah, but that's only his vice. Only his amusement. His
business,' Gumbril Senior hesitated.

'Well, what is his business?'

'Well, it seems to be everything. Patent medicine, trade news-papers, bankrupt tobacconist's stock – he's talked to me about those and heaps more. He seems to flit like a butterfly in search of honey, or rather money.'

'And he makes it?'

'Well, he pays my fees and he buys more Tudor houses, and he gives me luncheons at the Ritz. That's all I know.'

'Well, there's no harm in trying.'

'I'll write to him,' said Gumbril Senior. 'His name is Boldero. He'll either laugh at your idea or take it and give you nothing for it. Still,' he looked at his son over the top of his spectacles, 'if by any conceivable chance you ever should become rich; if, if, if ...' And he emphasized the remoteness of the conditional by raising his eyebrows a little higher, by throwing out his hands in a dubious gesture a little farther at every repetition of the word, 'if – why, then I've got exactly the thing for you. Look at this really delightful little idea I had this afternoon.' He put his hand in his coat pocket and after some sorting and sifting produced a sheet of squared paper on which was roughly drawn the elevation of a house. 'For any one with eight or ten thousand to spend, this would be – this would be ...' Gumbril Senior smoothed his hair and hesitated, searching for something strong enough to say of his little idea. 'Well, this would be much too good for most of the greasy devils who do have eight or ten thousand to spend.'

He passed the sheet to Gumbril Junior, who held it out so that both Mr Porteous and himself could look at it. Gumbril Senior got up from his chair and, standing behind them, leant over to elucidate and explain.

'You see the idea,' he said, anxious lest they should fail to understand. 'A central block of three stories, with low wings of only one, ending in pavilions with a second floor. And the flat roofs of the wings are used as gardens – you see? – protected from the north by a wall. In the east wing there is the kitchen and the garage, with the maids' rooms in the pavilion at the end. The west is a library, and it has an arcaded loggia along the front. And instead of a solid superstructure corresponding to the maids' rooms, there's a pergola with brick piers. You see? And in the main block there's a Spanish sort of balcony along the whole length at first-floor level; that gives a good horizontal line. And you get the perpendiculars with coigns and raised panels. And the roof's hidden by a balustrade, and there are balustrades along the open sides of the roof gardens on the wings. All in brick it is. This is the garden front; the entrance front will be admirable too. Do you like it?'

Gumbril Junior nodded. 'Very much,' he said.

His father sighed and taking the sketch put it back in his pocket. 'You must hurry up with your ten thousand,' he said. 'And you, Porteous, and you. I've been waiting so long to build your splendid house.'

Laughing, Mr Porteous got up from his chair. 'And long, dear Gumbril,' he said, 'may you continue to wait. For my splendid house won't be built this side of New Jerusalem, and you must go on living a long time yet. A long, long time,' Mr Porteous repeated; and carefully he buttoned up his double-breasted coat, carefully, as though he were adjusting an instrument of precision, he took out and replaced his monocle. Then, very erect and neat, very soldierly and pillar-boxical, he marched towards the door. 'You've kept me very late to-night,' he said. 'Unconscionably late.'

The front door closed heavily behind Mr Porteous's departure. Gumbril Senior came upstairs again into the big room on the first floor smoothing down his hair, which the impetuosity of his ascent had once more disarranged.

'That's a good fellow,' he said of his departed guest, 'a splendid fellow.'

'I always admire the monocle,' said Gumbril Junior irrelevantly. But his father turned the irrelevance into relevance.

'He couldn't have come through without it, I believe. It was a symbol, a proud flag. Poverty's squalid, not fine at all. The monocle made a kind of difference, you understand. I'm always so enormously thankful I had a little money. I couldn't have stuck it without. It needs strength, more strength than I've got.' He clutched his beard close under the chin and remained for a moment pensively silent. 'The advantage of Porteous's line of business,' he went on at last, reflectively, 'is that it can be carried

on by oneself, without collaboration. There's no need to appeal
to any one outside oneself, or to have any dealings with other
people at all, if one doesn't want to. That's so deplorable about
architecture. There's no privacy, so to speak; always this
horrible jostling with clients and builders and contractors and
people, before one can get anything done. It's really revolting.
I'm not good at people. Most of them I don't like at all, not at
all,' Mr Gumbril repeated with vehemence. 'I don't deal with
them very well; it isn't my business. My business is architecture.
But I don't often get a chance of practising it. Not properly.'

Gumbril Senior smiled rather sadly. 'Still,' he said, 'I can do
something. I have my talent, I have my imagination. They can't
take those from me. Come and see what I've been doing lately.'

He led the way out of the room and mounted, two steps at a
time, towards a higher floor. He opened the door of what should
have been, in a well-ordered house, the Best Bedroom, and
slipped into the darkness.

'Don't rush in,' he called back to his son, 'for God's sake
don't rush in. You'll smash something. Wait till I've turned on
the light. It's so like these asinine electricians to have hidden the
switch behind the door like this.' Gumbril Junior heard him
fumbling in the darkness; there was suddenly light. He stepped
in.

The only furniture in the room consisted of a couple of long
trestle tables. On these, on the mantelpiece and all over the floor,
were scattered confusedly, like the elements of a jumbled city, a
vast collection of architectural models. There were cathedrals,
there were town halls, universities, public libraries, there were
three or four elegant little sky-scrapers, there were blocks of
offices, huge warehouses, factories, and finally dozens of magnificent country mansions, complete with their terraced gardens,
their noble flights of steps, their fountains and ornamental waters
and grandly bridged canals, their little rococo pavilions and
garden houses.

'Aren't they beautiful?' Gumbril Senior turned enthusiastically towards his son. His long grey hair floated wispily about his
head, his spectacles flashed, and behind them his eyes shone with
emotion.

'Beautiful,' Gumbril Junior agreed.

'When you're really rich,' said his father, 'I'll build you one of these.' And he pointed to a little village of Chatsworths clustering, at one end of a long table, round the dome of a vaster and austerer St Peter's. 'Look at this one, for example.' He picked his way nimbly across the room, seized the little electric reading-lamp that stood between a railway station and a baptistery on the mantelpiece, and was back again in an instant, trailing behind him a long flex that, as it tautened out, twitched one of the crowning pinnacles off the top of a sky-scraper near the fireplace. 'Look,' he repeated, 'look.' He switched on the current, and moving the lamp back and forth, up and down in front of the miniature palace. 'See the beauty of the light and shade,' he said. 'There, underneath the great, ponderous cornice, isn't that fine? And look how splendidly the pilasters carry up the vertical lines. And then the solidity of it, the size, the immense, impending bleakness of it!' He threw up his arms, he turned his eyes upwards as though standing overwhelmed at the foot of some huge precipitous façade. The lights and shadows vacillated wildly through all the city of palaces and domes as he brandished the lamp in ecstasy above his head.

'And then,' he had suddenly stooped down, he was peering and pointing once more into the details of his palace, 'then there's the doorway – all florid and rich with carving. How magnificently and surprisingly it flowers out of the bare walls! Like the colossal writing of Darius, like the figures graven in the bald face of the precipice over Behistun – unexpected and beautiful and human, human in the surrounding emptiness.'

Gumbril Senior brushed back his hair and turned, smiling, to look at his son over the top of his spectacles.

'Very fine,' Gumbril Junior nodded to him. 'But isn't the wall a little too blank? You seem to allow very few windows in this vast palazzo.'

'True,' his father replied, 'very true.' He sighed. 'I'm afraid this design would hardly do for England. It's meant for a place where there's some sun – where you do your best to keep the light out, instead of letting it in, as you have to do here. Windows are the curse of architecture in this country. Your walls

have to be like sieves, all holes, it's heart-breaking. If you wanted me to build you this house, you'd have to live in Barbados or somewhere like that.'

'There's nothing I should like better,' said Gumbril Junior.

'Another great advantage of sunny countries,' Gumbril Senior pursued, 'is that one can really live like an aristocrat, in privacy, by oneself. No need to look out on the dirty world or to let the dirty world look in on you. Here's this great house, for example, looking out on the world through a few dark portholes and a single cavernous doorway. But look inside.' He held his lamp above the courtyard that was at the heart of the palace. Gumbril Junior leaned and looked, like his father. 'All the life looks inwards – into a lovely courtyard, a more than Spanish *patio*. Look there at the treble tiers of arcades, the vaulted cloisters for your cool peripatetic meditations, the central Triton spouting white water into a marble pool, the mosaic work on the floor and flowering up the walls, brilliant against the white stucco. And there's the archway that leads out into the gardens. And now you must come and have a look at the garden front.'

He walked round with his lamp to the other side of the table. There was suddenly a crash; the wire had twitched a cathedral from off the table. It lay on the floor in disastrous ruin as though shattered by some appalling cataclysm.

'Hell and death!' said Gumbril Senior in an outburst of Elizabethan fury. He put down the lamp and ran to see how irreparable the disaster had been. 'They're so horribly expensive, these models,' he explained, as he bent over the ruins. Tenderly he picked up the pieces and replaced them on the table. 'It might have been worse,' he said at last, brushing the dust off his hands. 'Though I'm afraid that dome will never be quite the same again.' Picking up the lamp once more, he held it high above his head and stood looking out, with a melancholy satisfaction, over his creations. 'And to think,' he said after a pause, 'that I've been spending these last days designing model cottages for workmen at Bletchley! I'm in luck to have got the job, of course, but really, that a civilized man should have to do jobs like that! It's too much. In the old days these creatures built their own hovels, and very nice and suitable they were too. The architects busied themselves with architecture – which is the expression of human dignity and greatness, which is man's protest, not his miserable acquiescence. You can't do much protesting in a model cottage at seven hundred pounds a time. A little, no doubt, you can protest a little; you can give your cottage decent proportions and avoid sordidness and vulgarity. But that's all; it's really a negative process. You can only begin to protest positively and actively when you abandon the petty human scale and build for giants – when you build for the spirit and the imagination of man, not for his little body. Model cottages, indeed!'

Mr Gumbril snorted with indignation. 'When I think of Alberti!' And he thought of Alberti – Alberti, the noblest Roman of them all, the true and only Roman. For the Romans themselves had lived their own actual lives, sordidly and extravagantly in the middle of a vulgar empire. Alberti and his followers in the Renaissance lived the ideal Roman life. They put Plutarch into their architecture. They took the detestable real Cato, the Brutus of history, and made of them Roman heroes to walk as guides and models before them. Before Alberti there were no true Romans, and with Piranesi's death the race began to wither towards extinction.

'And when I think of Brunelleschi!' Gumbril Senior went on to remember with passion the architect who had suspended on eight thin flying ribs of marble the lightest of all domes and the loveliest.

'And when of Michelangelo! The grim, enormous apse ... And of Wren and of Palladio, when I think of all these – ' Gumbril Senior waved his arms and was silent. He could not put into words what he felt when he thought of them.

Gumbril Junior looked at his watch. 'Half-past two,' he said. 'Time to go to bed.'

CHAPTER III

'MISTER GUMBRIL!' Surprise was mingled with delight. 'This is indeed a pleasure!' Delight was now the prevailing emotion expressed by the voice that advanced, as yet without a visible source, from the dark recesses of the shop.

'The pleasure, Mr Bojanus, is mine.' Gumbril closed the shop door behind him.

A very small man, dressed in a frock-coat, popped out from a canyon that opened, a mere black crevice, between two stratified precipices of mid-season suitings, and advancing into the open space before the door bowed with an old-world grace, revealing a nacreous scalp thinly mantled with long, damp creepers of brown hair.

'And to what, may I ask, do I owe this pleasure, sir?' Mr Bojanus looked up archly with a sideways cock of his head that tilted the rigid points of his waxed moustache. The fingers of his right hand were thrust into the bosom of his frock-coat and his toes were turned out in the dancing-master's First Position. 'A light spring great-coat, is it? Or a new suit? I notice,' his eye travelled professionally up and down Gumbril's long, thin form, 'I notice that the garments you are wearing at present, Mr Gumbril, look – how shall I say? – well, a trifle negleejay, as the French would put it, a trifle negleejay.'

Gumbril looked down at himself. He resented Mr Bojanus's negleejay, he was pained and wounded by the aspersion. Negleejay? And he had fancied that he really looked rather elegant and distinguished (but, after all, he always looked that, even in rags) – no, that he looked positively neat, like Mr Porteous, positively soldierly in his black jacket and his musical-comedy trousers and his patent-leather shoes. And the black felt hat – didn't that add just the foreign, the Southern touch which saved the whole composition from banality? He regarded himself, trying to see his clothes – garments, Mr Bojanus had called them; garments, good Lord! – through the tailor's expert eyes. There were sagging

259

folds about the overloaded pockets, there was a stain on his waistcoat, the knees of his trousers were baggy and puckered like the bare knees of Hélène Fourmont in Rubens's fur-coat portrait at Vienna. Yes, it was all horribly negleejay. He felt depressed; but looking at Mr Bojanus's studied and professional correctness, he was a little comforted. That frock-coat, for example. It was like something in a very modern picture – such a smooth, unwrinkled cylinder about the chest, such a sense of pure and abstract conic-ness in the sleekly rounded skirts! Nothing could have been less negleejay. He was reassured.

'I want you,' he said at last, clearing his throat importantly, 'to make me a pair of trousers to a novel specification of my own. It's a new idea.' And he gave a brief description of Gumbril's Patent Small-Clothes.

Mr Bojanus listened with attention.

'I can make them for you,' he said, when the description was finished. 'I can make them for you – if you *really* wish, Mr Gumbril,' he added.

'Thank you,' said Gumbril.

'And do you intend, may I ask, Mr Gumbril, to *wear* these ... these garments?'

Guiltily, Gumbril denied himself. 'Only to demonstrate the idea, Mr Bojanus. I am exploiting the invention commercially, you see.'

'Commercially? I see, Mr Gumbril.'

'Perhaps you would like a share,' suggested Gumbril.

Mr Bojanus shook his head. 'It wouldn't do for my cleeantail, I fear, Mr Gumbril. You could 'ardly expect the Best People to wear such things.'

'Couldn't you?'

Mr Bojanus went on shaking his head. 'I know them,' he said, 'I know the Best People. Well.' And he added with an irrelevance that was, perhaps, only apparent, 'Between ourselves, Mr Gumbril, I am a great admirer of Lenin ...'

'So am I,' said Gumbril, 'theoretically. But then I have so little to lose to Lenin. I can afford to admire him. But you, Mr Bojanus, you, the prosperous bourgeois – oh, purely in the economic sense of the word, Mr Bojanus ...'

Mr Bojanus accepted the explanation with one of his old-world bows.

'... you would be among the first to suffer if an English Lenin were to start his activities here.'

'There, Mr Gumbril, if I may be allowed to say so, you are wrong.' Mr Bojanus removed his hand from his bosom and employed it to emphasize the points of his discourse. 'When the revolution comes, Mr Gumbril – the great and necessary revolution, as Alderman Beckford called it – it won't be the owning of a little money that'll get a man into trouble. It'll be his class-habits, Mr Gumbril, his class-speech, his class-education. It'll be Shibboleth all over again, Mr Gumbril; mark my words. The Red Guards will stop people in the street and ask them to say some such word as "towel". If they call it "towel", like you and your friends, Mr Gumbril, why then ...' Mr Bojanus went through the gestures of pointing a rifle and pulling the trigger; he clicked his tongue against his teeth to symbolize the report. ... 'That'll be the end of them. But if they say "tèaul", like the rest of us, Mr Gumbril, it'll be: "Pass Friend and Long Live the Proletariat." Long live Tèaul.'

'I'm afraid you may be right,' said Gumbril.

'I'm convinced of it,' said Mr Bojanus. 'It's my clients, Mr Gumbril, it's the Best People that the other people resent. It's their confidence, their ease, it's the habit their money and their position give them of ordering people about, it's the way they take their place in the world for granted, it's their prestige, which the other people would like to deny, but can't – it's all that, Mr Gumbril, that's so galling.'

Gumbril nodded. He himself had envied his securer friends their power of ignoring the humanity of those who were not of their class. To do that really well, one must always have lived in a large house full of clockwork servants; one must never have been short of money, never at a restaurant ordered the cheaper thing instead of the more delicious; one must never have regarded a policeman as anything but one's paid defender against the lower orders, never for a moment have doubted one's divine right to do, within the accepted limits, exactly what one liked without a further thought to anything or any one but oneself and one's own enjoyment. Gumbril had been brought up among these blessed beings; but he was not one of them. Alas? or fortunately? He hardly knew which.

'And what good do you expect the revolution to do, Mr Bojanus?' he asked at last.

Mr Bojanus replaced his hand in his bosom. 'None whatever, Mr Gumbril,' he said. 'None whatever.'

'But Liberty,' Gumbril suggested, 'equality and all that. What about those, Mr Bojanus?'

Mr Bojanus smiled up at him tolerantly and kindly, as he might have smiled at some one who had suggested, shall we say, that evening trousers should be turned up at the bottom. 'Liberty, Mr Gumbril?' he said; 'you don't suppose any serious-minded person imagines a revolution is going to bring liberty, do you?'

'The people who make the revolution always seem to ask for liberty.'

'But do they ever get it, Mr Gumbril?' Mr Bojanus cocked his head playfully and smiled. 'Look at 'istory, Mr Gumbril, look at 'istory. First it's the French Revolution. They ask for political liberty. And they gets it. Then comes the Reform Bill, then Forty-Eight, then all the Franchise Acts and Votes for Women – always more and more political liberty. And what's the result, Mr Gumbril? Nothing at all. Who's freer for political liberty? Not a soul, Mr Gumbril. There was never a greater swindle 'atched in the 'ole of 'istory. And when you think 'ow those poor young men like Shelley talked about it – it's pathetic,' said Mr Bojanus, shaking his head, 'reelly pathetic. Political liberty's a swindle because a man doesn't spend his time being political. He spends it sleeping, eating, amusing himself a little and working – mostly working. When they'd got all the political liberty they wanted – or found they didn't want – they began to understand this. And so now it's all for the industrial revolution, Mr Gumbril. But bless you, that's as big a swindle as the other. How can there ever be liberty under any system? No amount of profit-sharing or self-government by the workers, no amount of hyjeenic conditions or cocoa villages or recreation grounds can get rid of the fundamental slavery – the necessity of working.

262

Liberty? why, it doesn't exist! There's no liberty in this world;
only gilded caiges. And then, Mr Gumbril, even suppose you
could somehow get rid of the necessity of working, suppose a
man's time were all leisure. Would he be free then? I say nothing
of the natural slavery of eating and sleeping and all that, Mr
Gumbril; I say nothing of that, because that, if I may say so,
would be too 'air-splitting and metaphysical. But what I do ask
you is this,' and Mr Bojanus wagged his forefinger almost
menacingly at the sleeping partner in this dialogue: 'would a
man with unlimited leisure be free, Mr Gumbril? I say he would
not. Not unless he 'appened to be a man like you or me, Mr
Gumbril, a man of sense, a man of independent judgment. An
ordinary man would not be free. Because he wouldn't know how
to occupy his leisure except in some way that would be forced on
'im by other people. People don't know 'ow to entertain themselves now; they leave it to other people to do it for them. They
swallow what's given them. They 'ave to swallow it, whether
they like it or not. Cinemas, newspapers, magazines, gramo-
phones, football matches, wireless, telephones – take them or
leave them, if you want to amuse yourself. The ordinary man
can't leave them. He takes; and what's that but slavery? And so
you see, Mr Gumbril,' Mr Bojanus smiled with a kind of roguish
triumph, 'you see that even in the purely 'ypothetical case of a
man with indefinite leisure, there still would be no freedom. ...
And the case, as I have said, is purely 'ypothetical; at any rate so
far as concerns the sort of people who want a revolution. And as
for the sort of people who do enjoy leisure, even now – why I
think, Mr Gumbril, you and I know enough about the Best
People to know that freedom, except possibly sexual freedom, is
not their strongest point. And sexual freedom – what's that?'
Mr Bojanus dramatically inquired. 'You and I, Mr Gumbril,' he
answered confidentially, 'we know. It's an 'orrible, 'ideous
slavery. That's what it is. Or am I wrong, Mr Gumbril?'

'Quite right, quite right, Mr Bojanus,' Gumbril hastened to
reply.

'From all of which,' continued Mr Bojanus, 'it follows that,
except for a few, a very few people like you and me, Mr Gumbril,
there's no such thing as liberty. It's an 'oax, Mr Gumbril. An

'orrible plant. And if I may be allowed to say so,' Mr Bojanus lowered his voice, but still spoke with emphasis, 'a bloody swindle.'

'But in that case, Mr Bojanus, why are you so anxious to have a revolution?' Gumbril inquired.

Thoughtfully, Mr Bojanus twisted to a finer point his waxed moustaches. 'Well,' he said at last, 'it would be a nice change. I was always one for change and a little excitement. And then there's the scientific interest. You never quite know 'ow an experiment will turn out, do you, Mr Gumbril? I remember when I was a boy, my old dad – a great gardener he was, a regular floriculturist, you might say, Mr Gumbril – he tried the experiment of grafting a sprig of Gloire de Dijon on to a black currant bush. And, would you believe it? the roses came out black, coal black, Mr Gumbril. Nobody would ever have guessed that if the thing had never been tried. And that's what I say about the revolution. You don't know what 'll come of it till you try. Black roses, blue roses – 'oo knows, Mr Gumbril, 'oo knows?'

'Who indeed?' Gumbril looked at his watch. 'About those trousers ...' he added.

'Those garments,' corrected Mr Bojanus. 'Ah, yes. Should we say next Tuesday?'

'Let us say next Tuesday.' Gumbril opened the shop door. 'Good morning, Mr Bojanus.'

Mr Bojanus bowed him out, as though he had been a prince of the blood.

The sun was shining and at the end of the street between the houses the sky was blue. Gauzily the distances faded to a soft, rich indistinctness; there were veils of golden muslin thickening down the length of every vista. On the trees in the Hanover Square gardens the young leaves were still so green that they seemed to be alight, green fire, and the sooty trunks looked blacker and dirtier than ever. It would have been a pleasant and apposite thing if a cuckoo had started calling. But though the cuckoo was silent it was a happy day. A day, Gumbril reflected, as he strolled idly along, to be in love.

From the world of tailors Gumbril passed into that of the artificial-pearl merchants, and with a still keener appreciation of

the amorous qualities of this clear spring day, he began a leisured
march along the perfumed pavements of Bond Street. He thought
with a profound satisfaction of those sixty-three papers on the
Risorgimento. How pleasant it was to waste time! And Bond
Street offered so many opportunities for wasting it agreeably.
He trotted round the Spring Exhibition at the Grosvenor and
came out, a little regretting, he had to confess, his eighteenpence
for admission. After that, he pretended that he wanted to buy a
grand piano. When he had finished practising his favourite
passages on the magnificent instrument to which they obse-
quiously introduced him, he looked in for a few moments at
Sotheby's, sniffed among the ancient books and strolled on
again, admiring the cigars, the lucid scent-bottles, the socks, the
old masters, the emerald necklaces – everything, in fact, in all the
shops he passed.

'Forthcoming Exhibition of Works by Casimir Lypiatt.' The
announcement caught his eye. And so poor old Lypiatt was on
the warpath again, he reflected, as he pushed open the doors of
the Albemarle Galleries. Poor old Lypiatt! Dear old Lypiatt,
even. He liked Lypiatt. Though he had his defects. It would be
fun to see him again.

Gumbril found himself in the midst of a dismal collection of
etchings. He passed them in review, wondering why it was that,
in these hard days when no painter can sell a picture, almost any
dull fool who can scratch a conventional etcher's view of two
boats, a suggested cloud and the flat sea should be able to get rid
of his prints by the dozen and at guineas apiece. He was interrupted in his speculations by the approach of the assistant in
charge of the gallery. He came up shyly and uncomfortably, but
with the conscientious determination of one ambitious to do his
duty and make good. He was a very young man with pale hair,
to which heavy oiling had given a curious greyish colour, and a
face of such childish contour and so imberb that he looked like a
little boy playing at grown-ups. He had only been at this job a
few weeks and he found it very difficult.

'This,' he remarked, with a little introductory cough, pointing to one view of the two boats and the flat sea, 'is an earlier
state than this.' And he pointed to another view, where the boats

were still two and the sea seemed just as flat – though possibly, on a closer inspection, it might really have been flatter.

'Indeed,' said Gumbril.

The assistant was rather pained by his coldness. He blushed; but constrained himself to go on. 'Some excellent judges,' he said, 'prefer the earlier state, though it is less highly finished.'

'Ah?'

'Beautiful atmosphere, isn't it?' The assistant put his head on one side and pursed his childish lips appreciatively.

Gumbril nodded.

With desperation, the assistant indicated the shadowed rump of one of the boats. 'A wonderful feeling in this passage,' he said, redder than ever.

'Very intense,' said Gumbril.

The assistant smiled at him gratefully. 'That's the word,' he said, delighted. 'Intense. That's it. Very intense.' He repeated the word several times, as though to make sure of remembering it for use when the occasion next presented itself. He was determined to make good.

'I see Mr Lypiatt is to have a show here soon,' remarked Gumbril, who had had enough of the boats.

'He is making the final arrangements with Mr Albemarle at this very moment,' said the assistant triumphantly, with the air of one who produces, at the dramatic and critical moment, a rabbit out of the empty hat.

'You don't say so?' Gumbril was duly impressed. 'Then I'll wait till he comes out,' he said, and sat down with his back to the boats.

The assistant returned to his desk and picked up the gold-belted fountain pen which his aunt had given him when he first went into business, last Christmas. 'Very intense,' he wrote in capitals on a half-sheet of notepaper. 'The feeling in this passage is very intense.' He studied the paper for a few moments, then folded it up carefully and put it away in his waistcoat pocket. 'Always make a note of it.' That was one of the business mottoes he had himself written out so laboriously in Indian ink and old English lettering. It hung over his bed between 'The Lord is my Shepherd', which his mother had given him, and a quotation from Dr Frank Crane, 'A smiling face sells more goods than a clever tongue'. Still, a clever tongue, the young assistant had often reflected, was a very useful thing, especially in this job. He wondered whether one could say that the composition of a picture was very intense. Mr Albemarle was very keen on the composition, he noticed. But perhaps it was better to stick to plain 'fine', which was a little commonplace, perhaps, but very safe. He would ask Mr Albemarle about it. And then there was all that stuff about plastic values and pure plasticity. He sighed. It was all very difficult. A chap might be as willing and eager to make good as he liked; but when it came to this about atmosphere and intense passages and plasticity – well, really, what could a chap do? Make a note of it. It was the only thing.

In Mr Albemarle's private room Casimir Lypiatt thumped the table. 'Size, Mr Albemarle,' he was saying, 'size and vehemence and spiritual significance – that's what the old fellows had, and we haven't. ...' He gesticulated as he talked, his face worked and his green eyes, set in their dark, charred orbits, were full of a troubled light. The forehead was precipitous, the nose long and sharp; in the bony and almost fleshless face, the lips of the wide mouth were surprisingly full.

'Precisely, precisely,' said Mr Albemarle in his juicy voice. He was a round, smooth, little man with a head like an egg; he spoke, he moved with a certain pomp, a butlerish gravity, that were evidently meant to be ducal.

'That's what I've set myself to recapture,' Lypiatt went on: 'the size, the masterfulness of the masters.' He felt a warmth running through him as he spoke, flushing his cheeks, pulsing hotly behind the eyes, as though he had drunk a draught of some heartening red wine. His own words elated him, and drunkenly gesticulating, he was as though drunken. The greatness of the masters – he felt it in him. He knew his own power, he knew, he knew. He could do all that they had done. Nothing was beyond his strength.

Egg-headed Albemarle confronted him, impeccably the butler, exacerbatingly serene. Albemarle too should be fired. He struck the table once more, he broke out again:

'It's been my mission,' he shouted, 'all these years.'

All these years. ... Time had worn the hair from his temples; the high, steep forehead seemed higher than it really was. He was forty now; the turbulent young Lypiatt who had once declared that no man could do anything worth doing after he was thirty, was forty now. But in these fiery moments he could forget the years, he could forget the disappointments, the unsold pictures, the bad reviews. 'My mission,' he repeated; 'and by God! I feel, I know I can carry it through.'

Warmly the blood pulsed behind his eyes.

'Quite,' said Mr Albemarle, nodding the egg. 'Quite.'

'And how small the scale is nowadays!' Lypiatt went on, rhapsodically. 'How trivial the conception, how limited the scope! You see no painter-sculptor-poets, like Michelangelo; no scientist-artists, like Leonardo; no mathematician-courtiers, like Boscovitch; no impresario-musicians, like Handel; no geniuses of all trades, like Wren. I have set myself against this abject specialization of ours. I stand alone, opposing it with my example.' Lypiatt raised his hand. Like the statue of Liberty, standing colossal and alone.

'Nevertheless,' began Mr Albemarle.

'Painter, poet, musician,' cried Lypiatt. 'I am all three. I ...'

' ... there is a danger of – how shall I put it – dissipating one's energies,' Mr Albemarle went on with determination. Discreetly, he looked at his watch. This conversation, he thought, seemed to be prolonging itself unnecessarily.

'There is a greater danger in letting them stagnate and atrophy,' Lypiatt retorted. 'Let me give you my experience.' Vehemently, he gave it.

Out in the gallery, among the boats, the views of the Grand Canal, and the Firth of Forth, Gumbril placidly ruminated. Poor old Lypiatt, he was thinking. Dear old Lypiatt, even, in spite of his fantastic egotism. Such a bad painter, such a bombinating poet, such a loud emotional improviser on the piano! And going on like this, year after year, pegging away at the same old things – always badly! And always without a penny, always living in the most hideous squalor! Magnificent and pathetic old Lypiatt!

A door suddenly opened and a loud, unsteady voice, now deep and harsh, now breaking to shrillness, exploded into the gallery.

268

' ... like a Veronese,' it was saying; 'enormous, vehement, a great swirling composition' ('swirling composition' – mentally, the young assistant made a note of that), 'but much more serious, of course, much more spiritually significant, much more – '

'Lypiatt!' Gumbril had risen from his chair, had turned, had advanced, holding out his hand.

'Why, it's Gumbril. Good Lord!' and Lypiatt seized the proffered hand with an excruciating cordiality. He seemed to be in exuberantly good spirits. 'We're settling about my show, Mr Albemarle and I,' he explained. 'You know Gumbril, Mr Albemarle?'

'Pleased to meet you,' said Mr Albemarle. 'Our friend, Mr Lypiatt,' he added richly, 'has the true artistic temp – '

'It's going to be magnificent.' Lypiatt could not wait till Mr Albemarle had finished speaking. He gave Gumbril a heroic blow on the shoulder.

' ... artistic temperament, as I was saying,' pursued Mr Albemarle. 'He is altogether too impatient and enthusiastic for us poor people. ...' a ducal smile of condescension accompanied this graceful act of self-abasement ... 'who move in the prosaic, practical, workaday world.'

Lypiatt laughed, a loud, discordant peal. He didn't seem to mind being accused of having an artistic temperament; he seemed, indeed, to enjoy it, if anything. 'Fire and water,' he said aphoristically, 'brought together, beget steam. Mr Albemarle and I go driving along like a steam engine. Psh, psh!' He worked his arms like a pair of alternate pistons. He laughed; but Mr Albemarle only coldly and courteously smiled. 'I was just telling Mr Albemarle about the great Crucifixion I've just been doing. It's as big and headlong as a Veronese, but much more serious, more. ...'

Behind them the little assistant was expounding to a new visitor the beauties of the etchings. 'Very intense,' he was saying, 'the feeling in this passage.' The shadow, indeed, clung with an insistent affection round the stern of the boat. 'And what a fine, what a—' he hesitated for an instant, and under his pale, oiled hair his face became suddenly very red – 'what a swirling com-

position.' He looked anxiously at the visitor. The remark had
been received without comment. He felt immensely relieved.

They left the galleries together. Lypiatt set the pace, striding
along at a great rate and with a magnificent brutality through the
elegant and leisured crowd, gesticulating and loudly talking as
he went. He carried his hat in his hand; his tie was brilliantly
orange. People turned to look at him as he passed and he liked it.
He had, indeed, a remarkable face – a face that ought by rights
to have belonged to a man of genius. Lypiatt was aware of it.
The man of genius, he liked to say, bears upon his brow a kind
of mark of Cain, by which men recognize him at once –‘ ‘and
having recognized, generally stone him,’ he would add with
that peculiar laugh he always uttered whenever he said anything
rather bitter or cynical; a laugh that was meant to show that the
bitterness, the cynicism, justifiable as events might have made
them, were really only a mask, and that beneath it the artist was
still serenely and tragically smiling. Lypiatt thought a great deal
about the ideal artist. That titanic abstraction stalked within his
own skin. He was it – a little too consciously, perhaps.

‘This time,’ he kept repeating, ‘they’ll be bowled over. This
time. ... It’s going to be terrific.’ And with the blood beating
behind his eyes, with the exultant consciousness and certainty of
power growing and growing in him with every word he spoke,
Lypiatt began to describe the pictures there would be at his show;
he talked about the preface he was writing to the catalogue, the
poems that would be printed in it by way of literary complement
to the pictures. He talked, he talked.

Gumbril listened, not very attentively. He was wondering
how any one could talk so loud, could boast so extravagantly. It
was as though the man had to shout in order to convince himself
of his own existence. Poor Lypiatt; after all these years, Gumbril supposed, he must have some doubts about it. Ah, but this
time, this time he was going to bowl them all over.

‘You’re pleased, then, with what you’ve done recently,’ he
said at the end of one of Lypiatt’s long tirades.

‘Pleased?’ exclaimed Lypiatt; ‘I should think I was.’

Gumbril might have reminded him that he had been as well
pleased in the past and that ‘they’ had by no means been bowled

over. He preferred, however, to say nothing. Lypiatt went on about the size and universality of the old masters. He himself, it was tacitly understood, was one of them.

They parted near the bottom of the Tottenham Court Road, Lypiatt to go northward to his studio off Maple Street, Gumbril to pay one of his secret visits to those rooms of his in Great Russell Street. He had taken them nearly a year ago now, two little rooms over a grocer's shop, promising himself goodness only knew what adventures in them. But somehow there had been no adventures. Still, it had pleased him, all the same, to be able to go there from time to time when he was in London and to think, as he sat in solitude before his gas fire, that there was literally not a soul in the universe who knew where he was. He had an almost childish affection for mysteries and secrets.

'Good-bye,' said Gumbril, raising his hand to the salute. 'And I'll beat up some people for dinner on Friday.' (For they had agreed to meet again.) He turned away, thinking that he had spoken the last words; but he was mistaken.

'Oh, by the way,' said Lypiatt, who had also turned to go, but who now came stepping quickly after his companion. 'Can you, by any chance, lend me five pounds? Only till after the exhibition, you know. I'm a bit short.'

Poor old Lypiatt! But it was with reluctance that Gumbril parted from his Treasury notes.

CHAPTER IV

LYPIATT had a habit, which some of his friends found rather trying – and not only friends, for Lypiatt was ready to let the merest acquaintances, the most absolute strangers, even, into the secrets of his inspiration – a habit of reciting at every possible opportunity his own verses. He would declaim in a voice loud and tremulous, with an emotion that never seemed to vary with the varying subject-matter of his poems, for whole quarters of an hour at a stretch; would go on declaiming till his auditors were overwhelmed with such a confusion of embarrassment and shame, that the blood rushed to their cheeks and they dared not meet one another's eyes.

He was declaiming now; not merely across the dinner-table to his own friends, but to the whole restaurant. For at the first reverberating lines of his latest, 'The Conquistador', there had been a startled turning of heads, a craning of necks from every corner of the room. The people who came to this Soho restaurant because it was, notoriously, so 'artistic', looked at one another significantly and nodded; they were getting their money's worth, this time. And Lypiatt, with a fine air of rapt unconsciousness, went on with his recitation.

'Look down on Mexico, Conquistador' – that was the refrain.

The Conquistador, Lypiatt had made it clear, was the Artist, and the Vale of Mexico on which he looked down, the towered cities of Tlacopan and Chalco, of Tenochtitlan and Iztapalapan symbolized – well, it was difficult to say precisely what. The universe, perhaps?

'Look down,' cried Lypiatt, with a quivering voice.

> 'Look down, Conquistador!
> There on the valley's broad green floor,
> There lies the lake; the jewelled cities gleam;
> Chalco and Tlacopan
> Await the coming Man.
> Look down on Mexico, Conquistador,
> Land of your golden dream.'

'Not "dream",' said Gumbril, putting down the glass from which he had been profoundly drinking. 'You can't possibly say "dream", you know.'

'Why do you interrupt me?' Lypiatt turned on him angrily. His wide mouth twitched at the corners, his whole long face worked with excitement. 'Why don't you let me finish?' He allowed his hand, which had hung awkwardly in the air above him, suspended, as it were, at the top of a gesture, to sink slowly to the table. 'Imbecile!' he said, and once more picked up his knife and fork.

'But really,' Gumbril insisted, 'you can't say "dream". Can you now, seriously?' He had drunk the best part of a bottle of Burgundy and he felt good-humoured, obstinate and a little bellicose.

'And why not?' Lypiatt asked.

'Oh, because one simply can't.' Gumbril leaned back in his chair, smiled and caressed his drooping blond moustache. 'Not in this year of grace, nineteen twenty-two.'

'But why?' Lypiatt repeated, with exasperation.

'Because it's altogether *too* late in the day,' declared precious Mr Mercaptan, rushing up to his emphasis with flutes and roaring, like a true Conquistador, to fall back, however, at the end of the sentence rather ignominiously into a breathless confusion. He was a sleek, comfortable young man with smooth brown hair parted in the centre and conducted in a pair of flowing curves across the temples, to be looped in damp curls behind his ears. His face ought to have been rather more exquisite, rather more refinedly *dix-huitième* than it actually was. It had a rather gross, snouty look, which was sadly out of harmony with Mr Mercaptan's inimitably graceful style. For Mr Mercaptan had a style and used it, delightfully, in his middle articles for the literary weeklies. His most precious work, however, was that little volume of essays, prose poems, vignettes and paradoxes, in which he had so brilliantly illustrated his favourite theme – the pettiness, the simian limitations, the insignificance and the absurd pretentiousness of *Homo* soi-disant *Sapiens*. Those who met Mr Mercaptan personally often came away with the feeling that perhaps, after all, he was right in judging so severely of humanity.

273

'*Too* late in the day,' he repeated. 'Times have changed. *Sunt lacrymae rerum, nos et mutamur in illis.*' He laughed his own applause.

'*Quot homines, tot disputandum est,*' said Gumbril, taking another sip of his Beaune Supérieure. At the moment, he was all for Mercaptan.

'But *why* is it too late?' Lypiatt insisted.

Mr Mercaptan made a delicate gesture. '*Ça se sent, mon cher ami,*' he said, '*ça ne s'explique pas.*' Satan, it is said, carries hell in his heart; so it was with Mr Mercaptan – wherever he was, it was Paris. 'Dreams in nineteen twenty-two. ...' He shrugged his shoulders.

'After you've accepted the war, swallowed the Russian famine,' said Gumbril. 'Dreams!'

'They belonged to the *Rostand* epoch,' said Mr Mercaptan, with a little titter. '*Le Rêve* – ah!'

Lypiatt dropped his knife and fork with a clatter and leaned forward, eager for battle. 'Now I have you,' he said, 'now I have you on the hip. You've given yourselves away. You've given away the secret of your spiritual poverty, your weakness and pettiness and impotence. ...'

'Impotence? You malign me, sir,' said Gumbril.

Shearwater ponderously stirred. He had been silent all this time, sitting with hunched shoulders, his elbows on the table, his big round head bent forward, absorbed, apparently, in the slow meticulous crumbling of a piece of bread. Sometimes he put a piece of crust in his mouth and under the bushy black moustache his jaw moved slowly, ruminatively, with a sideways motion, like a cow's. He nudged Gumbril with his elbow. 'Ass,' he said, 'be quiet.'

Lypiatt went on torrentially. 'You're afraid of ideals, that's what it is. You daren't admit to having dreams. Oh, I call them dreams,' he added parenthetically. 'I don't mind being thought a fool and old-fashioned. The word's shorter and more English. Besides, it rhymes with gleams. Ha, ha!' And Lypiatt laughed his loud Titan's laugh, the laugh of cynicism which seems to belie, but which, for those who have understanding, reveals the high, positive spirit within. 'Ideals – they're not sufficiently gen-

teel for you civilized young men. You've quite outgrown that
sort of thing. No dream, no religion, no morality.'

'I glory in the name of earwig,' said Gumbril. He was pleased
with that little invention. It was felicitous; it was well chosen.
'One's an earwig in sheer self-protection,' he explained.

But Mr Mercaptan refused to accept the name of earwig at any
price. '*What* there is to be ashamed of in being civilized, I *really*
don't know,' he said, in a voice that was now the bull's, now the
piping robin's. 'No, if I glory in anything, it's in my little rococo
boudoir, and the conversations across the polished mahogany,
and the delicate, lascivious, *witty* little flirtations on ample sofas
inhabited by the soul of Crebillon Fils. We needn't *all* be
Russians, I hope. These revolting Dostoievskys.' Mr Mercaptan
spoke with a profound feeling. 'Nor all Utopians. Homo *au
naturel* –' Mr Mercaptan applied his thumb and forefinger to his,
alas! too snout-like nose, '*ça pue.* And as for Homo à la H.G.
Wells *–ça ne pue pas assez.* What I glory in is the civilized, middle
way between stink and asepsis. Give me a little musk, a little
intoxicating feminine exhalation, the bouquet of old wine and
strawberries, a lavender bag under every pillow and potpourri
in the corners of the drawing-room. Readable books, amusing
conversation, civilized women, graceful art and dry vintage,
music, with a quiet life and reasonable comfort – that's *all* I ask
for.'

'Talking about comfort,' Gumbril put in, before Lypiatt had
time to fling his answering thunders, 'I must tell you about my
new invention. Pneumatic trousers,' he explained. 'Blow them
up. Perfect comfort. You see the idea? You're a sedentary man,
Mercaptan. Let me put you down for a couple of pairs.'

Mr Mercaptan shook his head. 'Too Wellsian,' he said. 'Too
horribly Utopian. They'd be ludicrously out of place in my
boudoir. And besides, my sofa is well enough sprung already,
thank you.'

'But what about Tolstoy?' shouted Lypiatt, letting out his
impatience in a violent blast.

Mr Mercaptan waved his hand. 'Russian,' he said, 'Russian.'
'And Michelangelo?'
'Alberti,' said Gumbril, very seriously, giving them all a piece

of his father's mind – 'Alberti was much the better architect, I assure you.'

'And pretentiousness for pretentiousness,' said Mr Mercaptan, 'I prefer old Borromini and the baroque.'

'What about Beethoven?' went on Lypiatt. 'What about Blake? Where do they come in under your scheme of things?'

Mr Mercaptan shrugged his shoulders. 'They stay in the hall,' he said. 'I don't let them into the boudoir.'

'You disgust me,' said Lypiatt, with rising indignation, and making wilder gestures. 'You disgust me – you and your odious little sham eighteenth-century civilization; your piddling little poetry; your art for art's sake instead of for God's sake; your nauseating little copulations without love or passion; your hoggish materialism; your bestial indifference to all that's unhappy and your yelping hatred of all that's great."

'Charming, charming,' murmured Mr Mercaptan, who was pouring oil on his salad.

'How can you ever hope to achieve anything decent or solid, when you don't even believe in decency or solidity? I look about me,' and Lypiatt cast his eyes wildly round the crowded room, 'and I find myself alone, spiritually alone. I strive on by myself, by myself.' He struck his breast, a giant, a solitary giant. 'I have set myself to restore painting and poetry to their rightful position among the great moral forces. They have been amusements, they have been mere games for too long. I am giving my life for that. My life.' His voice trembled a little. 'People mock me, hate me, stone me, deride me. But I go on, I go on. For I know I'm right. And in the end they too will recognize that I've been right.' It was a loud soliloquy. One could fancy that Lypiatt had been engaged in recognizing himself.

'All the same,' said Gumbril with a cheerful stubbornness, 'I persist that the word "dreams" is inadmissible.'

'*Inadmissible*,' repeated Mr Mercaptan, imparting to the word an additional significance by giving it its French pronunciation. 'In the age of Rostand, well and good. But now. ...'

'Now,' said Gumbril, 'the word merely connotes Freud.'

'It's a matter of literary tact,' explained Mr Mercaptan. 'Have you no literary tact?'

276

'No,' said Lypiatt, with emphasis, 'thank God, I haven't. I have no tact of any kind. I do things straightforwardly, frankly, as the spirit moves me. I don't like compromises.'

He struck the table. The gesture startlingly let loose a peal of cracked and diabolic laughter. Gumbril and Lypiatt and Mr Mercaptan looked quickly up; even Shearwater lifted his great spherical head and turned towards the sound the large disk of his face. A young man with a blond, fan-shaped beard stood by the table, looking down at them through a pair of bright blue eyes and smiling equivocally and disquietingly as though his mind were full of some nameless and fantastic malice.

'*Come sta la Sua Terribiltà?*' he asked; and, taking off his preposterous bowler hat, he bowed profoundly to Lypiatt. 'How I recognize my Buonarrotti!' he added affectionately.

Lypiatt laughed, rather uncomfortably, and no longer on the Titanic scale. 'How I recognize my Coleman!' he echoed, rather feebly.

'On the contrary,' Gumbril corrected, 'how almost completely I fail to recognize. This beard' – he pointed to the blond fan – 'why, may I ask?'

'More Russianism,' said Mr Mercaptan, and shook his head.

'Ah, why indeed?' Coleman lowered his voice to a confidential whisper. 'For religious reasons,' he said, and made the sign of the cross.

'Christlike is my behaviour,
Like every good believer,
I imitate the Saviour,
And cultivate a beaver.

There be beavers which have made themselves beavers for the kingdom of heaven's sake. But there are some beavers, on the other hand, which were so born from their mother's womb.' He burst into a fit of outrageous laughter which stopped as suddenly and as voluntarily as it had begun.

Lypiatt shook his head. 'Hideous,' he said, 'hideous.'

'Moreover,' Coleman went on, without paying any attention, 'I have other and, alas! less holy reasons for this change of face. It enables one to make such delightful acquaintances in the street. You hear some one saying, "Beaver", as you pass, and you

277

immediately have the right to rush up and get into conversation. I owe to this dear symbol,' and he caressed the golden beard tenderly with the palm of his hand, 'the most admirably dangerous relations.'

'Magnificent,' said Gumbril, drinking his own health. 'I shall stop shaving at once.'

Shearwater looked round the table with raised eyebrows and a wrinkled forehead. 'This conversation is rather beyond me,' he said gravely. Under the formidable moustache, under the thick, tufted eyebrows, the mouth was small and ingenuous, the mild grey eyes full of an almost childish inquiry. 'What does the word "beaver" signify in this context? You don't refer, I suppose, to the rodent, *Castor fiber*?'

'But this is a very great man,' said Coleman, raising his bowler. 'Tell me, who he is?'

'Our friend Shearwater,' said Gumbril, 'the physiologist.'

Coleman bowed. 'Physiological Shearwater,' he said. 'Accept my homage. To one who doesn't know what a beaver is, I resign all my claims to superiority. There's nothing else but beavers in all the papers. Tell me, do you never read the *Daily Express*?'

'No.'

'Nor the *Daily Mail*?'

Shearwater shook his head.

'Nor the *Mirror*? nor the *Sketch*? nor the *Graphic*? nor even (for I was forgetting that physiologists must surely have Liberal opinions) – even the *Daily News*?'

Shearwater continued to shake his large spherical head.

'Nor any of the evening papers?'

'No.'

Coleman once more lifted his hat. 'O eloquent, just and mighty Death!' he exclaimed, and replaced it on his head. 'You never read any papers at all – not even our friend Mercaptan's delicious little middles in the weeklies? How is your delicious little middle, by the way?' Coleman turned to Mr Mercaptan and with the point of his huge stick gave him a little prod in the stomach. '*Ça marche – les tripes? Hein?*' He turned back to Shearwater. 'Not even those?' he asked.

'Never,' said Shearwater. 'I have more serious things to think about than newspapers.'

'And what serious thing, may I ask?'

'Well, at the present moment,' said Shearwater, 'I am chiefly preoccupied with the kidneys.'

'The kidneys!' In an ecstasy of delight, Coleman thumped the floor with the ferrule of his stick. 'The kidneys! Tell me all about kidneys. This is of the first importance. This is really life. And I shall sit down at your table without asking permission of Buonarrotti here, and in the teeth of Mercaptan, and without so much as thinking about this species of Gumbril, who might as well not be there at all. I shall sit down and – '

'Talking of sitting,' said Gumbril, 'I wish I could persuade you to order a pair of my patent pneumatic trousers. They will – '

Coleman waved him away. 'Not now, not now,' he said. 'I shall sit down and listen to the physiologue talking about runions, while I myself actually eat them – *sautés*. *Sautés*, mark my words.'

Laying his hat and stick on the floor beside him, he sat down at the end of the table, between Lypiatt and Shearwater.

'Two believers,' he said, laying his hand for a moment on Lypiatt's arm, 'and three black-hearted unbelievers – confronted. Eh, Buonarrotti? You and I are both *croyants et pratiquants*, as Mercaptan would say. I believe in one devil, father quasi-almighty, Samael and his wife, the Woman of Whoredom. Ha, ha!' He laughed his ferocious, artificial laugh.

'Here's an end to any civilized conversation,' Mr Mercaptan complained, hissing on the *c*, labiating lingeringly on the *v* of 'civilized' and giving the first two *i*'s their fullest value. The word, in his mouth, seemed to take on a special and a richer significance.

Coleman ignored him. 'Tell me, you physiologue,' he went on, 'tell me about the physiology of the Archetypal Man. This is most important; Buonarotti shares my opinion about this, I know. Has the Archetypal Man a *boyau rectum*, as Mercaptan would say again, or not? Everything depends on this, as Voltaire realized ages ago. "His feet," as we know already on inspired authority, "were straight feet; and the soles of his feet were like the sole of a calf's foot." But the viscera, you must tell us something about the viscera. Mustn't he, Buonarrotti? And where are my *rognons sautés*?' he shouted at the waiter.

'You revolt me,' said Lypiatt.

'Not mortually, I 'ope?' Coleman turned with solicitude to his neighbour; then shook his head. 'Mortually I fear. Kiss me 'Ardy, and I die happy.' He blew a kiss into the air. 'But why is the physiologue so slow? Up, pachyderm, up! Answer. You hold the key to everything. The key, I tell you, the key. I remember, when I used to hang about the biological laboratories at school, eviscerating frogs – crucified with pins, they were, belly upwards, like little green Christs – I remember once, when I was sitting there, quietly poring over the entrails, in came the laboratory boy and said to the stinks usher: "Please, sir, may I have the key of the Absolute?" And, would you believe it, that usher calmly put his hand in his trouser pocket and fished out a small Yale key and gave it him without a word. What a gesture! The key of the Absolute. But it was only the absolute alcohol the urchin wanted – to pickle some loathsome fœtus in, I suppose. God rot his soul in peace! And now, Castor Fiber, out with your key. Tell us about the Archetypal Man, tell us about the primordial Adam. Tell us all about the *boyau rectum*.'

Ponderously, Shearwater moved his clumsy frame; leaning back in his chair he scrutinized Coleman with a large, benevolent curiosity. The eyes under the savage eyebrows were mild and gentle; behind the fearful disguise of the moustache he smiled poutingly, like a baby who sees the approaching bottle. The broad, domed forehead was serene. He ran his hand through his thick brown hair, scratched his head meditatively and then, when he had thoroughly examined, had comprehended and duly classified the strange phenomenon of Coleman, opened his mouth and uttered a little good-natured laugh of amusement.

'Voltaire's question,' he said at last, in his slow, deep voice, 'seemed at the time he asked it an unanswerable piece of irony. It would have seemed almost equally ironic to his contemporaries, if he had asked whether God had a pair of kidneys. We know a little more about the kidneys nowadays. If he had asked me, I should answer: why not? The kidneys are so beautifully organized; they do their work of regulation with such a miraculous – it's hard to find another word – such a positively divine precision, such knowledge and wisdom, that there's no reason why your archetypal man, whoever he is, or any one else, for that matter, should be ashamed of owning a pair.'

Coleman clapped his hands. 'The key,' he cried, 'the key. Out of the trouser pocket of babes and sucklings it comes. The genuine, the unique Yale. How right I was to come here to-night! But, holy Sephiroth, there's my trollop.'

He picked up his stick, jumped from his chair and threaded his way between the tables. A woman was standing near the door. Coleman came up to her, pointed without speaking to the table, and returned, driving her along in front of him, tapping her gently over the haunches with his stick, as one might drive a docile animal to the slaughter.

'Allow me to introduce,' said Coleman. 'The sharer of my joys and sorrows. *La compagne de mes nuits blanches et de mes jours plutôt sales.* In a word, Zoe. *Qui ne comprend pas le français, qui me déteste avec une passion égale à la mienne, et qui mangera, ma foi, des rognons pour faire honneur au physiologue.*'

'Have some Burgundy?' Gumbril proffered the bottle.

Zoe nodded and pushed forward her glass. She was dark-haired, had a pale skin and eyes like round blackberries. Her mouth was small and floridly curved. She was dressed, rather depressingly, like a picture by Augustus John, in blue and orange. Her expression was sullen and ferocious, and she looked about her with an air of profound contempt.

'Shearwater's no better than a mystic,' fluted Mr Mercaptan. 'A mystical scientist; really, one hadn't reckoned on that.'

'Like a Liberal Pope,' said Gumbril. 'Poor Metternich, you remember? Pio Nono.' And he burst into a fit of esoteric laughter. 'Of less than average intelligence,' he murmured delightedly, and refilled his glass.

'It's only the deliberately blind who wouldn't reckon on the combination,' Lypiatt put in, indignantly. 'What are science and art, what are religion and philosophy but so many expressions in human terms of some reality more than human? Newton and

Boehme and Michelangelo – what are they doing but expressing, in different ways, different aspects of the same thing?'

'Alberti, I beg you,' said Gumbril. 'I assure you he was the better architect.'

'*Fi donc!*' said Mr Mercaptan. 'San Carlo alle Quattro Fontane –' But he got no further. Lypiatt abolished him with a gesture.

'One reality,' he cried, 'there is only one reality.'

'One reality,' Coleman reached out a hand across the table and caressed Zoe's bare white arm, 'and that is callipygous.' Zoe jabbed at his hand with her fork.

'We are all trying to talk about it,' continued Lypiatt. 'The physicists have formulated their laws, which are after all no more than stammering provisional theories about a part of it. The physiologists are penetrating into the secrets of life, psychologists into the mind. And we artists are trying to say what is revealed to us about the moral nature, the personality of that reality, which is the universe.'

Mr Mercaptan threw up his hands in affected horror. 'Oh, *barbaridad, barbaridad*!' Nothing less than the pure Castilian would relieve his feelings. 'But all this is meaningless.'

'Quite right about the chemists and physicists,' said Shearwater. 'They're always trying to pretend that they're nearer the truth than we are. They take their crude theories as facts and try to make us accept them when we're dealing with life. Oh, they are sacred, their theories. Laws of Nature they call them; and they talk about their known truths and our romantic biological fancies. What a fuss they make when we talk about life! Bloody fools!' said Shearwater, mild and crushing. 'Nobody but a fool could talk of mechanism in face of the kidneys. And there are actually imbeciles who talk about the mechanism of heredity and reproduction.'

'All the same,' began Mr Mercaptan very earnestly, anxious to deny his own life, 'there are eminent authorities. I can only quote what they say, of course. I can't pretend to know anything about it myself. But – '

'Reproduction, reproduction,' Coleman murmured the word to himself ecstatically. 'Delightful and horrifying to think they all come to that, even the most virginal; that they were all made for that, little she-dogs, in spite of their china-blue eyes. What sort of a mandrake shall we produce, Zoe and I?' he asked, turning to Shearwater. 'How I should like to have a child,' he went on without waiting for an answer. 'I shouldn't teach it anything; no language, nothing at all. Just a child of nature. I believe it would really be the devil. And then what fun it would be if it suddenly started to say "Bekkos", like the children in Herodotus. And Buonarroti here would paint an allegorical picture of it and write an epic called "The Ignoble Savage". And Castor Fiber would come and sound its kidneys and investigate its sexual instincts. And Mercaptan would write one of his inimitable middle articles about it. And Gumbril would make it a pair of patent trousers. And Zoe and I would look parentally on and fairly swell with pride. Shouldn't we, Zoe?' Zoe preserved her expression of sullen, unchanging contempt and did not deign to answer. 'Ah, how delightful it would be! I long for posterity. I live in hopes. I stope against Stopes. I – '

Zoe threw a piece of bread, which caught him on the cheek, a little below the eye. Coleman leaned back and laughed and laughed till the tears rolled down his face.

CHAPTER V

ONE after another, they engaged themselves in the revolving doors of the restaurant, trotted round in the moving cage of glass and ejected themselves into the coolness and darkness of the street. Shearwater lifted up his large face and took two or three deep breaths. 'Too much carbon dioxide and ammonia in there,' he said.

'It is unfortunate that when two or three are gathered together in God's name, or even in the more civilized name of Mercaptan of the delicious middle,' Mercaptan dexterously parried the prod which Coleman aimed at him, 'it is altogether deplorable that they should necessarily empest the air.'

Lypiatt had turned his eyes heavenwards. 'What stars,' he said, 'and what prodigious gaps between the stars!'

'A real light opera summer night.' And Mercaptan began to sing, in fragmentary German, the 'Barcarolle' from the *Tales of Hoffmann*. 'Liebe Nacht, du schöne Nacht, oh stille mein tumpty-tum. Te, tum, Te tum. ... Delicious Offenbach. Ah, if only we could have a third Empire! Another comic Napoleon! That would make Paris look like Paris again. Tiddy, tumpty-ti-tum.'

They walked along without any particular destination, but simply for the sake of walking through this soft cool night. Coleman led the way, tapping the pavement at every step with the ferrule of his stick. 'The blind leading the blind,' he explained. 'Ah, if only there were a ditch, a crevasse, a great hole full of stinging centipedes and dung. How gleefully I should lead you all into it!'

'I think you would do well,' said Shearwater gravely, 'to go and see a doctor.'

Coleman gave vent to a howl of delight.

'Does it occur to you,' he went on, 'that at this moment we are walking through the midst of seven million distinct and separate individuals, each with distinct and separate lives and all completely indifferent to our existence? Seven million people, each one of whom thinks himself quite as important as each of us does. Millions of them are now sleeping in an empested atmosphere. Hundreds of thousands of couples are at this moment engaged in mutually caressing one another in a manner too hideous to be thought of, but in no way differing from the manner in which each of us performs, delightfully, passionately and beautifully, his similar work of love. Thousands of women are now in the throes of parturition, and of both sexes thousands are dying of the most diverse and appalling diseases, or simply because they have lived too long. Thousands are drunk, thousands have over-eaten, thousands have not had enough to eat. And they are all alive, all unique and separate and sensitive, like you and me. It's a horrible thought. Ah, if I could lead them all into that great hole of centipedes.'

He tapped and tapped on the pavement in front of him, as though searching for the crevasse. At the top of his voice he began to chant: 'O all ye Beasts and Cattle, curse ye the Lord: curse him and vilify him for ever.'

'All this religion,' sighed Mercaptan. 'What with Lypiatt on one side, being a muscular Christian artist, and Coleman on the other, howling the black mass. ... Really!' He elaborated an Italianate gesture, and turned to Zoe. 'What do you think of it all?' he asked.

Zoe jerked her head in Coleman's direction. 'I think 'e's a bloody swine,' she said. They were the first words she had spoken since she had joined the party.

'Hear, hear!' cried Coleman, and he waved his stick.

In the warm yellow light of the coffee-stall at Hyde Park Corner loitered a little group of people. Among the peaked caps and the chauffeurs' dust-coats, among the weather-stained workmen's jackets and the knotted handkerchiefs, there emerged an alien elegance. A tall tubed hat and a silk-faced overcoat, a cloak of flame-coloured satin, and in bright, coppery hair a great Spanish comb of carved tortoiseshell.

'Well, I'm damned,' said Gumbril as they approached. 'I believe it's Myra Viveash.'

'So it is,' said Lypiatt, peering in his turn. He began suddenly to walk with an affected swagger, kicking his heels at every step.

Looking at himself from outside, his divining eyes pierced through the veil of cynical *je-m'en-fichisme* to the bruised heart beneath. Besides, he didn't want any one to guess.

'The Viveash, is it?' Coleman quickened his rapping along the pavement. 'And who is the present incumbent?' He pointed at the top hat.

'Can it be Bruin Opps?' said Gumbril dubiously.

'Opps!' Coleman yelled out the name. 'Opps!'

The top hat turned, revealing a shirt front, a long grey face, a glitter of circular glass over the left eye. 'Who the devil are you?' The voice was harsh and arrogantly offensive.

'I am that I am,' said Coleman. 'But I have with me' – he pointed to Shearwater, to Gumbril, to Zoe – 'a physiologue, a pedagogue and a priapagogue; for I leave out of account mere artists and journalists whose titles do not end with the magic syllable. And finally,' indicating himself, 'plain Dog, which, being interpreted kabbalistically backwards, signifies God. All at your service.' He took off his hat and bowed.

The top hat turned back towards the Spanish comb. 'Who is this horrible drunk?' it inquired.

Mrs Viveash did not answer him, but stepped forward to meet the newcomers. In one hand she held a peeled, hard-boiled egg and a thick slice of bread and butter in the other, and between her sentences she bit at them alternately.

'Coleman!' she exclaimed, and her voice, as she spoke, seemed always on the point of expiring, as though each word were the last, utterly faintly and breakingly from a death-bed – the last, with all the profound and nameless significance of the ultimate word. 'It's a very long time since I heard you raving last. And you, Theodore darling, why do I never see you now?'

Gumbril shrugged his shoulders. 'Because you don't want to, I suppose,' he said.

Myra laughed and took another bite at her bread and butter. ... She laid the back of her hand – for she was still holding the butt end of her hard-boiled egg – on Lypiatt's arm. The Titan, who had been looking at the sky, seemed to be surprised to find her standing there. 'You?' he said, smiling and wrinkling up his forehead interrogatively.

286

'It's to-morrow I'm sitting for you, Casimir, isn't it?'

'Ah, you remembered.' The veil parted for a moment. Poor Lypiatt! 'And happy Mercaptan? Always happy?'

Gallantly Mercaptan kissed the back of the hand which held the egg. 'I might be happier,' he murmured, rolling up at her from the snouty face a pair of small brown eyes. '*Puis-je espérer?*'

Mrs Viveash laughed expiringly from her inward death-bed and turned on him, without speaking, her pale unwavering glance. Her eyes had a formidable capacity for looking and expressing nothing; they were like the pale blue eyes which peer out of the Siamese cat's black-velvet mask.

'Bellissima,' murmured Mercaptan, flowering under their cool light.

Mrs Viveash addressed herself to the company at large. 'We have had the most appalling evening,' she said. 'Haven't we, Bruin?'

Bruin Opps said nothing, but only scowled. He didn't like these damned intruders. The skin of his contracted brows oozed over the rim of his monocle, on to the shining glass.

'I thought it would be fun,' Myra went on, 'to go to that place at Hampton Court, where you have dinner on an island and dance. ...'

'What is there about islands,' put in Mercaptan, in a deliciously whimsical parenthesis, 'that makes them so peculiarly voluptuous? Cythera, Monkey Island, Capri. *Je me demande.*'

'Another charming middle.' Coleman pointed his stick menacingly; Mr Mercaptan stepped quickly out of range.

'So we took a cab,' Mrs Viveash continued, 'and set out. And what a cab, my God! A cab with only one gear, and that the lowest. A cab as old as the century, a museum specimen, a collector's piece.' They had been hours and hours on the way. And when they got there, the food they were offered to eat, the wine they were expected to drink! From her eternal death-bed Mrs Viveash cried out in unaffected horror. Everything tasted as though it had been kept soaking for a week in the river before being served up – rather weedy, with that delicious typhoid flavour of Thames water. There was Thames even in the champagne. They had not been able to eat so much as a crust of bread.

Hungry and thirsty, they had re-embarked in their antique taxi, and here, at last, they were, at the first outpost of civilization, eating for dear life.

'Oh, a terrible evening,' Mrs Viveash concluded. 'The only thing which kept up my spirits was the spectacle of Bruin's bad temper. You've no idea, Bruin, what an incomparable comic you can be.'

Bruin ignored the remark. With an expression of painfully repressed disgust he was eating a hard-boiled egg. Myra's caprices were becoming more and more impossible. That Hampton Court business had been bad enough; but when it came to eating in the street, in the middle of a lot of filthy workmen – well, really, that was rather too much.

Mrs Viveash looked about her. 'Am I never to know who this mysterious person is?' She pointed to Shearwater, who was standing a little apart from the group, his back leaning against the park railings and staring thoughtfully at the ground.

'The physiologue,' Coleman explained, 'and he has the key. The key, the key!' He hammered the pavement with his stick.

Gumbril performed the introduction in more commonplace style.

'You don't seem to take much interest in us, Mr Shearwater,' Myra called expiringly. Shearwater looked up; Mrs Viveash regarded him intently through pale, unwavering eyes, smiling as she looked that queer, downward-turning smile which gave to her face, through its mask of laughter, a peculiar expression of agony. 'You don't seem to take much interest in us,' she repeated.

Shearwater shook his heavy head. 'No,' he said, 'I don't think I do.'

'Why don't you?'

'Why should I? There's not time to be interested in everything. One can only be interested in what's worth while.'

'And we're not worth while?'

'Not to me personally,' replied Shearwater with candour. 'The Great Wall of China, the political situation in Italy, the habits of Trematodes – all these are most interesting in them-

288

selves. But they aren't interesting to me; I don't permit them to be. I haven't the leisure.'

'And what do you allow yourself to be interested in?'

'Shall we go?' said Bruin impatiently; he had succeeded in swallowing the last fragment of his hard-boiled egg. Mrs Viveash did not answer, did not even look at him.

Shearwater, who had hesitated before replying, was about to speak. But Coleman answered for him. 'Be respectful,' he said to Mrs Viveash. 'This is a great man. He reads no papers, not even those in which our Mercaptan so beautifully writes. He does not know what a beaver is. And he lives for nothing but the kidneys.'

Mrs Viveash smiled her smile of agony. 'Kidneys? But what a *memento mori*! There are other portions of the anatomy.' She threw back her cloak, revealing an arm, a bare shoulder, a slant of pectoral muscle. She was wearing a white dress that, leaving her back and shoulders bare, came up, under either arm, to a point in front and was held there by a golden thread about the neck. 'For example,' she said, and twisted her hand several times over and over, making the slender arm turn at the elbow, as though to demonstrate the movement of the articulations and the muscular play.

' *Memento vivere*,' Mr Mercaptan aptly commented. ' *Vivamus, mea Lesbia, atque amemus*.'

Mrs Viveash dropped her arm and pulled the cloak back into place. She looked at Shearwater, who had followed all her movements with conscientious attention, and who now nodded with an expression of interrogation on his face, as though to ask: what next?

'We all know that you've got beautiful arms,' said Bruin angrily. 'There's no need for you to make an exhibition of them in the street, at midnight. Let's get out of this.' He laid his hand on her shoulder and made as if to draw her away. 'We'd better be going. Goodness knows what's happening behind us.' He indicated with a little movement of the head the loiterers round the coffee-stall. 'Some disturbance among the *canaille*.'

Mrs Viveash looked round. The cab-drivers and the other consumers of midnight coffee had gathered in an interested circle, curious and sympathetic, round the figure of a woman

289

who was sitting, like a limp bundle tied up in black cotton and mackintosh, on the stall-keeper's high stool, leaning wearily against the wall of the booth. A man stood beside her drinking tea out of a thick white cup. Every one was talking at once.

'Mayn't the poor wretches talk?' asked Mrs Viveash, turning back to Bruin. 'I never knew any one who had the lower classes on the brain as much as you have.'

'I loathe them,' said Bruin. 'I hate every one poor, or ill, or old. Can't abide them; they make me positively sick.'

'*Quelle âme bien-née*,' piped Mr Mercaptan. 'And how well and frankly you express what we all feel and lack the courage to say.'

Lypiatt gave vent to indignant laughter.

'I remember when I was a little boy,' Bruin went on, 'my old grandfather used to tell me stories about his childhood. He told me that when he was about five or six, just before the passing of the Reform Bill of 'thirty-two, there was a song which all right-thinking people used to sing, with a chorus that went like this: "Rot the People, blast the People, damn the Lower Classes". I wish I knew the rest of the words and the tune. It must have been a good song.'

Coleman was enraptured with the song. He shouldered his walking-stick and began marching round and round the nearest lamp-post chanting the words to a stirring march tune. 'Rot the People, blast the People ...' He marked the rhythm with heavy stamps of his feet.

'Ah, if only they'd invent servants with internal combustion engines,' said Bruin, almost pathetically. 'However well trained they are, they always betray their humanity occasionally. And that is really intolerable.'

'How tedious is a guilty conscience!' Gumbril murmured the quotation.

'But Mr Shearwater,' said Myra, bringing back the conversation to more congenial themes, 'hasn't told us yet what he thinks of arms.'

'Nothing at all,' said Shearwater. 'I'm occupied with the regulation of the blood at the moment.'

'But is it true what he says, Theodore?' She appealed to Gumbril.

'I should think so.' Gumbril's answer was rather dim and remote. He was straining to hear the talk of Bruin's *canaille*, and
Mrs Viveash's question seemed a little irrelevant.

'I used to do cartin' jobs,' the man with the teacup was saying.
''Ad a van and a nold pony of me own. And didn't do so badly
neither. The only trouble was me lifting furniture and 'eavy
weights about the place. Because I 'ad malaria out in India, in the
war ...'

'Nor even — you compel me to violate the laws of modesty —
nor even,' Mrs Viveash went on, smiling painfully, speaking
huskily, expiringly, 'of legs?'

A spring of blasphemy was touched in Coleman's brain.
'Neither delighteth He in any man's legs,' he shouted, and with
an extravagant show of affection he embraced Zoe, who caught
hold of his hand and bit it.

'It comes back on you when you get tired like, malaria does.'
The man's face was sallow and there was an air of peculiar listlessness and hopelessness about his misery. 'It comes back on you,
and then you go down with fever and you're as weak as a child.'

Shearwater shook his head.

'Nor even of the heart?' Mrs Viveash lifted her eyebrows.
'Ah, now the inevitable word has been pronounced, the real sub-
ject of every conversation has appeared on the scene. Love, Mr
Shearwater!'

'But as I says,' recapitulated the man with the teacup, 'we
didn't do so badly after all. We 'ad nothing to complain about.
'Ad we, Florrie?'

The black bundle made an affirmative movement with its upper
extremity.

'That's one of the subjects,' said Shearwater, 'like the Great
Wall of China and the habits of Trematodes, I don't allow myself to be interested in.'

Mrs Viveash laughed, breathed out a little 'Good God!' of
incredulity and astonishment, and asked, 'Why not?'

'No time,' he explained. 'You people of leisure have nothing
else to do or think about. I'm busy, and so naturally less interested in the subject than you; and I take care, what's more, to
limit such interest as I have.'

'I was goin' up Ludgate 'Ill one day with a vanload of stuff for a chap in Clerkenwell. I was leadin' Jerry up the 'ill – Jerry's the name of our ole pony. ...'

'One can't have everything,' Shearwater was explaining, 'not all at the same time, in any case. I've arranged my life for work now. I'm quietly married, I simmer away domestically.'

'*Quelle horreur!*' said Mr Mercaptan. All the Louis Quinze Abbé in him was shocked and revolted by the thought.

'But love?' questioned Mrs Viveash. 'Love?'

'Love!' Lypiatt echoed. He was looking up at the Milky Way.

'All of a sudden out jumps a copper at me. "'Ow old is that 'orse?" 'e says. "It ain't fit to drawr a load, it limps in all four feet," 'e says. "No, it doesn't," I says. "None of your answerin' back," 'e says. "Take it outer the shafts at once."'

'But I know all about love already. I know precious little still about kidneys.'

'But, my good Shearwater, how can you know all about love before you've made it with all women?'

'Off we goes, me and the cop and the 'orse, up in front of the police-court magistrate. ...'

'Or are you one of those imbeciles,' Mrs Viveash went on, 'who speak of women with a large W and pretend we're all the same? Poor Theodore here might possibly think so in his feebler moments.' Gumbril smiled vaguely from a distance. He was following the man with the teacup into the magistrate's stuffy court. 'And Mercaptan certainly does, because all the women who ever sat on his *dix-huitième* sofa certainly were exactly like one another. And perhaps Casimir does too; all women look like his absurd ideal. But you, Shearwater, you're intelligent. Surely you don't believe anything so stupid?'

Shearwater shook his head.

'The cop, 'e gave evidence against me. "Limping in all four feet," 'e says. "It wasn't," I says, and the police-court vet, 'e bore me out. "The 'orse 'as been very well treated," 'e says. "But 'e's old, 'e's very old." "I know 'e's old," I says. "But where am I goin' to find the price for a young one?"'

'$x^2 - y^2$,' Shearwater was saying, '$= (x+y)(x-y)$. And the equation holds good whatever the values of x and y. ... It's the same with your love business, Mrs Viveash. The relation is still fundamentally the same, whatever the value of the unknown personal quantities concerned. Little individual tics and peculiarities – after all, what do they matter?'

'What indeed!' said Coleman. 'Tics, mere tics. Sheep ticks, horse ticks, bed bugs, tape worms, taint worms, guinea worms, liver flukes. ...'

' "The 'orse must be destroyed," says the beak. "'E's too old for work." "But I'm not," I says. "I can't get a old age pension at thirty-two, can I? 'Ow am I to earn my living if you take away what I earns my living by?"''

Mrs Viveash smiled agonizingly. 'Here's a man who thinks personal peculiarities are trivial and unimportant,' she said. 'You're not even interested in people, then?'

' " I don't know what you can do," 'e says. "I'm only 'ere to administer the law." "Seems a queer sort of law," I says. "What law is it?"''

Shearwater scratched his head. Under his formidable black moustache he smiled at last his ingenuous, childish smile. 'No,' he said. 'No, I suppose I'm not. It hadn't occurred to me, until you said it. But I suppose I'm not. No.' He laughed, quite delighted, it seemed, by this discovery about himself.

' "What law is it?" 'e says. "The Croolty to Animals law. That's what it is," 'e says.'

The smile of mockery and suffering appeared and faded. 'One of these days,' said Mrs Viveash, 'you may find them more absorbing than you do now.'

'Meanwhile,' said Shearwater ...

'I couldn't find a job 'ere, and 'aving been workin' on my own, my own master like, couldn't get unemployment pay. So when we 'eard of jobs at Portsmouth, we thought we'd try to get one, even if it did mean walkin' there.'

'Meanwhile, I have my kidneys.'

' "'Opeless," 'e says to me, "quite 'opeless. More than two hundred come for three vacancies." So there was nothing for it but to walk back again. Took us four days it did, this time. She was very bad on the way, very bad. Being nearly six months gone. Our first it is. Things will be 'arder still, when it comes.'

From the black bundle there issued a sound of quiet sobbing.

'Look here,' said Gumbril, making a sudden irruption into the conversation. 'This is really too awful.' He was consumed with indignation and pity; he felt like a prophet in Nineveh.

'There are two wretched people here,' and Gumbril told them breathlessly what he had overheard. It was terrible, terrible. 'All the way to Portsmouth and back again; on foot; without proper food; and the woman's with child.'

Coleman exploded with delight. 'Gravid,' he kept repeating, 'gravid, gravid. The laws of gravidy, first formulated by Newton, now recodified by the immortal Einstein. God said, Let Newstein be, and there was light. And God said, Let there be Light; and there was darkness o'er the face of the earth.' He roared with laughter.

Between them they raised five pounds. Mrs Viveash undertook to give them to the black bundle. The cabmen made way for her as she advanced; there was an uncomfortable silence. The black bundle lifted a face that was old and worn, like the face of a statue in the portal of a cathedral; an old face, but one was aware, somehow, that it belonged to a woman still young by the reckoning of years. Her hands trembled as she took the notes, and when she opened her mouth to speak her hardly articulate whisper of gratitude, one saw that she had lost several of her teeth.

The party disintegrated. All went their ways: Mr Mercaptan to his rococo boudoir, his sweet barocco bedroom in Sloane Street; Coleman and Zoe towards goodness only knew what scenes of intimate life in Pimlico; Lypiatt to his studio off the Tottenham Court Road, alone, silently brooding and perhaps too consciously bowed with unhappiness. But the unhappiness, poor Titan! was real enough, for had he not seen Mrs Viveash and the insufferable, the stupid and loutish Opps driving off in one taxi? 'Must finish up with a little dancing,' Myra had huskily uttered from that death-bed on which her restless spirit for ever and wearily exerted itself. Obediently, Bruin had given an address and they had driven off. But after the dancing? Oh, was it possible that that odious, bad-blooded young cad was her lover? And that she should like him? It was no wonder that Lypiatt should have walked, bent like Atlas under the weight of

a world. And when, in Piccadilly, a belated and still unsuccessful prostitute sidled out of the darkness, as he strode by unseeing in his misery when she squeaked up at him a despairing 'Cheer up, duckie,' Lypiatt suddenly threw up his head and laughed titanically, with the terrible bitterness of a noble soul in pain. Even the poor drabs at the street corners were affected by the unhappiness that radiated out from him, wave after throbbing wave, like music, he liked to fancy, into the night. Even the wretched drabs. He walked on, more desperately bowed than ever; but met no further adventure on his way.

Gumbril and Shearwater both lived in Paddington; they set off in company up Park Lane, walking in silence. Gumbril gave a little skip to get himself into step with his companion. To be out of step, when steps so loudly and flat-footedly flapped on empty pavements, was disagreeable, he found, was embarrassing, was somehow dangerous. Stepping, like this, out of time, one gave oneself away, so to speak, one made the night aware of two presences, when there might, if steps sounded in unison, be only one, heavier, more formidable, more secure than either of the separate two. In unison, then, they flapped up Park Lane. A policeman and the three poets, sulking back to back on their fountain, were the only human things besides themselves under the mauve electric moons.

'It's appalling, it's horrible,' said Gumbril at last, after a long, long silence, during which he had, indeed, been relishing to the full the horror of it all. Life, don't you know.

'What's appalling?' Shearwater inquired. He walked with his big head bowed, his hands clasped behind his back and clutching his hat; walked clumsily, with sudden lurches of his whole massive anatomy. Wherever he was, Shearwater always seemed to take up the space that two or three ordinary people would normally occupy. Cool fingers of wind passed refreshingly through his hair. He was thinking of the experiment he meant to try, in the next few days, down at the physiological laboratory. You'd put a man on an ergometer in a heated chamber and set him to work – hours at a time. He'd sweat, of course, prodigiously. You'd make arrangements for collecting the sweat, weighing it, analyzing it and so on. The interesting thing would be to see what happened at the end of a few days. The man would have got rid of so much of his salts, that the blood composition might be altered and all sorts of delightful consequences might follow. It ought to be a capital experiment. Gumbril's exclamation disturbed him. 'What's appalling?' he asked rather irritably.

'Those people at the coffee-stall,' Gumbril answered. 'It's appalling that human beings should have to live like that. Worse than dogs.'

'Dogs have nothing to complain of.' Shearwater went off at a tangent. 'Nor guinea-pigs, nor rats. It's these blasted anti-vivisection maniacs who make all the fuss.'

'But think,' cried Gumbril, 'what these wretched people have had to suffer! Walking all the way to Portsmouth in search of work; and the woman with child. It's horrifying. And then, the way people of that class are habitually treated. One has no idea of it until one has actually been treated that way oneself. In the war, for example, when one went to have one's mitral murmurs listened to by the medical board – they treated one then as though one belonged to the lower orders, like all the rest of the poor wretches. It was a real eye-opener. One felt like a cow being got into a train. And to think that the majority of one's fellow-beings pass their whole lives being shoved about like maltreated animals!'

'H'm,' said Shearwater. If you went on sweating indefinitely, he supposed, you would end by dying.

Gumbril looked through the railings at the profound darkness of the park. Vast it was and melancholy, with a string, here and there, of receding lights. 'Terrible,' he said, and repeated the word several times. 'Terrible, terrible.' All the legless soldiers grinding barrel-organs, all the hawkers of toys stamping their leaky boots in the gutters of the Strand; at the corner of Cursitor Street and Chancery Lane, the old woman with matches, for ever holding to her left eye a handkerchief as yellow and dirty as the winter fog. What was wrong with the eye? He had never dared to look, but hurried past as though she were not there, or some-times, when the fog was more than ordinarily cold and stifling, paused for an instant with averted eyes to drop a brown coin into her tray of matches. And then there were the murderers hanged at eight o'clock, while one was savouring, almost with voluptuous consciousness, the final dream-haunted doze. There was the phthisical charwoman who used to work at his father's house, until she got too weak and died. There were the lovers who turned on the gas and the ruined shopkeepers jumping in front of trains. Had one a right to be contented and well-fed, had one a right to one's education and good taste, a right to knowledge and conversation and the leisurely complexities of love?

He looked once more through the railings at the park's impenetrable, rustic night, at the lines of beaded lamps. He looked, and remembered another night, years ago, during the war, when there were no lights in the park and the electric moons above the roadway were in almost total eclipse. He had walked up this street alone, full of melancholy emotions which, though the cause of them was different, were in themselves much the same as the melancholy emotions which swelled windily up within him to-night. He had been most horribly in love.

'What did you think,' he asked abruptly, 'of Myra Viveash?'

'Think?' said Shearwater. 'I don't know that I thought very much about her. Not a case for ratiocination exactly, is she? She seemed to me entertaining enough, as women go. I said I'd lunch with her on Thursday.'

Gumbril felt, all of a sudden, the need to speak confidentially. 'There was a time,' he said in a tone that was quite unreally airy, off-hand and disengaged, 'years ago, when I totally lost my head about her. Totally.' Those tear-wet patches on his pillow, cold against his cheek in the darkness; and oh, the horrible pain of weeping, vainly, for something that was nothing, that was everything in the world! 'Towards the end of the war it was. I remember walking up this dismal street one night, in the pitch darkness, writhing with jealousy.' He was silent. Spectrally, like a dim, haunting ghost, he had hung about her; dumbly, dumbly imploring, appealing. 'The weak, silent man,' she used to call him. And once for two or three days, out of pity, out of affection, out of a mere desire, perhaps, to lay the tiresome ghost, she had given him what his mournful silence implored – only to take it back, almost as soon as accorded. That other night, when he had walked up this street before, desire had eaten out his vitals and his body seemed empty, sickeningly and achingly void; jealousy was busily reminding him, with an unflagging malice, of her beauty – of her beauty and the hateful, ruffian hands which now caressed, the eyes which looked on it. That was all long ago.

'She is certainly handsome,' said Shearwater, commenting, at one or two removes, on Gumbril's last remark. 'I can see that she might make any one who got involved with her decidedly uncomfortable.' After a day or two's continuous sweating, it suddenly occurred to him, one might perhaps find sea-water more refreshing than fresh water. That would be queer.

Gumbril burst out ferociously laughing. 'But there were other times,' he went on jauntily, 'when other people were jealous of me.' Ah, revenge, revenge. In the better world of the imagination it was possible to get one's own back. What fiendish vendettas were there carried to successful ends! 'I remember once writing her a quatrain in French.' (He had written it years after the whole thing was over, he had never sent it to any one at all; but that was all one.) 'How did it go? Ah, yes.' And he recited, with suitable gestures:

> '"Puisque nous sommes là, je dois
> Vous avertir, sans trop de honte,
> Que je n'égale pas le Comte
> Casanovesque de Sixfois."

Rather prettily turned, I flatter myself. Rather elegantly gross.'

Gumbril's laughter went hooting past the Marble Arch. It stopped rather suddenly, however, at the corner of the Edgware Road. He had suddenly remembered Mr Mercaptan, and the thought depressed him.

CHAPTER VI

I⊤ was between Whitfield Street and the Tottenham Court Road, in a 'heavenly Mews', as he liked to call it (for he had a characteristic weakness for philosophical paronomasia), that Casimir Lypiatt lived and worked. You passed under an archway of bald and sooty brick – and at night, when the green gaslamp underneath the arch threw livid lights and enormous architectural shadows, you could fancy yourself at the entrance of one of Piranesi's prisons – and you found yourself in a long cul-de-sac, flanked on either side by low buildings, having stabling for horses below and, less commodiously, stabling for human beings in the attics above. An old-fashioned smell of animals mingled with the more progressive stink of burnt oil. The air was a little thicker here, it seemed, than in the streets outside; looking down the mews on even the clearest day, you could see the forms of things dimming and softening, the colours growing richer and deeper with every yard of distance. It was the best place in the world, Lypiatt used to say, for studying aerial perspective; that was why he lived there. But you always felt about poor Lypiatt that he was facing misfortune with a jest a little too self-consciously.

Mrs Viveash's taxi drove in under the Piranesian arch, drove in slowly and as though with a gingerly reluctance to soil its white wheels on pavements so sordid. The cabman looked round inquiringly.

'This right?' he asked.

With a white-gloved finger Mrs Viveash prodded the air two or three times, indicating that he was to drive straight on. Halfway down the mews she rapped the glass; the man drew up.

'Never been down '*ere* before,' he said, for the sake of making a little conversation, while Mrs Viveash fumbled for her money. He looked at her with a polite and slightly ironic curiosity that was frankly mingled with admiration.

'You're lucky,' said Mrs Viveash. 'We poor decayed gentle-

299

women – you see what we're reduced to.' And she handed him a florin.

Slowly the taxi-man unbuttoned his coat and put the coin away in an inner pocket. He watched her as she crossed the dirty street, placing her feet with a meticulous precision one after the other in the same straight line, as though she were treading a knife edge between goodness only knew what invisible gulfs. Floating she seemed to go, with a little spring at every step and the skirt of her summery dress – white it was, with a florid pattern printed in black all over it – blowing airily out around her swaying march. Decayed gentlewomen indeed! The driver started his machine with an unnecessary violence; he felt, for some reason, positively indignant.

Between the broad double-doors through which the horses passed to their fodder and repose were little narrow human doors – for the Yahoos, Lypiatt used to say in his large allusive way; and when he said it he laughed with the loud and bell-mouthed cynicism of one who sees himself as a misunderstood and embittered Prometheus. At one of these little Yahoo doors Mrs Viveash halted and rapped as loudly as a small and stiff-hinged knocker would permit. Patiently she waited; several small and dirty children collected to stare at her. She knocked again, and again waited. More children came running up from the farther end of the mews; two young girls of fifteen or sixteen appeared at a neighbouring doorway and immediately gave tongue in whoops of mirthless, hyena-like laughter.

'Have you ever read about the Pied Piper of Hamelin?' Mrs Viveash asked the nearest child. Terrified, it shrank away. 'I thought not,' she said, and knocked again.

There was a sound, at last, of heavy feet slowly descending steep stairs; the door opened.

'Welcome to the palazzo!' It was Lypiatt's heroic formula of hospitality.

'Welcome at last,' Mrs Viveash corrected, and followed him up a narrow, dark staircase that was as steep as a ladder. He was dressed in a velveteen jacket and linen trousers that should have been white, but needed washing. He was dishevelled and his hands were dirty.

300

'Did you knock more than once?' he asked, looking back over his shoulder.

'More than twenty times,' Mrs Viveash justifiably exaggerated.

'I'm infinitely sorry,' protested Lypiatt. 'I get so deeply absorbed in my work, you know. Did you wait long?'

'The children enjoyed it, at any rate.' Mrs Viveash was irritated by a suspicion, which was probably, after all, quite unjustified, that Casimir had been rather consciously absorbed in his work; that he had heard her first knock and plunged the more profoundly into those depths of absorption where the true artist always dwells, or at any rate ought to dwell; to rise at her third appeal with a slow, pained reluctance, cursing, perhaps, at the importunity of a world which thus noisily interrupted the flow of his inspiration. 'Queer, the way they stare at one,' she went on, with a note in her dying voice of a petulance that the children had not inspired. 'Does one look such a guy?'

Lypiatt threw open the door at the head of the stairs and stood there on the threshold, waiting for her. 'Queer?' he repeated. 'Not a bit.' And as she moved past him into the room, he laid his hand on her shoulder and fell into step with her, leaving the door to slam behind them. 'Merely an example of the mob's instinctive dislike of the aristocratic individual. That's all. "Oh, why was I born with a different face?" Thank God I was, though. And so were you. But the difference has its disadvantages; the children throw stones.'

'They didn't throw stones.' Mrs Viveash was too truthful, this time.

They halted in the middle of the studio. It was not a very large room and there were too many things in it. The easel stood near the centre of the studio; round it Lypiatt kept a space permanently cleared. There was a broad fairway leading to the door, and another, narrower and tortuously winding between boxes and piled-up furniture and tumbled books, gave access to his bed. There was a piano and a table permanently set with dirty plates and strewed with the relics of two or three meals. Bookshelves stood on either side of the fireplace, and lying on the floor were still more books, piles on dusty piles. Mrs Viveash stood looking at the picture on the easel (abstract again – she

301

didn't like it), and Lypiatt, who had dropped his hand from her shoulder, and had stepped back the better to see her, stood earnestly looking at Mrs Viveash.

'May I kiss you?' he asked after a silence.

Mrs Viveash turned towards him, smiling agonizingly, her eyebrows ironically lifted, her eyes steady and calm and palely, brightly inexpressive. 'If it really gives you any pleasure,' she said. 'It won't, I may say, to me.'

'You make me suffer a great deal,' said Lypiatt, and said it so quietly and unaffectedly, that Myra was almost startled; she was accustomed, with Casimir, to noisier and more magniloquent protestations.

'I'm very sorry,' she said; and, really, she felt sorry. 'But I can't help it, can I?'

'I suppose you can't,' he said. 'You can't,' he repeated, and his voice had now become the voice of Prometheus in his bitterness. 'Nor can tigresses.' He had begun to pace up and down the unobstructed fairway between his easel and the door; Lypiatt liked pacing while he talked. 'You like playing with the victim,' he went on; 'he must die slowly.'

Reassured, Mrs Viveash faintly smiled. This was the familiar Casimir. So long as he could talk like this, could talk like an old-fashioned French novel, it was all right; he couldn't really be so very unhappy. She sat down on the nearest unencumbered chair. Lypiatt continued to walk back and forth, waving his arms as he walked.

'But perhaps it's good for one to suffer,' he went on, 'perhaps it's unavoidable and necessary. Perhaps I ought to thank you. Can an artist do anything if he's happy? Would he ever want to do anything? What is art, after all, but a protest against the horrible inclemency of life?' He halted in front of her, with arms extended in a questioning gesture. Mrs Viveash slightly shrugged her shoulders. She really didn't know; she couldn't answer. 'Ah, but that's all nonsense,' he burst out again, 'all rot. I want to be happy and contented and successful; and of course I should work better if I were. And I want, oh, above everything, everything, I want you: to possess you completely and exclusively and jealously and for ever. And the desire is like rust

302

corroding my heart, it's like moth eating holes in the fabric of my mind. And you merely laugh.' He threw up his hands and let them limply fall again.

'But I don't laugh,' said Mrs Viveash. On the contrary, she was very sorry for him; and, what was more, he rather bored her. For a few days, once, she had thought she might be in love with him. His impetuosity had seemed a torrent strong enough to carry her away. She had found out her mistake very soon. After that he had rather amused her: and now he rather bored her. No, decidedly, she never laughed. She wondered why she still went on seeing him. Simply because one must see some one? or why? 'Are you going to go on with my portrait?' she asked.

Lypiatt sighed. 'Yes,' he said, 'I suppose I'd better be getting on with my work. Work – it's the only thing. "Portrait of a Tigress".' The cynical Titan spoke again. 'Or shall I call it, "Portrait of a Woman who has never been in Love"?'

'That would be a very stupid title,' said Mrs Viveash.

'Or, "Portrait of the Artist's Heart Disease"? That would be good, that would be damned good!' Lypiatt laughed very loudly and slapped his thighs. He looked, Mrs Viveash thought, peculiarly ugly when he laughed. His face seemed to go all to pieces; not a corner of it but was wrinkled and distorted by the violent grimace of mirth. Even the forehead was ruined when he laughed. Foreheads are generally the human part of people's faces. Let the nose twitch and the mouth grin and the eyes twinkle as monkeyishly as you like; the forehead can still be calm and serene, the forehead still knows how to be human. But when Casimir laughed, his forehead joined in the general disintegrating grimace. And sometimes even when he wasn't laughing, when he was just vivaciously talking, his forehead seemed to lose its calm and would twitch and wrinkle itself in a dreadful kind of agitation. 'Portrait of the Artist's Heart Disease' – she didn't find it so very funny.

'The critics would think it was a problem picture,' Lypiatt went on. 'And so it would be, by God, so it would be. You *are* a problem. You're the Sphinx. I wish I were Œdipus and could kill you.'

All this mythology! Mrs Viveash shook her head.

He made his way through the intervening litter and picked up a canvas that was leaning with averted face against the wall near the window. He held it out at arm's length and examined it, his head critically cocked on one side. 'Oh, it's good,' he said softly. 'It's good. Look at it.' And, stepping out once more into the open, he propped it up against the table so that Mrs Viveash could see it without moving from her chair.

It was a stormy vision of her; it was Myra seen, so to speak, through a tornado. He had distorted her in the portrait, had made her longer and thinner than she really was, had turned her arms into sleek tubes and put a bright, metallic polish on the curve of her cheek. The figure in the portrait seemed to be leaning backwards a little from the surface of the canvas, leaning sideways too, with the twist of an ivory statuette carved out of the curving tip of a great tusk. Only somehow in Lypiatt's portrait the curve seemed to lack grace, it was without point, it had no sense.

'You've made me look,' said Mrs Viveash at last, 'as though I were being blown out of shape by the wind.' All this show of violence – what was the point of it? She didn't like it, she didn't like it at all. But Casimir was delighted with her comment. He slapped his thighs and once more laughed his restless, sharp-featured face to pieces.

'Yes, by God,' he shouted, 'by God, that's right! Blown out of shape by the wind. That's it: you've said it.' He began stamping up and down the room again, gesticulating. 'The wind, the great wind that's in me.' He struck his forehead. 'The wind of life, the wild west wind. I feel it inside me, blowing, blowing. It carries me along with it; for though it's inside me, it's more than I am, it's a force that comes from somewhere else, it's Life itself, it's God. It blows me along in the teeth of opposing fate, it makes me work on, fight on.' He was like a man who walks along a sinister road at night and sings to keep up his own spirits, to emphasize and magnify his own existence. 'And when I paint, when I write or improvise my music, it bends the things I have in my mind, it pushes them in one direction, so that everything I do has the look of a tree that streams north-east with all its branches and all its trunk from the root upwards, as though it were trying to run from before the Atlantic gale.'

Lypiatt stretched out his two hands and, with fingers splayed out to the widest and trembling in the excessive tension of the muscles, moved them slowly upwards and sideways, as though he were running his palms up the stem of a little wind-wizened tree on a hilltop above the ocean.

Mrs Viveash continued to look at the unfinished portrait. It was as noisy and easy and immediately effective as a Vermouth advertisement in the streets of Padua. Cinzano, Bonomelli, Campari – illustrious names. Giotto and Mantegna mouldered meanwhile in their respective chapels.

'And look at this,' Lypiatt went on. He took down the canvas that was clamped to the easel and held it out for her inspection. It was one of Casimir's abstract paintings: a procession of machine-like forms rushing up diagonally from right to left across the canvas, with as it were a spray of energy blowing back from the crest of the wave towards the top right-hand corner. 'In this painting,' he said, 'I symbolize the Artist's conquering spirit – rushing on the universe, making it its own.' He began to declaim:

> 'Look down, Conquistador,
> There on the valley's broad green floor,
> There lies the lake, the jewelled cities gleam,
> Chalco and Tlacopan
> Await the coming Man;
> Look down on Mexico, Conquistador,
> Land of your golden dream.

Or the same idea in terms of music—' and Lypiatt dashed to the piano and evoked a distorted ghost of Scriabin. 'You see?' he asked feverishly, when the ghost was laid again and the sad cheap jangling had faded again into silence. 'You *feel*? The artist rushes on the world, conquers it, gives it beauty, imposes a moral significance.' He returned to the picture. 'This will be fine when it's finished,' he said. 'Tremendous. You feel the wind blowing there, too.' And with a pointing finger he followed up the onrush of the forms. 'The great south-wester driving them on. "Like leaves from an enchanter fleeing." Only not chaotically, not in disorder. They're blown, so to speak in column of four – by a conscious wind.' He leaned the canvas against the table and was free again to march and brandish his conquering fists.

'Life,' he said, 'life – that's the great, essential thing. You've got to get life into your art, otherwise it's nothing. And life only comes out of life, out of passion and feeling; it can't come out of theories. That's the stupidity of all this chatter about art for art's sake and the æsthetic emotions and purely formal values and all that. It's only the formal relations that matter; one subject is just as good as another – that's the theory. You've only got to look at the pictures of the people who put it into practice to see that it won't do. Life comes out of life. You must paint with passion, and the passion will stimulate your intellect to create the right formal relations. And to paint with passion, you must paint things that passionately interest you, moving things, human things. Nobody, except a mystical pantheist, like Van Gogh, can seriously be as much interested in napkins, apples and bottles as in his lover's face, or the resurrection, or the destiny of man. Could Mantegna have devised his splendid compositions if he had painted arrangements of Chianti flasks and cheeses instead of Crucifixions, martyrs and triumphs of great men? Nobody but a fool could believe it. And could I have painted that portrait if I hadn't loved you, if you weren't killing me?'

Ah, Bonomelli and illustrious Cinzano!

'Passionately I paint passion. I draw life out of life. And I wish them joy of their bottles and their Canadian apples and their muddy table napkins with the beastly folds in them that look like loops of tripe.' Once more Lypiatt disintegrated himself with laughter; then was silent.

Mrs Viveash nodded, slowly and reflectively. 'I think you're right,' she said. Yes, he was surely right; there must be life, life was the important thing. That was precisely why his paintings were so bad – she saw now; there was no life in them. Plenty of noise there was, and gesticulation and a violent galvanized twitching; but no life, only the theatrical show of it. There was a flaw in the conduit; somewhere between the man and his work life leaked out. He protested too much. But it was no good; there was no disguising the deadness. Her portrait was a dancing mummy. He bored her now. Did she even posi--

tively dislike him? Behind her unchanging pale eyes Mrs Vive-ash wondered. But in any case, she reflected, one needn't always like the people with whom one associates. There are music-halls as well as confidential boudoirs; some people are admitted to the tea-party and the *tête-à-tête*, others, on a stage invisible, poor things! to themselves, do their little song-and-dance, roll out their characteristic patter, and having provided you with your entertainment are dismissed with their due share of applause. But then, what if they become boring?

'Well,' said Lypiatt at last – he had stood there, motionless, for a long time, biting his nails, 'I suppose we'd better begin our sitting.' He picked up the unfinished portrait and adjusted it on the easel. 'I've wasted a lot of time,' he said, 'and there isn't, after all, so much of it to waste.' He spoke gloomily, and his whole person had become, all of a sudden, curiously shrunken and deflated. 'There isn't so much of it,' he repeated, and sighed. 'I still think of myself as a young man, young and promising, don't you know. Casimir Lypiatt – it's a young, promising sort of name, isn't it? But I'm not young, I've passed the age of pro-mise. Every now and then I realize it, and it's painful, it's depressing.'

Mrs Viveash stepped up on to the model's dais and took her seat. 'Is that right?' she asked.

Lypiatt looked first at her, then at his picture. Her beauty, his passion – were they only to meet on the canvas? Opps was her lover. Time was passing; he felt tired. 'That'll do,' he said, and began painting. 'How young are you?' he asked after a moment.

'Twenty-five, I should imagine,' said Mrs Viveash.

'Twenty-five? Good Lord, it's nearly fifteen years since I was twenty-five. Fifteen years, fighting all the time. God, how I hate people sometimes! Everybody. It's not their malignity I mind; I can give them back as good as they give me. It's their power of silence and indifference, it's their capacity for making them-selves deaf. Here am I with something to say to them, something important and essential. And I've been saying it for more than fifteen years, I've been shouting it. They pay no attention. I bring them my head and heart on a charger, and they don't even notice that the things are there. I sometimes wonder how much longer I can manage to go on.' His voice had become very low, and it trembled. 'One's nearly forty, you know. ...' The voice faded huskily away into silence. Languidly and as though the business exhausted him, he began mixing colours on his palette.

Mrs Viveash looked at him. No, he wasn't young; at the moment, indeed, he seemed to have become much older than he really was. An old man was standing there, peaked and sharp and worn. He had failed, he was unhappy. But the world would have been unjuster, less discriminating if it had given him success.

'Some people believe in you,' she said; there was nothing else for her to say.

Lypiatt looked up at her. 'You?' he asked.

Mrs Viveash nodded, deliberately. It was a lie. But was it possible to tell the truth? 'And then there is the future,' she reassured him, and her faint death-bed voice seemed to prophesy with a perfect certainty. 'You're not forty yet; you've got twenty, thirty years of work in front of you. And there were others, after all, who had to wait – a long time – sometimes till after they were dead. Great men; Blake, for instance. ...' She felt positively ashamed; it was like a little talk by Doctor Frank Crane. But she felt still more ashamed when she saw that Casimir had begun to cry, and that the tears were rolling, one after another, slowly down his face.

He put down his palette, he stepped on to the dais, he came and knelt at Mrs Viveash's feet. He took one of her hands between his own and he bent over it, pressing it to his forehead, as though it were a charm against unhappy thoughts, sometimes kissing it; soon it was wet with tears. He wept almost in silence.

'It's all right,' Mrs Viveash kept repeating, 'it's all right,' and she laid her free hand on his bowed head, she patted it comfortingly as one might pat the head of a large dog that comes and thrusts its muzzle between one's knees. She felt, even as she made it, how meaningless and unintimate the gesture was. If she had liked him, she would have run her fingers through his hair; but somehow his hair rather disgusted her. 'It's all right, all right.' But, of course, it wasn't all right; and she was comforting him under false pretences and he was kneeling at the feet of somebody who simply wasn't there – so utterly detached, so far away she was from all this scene and all his misery.

'You're the only person,' he said at last, 'who cares or understands.'

Mrs Viveash could almost have laughed.

He began once more to kiss her hand.

'Beautiful and enchanting Myra – you were always that. But now you're good and dear as well, now I know you're kind.'

'Poor Casimir!' she said. Why was it that people always got involved in one's life? If only one could manage things on the principle of the railways! Parallel tracks – that was the thing. For a few miles you'd be running at the same speed. There'd be delightful conversation out of the windows; you'd exchange the omelette in your restaurant car for the vol-au-vent in theirs. And when you'd said all there was to say, you'd put on a little more steam, wave your hand, blow a kiss and away you'd go, forging ahead along the smooth, polished rails. But instead of that, there were these dreadful accidents; the points were wrongly set, the trains came crashing together; or people jumped on as you were passing through the stations and made a nuisance of themselves and wouldn't allow themselves to be turned off. Poor Casimir! But he irritated her, he was a horrible bore. She ought to have stopped seeing him.

'You can't wholly dislike me, then?'

'But of course not, my poor Casimir!'

'If you knew how horribly I loved you!' He looked up at her despairingly.

'But what's the good?' said Mrs Viveash.

'Have you ever known what it's like to love some one so much that you feel you could die of it? So that it hurts all the time. As though there were a wound. Have you ever known that?'

Mrs Viveash smiled her agonizing smile, nodded slowly and said, 'Perhaps. And one doesn't die, you know. One doesn't die.'

Lypiatt was leaning back, staring fixedly up at her. The tears were dry on his face, his cheeks were flushed. 'Do you know what it is,' he asked, 'to love so much that you begin to long for the anodyne of physical pain to quench the pain in the soul? You

309

don't know that.' And suddenly, with his clenched fist, he began to bang the wooden dais on which he was kneeling, blow after blow, with all his strength.

Mrs Viveash leant forward and tried to arrest his hand. 'You're mad, Casimir,' she said. 'You're mad. Don't do that.' She spoke with anger.

Lypiatt laughed till his face was all broken up with the grimace, and proffered for her inspection his bleeding knuckles. The skin hung in little white tags and tatters, and from below the blood was slowly oozing up to the surface. 'Look,' he said, and laughed again. Then suddenly, with an extraordinary agility, he jumped to his feet, bounded from the dais and began once more to stride up and down the fairway between his easel and the door.

'By God,' he kept repeating, 'by God, by God. I feel it in me. I can face the whole lot of you; the whole damned lot. Yes, and I shall get the better of you yet. An Artist' – he called up that traditional ghost and it comforted him; he wrapped himself with a protective gesture within the ample folds of its bright mantle – 'an Artist doesn't fail under unhappiness. He gets new strength from it. The torture makes him sweat new masterpieces. ...'

He began to talk about his books, his poems and pictures; all the great things in his head, the things he had already done. He talked about his exhibition – ah, by God, that would astonish them, that would bowl them over, this time. The blood mounted to his face; there was a flush over the high projecting cheek-bones. He could feel the warm blood behind his eyes. He laughed aloud; he was a laughing lion. He stretched out his arms; he was enormous, his arms reached out like the branches of a cedar. The Artist walked across the world and the mangy dogs ran yelping and snapping behind him. The great wind blew and blew, driving him on; it lifted him and he began to fly.

Mrs Viveash listened. It didn't look as though he would get much further with the portrait.

CHAPTER VII

IT was Press Day. The critics had begun to arrive; Mr Albemarle circulated among them with a ducal amiability. The young assistant hovered vaguely about, straining to hear what the great men had to say and trying to pretend that he wasn't eavesdropping. Lypiatt's pictures hung on the walls, and Lypiatt's catalogue, thick with its preface and its explanatory notes, was in all hands.

'Very strong,' Mr Albemarle kept repeating, 'very strong indeed!' It was his password for the day.

Little Mr Clew, who represented the *Daily Post*, was inclined to be enthusiastic. 'How well he writes!' he said to Mr Albemarle, looking up from the catalogue. 'And how well he paints! What *impasto*!'

Impasto, impasto – the young assistant sidled off unobtrusively to the desk and made a note of it. He would look the word up in Grubb's *Dictionary of Art and Artists* later on. He made his way back, circuitously, and as though by accident, into Mr Clew's neighbourhood.

Mr Clew was one of those rare people who have a real passion for art. He loved painting, all painting, indiscriminately. In a picture-gallery he was like a Turk in a harem; he adored them all. He loved Memling as much as Raphael, he loved Grünewald and Michelangelo, Holman Hunt and Manet, Romney and Tintoretto; how happy he could be with all of them! Sometimes, it is true, he hated; but that was only when familiarity had not yet bred love. At the first Post-Impressionist Exhibition, for example, in 1911, he had taken a very firm stand. 'This is an obscene farce,' he had written then. Now, however, there was no more passionate admirer of Matisse's genius. As a connoisseur and *kunstforscher*, Mr Clew was much esteemed. People would bring him dirty old pictures to look at, and he would exclaim at once: Why, it's an El Greco, a Piazzetta, or some other suitable name. Asked how he knew, he would shrug his shoulders and say: But it's signed all over. His certainty and his enthusiasm were in-

311

fectious. Since the coming of El Greco into fashion, he had discovered dozens of early works by that great artist. For Lord Petersfield's collection alone he had found four early El Grecos, all by pupils of Bassano. Lord Petersfield's confidence in Mr Clew was unbounded; not even that affair of the Primitives had shaken it. It was a sad affair: Lord Petersfield's Duccio had shown signs of cracking; the estate carpenter was sent for to take a look at the panel; he had looked. 'A worse-seasoned piece of Illinois hickory,' he said, 'I've never seen.' After that he looked at the Simone Martini; for that, on the contrary, he was full of praise. Smooth-grained, well-seasoned – it wouldn't crack, no, not in a hundred years. 'A nicer slice of board never came out of America.' He had a hyperbolical way of speaking. Lord Petersfield was extremely angry; he dismissed the estate carpenter on the spot. After that he told Mr Clew that he wanted a Giorgione, and Mr Clew went out and found him one which was signed all over.

'I like this very much,' said Mr Clew, pointing to one of the thoughts with which Lypiatt had prefaced his catalogue. ' "Genius," ' he adjusted his spectacles and began to read aloud, ' "is life. Genius is a force of nature. In art, nothing else counts. The modern impotents, who are afraid of genius and who are envious of it, have invented in self-defence the notion of the Artist. The Artist with his sense of form, his style, his devotion to pure beauty, et cetera, et cetera. But Genius includes the Artist; every Genius has, among very many others, the qualities attributed by the impotents to the Artist. The Artist without genius is a carver of fountains through which no water flows." Very true,' said Mr Clew, 'very true indeed.' He marked the passage with his pencil.

Mr Albemarle produced the password. 'Very strongly put,' he said.

'I have always felt that myself,' said Mr Clew. 'El Greco, for example ...'

'Good morning. What about El Greco?' said a voice, all in one breath. The thin, long, skin-covered skeleton of Mr Mallard hung over them like a guilty conscience. Mr Mallard wrote every week in the *Hebdomadal Digest*. He had an immense knowledge

312

of art, and a sincere dislike of all that was beautiful. The only modern painter whom he really admired was Hodler. All others were treated by him with a merciless savagery; he tore them to pieces in his weekly articles with all the holy gusto of a Calvinist iconoclast smashing images of the Virgin.

'What about El Greco?' he repeated. He had a peculiarly passionate loathing of El Greco.

Mr Clew smiled up at him propitiatingly; he was afraid of Mr Mallard. His enthusiasms were no match for Mr Mallard's erudite and logical disgusts. 'I was merely quoting him as an example,' he said.

'An example, I hope, of incompetent drawing, baroque composition, disgusting forms, garish colouring and hysterical subject-matter.' Mr Mallard showed his old ivory teeth in a menacing smile. 'Those are the only things which El Greco's work exemplifies.'

Mr Clew gave a nervous little laugh. 'What do you think of these?' he asked, pointing to Lypiatt's canvases.

'They look to me very ordinarily bad,' answered Mr Mallard.

The young assistant listened appalled. In a business like this, how was it possible to make good?

'All the same,' said Mr Clew courageously, 'I like that bowl of roses in the window with the landscape behind. Number twenty-nine.' He looked in the catalogue. 'And there's a really charming little verse about it:

"O beauty of the rose,
    Goodness as well as perfume exhaling!
    Who gazes on these flowers,
    On this blue hill and ripening field – he knows
    Where duty leads and that the nameless Powers
    In a rose can speak their will."

Really charming!' Mr Clew made another mark with his pencil.

'But commonplace, commonplace.' Mr Mallard shook his head. 'And in any case a verse can't justify a bad picture. What an unsubtle harmony of colour! And how uninteresting the composition is! That receding diagonal – it's been worked to death.' He too made a mark in his catalogue – a cross and a little circle, arranged like the skull and cross-bones on a pirate's flag.

Mr Mallard's catalogues were always covered with these little marks: they were his symbols of condemnation.

Mr Albemarle, meanwhile, had moved away to greet the new arrivals. To the critic of the *Daily Cinema* he had to explain that there were no portraits of celebrities. The reporter from the *Evening Planet* had to be told which were the best pictures.

'Mr Lypiatt,' he dictated, 'is a poet and philosopher as well as a painter. His catalogue is a – h'm – declaration of faith.'

The reporter took it down in shorthand. 'And very nice too,' he said. 'I'm most grateful to you, sir, most grateful.' And he hurried away, to get to the Cattle Show before the King should arrive. Mr Albemarle affably addressed himself to the critic of the *Morning Globe*.

'I *al*ways regard this gallery,' said a loud and cheerful voice, full of bulls and canaries in chorus, 'as positively a *mauvais lieu*. Such exhibitions!' And Mr Mercaptan shrugged his shoulders expressively. He halted to wait for his companion.

Mrs Viveash had lagged behind, reading the catalogue as she slowly walked along. 'It's a complete book,' she said, 'full of poems and essays and short stories even, so far as I can see.'

'Oh, the usual cracker mottoes.' Mr Mercaptan laughed. 'I know the sort of thing. "Look after the past and the future will look after itself." "God squared minus Man squared equals Art-plus-life times Art-minus-Life." "The Higher the Art the fewer the morals" – only that's too nearly good sense to have been invented by Lypiatt. But I know the sort of thing. I could go on like that for ever.' Mr Mercaptan was delighted with himself.

'I'll read you one of them,' said Mrs Viveash. ' "A picture is a chemical combination of plastic form and spiritual significance." '

'Crikey!' said Mr Mercaptan.

' "Those who think that a picture is a matter of nothing but plastic form are like those who imagine that water is made of nothing but hydrogen." '

Mr Mercaptan made a grimace. 'What writing!' he exclaimed; '*le style c'est l'homme*. Lypiatt hasn't got a style. Argal – inexorable conclusion – Lypiatt doesn't exist. My word, though. Look at those horrible great nudes there. Like Caraccis with cubical muscles.'

314

'Samson and Delilah,' said Mrs Viveash. 'Would you like me to read about them?'

'Certainly not.'

Mrs Viveash did not press the matter. Casimir, she thought, must have been thinking of her when he wrote this little poem about Poets and Women, crossed genius, torments, the sweating of masterpieces. She sighed. 'Those leopards are rather nice,' she said, and looked at the catalogue again. ' "An animal is a symbol and its form is significant. In the long process of adaptation, evolution has refined and simplified and shaped, till every part of the animal expresses one desire, a single idea. Man, who has become what he is, not by specialization, but by generalization, symbolizes with his body no one thing. He is a symbol of everything from the most hideous and ferocious bestiality to godhead." '

'Dear me,' said Mr Mercaptan.

A canvas of mountains and enormous clouds like nascent sculptures presented itself.

' "Aerial Alps" ' Mrs Viveash began to read.

> ' "Aerial Alps of amber and of snow,
> Junonian flesh, and bosomy alabaster
> Carved by the wind's uncertain hands ..." '

Mr Mercaptan stopped his ears. 'Please, please,' he begged.

'Number seventeen,' said Mrs Viveash, 'is called "Woman on a Cosmic Background." ' A female figure stood leaning against a pillar on a hilltop, and beyond was a blue night with stars. 'Underneath is written: "For one at least, she is more than the starry universe." ' Mrs Viveash remembered that Lypiatt had once said very much that sort of thing to her. 'So many of Casimir's things remind me,' she said, 'of those Italian vermouth advertisements. You know – Cinzano, Bonomelli and all those. I wish they didn't. This woman in white with her head in the Great Bear. ...' She shook her head. 'Poor Casimir.'

Mr Mercaptan roared and squealed with laughter. 'Bonomelli,' he said; 'that's precisely it. What a critic, Myra! I take off my hat.' They moved on. 'And what's this grand transformation scene?' he asked.

Mrs Viveash looked at the catalogue. 'It's called "The Sermon

315

on the Mount ",' she said. 'And really, do you know, I rather like
it. All that crowd of figures slanting up the hill and the single
figure on the top – it seems to me very dramatic.'

'My *dear*,' protested Mr Mercaptan.

'And in spite of everything,' said Mrs Viveash, feeling suddenly and uncomfortably that she had somehow been betraying
the man, 'he's really very nice, you know. Very nice indeed.'
Her expiring voice sounded very decidedly.

'Ah, *ces femmes*,' exclaimed Mr Mercaptan, '*ces femmes!*
They're all Pasiphaes and Ledas. They all in their hearts prefer
beasts to men, savages to civilized beings. *Even* you, Myra, I
really believe.' He shook his head.

Mrs Viveash ignored the outburst. 'Very nice, she repeated
thoughtfully. 'Only rather a bore. ...' Her voice expired
altogether.

They continued their round of the gallery.

CHAPTER VIII

CRITICALLY, in the glasses of Mr Bojanus's fitting-room, Gumbril examined his profile, his back view. Inflated, the Patent Small-Clothes bulged, bulged decidedly, though with a certain gracious opulence that might, in a person of the other sex, have seemed only deliciously natural. In him, however, Gumbril had to admit, the opulence seemed a little misplaced and paradoxical. Still, if one has to suffer in order to be beautiful, one must also expect to be ugly in order not to suffer. Practically, the trousers were a tremendous success. He sat down heavily on the hard wooden bench of the fitting-room and was received as though on a lap of bounding resiliency; the Patent Small-Clothes, there was no doubt, would be proof even against marble. And the coat, he comforted himself, would mask with its skirts the too decided bulge. Or if it didn't, well, there was no help for it. One must resign oneself to bulging, that was all.

'Very nice,' he declared at last.

Mr Bojanus, who had been watching his client in silence and with a polite but also, Gumbril could not help feeling, a somewhat ironical smile, coughed. 'It depends,' he said, 'precisely what you mean by "nice".' He cocked his head on one side, and the fine waxed end of his moustache was like a pointer aimed up at some remote star.

Gumbril said nothing, but catching sight once more of his own side view, nodded a dubious agreement.

'If by nice,' continued Mr Bojanus, 'you mean comfortable, well and good. If, however, you mean elegant, then, Mr Gumbril, I fear I must disagree.'

'But elegance,' said Gumbril, feebly playing the philosopher, 'is only relative, Mr Bojanus. There are certain African negroes among whom it is considered elegant to pierce the lips and distend them with wooden plates, until the mouth looks like a pelican's beak.'

Mr Bojanus placed his hand in his bosom and slightly bowed.

317

'Very possibly, Mr Gumbril,' he replied. 'But if you'll pardon my saying so, we are not African negroes.'

Gumbril was crushed, deservedly. He looked at himself again in the mirrors. 'Do you object,' he asked after a pause, 'to all eccentricities in dress, Mr Bojanus? Would you put us all into your elegant uniform?'

'Certainly not,' replied Mr Bojanus. 'There are certain walks of life in which eccentricity in appearance is positively a *sine qua non*, Mr Gumbril, and I might almost say *de rigueur*.'

'And which walks of life, Mr Bojanus, may I ask? You refer, perhaps, to the artistic walks? Sombreros and Byronic collars and possibly velveteen trousers? Though all that sort of thing is surely a little out of date, nowadays.'

Enigmatically Mr Bojanus smiled, a playful Sphinx. He thrust his right hand deeper into his bosom and with his left twisted to a finer needle the point of his moustache. 'Not artists, Mr Gumbril.' He shook his head. 'In practice they may show themselves a little eccentric and negleejay. But they have no need to look unusual on principle. It's only the politicians who need do it on principle. It's only *de rigueur*, as one might say, in the political walks, Mr Gumbril.'

'You surprise me,' said Gumbril. 'I should have thought that it was to the politician's interest to look respectable and normal.'

'But it is still more to his interest as a leader of men to look distinguished,' Mr Bojanus replied. 'Well, not precisely distinguished,' he corrected himself, 'because that implies that politicians look *distangay*, which I regret to say, Mr Gumbril, they very often don't. Distinguishable, is more what I mean.'

'Eccentricity is their badge of office?' suggested Gumbril. He sat down luxuriously on the Patent Small-Clothes.

'That's more like it,' said Mr Bojanus, tilting his moustaches. 'The leader has got to look different from the other ones. In the good old days they always wore their official badges. The leader 'ad his livery, like every one else, to show who he was. That was sensible, Mr Gumbril. Nowadays he has no badge – at least not for ordinary occasions – for I don't count Privy Councillors' uniforms and all that sort of once-a-year fancy dress. 'E's reduced to dressing in some eccentric way or making the most of the peculiarities of 'is personal appearance. A very 'apazard method of doing things, Mr Gumbril, very 'apazard.'

Gumbril agreed.

Mr Bojanus went on, making small, neat gestures as he spoke. 'Some of them,' he said, 'wear 'uge collars, like Mr Gladstone. Some wear orchids and eyeglasses, like Joe Chamberlain. Some let their 'air grow, like Lloyd George. Some wear curious 'ats, like Winston Churchill. Some put on black shirts, like this Mussolini, and some put on red ones, like Garibaldi. Some turn up their moustaches, like the German Emperor. Some turn them down, like Clemenceau. Some grow whiskers, like Tirpitz. I don't speak of all the uniforms, orders, ornaments, 'ead-dresses, feathers, crowns, buttons, tattooings, ear-rings, sashes, swords, trains, tiaras, urims, thummims and what not, Mr Gumbril, that 'ave been used in the past and in other parts of the world to distinguish the leader. We, 'oo know our 'istory, Mr Gumbril, we know all about that.'

Gumbril made a deprecating gesture. 'You speak for yourself, Mr Bojanus,' he said.

Mr Bojanus bowed.

'Pray continue,' said Gumbril.

Mr Bojanus bowed again. 'Well, Mr Gumbril,' he said, 'the point of all these things, as I've already remarked, is to make the leader look different, so that 'e can be recognized at the first *coop d'oil*, as you might say, by the 'erd 'e 'appens to be leading. For the 'uman 'erd, Mr Gumbril, is an 'erd which can't do without a leader. Sheep, for example: I never noticed that they 'ad a leader; nor rooks. Bees, on the other 'and, I take it, 'ave. At least when they're swarming. Correct me, Mr Gumbril, if I'm wrong. Natural 'istory was never, as you might say, my *forty*.'

'Nor mine,' protested Gumbril.

'As for elephants and wolves, Mr Gumbril, I can't pretend to speak of them with first-'and knowledge. Nor llamas, nor locusts, nor squab pigeons, nor lemmings. But 'uman beings, Mr Gumbril, those I can claim to talk of with authority, if I may say so in all modesty, and not as the scribes. I 'ave made a special study of them, Mr Gumbril. And my profession 'as brought me into contact with very numerous specimens.'

319

Gumbril could not help wondering where precisely in Mr Bojanus's museum he himself had his place.

'The 'uman 'erd,' Mr Bojanus went on, 'must have a leader. And a leader must have something to distinguish him from the 'erd. It's important for 'is interests that he should be recognized easily. See a baby reaching out of a bath and you immediately think of Pears' Soap; see the white 'air waving out behind, and you think of Lloyd George. That's the secret. But in my opinion, Mr Gumbril, the old system was much more sensible, give them regular uniforms and badges, I say; make Cabinet Ministers wear feathers in their 'air. Then the people will be looking to a real fixed symbol of leadership, not to the peculiarities of the mere individuals. Beards and 'air and funny collars change; but a good uniform is always the same. Give them feathers, that's what I say, Mr Gumbril. Feathers will increase the dignity of the State and lessen the importance of the individual. And that,' concluded Mr Bojanus with emphasis, 'that, Mr Gumbril, will be all to the good.'

'But you don't mean to tell me,' said Gumbril, 'that if I chose to show myself to the multitude in my inflated trousers, I could become a leader – do you?'

'Ah, no,' said Mr Bojanus. 'You'd 'ave to 'ave the talent for talking and ordering people about, to begin with. Feathers wouldn't give the genius, but they'd magnify the effect of what there was.'

Gumbril got up and began to divest himself of the Small-Clothes. He unscrewed the valve and the air whistled out, dyingly. He too sighed. 'Curious,' he said pensively, 'that I've never felt the need for a leader. I've never met any one I felt I could whole-heartedly admire or believe in, never any one I wanted to follow. It must be pleasant, I should think, to hand oneself over to somebody else. It must give you a warm, splendid, comfortable feeling.'

Mr Bojanus smiled and shook his head. 'You and I, Mr Gumbril,' he said, 'we're not the sort of people to be impressed with feathers or even by talking and ordering about. We may not be leaders ourselves. But at any rate we aren't the 'erd.'

'Not the main herd, perhaps.'

'Not any 'erd,' Mr Bojanus insisted proudly.

Gumbril shook his head dubiously and buttoned up his trousers. He was not sure, now he came to think of it, that he didn't belong to all the herds – by a sort of honorary membership and temporarily, as occasion offered, as one belongs to the Union at the sister university or to the Naval and Military Club while one's own is having its annual clean-out. Shearwater's herd, Lypiatt's herd, Mr Mercaptan's herd, Mrs Viveash's herd, the architectural herd of his father, the educational herd (but that, thank God! was now bleating on distant pastures), the herd of Mr Bojanus – he belonged to them all a little, to none of them completely. Nobody belonged to his herd. How could they? No chameleon can live with comfort on a tartan. He put on his coat.

'I'll send the garments this evening,' said Mr Bojanus.

Gumbril left the shop. At the theatrical wig-maker's in Leicester Square he ordered a blond fan-shaped beard to match his own hair and moustache. He would, at any rate, be his own leader; he would wear a badge, a symbol of authority. And Coleman had said that there were dangerous relations to be entered into by the symbol's aid.

Ah, now he was provisionally a member of Coleman's herd. It was all very depressing.

321

CHAPTER IX

FAN-SHAPED, blond, mounted on gauze and guaranteed un-detectable, it arrived from the wig-maker, preciously packed in a stout cardboard box six times too large for it and accompanied by a quarter of a pint of the choicest spirit gum. In the privacy of his bedroom Gumbril uncoffined it, held it out for his own admiration, caressed its silkiness, and finally tried it on, holding it provisionally to his chin, in front of the looking-glass. The effect, he decided immediately, was stunning, was grandiose. From melancholy and all too mild he saw himself transformed on the instant into a sort of jovial Henry the Eighth, into a massive Rabelaisian man, broad and powerful and exuberant with vitality and hair.

The proportions of his face were startlingly altered. The podium, below the mouth, had been insufficiently massive to carry the stately order of the nose; and the ratiocinative attic of the forehead, noble enough, no doubt, in itself, had been dis-proportionately high. The beard now supplied the deficiencies in the stylobate, and planted now on a firm basement of will, the order of the senses, the aerial attic of ideas, reared themselves with a more classical harmoniousness of proportion. It only re-mained for him to order from Mr Bojanus an American coat, padded out at the shoulders as squarely and heroically as a doublet of the Cinquecento, and he would look the complete Rabelaisian man. Great eater, deep drinker, stout fighter, pro-digious lover; clear thinker, creator of beauty, seeker of truth and prophet of heroic grandeurs. Fitted out with coat and beard, he could qualify for the next vacancy among the cœnobites of Thelema.

He removed his beard – 'put his beaver up,' as they used to say in the fine old days of chivalry; he would have to remember that little joke for Coleman's benefit. He put his beaver up – ha, ha! – and stared ruefully at the far from Rabelaisian figure which now confronted him. The moustache – that was genuine enough

322

– which had looked, in conjunction with the splendid work of art below, so fierce and manly, served by itself, he now perceived, only droopily to emphasize his native mildness and melancholy.

It was a dismal affair, which might have belonged to Maurice Barrès in youth; a slanting, flagging, sagging thing, such as could only grow on the lip of an assiduous Cultivator of the Me, and would become, as one grew older, ludicrously out of place on the visage of a roaring Nationalist. If it weren't that it fitted in so splendidly with the beard, if it weren't that it became so marvellously different in the new context he had now discovered for it, he would have shaved it off then and there.

Mournful appendage. But now he would transform it, he would add to it its better half. Zadig's quatrain to his mistress, when the tablet on which it was written was broken in two, became a treasonable libel on the king. So this moustache, thought Gumbril, as gingerly he applied the spirit gum to his cheeks and chin, this moustache which by itself serves only to betray me, becomes, as soon as it is joined to its missing context, an amorous arm for the conquest of the fair sex.

A little far-fetched, he decided; a little ponderous. And besides, as so few people had read Zadig, not much use in conversation. Cautiously and with neat, meticulous finger-tips he adjusted the transformation to his gummed face, pressed it firmly, held it while it stuck fast. The portals of Thelema opened before him; he was free of those rich orchards, those halls and courts, those broad staircases winding in noble spirals within the flanks of each of the fair round towers. And it was Coleman who had pointed out the way; he felt duly grateful. One last look at the Complete Man, one final and definitive constatation that the Mild and Melancholy one was, for the time at least, no more; and he was ready in all confidence to set out. He selected a loose, light great-coat – not that he needed a coat at all, for the day was bright and warm; but until Mr Bojanus had done his labour of padding he would have to broaden himself out in this way, even if it did mean that he might be uncomfortably hot. To fall short of Complete Manhood for fear of a little inconvenience would be absurd. He slipped, therefore, into his light coat – a toga, Mr

Bojanus called it, a very neat toga in real West Country whip-cord. He put on his broadest and blackest felt hat, for breadth above everything was what he needed to give him completeness – breadth of stature, breadth of mind, breadth of human sympathy, breadth of smile, breadth of humour, breadth of everything. The final touch was a massive and antique Malacca cane belonging to his father. If he had possessed a bulldog, he would have taken it out on a leash. But he did not. He issued into the sunshine, unaccompanied.

But unaccompanied he did not mean to remain for long. These warm, bright May days were wonderful days for being in love on. And to be alone on such days was like a malady. It was a malady from which the Mild and Melancholy Man suffered all too frequently. And yet there were millions of superfluous women in the country; millions of them. Every day, in the streets, one saw thousands of them passing; and some were exquisite, were ravishing, the only possible soul-mates. Thousands of unique soul-mates every day. The Mild and Melancholy one allowed them to pass – for ever. But to-day – to-day he was the complete and Rabelaisian man; he was bearded to the teeth; the imbecile game was at its height; there would be opportunities, and the Complete Man could know how to take them. No, he would not be unaccompanied for long.

Outside in the square the fourteen plane-trees glowed in their young, unsullied green. At the end of every street the golden muslin of the haze hung in an unwrinkled curtain that thinned away above the sky's gauzy horizon to transparent nothing against the intenser blue. The dim, conch-like murmur that in a city is silence seemed hazily to identify itself with the golden mistiness of summer, and against this dim, wide background the yells of the playing children detached themselves, distinct and piercing. 'Beaver,' they shouted, 'beaver!' and, 'Is it cold up there?' Full of playful menace, the Complete Man shook at them his borrowed Malacca. He accepted their prompt hail as the most favourable of omens.

At the first tobacconist's Gumbril bought the longest cigar he could find, and trailing behind him expiring blue wreaths of Cuban smoke, he made his way slowly and with an ample swagger towards the park. It was there, under the elms, on the shores of the ornamental waters, that he expected to find his opportunity, that he intended – how confidently behind his Gargantuan mask! – to take it.

The opportunity offered itself sooner than he expected.

He had just turned into the Queen's Road and was sauntering past Whiteley's with the air of one who knows that he has a right to a good place, to two or three good places even, in the sun, when he noticed just in front of him, peering intently at the New Season's Models, a young woman whom in his mild and melancholy days he would have only hopelessly admired, but who now, to the Complete Man, seemed a destined and accessible prey. She was fairly tall, but seemed taller than she actually was, by reason of her remarkable slenderness. Not that she looked disagreeably thin, far from it. It was a rounded slenderness. The Complete Man decided to consider her as tubular – flexible and tubular, like a section of boa constrictor, should one say? She was dressed in clothes that emphasized this serpentine slimness: in a close-fitting grey jacket that buttoned up to the neck and a long, narrow grey skirt that came down to her ankles. On her head was a small, sleek black hat, that looked almost as though it were made of metal. It was trimmed on one side with a bunch of dull golden foliage.

Those golden leaves were the only touch of ornament in all the severe smoothness and unbroken tubularity of her person. As for her face, that was neither strictly beautiful nor strictly ugly, but combined elements of both beauty and ugliness into a whole that was unexpected, that was oddly and somehow unnaturally attractive.

Pretending, he too, to take an interest in the New Season's Models, Gumbril made, squinting sideways over the burning tip of his cigar, an inventory of her features. The forehead, that was mostly hidden by her hat; it might be pensively and serenely high, it might be of that degree of lowness which in men is villainous, but in women is only another – a rather rustic one perhaps, rather *canaille* even, but definitely another – attraction. There was no telling. As for her eyes, they were green, and limpid; set wide apart in her head, they looked out from under heavy lids and through openings that slanted up towards the outer corners. Her nose was slightly aquiline. Her mouth was full-lipped, but straight and unexpectedly wide. Her chin was small, round and firm. She had a pale skin, a little flushed over the cheek-bones, which were prominent.

On the left cheek, close under the corner of the slanting eye, she had a brown mole. Such hair as Gumbril could see beneath her hat was pale and inconspicuously blond. When she had finished looking at the New Season's Models she moved slowly on, halting for a moment before the travelling-trunks and the fitted picnic-baskets; dwelling for a full minute over the corsets, passing the hats, for some reason, rather contemptuously, but pausing, which seemed strange, for a long pensive look at the cigars and wine. As for the tennis rackets and cricket bats, the school outfits and the gentleman's hosiery – she hadn't so much as a look for one of them. But how lovingly she lingered before the boots and shoes! Her own feet, the Complete Man noticed with satisfaction, had an elegance of florid curves. And while other folk walked on neat's leather she was content to be shod with nothing coarser than mottled serpent's skin.

Slowly they drifted up Queen's Road, lingering before every jeweller's, every antiquarian's, every milliner's on the way. The stranger gave him no opportunity, and indeed, Gumbril reflected, how should she? For the imbecile game on which he was relying is a travelling piquet for two players, not a game of patience. No sane human being could play it in solitude. He would have to make the opportunity himself.

All that was mild in him, all that was melancholy, shrank with a sickened reluctance from the task of breaking – with what consequences delicious and perilous in the future or, in the case of the deserved snub, immediately humiliating? – a silence which, by the tenth or twelfth shop window, had become quite unbearably significant. The Mild and Melancholy one would have drifted to the top of the road, sharing, with that community of tastes which is the basis of every happy union, her enthusiasm for brass candlesticks and toasting-forks, imitation Chippendale furniture, gold watch-bracelets and low-waisted summer frocks; would have drifted to the top of the road and watched her,

dumbly, disappearing for ever into the green park or along the blank pavements of the Bayswater Road; would have watched her for ever disappear and then, if the pubs had happened to be open, would have gone and ordered a glass of port, and sitting at the bar would have savoured, still dumbly, among the other drinkers, the muddy grapes of the Douro, and his own unique loneliness.

That was what the Mild and Melancholy one would have done. But the sight, as he gazed earnestly into an antiquary's window, of his own powerful bearded face reflected in a sham Heppelwhite mirror, reminded him that the Mild and Melancholy one was temporarily extinct, and that it was the Complete Man who now dawdled, smoking his long cigar, up the Queen's Road towards the Abbey of Thelema.

He squared his shoulders; in that loose toga of Mr Bojanus's he looked as copious as François Premier. The time, he decided, had come.

It was at this moment that the reflection of the stranger's face joined itself in the little mirror, as she made a little movement away from the Old Welsh dresser in the corner, to that of his own. She looked at the spurious Heppelwhite. Their eyes met in the hospitable glass. Gumbril smiled. The corners of the stranger's wide mouth seemed faintly to move; like petals of the magnolia, her eyelids came slowly down over her slanting eyes. Gumbril turned from the reflection to the reality.

'If you want to say Beaver,' he said, 'you may.'

The Complete Man had made his first speech.

'I want to say nothing,' said the stranger. She spoke with a charming precision and distinctness, lingering with a pretty emphasis on the *n* of nothing. 'N – n – nothing' – it sounded rather final. She turned away, she moved on.

But the Complete Man was not one to be put off by a mere ultimatum. 'There,' he said, falling into step with her, 'now I've had it – the deserved snub. Honour is saved, prestige duly upheld. Now we can get on with our conversation.'

The Mild and Melancholy one stood by, gasping with astonished admiration.

'You are v – very impertinent,' said the stranger, smiling and looking up from under the magnolia petals.

327

'It is in my character,' said the Complete Man. 'You mustn't blame me. One cannot escape from one's heredity; that's one's share of original sin.'

'There is always grace,' said the stranger.

Gumbril caressed his beard. 'True,' he replied.

'I advise you to pr—ray for it.'

His prayer, the Mild and Melancholy one reflected, had already been answered. The original sin in him had been self-corrected.

'Here is another antique shop,' said Gumbril. 'Shall we stop and have a look at it?'

The stranger glanced at him doubtfully. But he looked quite serious. They stopped.

'How revolting this sham cottage furniture is,' Gumbril remarked. The shop, he noticed, was called 'Ye Olde Farme House'.

The stranger, who had been on the point of saying how much she liked those lovely Old Welsh dressers, gave him her heartiest agreement. 'So v—vulgar.'

'So horribly refined. So refined and artistic.'

She laughed on a descending chromatic scale. This was excitingly new. Poor Aunt Aggie with her Arts and Crafts, and her old English furniture. And to think she had taken them so seriously! She saw in a flash the fastidious lady that she now was – with Louis whatever-it-was furniture at home, and jewels, and young poets to tea, and real artists. In the past, when she had imagined herself entertaining real artists, it had always been among really artistic furniture. Aunt Aggie's furniture. But now – no, oh no. This man was probably an artist. His beard; and that big black hat. But not poor; very well dressed.

'Yes, it's funny to think that there are people who call that sort of thing artistic. One's quite s—sorry for them,' she added, with a little hiss.

'You have a kind heart,' said Gumbril. 'I'm glad to see that.'

'Not v—very kind, I'm af—fraid.' She looked at him sideways, and significantly as the fastidious lady would have looked at one of the poets.

'Well, kind enough, I hope,' said the Complete Man. He was delighted with his new acquaintance.

Together they disembogued into the Bayswater Road. It was here, Gumbril reflected, that the Mild and Melancholy one would dumbly have slunk away to his glass of port and his loneliness among the alien topers at the bar. But the Complete Man took his new friend by the elbow, and steered her into the traffic. Together they crossed the road, together entered the park.

'I still think you are v–very impertinent,' said the lady. 'What induced you to follow me?'

With a single comprehensive gesture, Gumbril indicated the sun, the sky, the green trees airily glittering, the grass, the emerald lights and violet shadows of the rustic distance. 'On a day like this,' he said, 'how could I help it?'

'Original sin?'

'Oh,' the Complete Man modestly shook his head, 'I lay no claim to originality in this.'

The stranger laughed. This was nearly as good as a young poet at the tea-table. She was very glad that she'd decided, after all, to put on her best suit this afternoon, even if it was a little stuffy for the warmth of the day. He, too, she noticed, was wearing a great-coat; which seemed rather odd.

'Is it original,' he went on, 'to go and tumble stupidly like an elephant into a pitfall, head over ears, at first sight ...?'

She looked at him sideways, then closed down the magnolia petals, and smiled. This was going to be the real thing – one of those long, those interminable, or, at any rate, indefinitely re-newable conversations about love; witty, subtle, penetrating and bold, like the conversations in books, like the conversations across the tea-table between brilliant young poets and ladies of quality, grown fastidious through an excessive experience, fasti-dious and a little weary, but still, in their subtle way, insatiably curious.

'Suppose we sit down,' suggested Gumbril, and he pointed to a couple of green iron chairs, standing isolated in the middle of the grass close together and with their fronts slanting inwards a little towards one another in a position that suggested a con-fidential intimacy. At the prospect of the conversation that, inevitably, was about to unroll iself, he felt decidedly less elated than did his new friend. If there was anything he disliked it was conversations about love. It bored him, oh, it bored him most horribly, this minute analysis of the passion that young women always seemed to expect one, at some point or other in one's relation with them, to make. How love alters the character for both good and bad; how physical passion need not be incompatible with the spiritual; how a hateful and tyrannous possessiveness can be allied in love with the most unselfish solicitude for the other party – oh, he knew all this and much more, so well, so well. And whether one can be in love with more than one person at a time, whether love can exist without jealousy, whether pity, affection, desire can in any way replace the full and genuine passion – how often he had had to thrash out these dreary questions!

And all the philosophic speculations were equally familiar, all the physiological and anthropological and psychological facts. In the theory of the subject he had ceased to take any interest. Unhappily, a discussion of the theory always seemed to be an essential preliminary to the practice of it. He sighed a little wearily as he took his seat on the green iron chair. But then, recollecting that he was now the Complete Man, and that the Complete Man must do everything with a flourish and a high hand, he leaned forward and, smiling with a charming insolence through his beard, began:

'Tiresias, you may remember, was granted the singular privilege of living both as a man and a woman.'

Ah, this was the genuine young poet. Supporting an elbow on the back of her chair and leaning her cheek against her hand, she disposed herself to listen and, where necessary, brilliantly to interpellate; it was through half-closed eyes that she looked at him, and she smiled faintly in a manner which she knew, from experience, to be enigmatic, and though a shade haughty, though a tiny bit mocking and ironical, exceedingly attractive.

An hour and a half later they were driving towards an address in Bloxam Gardens, Maida Vale. The name seemed vaguely familiar to Gumbril. Bloxam Gardens – perhaps one of his aunts had lived there once?

'It's a dr–dreadful little maisonnette,' she explained. 'Full of

330

awful things. We had to take it furnished. It's so impossible to find anything now.'

Gumbril leaned back in his corner, wondering, as he studied that averted profile, who or what this young woman could be. She seemed to be in the obvious movement, to like the sort of things one would expect people to like; she seemed to be as highly civilized, in Mr Mercaptan's rather technical sense of the term, as free of all prejudices as the great exponent of civilization himself.

She seemed, from her coolly dropped hints, to possess all the dangerous experience, all the assurance and easy ruthlessness of a great lady whose whole life is occupied in the interminable affairs of the heart, the senses and the head. But, by a strange contradiction, she seemed to find her life narrow and uninteresting. She had complained in so many words that her husband misunderstood and neglected her, had complained, by implication, that she knew very few interesting people.

The maisonnette in Bloxam Gardens was certainly not very splendid – six rooms on the second and third floors of a peeling stucco house. And the furniture – decidedly Hire Purchase. And the curtains and cretonnes – brightly 'modern', positively 'futurist'.

'What one has to put up with in furnished flats!' The lady made a grimace as she ushered him into the sitting-room. And while she spoke the words, she really managed to persuade herself that the furniture wasn't theirs, that they had found all this sordid stuff cluttering up the rooms, not chosen it, oh and with pains! themselves, not doggedly paid for it, month by month.

'Our own things,' she murmured vaguely, 'are stored. In the Riviera.' It was there, under the palms, among the gaudy melon flowers and the croupiers that the fastidious lady had last held her salon of young poets. In the Riviera – that would explain, now she came to think of it, a lot of things, if explanation ever became necessary.

The Complete Man nodded sympathetically. 'Other people's tastes,' he held up his hands, they both laughed. 'But why do we think of other people?' he added. And coming forward with a conquering impulsiveness, he took both her long, fine hands in his and raised them to his bearded mouth.

She looked at him for a second, then dropped her eyelids, took back her hands. 'I must go and make the tea,' she said. 'The servants' – the plural was a pardonable exaggeration – 'are out.'

Gallantly, the Complete Man offered to come and help her. These scenes of intimate life had a charm all their own. But she would not allow it. 'No, no,' she was very firm, 'I simply forbid you. You must stay here. I won't be a moment,' and she was gone, closing the door carefully behind her.

Left to himself, Gumbril sat down and filed his nails.

As for the young lady, she hurried along to her dingy little kitchen, lit the gas, put the kettle on, set out the teapot and the cups on a tray, and from the biscuit-box, where it was stored, took out the remains of a chocolate cake, which had already seen service at the day-before-yesterday's tea-party. When all was ready here, she tip-toed across to her bedroom and sitting down at her dressing-table, began with hands that trembled a little with excitement to powder her nose and heighten the colour of her cheeks. Even after the last touch had been given, she still sat there, looking at her image in the glass.

The lady and the poet, she was thinking, the *grande dame* and the brilliant young man of genius. She liked young men with beards. But he was not an artist, in spite of the beard, in spite of the hat. He was a writer of sorts. So she gathered; but he was reticent, he was delightfully mysterious. She too, for that matter. The great lady slips out, masked, into the street; touches the young man's sleeve: Come with me. She chooses, does not let herself passively be chosen. The young poet falls at her feet; she lifts him up. One is accustomed to this sort of thing.

She opened her jewel-box, took out all her rings – there were not many of them, alas! – and put them on. Two or three of them, on second thoughts, she took off again; they were a little, she suspected with a sudden qualm, in other people's taste.

He was very clever, very artistic – only that seemed to be the wrong word to use; he seemed to know all the new things, all the interesting people. Perhaps he would introduce her to some of them. And he was so much at ease behind his knowledge, so well assured. But for her part, she felt pretty certain, she had made no stupid mistakes. She too had been, had looked at any rate – which was the important thing – very much at ease.

She liked young men with beards. They looked so Russian. Catherine of Russia had been one of the great ladies with caprices. Masked in the streets. Young poet, come with me. Or even, Young butcher's boy. But that, no, that was going too far, too low. Still, life, life – it was there to be lived – life – to be enjoyed. And now, and now? She was still wondering what would happen next, when the kettle, which was one of those funny ones which whistle when they come to the boil, began, fitfully at first, then, under full steam, unflaggingly, to sound its mournful, other-worldly note. She sighed and bestirred herself to attend to it.

'Let me help you.' Gumbril jumped up as she came into the room. 'What can I do?' He hovered rather ineptly round her.

The lady put down her tray on the little table. 'N–nothing,' she said.

'N–nothing?' he imitated her with a playful mockery. 'Am I good for n–nothing at all?' He took one of her hands and kissed it.

'Nothing that's of the l–least importance.' She sat down and began to pour out the tea.

The Complete Man also sat down. 'So to adore at first sight,' he asked, 'is not of the l–least importance?'

She shook her head, smiled, raised and lowered her eyelids. One was so well accustomed to this sort of thing; it had no importance. 'Sugar?' she asked. The young poet was safely there, sparkling across the tea-table. He offered love and she, with the easy heartlessness of one who is so well accustomed to this sort of thing, offered him sugar.

He nodded. 'Please. But if it's of no importance to you,' he went on, 'then I'll go away at once.'

The lady laughed her section of a descending chromatic scale. 'Oh, no, you won't,' she said. 'You can't.' And she felt that the *grande dame* had made a very fine stroke.

'Quite right,' the Complete Man replied; 'I couldn't.' He stirred his tea. 'But who are you,' he looked up at her suddenly,

333

'you devilish female?' He was genuinely anxious to know; and besides, he was paying her a very pretty compliment. 'What do you do with your dangerous existence?'

'I enjoy life,' she said. 'I think one ought to enjoy life. Don't you? I think it's one's first duty.' She became quite grave. 'One ought to enjoy every moment of it,' she said. 'Oh, passionately, adventurously, newly, excitingly, uniquely.'

The Complete Man laughed. 'A conscientious hedonist. I see.'

She felt uncomfortably that the fastidious lady had not quite lived up to her character. She had spoken more like a young woman who finds life too dull and daily, and would like to get on to the cinema. 'I am very conscientious,' she said, making significant play with the magnolia petals and smiling her riddling smile. She must retrieve the Great Catherine's reputation.

'I could see that from the first,' mocked the Complete Man with a triumphant insolence. 'Conscience doth make cowards of us all.'

The fastidious lady only contemptuously smiled. 'Have a little chocolate cake,' she suggested. Her heart was beating. She wondered, she wondered.

There was a long silence. Gumbril finished his chocolate cake, gloomily drank his tea and did not speak. He found, all at once, that he had nothing to say. His jovial confidence seemed, for the moment, to have deserted him. He was only the Mild and Melancholy one foolishly disguised as a Complete Man; a sheep in beaver's clothing. He entrenched himself behind his formidable silence and waited; waited, at first, sitting in his chair, then, when this total inactivity became unbearable, striding about the room.

She looked at him, for all her air of serene composure, with a certain disquiet. What on earth was he up to now? What could he be thinking about? Frowning like that, he looked like a young Jupiter, bearded and burly (though not, she noticed, quite so burly as he had appeared in his overcoat), making ready to throw a thunderbolt. Perhaps he was thinking of her – suspecting her, seeing through the fastidious lady and feeling angry at her attempted deception. Or perhaps he was bored with her, perhaps he was wanting to go away. Well, let him go; she didn't mind. Or perhaps he was just made like that – a moody young poet; that seemed, on the whole, the most likely explanation; it was also the most pleasing and romantic. She waited. They both waited.

Gumbril looked at her and was put to shame by the spectacle of her quiet serenity. He must do something, he told himself; he must recover the Complete Man's lost morale. Desperately he came to a halt in front of the one decent picture hanging on the walls. It was an eighteenth-century engraving of Raphael's 'Transfiguration' – better, he always thought, in black and white than in its bleakly-coloured original.

'That's a nice engraving,' he said. 'Very nice.' The mere fact of having uttered at all was a great comfort to him, a real relief.

'Yes,' she said. 'That belongs to me. I found it in a second-hand shop, not far from here.'

'Photography,' he pronounced, with that temporary earnestness which made him seem an enthusiast about everything, 'is a mixed blessing. It has made it possible to reproduce pictures so easily and cheaply, that all the bad artists who were well occupied in the past, making engravings of good men's paintings, are now free to do bad original work of their own.' All this was terribly impersonal, he told himself, terribly off the point. He was losing ground. He must do something drastic to win it back. But what?

She came to his rescue. 'I bought another at the same time,' she said. ' "The Last Communion of St Jerome", by – who is it? I forget.'

'Ah, you mean Domenichino's "St Jerome"?' The Complete Man was afloat again. 'Poussin's favourite picture. Mine too, very nearly. I'd like to see that.'

'It's in my room, I'm afraid. But if you don't mind.'

He bowed. 'If *you* don't.'

She smiled graciously to him and got up. 'This way,' she said, and opened the door.

'It's a lovely picture,' Gumbril went on, loquaciously now, behind her, as they walked down the dark corridor. 'And besides, I have a sentimental attachment to it. There used to be a copy of an engraving of it at home, when I was a child. And I remember wondering and wondering – oh, it went on for years – every time I saw the picture; wondering why on earth that old bishop (for I did know it was a bishop) should be handing the naked old man a five-shilling piece.'

She opened a door; they were in her very pink room. Grave in its solemn and subtly harmonious beauty, the picture hung over the mantelpiece, hung there, among the photographs of the little friends of her own age, like some strange object from another world. From within that chipped gilt frame all the beauty, all the grandeur of religion looked darkly out upon the pink room. The little friends of her own age, all deliciously nubile, sweetly smiled, turned up their eyes, clasped Persian cats or stood jauntily, feet apart, hand in the breeches pocket of the land-girl's uniform; the pink roses on the wallpaper, the pink and white curtains, the pink bed, the strawberry-coloured carpet, filled all the air with the rosy reflections of nakedness and life.

And utterly remote, absorbed in their grave, solemn ecstasy, the robed and mitred priest held out, the dying saint yearningly received, the body of the Son of God. The ministrants looked gravely on, the little angels looped in the air above a gravely triumphant festoon, the lion slept at the saint's feet, and through the arch beyond, the eye travelled out over a quiet country of dark trees and hills.

'There it is,' she waved towards the mantelpiece.

But Gumbril had taken it all in long ago. 'You see what I mean by the five-shilling piece.' And stepping up to the picture, he pointed to the round bright wafer which the priest holds in his hand and whose averted disk is like the essential sun at the centre of the picture's harmonious universe. 'Those were the days of five-shilling pieces,' he went on. 'You're probably too young to remember those large, lovely things. They came my way occasionally, and consecrated wafers didn't. So you can understand how much the picture puzzled me. A bishop giving a naked old man five shillings in a church, with angels fluttering overhead, and a lion sleeping in the foreground. It was obscure, it was horribly obscure.' He turned away from the picture and confronted his hostess, who was standing a little way behind him smiling enigmatically and invitingly.

336

'Obscure,' he repeated. 'But so is everything. So is life in general. And you,' he stepped towards her, 'you in particular.'

'Am I?' she lifted her limpid eyes at him. Oh, how her heart was beating, how hard it was to be the fastidious lady, calmly satisfying her caprice. How difficult it was to be accustomed to this sort of thing. What was going to happen next?

What happened next was that the Complete Man came still closer, put his arms round her, as though he were inviting her to the fox-trot, and began kissing her with a startling violence. His beard tickled her neck; shivering a little, she brought down the magnolia petals across her eyes. The Complete Man lifted her up, walked across the room carrying the fastidious lady in his arms and deposited her on the rosy catafalque of the bed. Lying there with her eyes shut, she did her best to pretend she was dead.

Gumbril had looked at his wrist watch and found that it was six o'clock. Already? He prepared himself to take his departure. Wrapped in a pink kimono, she came out into the hall to wish him farewell.

'When shall I see you again, Rosie?' He had learnt that her name was Rosie.

She had recovered her great lady's equanimity and detachment, and was able to shrug her shoulders and smile. 'How should I know?' she asked, implying that she could not foresee what her caprice might be an hour hence.

'May I write, then, and ask one of these days if you do know?'

She put her head on one side and raised her eyebrows, doubtfully. At last nodded. 'Yes, you can write,' she permitted.

'Good,' said the Complete Man, and picked up his wide hat. She held out her hand to him with stateliness, and with a formal gallantry he kissed it. He was just closing the front door behind him, when he remembered something. He turned round. 'I say,' he called after the retreating pink kimono. 'It's rather absurd. But how can I write? I don't know your name. I can't just address it "Rosie".'

The great lady laughed delightedly. This had the real *capriccio* flavour. 'Wait,' she said, and she ran into the sitting-room. She

337

was back again in a moment with an oblong of pasteboard. 'There,' she said, and dropped it into his great-coat pocket. Then blowing a kiss she was gone.

The Complete Man closed the door and descended the stairs. Well, well, he said to himself; well, well. He put his hand in his coat pocket and took out the card. In the dim light of the staircase he read the name on it with some difficulty. Mrs James — but no, but no. He read again, straining his eyes; there was no question of it. Mrs James Shearwater.

Mrs James Shearwater.

That was why he had vaguely known the name of Bloxam Gardens.

Mrs James Shear — . Step after step he descended, ponderously. 'Good Lord,' he said out loud. 'Good Lord.'

But why had he never seen her? Why did Shearwater never produce her? Now he came to think of it, he hardly ever spoke of her.

Why had she said the flat wasn't theirs? It was; he had heard Shearwater talk about it.

Did she make a habit of this sort of thing?

Could Shearwater be wholly unaware of what she was really like? But, for that matter, what *was* she really like?

He was half-way down the last flight, when with a rattle and a squeak of hinges the door of the house, which was only separated by a short lobby from the foot of the stairs, opened, revealing, on the doorstep, Shearwater and a friend, eagerly talking.

'... I take my rabbit,' the friend was saying — he was a young man with dark, protruding eyes, and staring, doggy nostrils; very eager, lively and loud. 'I take my rabbit and I inject into it the solution of eyes, pulped eyes of another dead rabbit. You see?'

Gumbril's first instinct was to rush up the stairs and hide in the first likely-looking corner. But he pulled himself together at once. He was a Complete Man, and Complete Men do not hide; moreover, he was sufficiently disguised to be quite unrecognizable. He stood where he was, and listened to the conversation.

'The rabbit,' continued the young man, and with his bright eyes and staring, sniffing nose, he looked like a poacher's terrier

ready to go barking after the first white tail that passed his way;
'the rabbit naturally develops the appropriate resistance, develops
a specific anti-eye to protect itself. I then take some of its anti-
eye serum and inject it into my female rabbit; I then immediately
breed from her.' He paused.

'Well?' asked Shearwater, in his slow, ponderous way. He
lifted his great round head inquiringly and looked at the doggy
young man from under his bushy eyebrows.

The doggy young man smiled triumphantly. 'The young
ones,' he said, emphasizing his words by striking his right fist
against the extended palm of his left hand, 'the young ones are
born with defective sight.'

Thoughtfully Shearwater pulled at his formidable moustache.
'H'm,' he said slowly. 'Very remarkable.'

'You realize the full significance of it?' asked the young man.
'We seem to be affecting the germ-plasm directly. We have
found a way of making acquired characteristics ...'

'Pardon me,' said Gumbril. He had decided that it was time
to be gone. He ran down the stairs and across the tiled hall, he
pushed his way firmly but politely between the talkers.

'... heritable,' continued the young man, imperturbably eager,
speaking through and over and round the obstacle.

'Damn!' said Shearwater. The Complete Man had trodden on
his toe. 'Sorry,' he added, absent-mindedly apologizing for the
injury he had received.

Gumbril hurried off along the street. 'If we really have found
out a technique for influencing the germ-plasm directly ...' he
heard the doggy young man saying; but he was already too far
away to catch the rest of the sentence. There are many ways, he
reflected, of spending an afternoon.

The doggy young man refused to come in, he had to get in
his game of tennis before dinner. Shearwater climbed the stairs
alone. He was taking off his hat in the little hall of his own apartment, when Rosie came out of the sitting-room with a trayful
of tea-things.

'Well?' he asked, kissing her affectionately on the forehead.
'Well? People to tea?'

'Only one,' Rosie replied. 'I'll go and make you a fresh cup.'

339

She glided off, rustling in her pink kimono towards the kitchen.

Shearwater sat down in the sitting-room. He had brought home with him from the library the fifteenth volume of the *Journal of Biochemistry*. There was something in it he wanted to look up. He turned over the pages. Ah, here it was. He began reading. Rosie came back again.

'Here's your tea,' she said.

He thanked her without looking up. The tea grew cold on the little table at his side.

Lying on the sofa, Rosie pondered and remembered. Had the events of the afternoon, she asked herself, really happened? They seemed very improbable and remote, now, in this studious silence. She couldn't help feeling a little disappointed. Was it only this? So simple and obvious? She tried to work herself up into a more exalted mood. She even tried to feel guilty; but there she failed completely. She tried to feel rapturous; but without much more success. Still, he certainly had been a most extraordinary man. Such impudence, and at the same time such delicacy and tact.

It was a pity she couldn't afford to change the furniture. She saw now that it wouldn't do at all. She would go and tell Aunt Aggie about the dreadful middle-classness of her Art and Craftiness.

She ought to have an Empire *chaise longue*. Like Madame Récamier. She could see herself lying there, dispensing tea. 'Like a delicious pink snake.' He had called her that.

Well, really, now she came to think of it all again, it had been too queer, too queer.

'What's a hedonist?' she suddenly asked.

Shearwater looked up from the *Journal of Biochemistry*. 'What?' he said.

'A hedonist.'

'A man who holds that the end of life is pleasure.'

A 'conscientious hedonist' – ah, that was good.

'This tea is cold,' Shearwater remarked.

'You should have drunk it before,' she said. The silence renewed and prolonged itself.

Rosie was getting much better, Shearwater reflected, as he washed his hands before supper, about not interrupting him when he was busy. This evening she had really not disturbed him at all, or at most only once, and that not seriously. There had been times in the past when the child had really made life almost impossible. There were those months at the beginning of their married life, when she had thought she would like to study physiology herself and be a help to him. He remembered the hours he had spent trying to teach her elementary facts about the chromosomes. It had been a great relief when she abandoned the attempt. He had suggested she should go in for stencilling patterns on Government linen. Such pretty curtains and things one could make like that. But she hadn't taken very kindly to the idea. There had followed a long period when she seemed to have nothing to do but prevent him from doing anything. Ringing him up at the laboratory, invading his study, sitting on his knee, or throwing her arms round his neck, or pulling his hair, or asking ridiculous questions when he was trying to work.

Shearwater flattered himself that he had been extremely patient. He had never got cross. He had just gone on as though she weren't there. As though she weren't there.

'Hurry up,' he heard her calling. 'The soup's getting cold.'

'Coming,' he shouted back, and began to dry his large, blunt hands.

She seemed to have been improving lately. And to-night, to-night she had been a model of non-existence.

He came striding heavily into the dining-room. Rosie was sitting at the head of the table, ladling out the soup. With her left hand she held back the flowing pink sleeve of her kimono so that it should not trail in the plates or the tureen. Her bare arm showed white and pearly through the steam of lentils.

How pretty she was! He could not resist the temptation, but coming up behind her bent down and kissed her, rather clumsily, on the back of her neck.

Rosie drew away from him. 'Really, Jim,' she said, disapprovingly. 'At meal-times!' The fastidious lady had to draw the line at these ill-timed, tumbling familiarities.

'And what about work-times?' Shearwater asked laughing.

341

'Still, you were wonderful this evening, Rosie, quite wonderful.' He sat down and began eating his soup. 'Not a sound all the time I was reading; or, at any rate, only one sound, so far as I remember.'

The great lady said nothing, but only smiled – a little contemptuously and with a touch of pity. She pushed away the plate of soup unfinished and planted her elbows on the table. Slipping her hands under the sleeves of her kimono, she began, lightly, delicately, with the tips of her fingers, to caress her own arms.

How smooth they were, how soft and warm and how secret under the sleeves. And all her body was as smooth and warm, was as soft and secret, still more secret beneath the pink folds. Like a warm serpent hidden away, secretly, secretly.

CHAPTER X

MR BOLDERO liked the idea of the Patent Small-Clothes. He liked it immensely, he said, immensely.

'There's money in it,' he said.

Mr Boldero was a small dark man of about forty-five, active as a bird and with a bird's brown, beady eyes, a bird's sharp nose. He was always busy, always had twenty different irons in the fire at once, was always fresh, clear-headed, never tired. He was also always unpunctual, always untidy. He had no sense of time or of order. But he got away with it, as he liked to say. He delivered the goods – or rather the goods, in the convenient form of cash, delivered themselves, almost miraculously it always seemed, to him.

He was like a bird in appearance. But in mind, Gumbril found, after having seen him once or twice, he was like a caterpillar: he ate all that was put before him, he consumed a hundred times his own mental weight every day. Other people's ideas, other people's knowledge – they were his food. He devoured them and they were at once his own. All that belonged to other people he annexed without a scruple or a second thought, quite naturally, as though it were already his own. And he absorbed it so rapidly and completely, he laid public claim to it so promptly that he sometimes deceived people into believing that he had really anticipated them in their ideas, that he had known for years and years the things they had just been telling him, and which he would at once airily repeat to them with the perfect assurance of one who knows – knows by instinct, as it were, by inheritance.

At their first luncheon he had asked Gumbril to tell him all about modern painting. Gumbril had given him a brief lecture; before the savoury had appeared on the table, Mr Boldero was talking with perfect familiarity of Picasso and Derain. He almost made it understood that he had a fine collection of their works in his drawing-room at home. Being a trifle deaf, however, he was not very good at names, and Gumbril's all-too-tactful correc-

343

tions were lost on him. He could not be induced to abandon his Bacosso in favour of any other version of the Spaniard's name. Bacosso – why, he had known all about Bacosso since he was a schoolboy! Bacosso was an old master, already.

Mr Boldero was very severe with the waiters and knew so well how things ought to be done at a good restaurant, that Gumbril felt sure he must recently have lunched with some meticulous gormandizer of the old school. And when the waiter made as though to serve them with brandy in small glasses, Mr Boldero was so passionately indignant that he sent for the manager.

'Do you mean to tell me,' he shouted in a perfect frenzy of righteous anger, 'that you don't yet know how brandy ought to be drunk?'

Perhaps it was only last week that he himself, Gumbril reflected, had learned to aerate his cognac in Gargantuan beakers.

Meanwhile, of course, the Patent Small-Clothes were not neglected. As soon as he had been told about the things, Mr Boldero began speaking of them with a perfect and practised familiarity. They were already his, mentally his. And it was only Mr Boldero's generosity that prevented him from making the Small-Clothes more effectively his own.

'If it weren't for the friendship and respect which I feel for your father, Mr Gumbril,' he said, twinkling genially over the brandy, 'I'd just annex your Small-Clothes. Bag and baggage. Just annex them.'

'Ah, but they're my patent,' said Gumbril. 'Or at least they're in process of being patented. The agents are at work.'

Mr Boldero laughed. 'Do you suppose that would trouble me if I wanted to be unscrupulous? I'd just take the idea and manufacture the article. You'd bring an action. I'd have it defended with all the professional erudition that could be brought. You'd find yourself let in for a case that might cost thousands. And how would you pay for it? You'd be forced to come to an agreement out of court, Mr Gumbril. That's what you'd have to do. And a damned bad agreement it would be for you, I can tell you.' Mr Boldero laughed very cheerfully at the thought of the badness of this agreement. 'But don't be alarmed,' he said. 'I shan't do it, you know.'

Gumbril was not wholly reassured. Tactfully, he tried to find out what terms Mr Boldero was prepared to offer. Mr Boldero was nebulously vague.

They met again in Gumbril's rooms. The contemporary drawings on the walls reminded Mr Boldero that he was now an art expert. He told Gumbril all about it – in Gumbril's own words. Every now and then, it was true, Mr Boldero made a little slip. Bacosso, for example, remained unshakably Bacosso. But on the whole the performance was most impressive. It made Gumbril feel very uncomfortable, however, while it lasted. For he recognized in this characteristic of Mr Boldero a horrible caricature of himself. He too was an assimilator; more discriminating, no doubt, more tactful, knowing better than Mr Boldero how to turn the assimilated experience into something new and truly his own; but still a caterpillar, definitely a caterpillar. He began studying Mr Boldero with a close and disgustful attention, as one might pore over some repulsive *memento mori*.

It was a relief when Mr Boldero stopped talking art and consented to get down to business. Gumbril was wearing for the occasion the sample pair of Small-Clothes which Mr Bojanus had made for him. For Mr Boldero's benefit he put them, so to speak, through their paces. He allowed himself to drop with a bump on to the floor – arriving there bruiseless and unjarred. He sat in complete comfort for minutes at a stretch on the edge of the ornamental iron fender. In the intervals he paraded up and down before Mr Boldero like a mannequin. 'A trifle bulgy,' said Mr Boldero. 'But still ...' He was, taking it all round, favourably impressed. It was time, he said, to begin thinking of details. They would have to begin by making experiments with the bladders to discover a model combining, as Mr Boldero put it, 'maximum efficiency with minimum bulge'. When they had found the right thing, they would have it made in suitable quantities by any good rubber firm. As for the trousers themselves, they could rely for those on sweated female labour in the East End. 'Cheap and good,' said Mr Boldero.

'It sounds ideal,' said Gumbril.

'And then,' said Mr Boldero, 'there's our advertising campaign. On that I may say,' he went on with a certain solemnity, 'will depend the failure or success of our enterprise. I consider it of the first importance.'

'Quite,' said Gumbril, nodding importantly and with intelligence.

'We must set to work,' said Mr Boldero, 'sci – en – tifically.' Gumbril nodded again.

'We have to appeal,' Mr Boldero went on so glibly that Gumbril felt sure he must be quoting somebody else's words, 'to the great instincts and feelings of humanity. ... They are the sources of action. They spend the money, if I may put it like that.'

'That's all very well,' said Gumbril. 'But how do you propose to appeal to the most important of the instincts? I refer, as you may well imagine, to sex.'

'I was just going to come to that,' said Mr Boldero, raising his hand as though to ask for a patient hearing. 'Alas! we can't. I don't see any way of hanging our Small-Clothes on the sexual peg.'

'Then we are undone,' said Gumbril, too dramatically.

'No, no.' Mr Boldero was reassuring. 'You make the error of the Viennese. You exaggerate the importance of sex. After all, my dear Mr Gumbril, there is also the instinct of self-preservation; there is also,' he leaned forward, wagging his finger, 'the social instinct, the instinct of the herd.'

'True.'

'Both of them as powerful as sex. What are the Professor's famous Censors but forbidding suggestions from the herd without, made powerful and entrenched by the social instinct within?'

Gumbril had no answer; Mr Boldero continued, smiling:

'So that we shall be all right if we stick to self-preservation and the herd. Rub in the comfort and the utility, the hygienic virtues of our Small-Clothes; that will catch their self-preservatory feelings. Aim at their dread of public opinion, at their ambition to be one better than their fellows and their terror of being different – at all the ludicrous weaknesses a well-developed social instinct exposes them to. We shall get them, if we set to work scientifically.' Mr Boldero's bird-like eyes twinkled very brightly. 'We shall get them,' he repeated, and he laughed a

346

happy little laugh, full of such a childlike diabolism, such an innocent gay malignity, that it seemed as though a little leprechaun had suddenly taken the financier's place in Gumbril's best arm-chair.

Gumbril laughed too; for this leprechaunish mirth was infectious. 'We shall get them,' he echoed. 'Oh, I'm sure we shall, if you set about it, Mr Boldero.'

Mr Boldero acknowledged the compliment with a smile that expressed no false humility. It was his due, and he knew it.

'I'll give you some of my ideas about the advertising campaign,' he said. 'Just to give you a notion. You can think them over, quietly, and make suggestions.'

'Yes, yes,' said Gumbril, nodding.

Mr Boldero cleared his throat. 'We shall begin,' he said, 'by making the most simple elementary appeal to their instinct of self-preservation: we shall point out that the Patent Small-Clothes are comfortable; that to wear them is to avoid pain. A few striking slogans about comfort – that's all we want. Very simple indeed. It doesn't take much to persuade a man that it's pleasanter to sit on air than on wood. But while we're on the subject of hard seats we shall have to glide off subtly at a tangent to make a flank attack on the social instincts.' And joining the tip of his forefinger to the tip of his thumb, Mr Boldero moved his hand delicately sideways, as though he were sliding it along a smooth brass rail. 'We shall have to speak about the glories and the trials of sedentary labour. We must exalt its spiritual dignity and at the same time condemn its physical discomforts. "The seat of honour", don't you know. We could talk about that. "The Seats of the Mighty." "The seat that rules the office rocks the world." All those lines might be made something of. And then we could have little historical chats about thrones; how dignified, but how uncomfortable they've been. We must make the bank clerk and the civil servant feel proud of being what they are and at the same time feel ashamed that, being such splendid people, they should have to submit to the indignity of having blistered hind-quarters. In modern advertising you must flatter your public – not in the oily, abject, tradesman-like style of the old advertisers, crawling before clients who were their social

347

superiors; that's all over now. It's we who are the social superiors
– because we've got more money than the bank clerks and the
civil servants. Our modern flattery must be manly, straight-
forward, sincere, the admiration of equal for equal – all the more
flattering as we aren't equals.' Mr Boldero laid a finger to his
nose. 'They're dirt and we're capitalists. ...' He laughed.

Gumbril laughed too. It was the first time that he had ever
thought of himself as a capitalist, and the thought was exhilarating.

'We flatter them,' went on Mr Boldero. 'We say that honest
work is glorious and ennobling – which it isn't; it's merely dull
and cretinizing. And then we go on to suggest that it would be
finer still, more ennobling, because less uncomfortable, if they
wore Gumbril's Patent Small-Clothes. You see the line?'

Gumbril saw the line.

'After that, said Mr Boldero, 'we get on to the medical side of
the matter. The medical side, Mr Gumbril – that's most important. Nobody feels really well nowadays – at any rate, nobody
who lives in a big town and does the kind of loathsome work
that the people we're catering for does. Keeping this fact before
our eyes, we have to make it clear that only those can expect to
be healthy who wear pneumatic trousers.'

'That will be a little difficult, won't it?' questioned Gumbril.

'Not a bit of it!' Mr Boldero laughed with an infectious confidence. 'All we have to do is to talk about the great nerve-centres
of the spine: the shocks they get when you sit down too hard;
the wearing exhaustion to which long-protracted sitting on un-
padded seats subjects them. We'll have to talk very scientifically
about the great lumbar ganglia – if there are such things, which I
really don't pretend to know. We'll even talk almost mystically
about the ganglia. You know that sort of ganglion philosophy?'

Mr Boldero went on parenthetically. 'Very interesting it is,
sometimes, I think. We could put in a lot about the dark, powerful sense-life, sex-life, instinct-life which is controlled by the
lumbar ganglion. How important it is that that shouldn't be
damaged. That already our modern conditions of civilization
tend unduly to develop the intellect and the thoracic ganglia
controlling the higher emotions. That we're wearing out, growing feeble, losing our balance in consequence. And that the only

cure – if we are to continue our present mode of civilized life – is to be found in Gumbril's Patent Small-Clothes.' Mr Boldero brought his hand with an emphatic smack on to the table as he spoke, as he fairly shouted these last words.

'Magnificent,' said Gumbril, with genuine admiration.

'This sort of medical and philosophical dope,' Mr Boldero went on, 'is always very effective, if it's properly used. The public to whom we are making our appeal is, of course, almost absolutely ignorant on these, or, indeed, on almost all other subjects. It is therefore very much impressed by the unfamiliar words; particularly if they have such a good juicy sound as the word "ganglia".'

'There was a young man of East Anglia, whose loins were a tangle of ganglia,' murmured Gumbril, *improvvisatore.*

'Precisely,' said Mr Boldero. 'Precisely. You see how juicy it is? Well, as I say, they're impressed. And they're also grateful. They're grateful to us for having given them a piece of abstruse, unlikely information which they can pass on to their wives, or to such friends as they know don't read the paper in which our advertisement appears – can pass on airily, don't you know, with easy erudition, as though they'd known all about ganglia from their childhood. And they'll feel such a flow of superiority as they hand on the metaphysics and the pathology, that they'll always think of us with affection. They'll buy our breeks and they'll get other people to buy. That's why,' Mr Boldero went off again on an instructive tangent, 'that's why the day of secret patent medicines is really over. It's no good saying you have rediscovered some secret known only, in the past, to the Egyptians. People don't know anything about Egyptology; but they have an inkling that such a science exists. And that if it does exist, it's unlikely that patent-medicine makers should have found out facts unknown to the professors at the universities. And it's much the same even with secrets that don't come from Egypt. People know there's such a thing as medical science and they again feel it's improbable that manufacturers should know things ignored by the doctors. The modern democratic advertiser is entirely above-board. He tells you all about it. He explains that the digestive juices acting on bismuth give rise to a disinfectant acid. He points out that lactic ferment gets destroyed before it reaches the large intestine, so that Metchnikoff's cure generally won't work. And he goes on to explain that the only way of getting the ferment there is to mix it with starch and paraffin: starch to feed the ferment on, paraffin to prevent the starch being digested before it gets to the intestine. And, in consequence, he convinces you that a mixture of starch, paraffin and ferment is the only thing that's any good at all. Consequently you buy it; which you would never have done without the explanation. In the same way, Mr Gumbril, we mustn't ask people to take our trousers on trust. We must explain scientifically why these trousers will be good for their health. And by means of the ganglia, as I've pointed out, we can even show that the trousers will be good for their souls and the whole human race at large. And as you probably know, Mr Gumbril, there's nothing like a spiritual message to make things go. Combine spirituality with practicality and you've fairly got them. Got them, I may say, on toast. And that's what we can do with our trousers; we can put a message into them, a big, spiritual message. Decidedly,' he concluded, 'we shall have to work those ganglia all we can.'

'I'll undertake to do that,' said Gumbril, who felt very buoyant and self-assured. Mr Boldero's hydrogenous conversation had blown him up like a balloon.

'And I'm sure you'll do it well,' said Mr Boldero encouragingly. 'There is no better training for modern commerce than a literary education. As a practical business man, I always uphold the ancient universities, especially in their teaching of the Humanities.'

Gumbril was much flattered. At the moment, it seemed supremely satisfying to be told that he was likely to make a good business man. The business man took on a radiance, began to glow, as it were, with a phosphorescent splendour.

'Then it's very important,' continued Mr Boldero, 'to play on their snobbism; to exploit that painful sense of inferiority which the ignorant and ingenuous always feel in the presence of the knowing. We've got to make our trousers the Thing – socially right as well as merely personally comfortable. We've got to imply somehow that it's bad form not to wear them. We've got to make those who don't wear them feel rather uncomfortable. Like that film of Charlie Chaplin's, where he's the absent-minded young man about town who dresses for dinner immaculately, from the waist up – white waistcoat, tail coat, stiff shirt, top-hat – and only discovers, when he gets down into the hall of the hotel, that he's forgotten to put on his trousers. We've got to make them feel like that. That's always very successful. You know those excellent American advertisements about young ladies whose engagements are broken off because they perspire too freely or have an unpleasant breath? How horribly uncomfortable those make you feel! We've got to do something of the same sort for our trousers. Or more immediately applicable would be those tailor's advertisements about correct clothes. "Good clothes make you feel good." You know the sort of line. And then those grave warning sentences in which you're told that a correctly cut suit may make the difference between an appointment gained and an appointment lost, an interview granted and an interview refused. But the most masterly examples I can think of,' Mr Boldero went on with growing enthusiasm, 'are those American advertisements of spectacles, in which the manufacturers first assume the existence of a social law about goggles, and then proceed to invoke all the sanctions which fall on the head of the committer of a solecism upon those who break it. It's masterly. For sport or relaxation, they tell you, as though it was a social axiom, you must wear spectacles of pure tortoiseshell. For business, tortoiseshell rims and nickel ear-pieces lend incisive poise – incisive poise, we must remember that for our ads, Mr Gumbril. "Gumbril's Patent Small-Clothes lend incisive poise to business men." For semi-evening dress, shell rims with gold ear-pieces and gold nose-bridge. And for full dress, gold-mounted rimless pince-nez are refinement itself, and absolutely correct. Thus we see, a social law has been created, according to which every self-respecting myope or astigmat must have four distinct pairs of glasses. Think if he should wear the all-shell sports model with full dress! Revolting solecism! The people who read advertisements like that begin to feel uncomfortable; they have only one pair of glasses, they are afraid of being laughed at, thought low-class and ignorant and suburban. And since there are few who would not rather be taken in adultery than in provincialism, they rush out to buy four new pairs of spectacles. And the manufacturer gets rich, Mr Gumbril. Now, we must do something of the kind with our trousers. Imply somehow that they're correct, that you're undressed without, that your fiancée would break off the engagement if she saw you sitting down to dinner on anything but air.' Mr Boldero shrugged his shoulders, vaguely waved his hand.

'It may be rather difficult,' said Gumbril, shaking his head.

'It may,' Mr Boldero agreed. 'But difficulties are made to be overcome. We must pull the string of snobbery and shame: it's essential. We must find out methods for bringing the weight of public opinion to bear mockingly on those who do not wear our trousers. It is difficult at the moment to see how it can be done. But it will have to be done, it will have to be done,' Mr Boldero repeated emphatically. 'We might even find a way of invoking patriotism to our aid. "English trousers filled with English air for English men." A little far-fetched, perhaps. But there might be something in it.'

Gumbril shook his head doubtfully.

'Well, it's one of the things we've got to think about in any case,' said Mr Boldero. 'We can't afford to neglect such powerful social emotions as these. Sex, as we've seen, is almost entirely out of the question. We must run the rest, therefore, as hard as we can. For instance, there's the novelty business. People feel superior if they possess something new which their neighbours haven't got. The mere fact of newness is an intoxication. We must encourage that sense of superiority, brew up that intoxication. The most absurd and futile objects can be sold because they're new. Not long ago I sold four million patent soap-dishes of a new and peculiar kind. The point was that you didn't screw the fixture into the bathroom wall: you made a hole in the wall and built the soap-dish into a niche, like a holy water stoup. My soap-dishes possessed no advantages over other kinds of soap-dishes, and they cost a fantastic amount to instal. But I managed to put them across, simply because they were new. Four million of them.' Mr Boldero smiled with satisfaction at the

352

recollection. 'We shall do the same, I hope, with our trousers. People may be shy of being the first to appear in them; but the shyness will be compensated for by the sense of superiority and elation produced by the consciousness of the newness of the things.'

'Quite so,' said Gumbril.

'And then, of course, there's the economy slogan. "One pair of Gumbril's Patent Small-Clothes will outlast six pairs of ordinary trousers." That's easy enough. So easy that it's really uninteresting.' Mr Boldero waved it away.

'We shall have to have pictures,' said Gumbril, parenthetically. He had an idea.

'Oh, of course.'

'I believe I know of the very man to do them,' Gumbril went on. 'His name's Lypiatt. A painter. You've probably heard of him.'

'Heard of him!' exclaimed Mr Boldero. He laughed. 'But who hasn't heard of Lydgate.'

'Lypiatt.'

'Lypgate, I mean, of course.'

'I think he'd be the very man,' said Gumbril.

'I'm certain he would,' said Mr Boldero, not a whit behind-hand.

Gumbril was pleased with himself. He felt he had done some one a good turn. Poor old Lypiatt; be glad of the money. Gumbril remembered also his own fiver. And remembering his own fiver, he also remembered that Mr Boldero had as yet made no concrete suggestion about terms. He nerved himself at last to suggest to Mr Boldero that it was time to think of this little matter. Ah, how he hated talking about money! He found it so hard to be firm in asserting his rights. He was ashamed of showing himself grasping. He always thought with consideration of the other person's point of view – poor devil, could he afford to pay? And he was always swindled and always conscious of the fact. Lord, how he hated life on these occasions! Mr Boldero was still evasive.

'I'll write you a letter about it,' he said at last.

Gumbril was delighted. 'Yes, do,' he said enthusiastically,

'do.' He knew how to cope with letters all right. He was a devil with the fountain-pen. It was these personal, hand-to-hand combats that he couldn't manage. He could have been, he always felt, such a ruthless critic and satirist, such a violent, unscrupulous polemical writer. And if ever he committed his autobiography to paper, how breath-takingly intimate, how naked – naked without so much as a healthy sunburn to colour the whiteness – how quiveringly a sensitive jelly it would be! All the things he had never told any one would be in it. Confession at long range – if anything, it would be rather agreeable.

'Yes, do write me a letter,' he repeated. 'Do.'

Mr Boldero's letter came at last, and the proposals it contained were derisory. A hundred pounds down and five pounds a week when the business should be started. Five pounds a week – and for that he was to act as a managing director, writer of advertisements and promoter of foreign sales. Gumbril felt thankful that Mr Boldero had put the terms in a letter. If they had been offered point-blank across the luncheon table, he would probably have accepted them without a murmur. He wrote a few neat, sharp phrases saying that he could not consider less than five hundred pounds down and a thousand a year. Mr Boldero's reply was amiable; would Mr Gumbril come and see him?

See him? Well, of course, it was inevitable. He would have to see him again some time. But he would send the Complete Man to deal with the fellow. A Complete Man matched with a leprechaun – there could be no doubt as to the issue.

'DEAR MR BOLDERO,' he wrote back, 'I should have come to talk over matters before this. But I have been engaged during the last few days in growing a beard and until this has come to maturity, I cannot, as you will easily be able to understand, leave the house. By the day after to-morrow, however, I hope to be completely presentable and shall come to see you at your office at about three o'clock, if that is convenient to you. I hope we shall be able to arrange matters satisfactorily. – Believe me, dear Mr Boldero, yours very truly, THEODORE GUMBRIL, JR.'

The day after to-morrow became in due course to-day; splendidly bearded and Rabelaisianly broad in his whipcord toga, Gumbril presented himself at Mr Boldero's office in Queen Victoria Street.

'I should hardly have recognized you,' exclaimed Mr Boldero as he shook hands. 'How it does alter you, to be sure!'

'Does it?' The Complete Man laughed with a significant joviality.

'Won't you take off your coat?'

'No, thanks,' said Gumbril. 'I'll keep it on.'

'Well,' said the leprechaun, leaning back in his chair and twinkling, bird-like, across the table.

'Well,' repeated Gumbril on a different tone from behind the stooks of his corn-like beard. He smiled, feeling serenely strong and safe.

'I'm sorry we should have disagreed,' said Mr Boldero.

'So am I,' the Complete Man replied. 'But we shan't disagree for long,' he added, with significance; and as he spoke the words he brought down his fist with such a bang, that the inkpots on Mr Boldero's very solid mahogany writing-table trembled and the pens danced, while Mr Boldero himself started with a genuine alarm. He had not expected them. And now he came to look at him more closely, this young Gumbril was a great, hulking, dangerous-looking fellow. He had thought he would be easy to manage. How could he have made such a mistake?

Gumbril left the office with Mr Boldero's cheque for three hundred and fifty pounds in his pocket and an annual income of eight hundred. His bruised right hand was extremely tender to the touch. He was thankful that a single blow had been enough.

355

CHAPTER XI

GUMBRIL had spent the afternoon at Bloxam Gardens. His chin was still sore from the spirit gum with which he had attached to it the symbol of the Complete Man; he was feeling also a little fatigued. Rosie had been delighted to see him; St Jerome had gone on solemnly communicating all the time.

His father had gone out to dine, and Gumbril had eaten his rump steak and drunk his bottle of stout alone. He was sitting now in front of the open french windows which led from his father's workroom on to the balcony, with a block on his knee and a fountain-pen in his hand, composing advertisements for the Patent Small-Clothes. Outside, in the plane-trees of the square, the birds had gone through their nightly performance. But Gumbril had paid no attention to them. He sat there, smoking, sometimes writing a word or two – sunk in the quagmire of his own drowsy and comfortable body. The flawless weather of the day had darkened into a blue May evening. It was agreeable merely to be alive.

He sketched out two or three advertisements in the grand idealistic transatlantic style. He imagined one in particular with a picture of Nelson at the head of the page and 'England expects ...' printed large beneath it. 'England ... Duty ... these are solemn words.' That was how it would begin. 'These are solemn words, and we use them solemnly as men who realize what Duty is, and who do all that in them lies to perform it as Englishmen should. The Manufacturer's is a sacred trust. The guide and ruler of the modern world, he has, like the Monarch of other days, responsibilities towards his people; he has a Duty to fulfil. He rules, but he must also serve. We realize our responsibilities, we take them seriously. Gumbril's Patent Small-Clothes have been brought into the world that they may serve. Our Duty towards you is a Duty of Service. Our proud boast is that we perform it. But besides his Duty towards Others, every man has a duty towards Himself. What is that Duty? It is to keep

356

himself in the highest possible state of physical and spiritual fitness. Gumbril's Patent Small-Clothes protect the lumbar ganglia. ...' After that it would be plain medical and mystical sailing.

As soon as he got to the ganglia, Gumbril stopped writing. He put down the block, sheathed his pen, and abandoned himself to the pleasures of pure idleness. He sat, he smoked his cigar. In the basement, two floors down, the cook and the house-parlourmaid were reading – one the *Daily Mirror*, the other the *Daily Sketch*. For them, Her Majesty the Queen spoke kindly words to crippled female orphans; the jockeys tumbled at the jumps; Cupid was busy in Society, and the murderers who had disembowelled their mistresses were at large. Above him was the city of models, was a bedroom, a servant's bedroom, an attic of tanks and ancient dirt, the roof and, after that, two or three hundred light-years away, a star of the fourth magnitude. On the other side of the party-wall on his right, a teeming family of Jews led their dark, compact, Jewish lives with a prodigious intensity. At this moment they were all passionately quarrelling. Beyond the wall on the left lived the young journalist and his wife. To-night it was he who had cooked the supper. The young wife lay on the sofa, feeling horribly sick; she was going to have a baby, there could be no doubt about it now. They had meant not to have one; it was horrible. And, outside, the birds were sleeping in the trees, the invading children from the slum tumbled and squealed. Ships meanwhile were walloping across the Atlantic freighted with more cigars. Rosie at this moment was probably mending Shearwater's socks. Gumbril sat and smoked, and the universe arranged itself in a pattern about him, like iron filings round a magnet.

The door opened, and the house-parlourmaid intruded Shearwater upon his lazy felicity, abruptly, in her unceremonious old way, and hurried back to the *Daily Sketch*.

'Shearwater! This is very agreeable,' said Gumbril. 'Come and sit down.' He pointed to a chair.

Clumsily, filling the space that two ordinary men would occupy, Shearwater came zigzagging and lurching across the room, bumped against the work-table and the sofa as he passed, and finally sat down in the indicated chair.

It suddenly occurred to Gumbril that this was Rosie's husband: he had not thought of that before. Could it be in the marital capacity that he presented himself so unexpectedly now? After this afternoon. ... He had come home; Rosie had confessed all. ... Ah! but then she didn't know who he was. He smiled to himself at the thought. What a joke! Perhaps Shearwater had come to complain to him of the unknown Complete Man – to him! It was delightful. Anon – the author of all those ballads in the *Oxford Book of English Verse*: the famous Italian painter – Ignoto. Gumbril was quite disappointed when his visitor began to talk of other themes than Rosie. Sunk in the quagmire of his own comfortable guts, he felt good-humouredly obscene. The dramatic scabrousness of the situation would have charmed him in his present mood. Good old Shearwater – but what an ox of a man! If he, Gumbril, took the trouble to marry a wife, he would at least take some interest in her.

Shearwater had begun to talk in general terms about life. What could he be getting at, Gumbril wondered? What particulars were ambushed behind these generalizations? There were silences. Shearwater looked, he thought, very gloomy. Under his thick moustache the small, pouting, babyish mouth did not smile. The candid eyes had a puzzled, tired expression in them.

'People are queer,' he said after one of his silences. 'Very queer. One has no idea how queer they are.'

Gumbril laughed. 'But I have a very clear idea of their queerness,' he said. 'Everyone's queer, and the ordinary, respectable, bourgeois people are the queerest of the lot. How do they manage to live like that? It's astonishing. When I think of all my aunts and uncles ...' He shook his head.

'Perhaps it's because I'm rather incurious,' said Shearwater. 'One ought to be curious, I think. I've come to feel lately that I've not been curious enough about people.' The particulars began to peep, alive and individual, out of the vagueness, like rabbits; Gumbril saw them in his fancy, at the fringe of a wood.

'Quite,' he said encouragingly. 'Quite.'

'I think too much of my work,' Shearwater went on, frowning. 'Too much physiology. There's also psychology. People's minds as well as their bodies. ... One shouldn't be limited. Not too much, at any rate. People's minds ...' He was silent for a moment. 'I can imagine,' he went on at last, as in the tone of one who puts a very hypothetical case, 'I can imagine one's getting so much absorbed in somebody else's psychology that one could really think of nothing else.' The rabbits seemed ready to come out into the open.

'That's a process,' said Gumbril, with middle-aged jocularity, speaking out of his private warm morass, 'that's commonly called falling in love.'

There was another silence. Shearwater broke it to begin talking about Mrs Viveash. He had lunched with her three or four days running. He wanted Gumbril to tell him what she was really like. 'She seems to me a very extraordinary woman,' he said.

'Like everybody else,' said Gumbril irritatingly. It amused him to see the rabbits scampering about at last.

'I've never known a woman like that before.'

Gumbril laughed. 'You'd say that of any woman you happened to be interested in,' he said. 'You've never known any women at all.' He knew much more about Rosie, already, than Shearwater did, or probably ever would.

Shearwater meditated. He thought of Mrs Viveash, her cool, pale, critical eyes; her laughter, faint and mocking; her words that pierced into the mind, goading it into thinking unprecedented thoughts.

'She interests me,' he repeated. 'I want you to tell me what she's really like.' He emphasized the word really, as though there must, in the nature of things, be a vast difference between the apparent and the real Mrs Viveash.

Most lovers, Gumbril reflected, picture to themselves, in their mistresses, a secret reality, beyond and different from what they see every day. They are in love with somebody else – their own invention. And sometimes there is a secret reality; and sometimes reality and appearance are the same. The discovery, in either case, is likely to cause a shock. 'I don't know,' he said. 'How should I know? You must find out for yourself.'

'But you know her, you know her well,' said Shearwater, almost with anxiety in his voice.

'Not so well as all that.'

Shearwater sighed profoundly, like a whale in the night. He felt restless, incapable of concentrating. His mind was full of a horrible confusion. A violent eruptive bubbling up from below had shaken its calm clarity to pieces. All this absurd business of passion – he had always thought it nonsense, unnecessary. With a little strength of will one could shut it out. Women – only for half an hour out of the twenty-four. But she had laughed, and his quiet, his security had vanished. 'I can imagine,' he had said to her yesterday, 'I can imagine myself giving up everything, work and all, to go running round after you.' 'And do you suppose I should enjoy that?' Mrs Viveash had asked. 'It would be ridiculous,' he said, 'it would be almost shameful.' And she had thanked him for the compliment. 'And at the same time,' he went on, 'I feel that it might be worth it. It might be the only thing.' His mind was confused, full of new thoughts. 'It's difficult,' he said after a pause, 'arranging things. Very difficult. I thought I had arranged them so well ...'

'I never arrange anything,' said Gumbril, very much the practical philosopher. 'I take things as they come.' And as he spoke the words, suddenly he became rather disgusted with himself. He shook himself; he climbed up out of his own morass. 'It would be better, perhaps, if I arranged things more,' he added.

'Render therefore unto Cæsar the things which are Cæsar's,' said Shearwater, as though to himself; 'and to God, and to sex, and to work. ... There must be a working arrangement.' He sighed again. 'Everything in proportion. In proportion,' he repeated, as though the word were magical and had power. 'In proportion.'

'Who's talking about proportion?' They turned round. In the doorway Gumbril Senior was standing, smoothing his ruffled hair and tugging at his beard. His eyes twinkled cheerfully behind his spectacles. 'Poaching on my architectural ground?' he said.

'This is Shearwater,' Gumbril Junior put in, and explained who he was.

360

The old gentleman sat down. 'Proportion,' he said – 'I was just thinking about it, now, as I was walking back. You can't help thinking about it in these London streets, where it doesn't exist. You can't help pining for it. There are some streets ... oh, my God!' And Gumbril Senior threw up his hands in horror. 'It's like listening to a symphony of cats to walk along them. Senseless discords and a horrible disorder all the way. And the one street that was really like a symphony by Mozart – how busily and gleefully they're pulling it down now! Another year and there'll be nothing left of Regent Street. There'll only be a jumble of huge, hideous buildings at three-quarters of a million apiece. A concert of Brobdingnagian cats. Order has been turned into a disgusting chaos. We need no barbarians from outside; they're on the premises, all the time.'

The old man paused and pulled his beard meditatively. Gumbril Junior sat in silence, smoking; and in silence Shearwater revolved within the walls of his great round head his agonizing thoughts of Mrs Viveash.

'It has always struck me as very curious,' Gumbril Senior went on, 'that people are so little affected by the vile and discordant architecture around them. Suppose, now, that all these brass bands of unemployed ex-soldiers that blow so mournfully at all the street corners were suddenly to play nothing but a series of senseless and devilish discords – why, the first policeman would move them on, and the second would put them under arrest, and the passers-by would try to lynch them on their way to the police station. There would be a real spontaneous outcry of indignation. But when at these same street corners the contractors run up enormous palaces of steel and stone that are every bit as stupid and ignoble and inharmonious as ten brass bandsmen each playing a different tune in a different key, there is no outcry. The police don't arrest the architect; the passing pedestrians don't throw stones at the workmen. They don't notice that anything's wrong. It's odd,' said Gumbril Senior. 'It's very odd.'

'Very odd,' Gumbril Junior echoed.

'The fact is, I suppose,' Gumbril Senior went on, smiling with a certain air of personal triumph, 'the fact is that architecture is a more difficult and intellectual art than music. Music – that's just a faculty you're born with, as you might be born with a snub nose. But the sense of plastic beauty – though that's, of course, also an inborn faculty – is something that has to be developed and intellectually ripened. It's an affair of the mind; experience and thought have to draw it out. There are infant prodigies in music; but there are no infant prodigies in architecture.' Gumbril Senior chuckled with a real satisfaction. 'A man can be an excellent musician and a perfect imbecile. But a good architect must also be a man of sense, a man who knows how to think and to profit by experience. Now, as almost none of the people who pass along the streets in London, or any other city of the world, do know how to think or to profit by experience, it follows that they cannot appreciate architecture. The innate faculty is strong enough in them to make them dislike discord in music; but they haven't the wits to develop that other innate faculty – the sense of plastic beauty – which would enable them to see and disapprove of the same barbarism in architecture. Come with me,' Gumbril Senior added, getting up from his chair, 'and I'll show you something that will illustrate what I've been saying. Something you'll enjoy, too. Nobody's seen it yet,' he said mysteriously as he led the way upstairs. 'It's only just finished – after months and years. It'll cause a stir when they see it – when I let them see it, if ever I do, that is. The dirty devils!' Gumbril Senior added good-humouredly.

On the landing of the next floor he paused, felt in his pocket, took out a key and unlocked the door of what should have been the second best bedroom. Gumbril Junior wondered, without very much curiosity, what the new toy would turn out to be. Shearwater wondered only how he could possess Mrs Viveash.

'Come on,' called Gumbril Senior from inside the room. He turned on the light. They entered.

It was a big room; but almost the whole of the floor was covered by an enormous model, twenty feet long by ten or twelve wide, of a complete city traversed from end to end by a winding river and dominated at its central point by a great dome. Gumbril Junior looked at it with surprise and pleasure. Even

Shearwater was roused from his bitter ruminations of desire to look at the charming city spread out at his feet.

'It's exquisite,' said Gumbril Junior. 'What is it? The capital of Utopia, or what?'

Delighted, Gumbril Senior laughed. 'Don't you see something rather familiar in the dome?' he asked.

'Well, I had thought ...' Gumbril Junior hesitated, afraid that he might be going to say something stupid. He bent down to look more closely at the dome. 'I had thought it looked rather like St Paul's – and now I see that it is St Paul's.'

'Quite right,' said his father. 'And this is London.'

'I wish it were,' Gumbril Junior laughed.

'It's London as it might have been if they'd allowed Wren to carry out his plans of rebuilding after the Great Fire.'

'And why didn't they allow him to?' Shearwater asked.

'Chiefly,' said Gumbril Senior, 'because, as I've said before, they didn't know how to think or profit by experience. Wren offered them open spaces and broad streets; he offered them sunlight and air and cleanliness; he offered them beauty, order and grandeur. He offered to build for the imagination and the ambitious spirit of man, so that even the most bestial, vaguely and remotely, as they walked those streets, might feel that they were of the same race – or very nearly – as Michelangelo; that they too might feel themselves, in spirit at least, magnificent, strong and free. He offered them all these things; he drew a plan for them, walking in peril among the still smouldering ruins. But they preferred to re-erect the old intricate squalor; they preferred the mediæval darkness and crookedness and beastly irregular quaintness; they preferred holes and crannies and winding tunnels; they preferred foul smells, sunless, stagnant air, phthisis and rickets; they preferred ugliness and pettiness and dirt; they preferred the wretched human scale, the scale of the sickly body, not of the mind. Miserable fools! But I suppose,' the old man continued, shaking his head, 'we can't blame them.' His hair had blown loose from its insecure anchorage; with a gesture of resignation he brushed it back into place. 'We can't blame them. We should have done the same in the circumstances – undoubtedly. People offer us reason and beauty; but we will have

363

none of them, because they don't happen to square with the notions that were grafted into our souls in youth, that have grown there and become a part of us. *Experientia docet* – nothing falser, so far as most of us are concerned, was ever said. You, no doubt, my dear Theodore, have often in the past made a fool of yourself with women. ...'

Gumbril Junior made an embarrassed gesture that half denied, half admitted the soft impeachment. Shearwater turned away, painfully reminded of what, for a moment, he had half forgotten. Gumbril Senior swept on.

'Will that prevent you from making as great a fool of yourself again to-morrow? It will not. It will most assuredly not.' Gumbril Senior shook his head. 'The inconveniences and horrors of the pox are perfectly well known to every one; but still the disease flourishes and spreads. Several million people were killed in a recent war and half the world ruined; but we all busily go on in courses that make another event of the same sort inevitable. *Experientia docet? Experientia* doesn't. And that is why we must not be too hard on these honest citizens of London who, fully appreciating the inconveniences of darkness, disorder and dirt, manfully resisted any attempt to alter conditions which they had been taught from childhood onwards to consider as necessary, right and belonging inevitably to the order of things. We must not be too hard. We are doing something even worse ourselves. Knowing by a century of experience how beautiful, how graceful, how soothing to the mind is an ordered piece of town-planning, we pull down almost the only specimen of it we possess and put up in its place a chaos of Portland stone that is an offence against civilization. But let us forget about these old citizens and the labyrinth of ugliness and inconvenience which we have inherited from them, and which is called London. Let us forget the contemporaries who are making it still worse than it was. Come for a walk with me through this ideal city. Look.'

And Gumbril Senior began expounding it to them.

In the middle, there, of that great elliptical Piazza at the eastern end of the new City, stands, four-square, the Royal Exchange. Pierced only with small dark windows, and built of rough ashlars of the silvery Portland stone, the ground floor serves as a massy foundation for the huge pilasters that slide up, between base and capital, past three tiers of pedimented windows. Upon them rest the cornice, the attic and the balustrade, and on every pier of the balustrade a statue holds up its symbol against the sky. Four great portals, rich with allegory, admit to the courtyard with its double tier of coupled columns, its cloister and its gallery. The statue of Charles the Martyr rides triumphantly in the midst, and within the windows one guesses the great rooms, rich with heavy garlands of plaster, panelled with carved wood.

Ten streets give on to the Piazza, and at either end of its ellipse the water of sumptuous fountains ceaselessly blows aloft and falls. Commerce, in that to the north of the Exchange, holds up her cornucopia, and from the midst of its grapes and apples the master jet leaps up; from the teats of all the ten Useful Arts, grouped with their symbols about the central figure, there spouts a score of fine subsidiary streams. The dolphins, the sea-horses and the Tritons sport in the basin below. To the south, the ten principal cities of the Kingdom stand in a family round the Mother London, who pours from her urn an inexhaustible Thames.

Ranged round the Piazza are the Goldsmiths' Hall, the Office of Excise, the Mint, the Post Office. Their flanks are curved to the curve of the ellipse. Between pilasters, their windows look out on to the Exchange, and the sister statues on the balustrades beckon to one another across the intervening space.

Two master roads of ninety feet from wall to wall run west-wards from the Exchange. New Gate ends the more northern vista with an Arch of Triumph, whose three openings are deep, shadowy and solemn as the entries of caverns. The Guildhall and the halls of the twelve City Companies in their livery of rose-red brick, with their lacings of white stone at the coigns and round the windows, lend to the street an air of domestic and comfort-able splendour. And every two or three hundred paces the line of the houses is broken, and in the indentation of a square recess there rises, conspicuous and insular, the fantastic tower of a parish church. Spire out of dome; octagon on octagon diminish-ing upwards; cylinder on cylinder; round lanterns, lanterns of many sides; towers with airy pinnacles; clusters of pillars linked by incurving cornices, and above them, four more clusters and above once more; square towers pierced with pointed windows; spires uplifted on flying buttresses; spires bulbous at the base – the multitude of them beckons, familiar and friendly, on the sky. From the other shore, or sliding along the quiet river, you see them all, you tell over their names; and the great dome swells up in the midst overtopping them all.

The dome of St. Paul's.

The other master street that goes westward from the Piazza of the Exchange slants down towards it. The houses are of brick, plain-faced and square, arcaded at the base, so that the shops stand back from the street and the pedestrian walks dry-shod under the harmonious succession of the vaultings. And there at the end of the street, at the base of a triangular space formed by the coming together of this with another master street that runs eastwards to Tower Hill, there stands the Cathedral. To the north of it is the Deanery and under the arcades are the booksellers' shops.

From St Paul's the main road slopes down under the swaggering Italianate arches of Ludgate, past the wide lime-planted boulevards that run north and south within and without the city wall, to the edge of the Fleet Ditch – widened now into a noble canal, on whose paved banks the barges unload their freights of country stuff – leaps it on a single flying arch to climb again to a round circus, a little to the east of Temple Bar, from which, in a pair of diagonally superimposed crosses, eight roads radiate: three northwards towards Holborn, three from the opposite arc towards the river, one eastward to the City, and one past Lincoln's Inn Fields to the west. The piazza is all of brick and the houses that compose it are continuous above the ground-floor level; for the roads lead out under archways. To one who stands in the centre at the foot of the obelisk that commemorates the victory over the Dutch, it seems a smooth well of brickwork pierced by eight arched conduits at the base and diversified above by the three tiers of plain, unornamented windows.

Who shall describe all the fountains in the open places, all the statues and monuments? In the circus north of London Bridge, where the four roads come together, stands a pyramid of nymphs and Tritons – river goddesses of Polyolbion, sea-gods of the island beaches – bathing in a ceaseless tumble of white water. And here the city griffon spouts from its beak, the royal lion from between its jaws. St George at the foot of the Cathedral rides down a dragon whose nostrils spout, not fire, but the clear water of the New River. In front of the India House, four elephants of black marble, endorsed with towers of white, blow through their upturned trunks the copious symbol of Eastern wealth. In the gardens of the Tower sits Charles the Second, enthroned among a troop of Muses, Cardinal Virtues, Graces and Hours. The tower of the Customs-House is a pharos. A great water-gate, the symbol of naval triumph, spans the Fleet at its junction with the Thames. The river is embanked from Blackfriars to the Tower, and at every twenty paces a grave stone angel looks out from the piers of the balustrade across the water. ...

Gumbril Senior expounded his city with passion. He pointed to the model on the ground, he lifted his arms and turned up his eyes to suggest the size and splendour of his edifices. His hair blew wispily loose and fell into his eyes, and had to be brushed impatiently back again. He pulled at his beard; his spectacles flashed, as though they were living eyes. Looking at him, Gumbril Junior could imagine that he saw before him the passionate and gesticulating silhouette of one of those old shepherds who stand at the base of Piranesi's ruins demonstrating obscurely the prodigious grandeur and the abjection of the human race.

CHAPTER XII

'You? Is it you?' She seemed doubtful.

Gumbril nodded. 'It's me,' he reassured her. 'I've shaved; that's all.' He had left his beard in the top right-hand drawer of the chest of drawers, among the ties and the collars.

Emily looked at him judicially. 'I like you better without it,' she decided at last. 'You look nicer. Oh no, I don't mean to say you weren't nice before,' she hastened to add. 'But – you know – gentler—' She hesitated. 'It's a silly word,' she said, 'but there it is: sweeter.'

That was the unkindest cut of all. 'Milder and more melancholy?' he suggested.

'Well, if you like to put it like that,' Emily agreed.

He took her hand and raised it to his lips. 'I forgive you,' he said.

He could forgive her anything for the sake of those candid eyes, anything for the grave, serious mouth, anything for the short brown hair that curled – oh, but never seriously, never gravely – with such a hilarious extravagance round her head. He had met her, or rather the Complete Man, flushed with his commercial triumphs as he returned from his victory over Mr Boldero, had met her at the National Gallery. 'Old Masters, young mistresses'; Coleman had recommended the National Gallery. He was walking up the Venetian Room, feeling as full of swaggering vitality as the largest composition of Veronese, when he heard, gigglingly whispered just behind him, his Open Sesame to new adventure, 'Beaver'. He spun round on his tracks and found himself face to face with two rather startled young women. He frowned ferociously: he demanded satisfaction for the impertinence. They were both, he noticed, of gratifyingly pleasing appearance and both extremely young. One of them, the elder it seemed, and the more charming, as he had decided from the first, of the two, was dreadfully taken aback; blushed to the eyes, stammered apologetically. But the other, who had obviously pronounced the word, only laughed. It was she who made easy the forming of an acquaintance which ripened, half an hour later, over the tea-cups and to the strains of the most classy music on the fifth floor of Lyons' Strand Corner House.

Their names were Emily and Molly. Emily, it seemed, was married. It was Molly who let that out, and the other had been angry with her for what was evidently an indiscretion. The bald fact that Emily was married had at once been veiled with mysteries, surrounded and protected by silences; whenever the Complete Man asked a question about it, Emily did not answer and Molly only giggled. But if Emily was married and the elder of the two, Molly was decidedly the more knowledgeable about life; Mr Mercaptan would certainly have set her down as the more civilized. Emily didn't live in London; she didn't seem to live anywhere in particular. At the moment she was staying with Molly's family at Kew.

He had seen them the next day, and the day after, and the day after that; once at lunch, to desert them precipitately for his afternoon with Rosie; once at tea in Kew Gardens; once at dinner, with a theatre to follow and an extravagant taxi back to Kew at midnight. The tame decoy allays the fears of the shy wild birds; Molly, who was tame, who was frankly a flirting little wanton, had served the Complete Man as a decoy for the ensnaring of Emily. When Molly went away to stay with friends in the country, Emily was already inured and accustomed to the hunter's presence; she accepted the playful attitude of gallantry, which the Complete Man, at the invitation of Molly's rolling eyes and provocative giggle, had adopted from the first, as natural and belonging to the established order of things. With giggling Molly to give her a lead, she had gone in three days much further along the path of intimacy than, by herself, she would have advanced in ten times the number of meetings.

'It seems funny,' she had said the first time they met after Molly's departure, 'it seems funny to be seeing you without Molly.'

'It seemed funnier with Molly,' said the Complete Man. 'It wasn't Molly I wanted to see.'

'Molly's a very nice, dear girl,' she declared loyally. 'Besides, she's amusing and can talk. And I can't; I'm not a bit amusing.'

It wasn't difficult to retort to that sort of thing; but Emily didn't believe in compliments; oh, quite genuinely not.

He set out to make the exploration of her; and now that she was inured to him, no longer too frightened to let him approach, now, moreover, that he had abandoned the jocular insolences of the Complete Man in favour of a more native mildness, which he felt instinctively was more suitable in this particular case, she laid no difficulties in his way. She was lonely, and he seemed to understand everything so well; in the unknown country of her spirit and her history she was soon going eagerly before him a his guide.

She was an orphan. Her mother she hardly remembered. Her father had died of influenza when she was fifteen. One of his business friends used to come and see her at school, take her out for treats and give her chocolates. She used to call him Uncle Stanley. He was a leather merchant, fat and jolly with a rather red face, very white teeth and a bald head that was beautifully shiny. When she was seventeen and a half he asked her to marry him, and she had said yes.

'But why?' Gumbril asked. 'Why on earth?' he repeated.

'He said he'd take me round the world; it was just when the war had come to an end. Round the world, you know; and I didn't like school. I didn't know anything about it and he was very nice to me; he was very pressing. I didn't know what marriage meant.'

'Didn't know?'

She shook her head; it was quite true. 'But not in the least.'

And she had been born within the twentieth century. It seemed a case for the text-books of sexual psychology. 'Mrs Emily X, born in 1901, was found to be in a state of perfect innocence and ignorance at the time of the Armistice, 11th November 1918,' etc.

'And so you married him?'

She had nodded.

'And then?'

She had covered her face with her hands, she had shuddered.

The amateur uncle, now professionally a husband, had come to claim his rights – drunk. She had fought him, she had eluded him, had run away and locked herself into another room. On the second night of her honeymoon he gave her a bruise on the forehead and a bite on the left breast which had gone on septic- ally festering for weeks. On the fourth, more determined than ever, he seized her so violently by the throat, that a blood-vessel broke and she began coughing bright blood over the bed- clothes. The amateur uncle had been reduced to send for a doctor and Emily had spent the next few weeks in a nursing home. That was four years ago; her husband had tried to induce her to come back, but Emily had refused. She had a little money of her own; she was able to refuse. The amateur uncle had con- soled himself with other and more docile nieces.

'And has nobody tried to make love to you since then?' he asked.

'Oh, lots of them have tried.'

'And not succeeded?'

She shook her head. 'I don't like men,' she said. 'They're hateful, most of them. They're brutes.'

'*Anch' io?*'

'What?' she asked, puzzled.

'Am I a brute too?' And behind his beard, suddenly, he felt rather a brute.

'No,' said Emily, after a little hesitation, 'you're different. At least I think you are; though sometimes,' she added candidly, 'sometimes you do and say things which make me wonder if you really are different.'

The Complete Man laughed.

'Don't laugh like that,' she said. 'It's rather stupid.'

'You're perfectly right,' said Gumbril. 'It is.'

And how did she spend her time? He continued the explora- tion.

Well, she read a lot of books; but most of the novels she got from Boots' seemed to her rather silly.

'Too much about the same thing. Always love.'

The Complete Man gave a shrug. 'Such is life.'

'Well, it oughtn't to be,' said Emily.

371

And then, when she was in the country – and she was often in the country, taking lodgings here and there in little villages, weeks and months at a time – she went for long walks. Molly couldn't understand why she liked the country; but she did. She was very fond of flowers. She liked them more than people, she thought.

'I wish I could paint,' she said. 'If I could, I'd be happy for ever, just painting flowers. But I can't paint.' She shook her head. 'I've tried so often. Such dirty, ugly smudges come out on the paper; and it's all so lovely in my head, so lovely out in the fields.'

Gumbril began talking with erudition about the flora of West Surrey: where you could find butterfly orchis and green man and the bee, the wood where there was actually wild columbine growing, the best localities for butcher's broom, the outcrops of clay where you get wild daffodils. All this odd knowledge came spouting up into his mind from some underground source of memory. Flowers – he never thought about flowers nowadays from one year's end to the other. But his mother had liked flowers. Every spring and summer they used to go down to stay at their cottage in the country. All their walks, all their drives in the governess cart had been hunts after flowers. And naturally the child had hunted with all his mother's ardour. He had kept books of pressed flowers, he had mummified them in hot sand, he had drawn maps of the country and coloured them elaborately with different coloured inks to show where the different flowers grew. How long ago all that was! Horribly long ago! Many seeds had fallen in the stony places of his spirit, to spring luxuriantly up into stalky plants and wither again because they had no deepness of earth; many had been sown there and had died, since his mother scattered the seeds of the wild flowers.

'And if you want sundew,' he wound up, 'you'll find it in the Punch Bowl, under Hindhead. Or round about Frensham. The Little Pond, you know, not the Big.'

'But you know all about them,' Emily exclaimed in delight. 'I'm ashamed of my poor little knowledge. And you must really love them as much as I do.'

Gumbril did not deny it; they were linked henceforth by a chain of flowers.

But what else did she do?

Oh, of course she played the piano a great deal. Very badly; but at any rate it gave her pleasure. Beethoven: she liked Beethoven best. More or less, she knew all the sonatas, though she could never keep up anything like the right speed in the difficult parts.

Gumbril had again shown himself wonderfully at home. 'Aha!' he said. 'I bet you can't shake that low B in the last variation but one of Op. 106 so that it doesn't sound ridiculous.'

And of course she couldn't, and of course she was glad that he knew all about it and how impossible it was.

In the cab, as they drove back to Kew that evening, the Complete Man had decided it was time to do something decisive. The parting kiss – more of a playful sonorous buss than a serious embracement – that was already in the protocol, as signed and sealed before her departure by giggling Molly. It was time, the Complete Man considered, that this salute should take on a character less formal and less playful. One, two, three and, decisively, as they passed through Hammersmith Broadway, he risked the gesture. Emily burst into tears. He was not prepared for that, though perhaps he should have been. It was only by imploring, only by almost weeping himself, that Gumbril persuaded her to revoke her decision never, never to see him again.

'I had thought you were different,' she sobbed. 'And now, now –'

'Please, please,' he entreated. He was on the point of tearing off his beard and confessing everything there and then. But that, on second thoughts, would probably only make things worse.

'Please, I promise.'

In the end, she had consented to see him once again, provisionally, in Kew Gardens, on the following day. They were to meet at the little temple that stands on the hillock above the valley of the heathers.

And now, duly, they had met. The Complete Man had been left at home in the top right-hand drawer, along with the ties and collars. She would prefer, he guessed, the Mild and Melancholy

373

one; he was quite right. She had thought him 'sweeter' at a first glimpse.

'I forgive you,' he said, and kissed her hand. 'I forgive you.'

Hand in hand they walked down towards the valley of the heaths.

'I don't know why you should be forgiving me,' she said, laughing. 'It seems to me that I ought to be doing the forgiving. After yesterday.' She shook her head at him. 'You made me so wretched.'

'Ah, but you've already done your forgiving.'

'You seem to take it very much for granted,' said Emily. 'Don't be too sure.'

'But I am sure,' said Gumbril. 'I can see –'

Emily laughed again. 'I feel happy,' she declared.

'So do I.'

'How green the grass is!'

Green, green – after these long damp months it glowed in the sunlight, as though it were lighted from inside.

'And the trees!'

The pale, high, clot-polled trees of the English spring; the dark, symmetrical pine trees, islanded here and there on the lawns, each with its own separate profile against the sky and its own shadow, impenetrably dark or freckled with moving lights, on the grass at its feet.

They walked on in silence. Gumbril took off his hat, breathed the soft air that smelt of the greenness of the garden.

'There are quiet places also in the mind,' he said meditatively. 'But we build bandstands and factories on them. Deliberately – to put a stop to the quietness. We don't like the quietness. All the thoughts, all the preoccupations in my head – round and round, continually.' He made a circular motion with his hand. 'And the jazz bands, the music-hall songs, the boys shouting the news. What's it for? what's it all for? To put an end to the quiet, to break it up and disperse it, to pretend at any cost it isn't there. Ah, but it is; it is there, in spite of everything, at the back of everything. Lying awake at night, sometimes – not restlessly, but serenely, waiting for sleep – the quiet re-establishes itself, piece by piece; all the broken bits, all the fragments of it we've been so

374

busily dispersing all day long. It re-establishes itself, an inward quiet, like this outward quiet of grass and trees. It fills one, it grows – a crystal quiet, a growing, expanding crystal. It grows, it becomes more perfect; it is beautiful and terrifying, yes, terrifying as well as beautiful. For one's alone in the crystal and there's no support from outside, there's nothing external and important, nothing external and trivial to pull oneself up by or to stand on, superiorly, contemptuously, so that one can look down. There's nothing to laugh at or feel enthusiastic about. But the quiet grows and grows. Beautifully and unbearably. And at last you are conscious of something approaching; it is almost a faint sound of footsteps. Something inexpressibly lovely and wonderful advances through the crystal, nearer, nearer. And, oh, inexpressibly terrifying. For if it were to touch you, if it were to seize and engulf you, you'd die; all the regular, habitual, daily part of you would die. There would be an end of bandstands and whizzing factories, and one would have to begin living arduously in the quiet, arduously in some strange, unheard-of manner. Nearer, nearer come the steps; but one can't face the advancing thing. One daren't. It's too terrifying, it's too painful to die. Quickly, before it is too late, start the factory wheels, bang the drum, blow up the saxophone. Think of the women you'd like to sleep with, the schemes for making money, the gossip about your friends, the last outrage of the politicians. Anything for a diversion. Break the silence, smash the crystal to pieces. There, it lies in bits; it is easily broken, hard to build up and easy to break. And the steps? Ah, those have taken themselves off, double quick. Double quick, they were gone at the first flawing of the crystal. And by this time the lovely and terrifying thing is three infinities away, at least. And you lie tranquilly on your bed, thinking of what you'd do if you had ten thousand pounds, and of all the fornications you'll never commit.' He thought of Rosie's pink underclothes.

'You make things very complicated,' she said, after a silence.

Gumbril spread out his great-coat on a green bank and they sat down. Leaning back, his hands under his head, he watched her sitting there beside him. She had taken off her hat; there was a stir of wind in those childish curls, and at the nape, at the temples, where the hair had sleaved out thin and fine, the sunlight made little misty haloes of gold. Her hands clasped round her knees, she sat quite still, looking out across the green expanses, at the trees, at the white clouds on the horizon. There was quiet in her mind, he thought. She was native to that crystal world; for her, the steps came comfortingly through the silence and the lovely thing brought with it no terrors. It was all so easy for her and simple.

Ah, so simple, so simple; like the Hire Purchase System on which Rosie had bought her pink bed. And how simple it was, too, to puddle clear waters and unpetal every flower! – every wild flower, by God! one ever passed in a governess cart at the heels of a barrel-bellied pony. How simple to spit on the floors of churches! *Si prega di non sputare.* Simple to kick one's legs and enjoy oneself – dutifully – in pink underclothing. Perfectly simple.

'It's like the Arietta, don't you think?' said Emily suddenly, 'the Arietta of Op. 111.' And she hummed the first bars of the air. 'Don't you feel it's like that?'

'What's like that?'

'Everything,' said Emily. 'To-day, I mean. You and me. These gardens –' And she went on humming.

Gumbril shook his head. 'Too simple for me,' he said.

Emily laughed. 'Ah, but then think how impossible it gets a little farther on.' She agitated her fingers wildly, as though she were trying to play the impossible passages. 'It begins easily for the sake of poor imbeciles like me; but it goes on, it goes on, more and more fully and subtly and abstrusely and embracingly. But it's still the same movement.'

The shadows stretched farther and farther across the lawns, and as the sun declined the level light picked out among the grasses innumerable stipplings of shadow; and in the paths, that had seemed under the more perpendicular rays as level as a table, a thousand little shadowy depressions and sun-touched mountains were now apparent. Gumbril looked at his watch.

'Good Lord!' he said, 'we must fly.' He jumped up. 'Quick, quick!'

'But why?'

'We shall be late.' He wouldn't tell her for what. 'Wait and see' was all that Emily could get out of him by her questioning. They hurried out of the gardens, and in spite of her protests he insisted on taking a taxi into town. 'I have such a lot of unearned increment to get rid of,' he explained. The Patent Small-Clothes seemed at the moment remoter than the farthest stars.

CHAPTER XIII

In spite of the taxi, in spite of the gobbled dinner, they were late. The concert had begun.

'Never mind,' said Gumbril. 'We shall get in in time for the minuetto. It's then that the fun really begins.'

'Sour grapes,' said Emily, putting her ear to the door. 'It sounds to me simply too lovely.'

They stood outside, like beggars waiting abjectly at the doors of a banqueting-hall – stood and listened to the snatches of music that came out tantalizingly from within. A rattle of clapping announced at last that the first movement was over; the doors were thrown open. Hungrily they rushed in. The Sclopis Quartet and a subsidiary viola were bowing from the platform. There was a chirrup of tuning, then preliminary silence. Sclopis nodded and moved his bow. The minuetto of Mozart's G minor Quintet broke out, phrase after phrase, short and decisive, with every now and then a violent sforzando chord, startling in its harsh and sudden emphasis.

Minuetto – all civilization, Mr Mercaptan would have said, was implied in the delicious word, the delicate, pretty thing. Ladies and precious gentlemen, fresh from the wit and gallantry of Crebillon-haunted sofas, stepping gracefully to a pattern of airy notes. To this passion of one who cries out, to this obscure and angry argument with fate how would they, Gumbril wondered, how would they have tripped it?

How pure the passion, how unaffected, clear and without clot or pretension the unhappiness of that slow movement which followed! Blessed are the pure in heart, for they shall see God. Pure and unsullied; pure and unmixed, unadulterated. 'Not passionate, thank God; only sensual and sentimental.' In the name of earwig. Amen. Pure, pure. Worshippers have tried to rape the statues of the gods; the statuaries who made the images were generally to blame. And how deliciously, too, an artist can suffer! and, in the face of the whole Albert Hall, with what an effective gesture and grimace! But blessed are the pure in heart, for they shall see God. The instruments come together and part again. Long silver threads hang aerially over a murmur of waters; in the midst of muffled sobbing a cry. The fountains blow their architecture of slender pillars, and from basin to basin the waters fall; from basin to basin, and every fall makes somehow possible a higher leaping of the jet, and at the last fall the mounting column springs up into the sunlight, and from water the music has modulated up into a rainbow. Blessed are the pure in heart, for they shall see God; they shall make God visible, too, to other eyes.

Blood beats in the ears. Beat, beat, beat. A slow drum in the darkness, beating in the ears of one who lies wakeful with fever, with the sickness of too much misery. It beats unceasingly, in the ears, in the mind itself. Body and mind are indivisible, and in the spirit blood painfully throbs. Sad thoughts droop through the mind. A small, pure light comes swaying down through the darkness, comes to rest, resigning itself to the obscurity of its misfortune. There is resignation, but blood still beats in the ears. Blood still painfully beats, though the mind has acquiesced. And then, suddenly, the mind exerts itself, throws off the fever of too much suffering and laughing, commands the body to dance. The introduction to the last movement comes to its suspended, throbbing close. There is an instant of expectation, and then, with a series of mounting trochees and a downward hurrying, step after tiny step, in triple time, the dance begins. Irrelevant, irreverent, out of key with all that has gone before. But man's greatest strength lies in his capacity for irrelevance. In the midst of pestilences, wars and famines, he builds cathedrals; and a slave, he can think the irrelevant and unsuitable thoughts of a free man. The spirit is slave to fever and beating blood, at the mercy of an obscure and tyrannous misfortune. But irrelevantly, it elects to dance in triple measure – a mounting skip, a patter of descending feet.

The G minor Quintet is at an end; the applause rattles out loudly. Enthusiasts stand up and cry bravo. And the five men on the platform rise and bow their acknowledgments. Great Sclopis himself receives his share of the plaudits with a weary condescension; weary are his poached eyes, weary his disillusioned smile. It is only his due, he knows; but he has had so much clapping, so many lovely women. He has a Roman nose, a colossal brow and, though the tawny musical mane does much to conceal the fact, no back to his head. Garofalo, the second fiddle, is black, beady-eyed and pot-bellied. The convex reflections of the electroliers slide back and forth over his polished bald head, as he bends, again, again, in little military salutes. Peperkoek, two metres high, bows with a sinuous politeness. His face, his hair are all of the same greyish buff colour; he does not smile, his appearance is monolithic and grim. Not so exuberant Knoedler, who sweats and smiles and embraces his 'cello and lays his hand to his heart and bows almost to the ground as though all this hullabaloo were directed only at him. As for poor little Mr Jenkins, the subsidiary viola, he has slid away into the background, and feeling that this is really the Sclopis's show and that he, a mere intruder, has no right to any of these demonstrations, he hardly bows at all, but only smiles, vaguely and nervously, and from time to time makes a little spasmodic twitch to show that he isn't really ungrateful or haughty, as you might think, but that he feels in the circumstances – the position is a little embarrassing – it is hard to explain. ...

'Strange,' said Gumbril, 'to think that those ridiculous creatures could have produced what we've just been hearing.'

The poached eye of Sclopis lighted on Emily, flushed and ardently applauding. He gave her, all to herself, a weary smile. He would have a letter, he guessed, to-morrow morning signed 'Your little Admirer in the Third Row'. She looked a choice little piece. He smiled again to encourage her. Emily, alas! had not even noticed. She was applauding the music.

'Did you enjoy it?' he asked, as they stepped out into a deserted Bond Street.

'Did I ...?' Emily laughed expressively. 'No, I didn't enjoy,' she said. 'Enjoy isn't the word. You enjoy eating ices. It made me happy. It's unhappy music, but it made me happy.'

Gumbril hailed a cab and gave the address of his rooms in Great Russell Street. 'Happy,' he repeated, as they sat there side by side in the darkness. He, too, was happy.

380

'Where are we going?' she asked.

'To my rooms,' said Gumbril, 'we shall be quiet there.' He was afraid she might object to going there – after yesterday. But she made no comment.

'Some people think that it's only possible to be happy if one makes a noise,' she said, after a pause. 'I find it's too delicate and melancholy for noise. Being happy is rather melancholy – like the most beautiful landscape, like those trees and the grass and the clouds and the sunshine to-day.'

'From the outside,' said Gumbril, 'it even looks rather dull.' They stumbled up the dark staircase to his rooms. Gumbril lit a pair of candles and put the kettle on the gas ring. They sat together on the divan sipping tea. In the rich, soft light of the candles she looked different, more beautiful. The silk of her dress seemed wonderfully rich and glossy, like the petals of a tulip, and on her face, on her bare arms and neck the light seemed to spread an impalpable bright bloom. On the wall behind them, their shadows ran up towards the ceiling, enormous and profoundly black.

'How unreal it is,' Gumbril whispered. 'Not true. This remote secret room. These lights and shadows out of another time. And you out of nowhere and I, out of a past utterly remote from yours, sitting together here, together – and being happy. That's the strangest thing of all. Being quite senselessly happy It's unreal, unreal.'

'But why,' said Emily, 'why? It's here and happening now. It *is* real.'

'It all might vanish, at any moment,' he said.

Emily smiled rather sadly. 'It'll vanish in due time,' she said. 'Quite naturally, not by magic; it'll vanish the way everything else vanishes and changes. But it's here now.'

They gave themselves up to the enchantment. The candles burned, two shining eyes of flame, without a wink, minute after minute. But for them there were no longer any minutes. Emily leaned against him, her body held in the crook of his arm, her head resting on his shoulder. He caressed his cheek against her hair; sometimes, very gently, he kissed her forehead or her closed eyes.

381

'If I had known you years ago ...' she sighed. 'But I was a silly little idiot then. I shouldn't have noticed any difference between you and anybody else.'

'I shall be very jealous,' Emily spoke again after another timeless silence. 'There must never be anybody else, never the shadow of anybody else.'

'There never will be anybody else,' said Gumbril.

Emily smiled and opened her eyes, looked up at him. 'Ah, not here,' she said, 'not in this real unreal room. Not during this eternity. But there will be other rooms just as real as this.'

'Not so real, not so real.' He bent his face towards hers. She closed her eyes again, and the lids fluttered with a sudden tremulous movement at the touch of his light kiss.

For them there were no more minutes. But time passed, time passed flowing in a dark stream, stanchlessly, as though from some profound mysterious wound in the world's side, bleeding, bleeding for ever. One of the candles had burned down to the socket and the long, smoky flame wavered unsteadily. The flickering light troubled their eyes; the shadows twitched and stirred uneasily. Emily looked up at him.

'What's the time?' she said.

Gumbril looked at his watch. It was nearly one o'clock. 'Too late for you to get back,' he said.

'Too late?' Emily sat up. Ah, the enchantment was breaking, was giving way, like a film of ice beneath a weight, like a web before a thrust of the wind. They looked at one another. 'What shall I do?' she asked.

'You could sleep here,' Gumbril answered in a voice that came from a long way away.

She sat for a long time in silence, looking through half-closed eyes at the expiring candle flame. Gumbril watched her in an agony of suspense. Was the ice to be broken, the web-work finally and for ever torn? The enchantment could still be prolonged, the eternity renewed. He felt his heart beating in his breast; he held his breath. It would be terrible if she were to go now, it would be a kind of death. The flame of the candle flickered more violently, leaping up in a thin, long, smoky flare,

sinking again almost to darkness. Emily got up and blew out the candle. The other still burned calmly and steadily.

'May I stay?' she asked. 'Will you allow me?'

He understood the meaning of her question, and nodded. 'Of course,' he said.

'Of course? Is it as much of course as all that?'

'When I say so.' He smiled at her. The eternity had been renewed, the enchantment prolonged. There was no need to think of anything now but the moment. The past was forgotten, the future abolished. There was only this secret room and the candlelight and the unreal, impossible happiness of being two. Now that this peril of a disenchantment had been averted, it would last for ever. He got up from the couch, crossed the room, he took her hands and kissed them.

'Shall we sleep now?' she asked.

Gumbril nodded.

'Do you mind if I blow out the light?' And without waiting for his answer, Emily turned, gave a puff, and the room was in darkness. He heard the rustling of her undressing. Hastily he stripped off his own clothes, pulled back the coverlet from the divan. The bed was made and ready; he opened it and slipped between the sheets. A dim greenish light from the gas lamp in the street below came up between the parted curtains illuminating faintly the farther end of the room. Against this tempered darkness he could see her, silhouetted, standing quite still, as if hesitating on some invisible brink.

'Emily,' he whispered.

'I'm coming,' Emily answered. She stood there, unmoving, a few seconds longer, then overstepped the brink. She came silently across the room, and sat down on the edge of the low couch. Gumbril lay perfectly still, without speaking, waiting in the enchanted timeless darkness. Emily lifted her knees, slid her feet in under the sheet, then stretched herself out beside him, her body, in the narrow bed, touching his. Gumbril felt that she was trembling; trembling, a sharp involuntary start, a little shudder, another start.

'You're cold,' he said, and slipping one arm beneath her shoulders he drew her, limp and unresisting, towards him. She lay there, pressed against him. Gradually the trembling ceased. Quite still, quite still in the calm of the enchantment. The past is forgotten, the future abolished; there is only this dark and ever-lasting moment. A drugged and intoxicated stupor of happiness possessed his spirit; a numbness, warm and delicious, lay upon him. And yet through the stupor he knew with a dreadful anxious certainty that the end would soon be there. Like a man on the night before his execution, he looked forward through the endless present; he foresaw the end of his eternity. And after? Everything was uncertain and unsafe.

Very gently, he began caressing her shoulder, her long slender arm, drawing his finger-tips lightly and slowly over her smooth skin; slowly from her neck, over her shoulder, lingeringly round the elbow to her hand. Again, again: he was learning her arm. The form of it was part of the knowledge, now, of his finger-tips; his fingers knew it as they knew a piece of music, as they knew Mozart's Twelfth Sonata, for example. And the themes that crowd so quickly one after another at the beginning of the first movement played themselves aerially, glitteringly in his mind; they became a part of the enchantment.

Through the silk of her shift he learned her curving side, her smooth straight back and the ridge of her spine. He stretched down, touched her feet, her knees. Under the smock he learned her warm body, lightly, slowly caressing. He knew her, his fingers, he felt, could build her up, a warm and curving statue in the darkness. He did not desire her; to desire would have been to break the enchantment. He let himself sink deeper and deeper into his dark stupor of happiness. She was asleep in his arms; and soon he too was asleep.

CHAPTER XIV

MRS VIVEASH descended the steps into King Street, and standing there on the pavement looked dubiously first to the right and then to the left. Little and loud, the taxis rolled by on their white wheels, the long-snouted limousines passed with a sigh. The air smelt of watered dust, tempered in Mrs Viveash's immediate neighbourhood by those memories of Italian jasmines which were her perfume. On the opposite pavement, in the shade, two young men, looking very conscious of their grey top-hats, marched gravely along.

Life, Mrs Viveash thought, looked a little dim this morning, in spite of the fine weather. She glanced at her watch; it was one o'clock. Soon one would have to eat some lunch. But where, and with whom? Mrs Viveash had no engagements. All the world was before her, she was absolutely free, all day long. Yesterday, when she declined all those pressing invitations, the prospect had seemed delightful. Liberty, no complications, no contacts; a pre-Adamite empty world to do what she liked in.

But to-day, when it came to the point, she hated her liberty. To come out like this at one o'clock into a vacuum – it was absurd, it was appalling. The prospect of immeasurable boredom opened before her. Steppes after steppes of ennui, horizon beyond horizon, for ever the same. She looked again to the right and again to the left. Finally she decided to go to the left. Slowly, walking along her private knife-edge between her personal abysses, she walked towards the left. She remembered suddenly one shining day like this in the summer of 1917, when she had walked along this same street, slowly, like this, on the sunny side, with Tony Lamb. All that day, that night, it had been one long good-bye. He was going back the next morning. Less than a week later he was dead. Never again, never again: there had been a time when she could make herself cry, simply by saying those two words once or twice, under her breath. Never again, never again. She repeated them softly now. But she felt no tears behind her eyes. Grief doesn't kill, love doesn't kill; but time kills everything, kills desire, kills sorrow, kills in the end the mind that feels them; wrinkles and softens the body while it still lives, rots it like a medlar, kills it too at last. Never again, never again. Instead of crying, she laughed, laughed aloud. The pigeon-breasted old gentleman who had just passed her, twirling between his finger and thumb the ends of a white military moustache, turned round startled. Could she be laughing at him?

'Never again,' murmured Mrs Viveash.

'I beg your pardon?' queried the martial gentleman, in a rich, port-winey, cigary voice.

Mrs Viveash looked at him with such wide-eyed astonishment that the old gentleman was quite taken aback. 'A thousand apologies, dear lady. Thought you were addressing ... H'm, ah'm.' He replaced his hat, squared his shoulders and went off smartly, left, right, bearing preciously before him his pigeon breast. Poor thing, he thought, poor young thing. Talking to herself. Must be cracked, must be off her head. Or perhaps she took drugs. That was more likely: that was much more likely. Most of them did nowadays. Vicious young women. Lesbians, drug-fiends, nymphomaniacs, dipsos – thoroughly vicious, nowadays, thoroughly vicious. He arrived at his club in an excellent temper.

Never again, never, never again. Mrs Viveash would have liked to be able to cry.

St James's Square opened before her. Romantically under its trees the statue pranced. The trees gave her an idea: she might go down into the country for the afternoon, take a cab and drive out, out, goodness only knew where! To the top of a hill somewhere. Box Hill, Leith Hill, Holmbury Hill, Ivinghoe Beacon – any hill where one could sit and look out over plains. One might do worse than that with one's liberty.

But not much worse, she reflected.

Mrs Viveash had turned up towards the northern side of the square and was almost at its north-western corner when, with a thrill of genuine delight, with a sense of the most profound relief she saw a familiar figure, running down the steps of the London Library.

'Theodore!' she hallooed faintly but penetratingly, from her inward death-bed. 'Gumbril!' She waved her parasol.

Gumbril halted, looked around, came smiling to meet her. 'How delightful,' he said, 'but how unfortunate.'

'Why unfortunate?' asked Mrs Viveash. 'Am I of evil omen?'

'Unfortunate,' Gumbril explained, 'because I've got to catch a train and can't profit by this meeting.'

'Ah no, Theodore,' said Mrs Viveash, 'you're not going to catch a train. You're going to come and lunch with me. Providence has decreed it. You can't say no to Providence.'

'I must,' Gumbril shook his head. 'I've said yes to somebody else.'

'To whom?'

'Ah!' said Gumbril, with a coy and saucy mysteriousness.

'And where are you going in your famous train?'

'Ah again,' Gumbril answered.

'How intolerably tiresome and silly you are!' Mrs Viveash declared. 'One would think you were a sixteen-year-old schoolboy going out for his first assignation with a shop girl. At your age, Gumbril!' She shook her head, smiled agonizingly and with contempt. 'Who is she? What sordid pick-up?'

'Not sordid in the least,' protested Gumbril.

'But decidedly a pick-up. Eh?' A banana-skin was lying, like a bedraggled starfish, in the gutter, just in front of where they were standing. Mrs Viveash stepped forward and with the point of her parasol lifted it carefully up and offered it to her companion.

'*Merci*,' Gumbril bowed.

She tossed the skin back again into the gutter. 'In any case,' she said, 'the young lady can wait while we have luncheon.'

Gumbril shook his head. 'I've made the arrangement,' he said. Emily's letter was in his pocket. She had taken the loveliest cottage just out of Robertsbridge, in Sussex. Ah, but the loveliest imaginable. For the whole summer. He could come and see her there. He had telegraphed that he would come to-day, this afternoon, by the two o'clock from Charing Cross.

Mrs Viveash took him by the elbow. 'Come along,' she said. 'There's a post office in that passage going from Jermyn Street to Piccadilly. You can wire from there your infinite regrets.

These things always improve with a little keeping. There will be raptures when you *do* go to-morrow.'

Gumbril allowed himself to be led along. 'What an insuffer-able woman you are,' he said, laughing.

'Instead of being grateful to me for asking you to luncheon!'

'Oh, I am grateful,' said Gumbril. 'And astonished.'

He looked at her. Mrs Viveash smiled and fixed him for a moment with her pale, untroubled eyes. ... She said nothing.

'Still,' Gumbril went on, 'I must be at Charing Cross by two, you know.'

'But we're lunching at Verrey's.'

Gumbril shook his head.

They were at the corner of Jermyn Street. Mrs Viveash halted and delivered her ultimatum, the more impressive for being spoken in that expiring voice of one who says *in articulo* the final and supremely important things. 'We lunch at Verrey's, Theodore, or I shall never, never speak to you again.'

'But be reasonable, Myra,' he implored. If only he'd told her that he had a business appointment. ... Imbecile, to have dropped those stupid hints – in that tone!

'I prefer not to be,' said Mrs Viveash.

Gumbril made a gesture of despair and was silent. He thought of Emily in her native quiet among the flowers; in a cottage altogether too cottagey, with honeysuckles and red ramblers and hollyhocks – though, on second thoughts, none of them would be blooming yet, would they? – happily, in white muslin, ex-tracting from the cottage piano the easier sections of the Arietta. A little absurd, perhaps, when you considered her like that; but exquisite, but adorable, but pure of heart and flawless in her bright pellucid integrity, complete as a crystal in its faceted per-fection. She would be waiting for him, expecting him; and they would walk through the twiddly lanes – or perhaps there would be a governess cart for hire, with a fat pony like a tub on legs to pull it – they would look for flowers in the woods and perhaps he would still remember what sort of noise a whitethroat makes; or even if he didn't remember, he could always magisterially say he did. 'That's a whitethroat, Emily. Do you hear? The one that goes "Tweedly, weedly, weedledy dee".'

388

'I'm waiting,' said Mrs Viveash. 'Patiently, however.'

Gumbril looked at her and found her smiling like a tragic mask. After all, he reflected, Emily would still be there if he went down to-morrow. It would be stupid to quarrel with Myra about something that was really, when he came to think of it, not of enormous importance. It was stupid to quarrel with any one about anything; and with Myra and about this, particularly so. In this white dress patterned with flowing arabesques of black she looked, he thought, more than ever enchanting. There had been times in the past. ... The past leads on to the present. ... No; but in any case she was excellent company.

'Well,' he said, sighing decisively, 'let's go and send my wire.'

Mrs Viveash made no comment, and traversing Jermyn Street they walked up the narrow passage under the lee of Wren's bald barn of St James's, to the post office.

'I shall pretext a catastrophe,' said Gumbril, as they entered; and going to the telegraph desk he wrote: 'Slight accident on way to station not serious at all but a little indisposed come same train to-morrow.' He addressed the form and handed it in.

'A little what?' asked the young lady behind the bars, as she read it through, prodding each successive word with the tip of her blunt pencil.

'A little indisposed,' said Gumbril, and he felt suddenly very much ashamed of himself. 'A little indisposed,' – no, really, that was too much. He'd withdraw the telegram, he'd go after all.

'Ready?' asked Mrs Viveash, coming up from the other end of the counter where she had been buying stamps.

Gumbril pushed a florin under the bars.

'A little indisposed,' he said, hooting with laughter, and he walked towards the door leaning heavily on his stick and limping. 'Slight accident,' he explained.

'What is the meaning of this clownery?' Mrs Viveash inquired.

'What indeed?' Gumbril had limped up to the door and stood there, holding it open for her. He was taking no responsibility for himself. It was the clown's doing, and the clown, poor creature, was *non compos*, not entirely there, and couldn't be called to account for his actions. He limped after her towards Piccadilly.

'*Giudicato guarabile in cinque giorni*,' Mrs Viveash laughed. 'How charming that always is in the Italian papers. The fickle lady, the jealous lover, the stab, the *colpo di rivoltella*, the mere Anglo-Saxon black eye – all judged by the house surgeon at the Misericordia curable in five days. And you, my poor Gumbril, are you curable in five days?'

'That depends,' said Gumbril. 'There may be complications.'

Mrs Viveash waved her parasol; a taxi came swerving to the pavement's edge in front of them. 'Meanwhile,' she said, 'you can't be expected to walk.'

At Verrey's they lunched off lobsters and white wine. 'Fish suppers,' Gumbril quoted jovially from the Restoration, 'fish suppers will make a man hop like a flea.' Through the whole meal he clowned away in the most inimitable style. The ghost of a governess cart rolled along the twiddly lanes of Robertsbridge. But one can refuse to accept responsibility; a clown cannot be held accountable. And besides, when the future and the past are abolished, when it is only the present instant, whether enchanted or unenchanted, that counts, when there are no causes or motives, no future consequences to be considered, how can there be responsibility, even for those who are not clowns? He drank a great deal of hock, and when the clock struck two and the train had begun to snort out of Charing Cross, he could not refrain from proposing the health of Viscount Lascelles. After that he began telling Mrs Viveash about his adventure as a Complete Man.

'You should have seen me,' he said, describing his beard.

'I should have been bowled over.'

'You shall see me, then,' said Gumbril. 'Ah, what a Don Giovanni. *La ci darem la mano, La mi dirai di si, Vieni, non e lontano, Partiam, ben mio, da qui.* And they came, they came. Without hesitation. No "*vorrei e non vorrei*", no "*mi trema un poco il cor.*" Straight away.'

'*Felice, io so, sarei*,' Mrs Viveash sang very faintly under her breath, from a remote bed of agony.

Ah, happiness, happiness; a little dull, some one had wisely

390

said, when you looked at it from outside. An affair of duets at the cottage piano, of collecting specimens, hand in hand, for the *hortus siccus*. A matter of integrity and quietness.

'Ah, but the history of the young woman who was married four years ago,' exclaimed Gumbril with clownish rapture, 'and remains to this day a virgin – what an episode in my memoirs!' In the enchanted darkness he had learned her young body. He looked at his fingers; her beauty was a part of their knowledge. On the tablecloth he drummed out the first bars of the Twelfth Sonata of Mozart. 'And even after singing her duet with the Don,' he continued, 'she is still virgin. There are chaste pleasures, sublimated sensualities. More thrillingly voluptuous,' with the gesture of a restaurant-keeper who praises the speciality of the house, he blew a treacly kiss, 'than any of the grosser deliriums.'

'What is all this about?' asked Mrs Viveash.

Gumbril finished off his glass. 'I am talking esoterically,' he said, 'for my own pleasure, not yours.'

'But tell me more about the beard,' Mrs Viveash insisted. 'I liked the beard so much.'

'All right,' said Gumbril, 'let us try to be unworthy with coherence.'

They sat for a long time over their cigarettes; it was half past three before Mrs Viveash suggested they should go.

'Almost time,' she said, looking at her watch, 'to have tea. One damned meal after another. And never anything new to eat. And every year one gets bored with another of the old things. Lobster, for instance, how I used to adore lobster once! But to-day – well, really, it was only your conversation, Theodore, that made it tolerable.'

Gumbril put his hand to his heart and bowed. He felt suddenly extremely depressed.

'And wine: I used to think Orvieto so heavenly. But this spring, when I went to Italy, it was just a bad muddy sort of Vouvray. And those soft caramels they call Fiats; I used to eat those till I was sick. I was at the sick stage before I'd finished one of them, this time in Rome.' Mrs Viveash shook her head. 'Disillusion after disillusion.'

They walked down the dark passage into the street.

'We'll go home,' said Mrs Viveash. 'I really haven't the spirit to do anything else this afternoon.' To the commissionaire who opened the door of the cab she gave the address of her house in St James's.

'Will one ever recapture the old thrills?' she asked rather fatiguedly as they drove slowly through the traffic of Regent Street.

'Not by chasing after them,' said Gumbril, in whom the clown had quite evaporated. 'If one sat still enough they might perhaps come back of their own accord. ...' There would be the faint sound as it were of feet approaching through the quiet.

'It isn't only food,' said Mrs Viveash, who had closed her eyes and was leaning back in her corner.

'So I can well believe.'

'It's everything. Nothing's the same now. I feel it never will be.'

'Never more,' croaked Gumbril.

'Never again,' Mrs Viveash echoed. 'Never again.' There were still no tears behind her eyes. 'Did you ever know Tony Lamb?' she asked.

'No,' Gumbril answered from his corner. 'What about him?'

Mrs Viveash did not answer. What, indeed, about him? She thought of his very clear blue eyes and the fair, bright hair that had been lighter than his brown face. Brown face and neck, red-brown hands; and all the rest of his skin was as white as milk. 'I was very fond of him,' she said at last. 'That's all. He was killed in 1917, just about this time of the year. It seems a very long time ago, don't you think?'

'Does it?' Gumbril shrugged his shoulders. 'I don't know. The past is abolished. *Vivamus, mea Lesbia.* If I weren't so horribly depressed, I'd embrace you. That would be some slight compensation for my' – he tapped his foot with the end of his walking-stick – 'my accident.'

'You're depressed too?'

'One should never drink at luncheon,' said Gumbril. 'It wrecks the afternoon. One should also never think of the past and never for one moment consider the future. These are treasures of ancient wisdom. But perhaps after a little tea –' He leaned forward to look at the figures on the taximeter, for the cab had come to a standstill –'after a nip of the tannin stimulant' – he threw open the door – 'we may feel rather better.'

Mrs Viveash smiled excruciatingly. 'For me,' she said, as she stepped out on to the pavement, 'even tannin has lost its virtues now.'

Mrs Viveash's drawing-room was tastefully in the movement. The furniture was upholstered in fabrics designed by Dufy – racehorses and roses, little tennis players clustering in the midst of enormous flowers, printed in grey and ochre on a white ground. There were a couple of lamp-shades by Balla. On the pale rose-stippled walls hung three portraits of herself by three different and entirely incongruous painters, a selection of the usual oranges and lemons, and a rather forbidding contemporary nude painted in two tones of green.

'And how bored I am with this room and all these beastly pictures!' exclaimed Mrs Viveash as she entered. She took off her hat and, standing in front of the mirror above the mantelpiece, smoothed her coppery hair.

'You should take a cottage in the country,' said Gumbril, 'buy a pony and a governess cart and drive along the twiddly lanes looking for flowers. After tea you open the cottage piano,' and suiting his action to the words, Gumbril sat down at the long-tailed Blüthner, 'and you play, you play.' Very slowly and with parodied expressiveness he played the opening theme of the Arietta. 'You wouldn't be bored then,' he said, turning round to her, when he had finished.

'Ah, wouldn't I!' said Mrs Viveash. 'And with whom do you propose that I should share my cottage?'

'Any one you like,' said Gumbril. His fingers hung, as though meditating over the keys.

'But I don't like any one,' cried Mrs Viveash with a terrible vehemence from her death-bed. ... Ah, now it had been said, the truth. It sounded like a joke. Tony had been dead five years now. Those bright blue eyes – ah, never again. All rotted away to nothing.

'Then you should try,' said Gumbril, whose hands had begun

to creep softly forward into the Twelfth Sonata. 'You should try.'

'But I do try,' said Mrs Viveash. Her elbows propped on the mantelpiece, her chin resting on her clasped hands, she was looking fixedly at her own image in the glass. Pale eyes looked unwaveringly into pale eyes. The red mouth and its reflection exchanged their smiles of pain. She had tried; it revolted her now to think how often she had tried; she had tried to like some-one, any one, as much as Tony. She had tried to recapture, to re-evoke, to revivify. And there had never been anything, really, but a disgust. 'I haven't succeeded,' she added, after a pause.

The music had shifted from F major to D minor; it mounted in leaping anapæsts to a suspended chord, ran down again, mounted once more, modulating to C minor, then, through a passage of trembling notes to A flat major, to the dominant of D flat, to the dominant of C, to C minor, and at last, to a new clear theme in the major.

'Then I'm sorry for you,' said Gumbril, allowing his fingers to play on by themselves. He felt sorry, too, for the subjects of Mrs Viveash's desperate experiments. She mightn't have suc-ceeded in liking them – for their part, poor devils, they in general only too agonizingly liked her. ... Only too ... He remembered the cold, damp spots on his pillow, in the darkness. Those hope-less, angry tears. 'You nearly killed me once,' he said.

'Only time kills,' said Mrs Viveash, still looking into her own pale eyes. 'I have never made any one happy,' she added, after a pause. 'Never any one,' she thought, except Tony, and Tony they had killed, shot him through the head. Even the bright eyes had rotted, like any other carrion. She too had been happy then. Never again.

A maid came in with the tea-things.

'Ah, the tannin!' exclaimed Gumbril with enthusiasm, and broke off his playing. 'The one hope of salvation.' He poured out two cups, and picking up one of them he came over to the fireplace and stood behind her, sipping slowly at the pale brew-age and looking over her shoulder at their two reflections in the mirror.

'*La ci darem*,' he hummed. 'If only I had my beard!' He

stroked his chin and with the tip of his forefinger brushed up the drooping ends of his moustache. 'You'd come trembling like Zerlina, in under its golden shadow.'

Mrs Viveash smiled. 'I don't ask for anything better,' she said. 'What more delightful part! *Felice, io so, sarei: Batti, batti, o bel Mazetto.* Enviable Zerlina!'

The servant made another silent entry.

'A gentleman,' she said, 'called Mr Shearwater would like –'

'Tell him I'm not at home,' said Mrs Viveash, without looking round.

There was a silence. With raised eyebrows Gumbril looked over Mrs Viveash's shoulder at her reflection. Her eyes were calm and without expression, she did not smile or frown. Gumbril still questioningly looked. In the end he began to laugh.

CHAPTER XV

THEY were playing that latest novelty from across the water
'What's he to Hecuba?' Sweet, sweet and piercing, the saxophone pierced into the very bowels of compassion and tenderness, pierced like a revelation from heaven, pierced like the
angel's treacly dart into the holy Teresa's quivering and ecstasi-
ated flank. More ripely and roundly, with a kindly and less
agonizing voluptuousness, the 'cello meditated those Moham-
medan ecstasies that last, under the green palms of Paradise, six
hundred inenarrable years apiece. Into this charged atmosphere
the violin admitted refreshing draughts of fresh air, cool and thin
like the breath from a still damp squirt. And the piano hammered
and rattled away unmindful of the sensibilities of the other
instruments, banged away all the time, reminding every one
concerned, in a thoroughly business-like way, that this was a
cabaret where people came to dance the fox-trot; not a baroque
church for female saints to go into ecstasies in, not a mild, happy
valley of tumbling houris.

At each recurrence of the refrain the four negroes of the
orchestra, or at least the three of them who played with their
hands alone – for the saxophonist always blew at this point with a
redoubled sweetness, enriching the passage with a warbling con-
trapuntal soliloquy that fairly wrung the entrails and transported
the pierced heart – broke into melancholy and drawling song:

> 'What's he to Hecuba?
> Nothing at all.
> That's why there'll be no wedding on Wednesday week,
> Way down in old Bengal.'

'What unspeakable sadness,' said Gumbril, as he stepped,
stepped through the intricacies of the trot. 'Eternal passion,
eternal pain. *Les chants désespérés sont les chants les plus beaux,
Et j'en sais d'immortels qui sont de purs sanglots.* Rum tiddle-um-
tum, pom-pom. Amen. What's he to Hecuba? Nothing at all.
Nothing, mark you. Nothing, nothing.'

396

'Nothing,' repeated Mrs Viveash. 'I know all about that.' She sighed.

'I am nothing to you,' said Gumbril, gliding with skill between the wall and the Charybdis of a couple dangerously experimenting with a new step. 'You are nothing to me. Thank God. And yet here we are, two bodies with but a single thought, a beast with two backs, a perfectly united centaur trotting, trotting.' They trotted.

'What's he to Hecuba?' The grinning blackamoors repeated the question, reiterated the answer on a tone of frightful unhappiness. The saxophone warbled on the verge of anguish. The couples revolved, marked time, stepped and stepped with an habitual precision, as though performing some ancient and profoundly significant rite. Some were in fancy dress, for this was a gala night at the cabaret. Young women disguised as callipygous Florentine pages, blue-breeched Gondoliers, black-breeched Toreadors circulated, moon-like, round the hall, clasped sometimes in the arms of Arabs, or white clowns, or more often of untravestied partners. The faces reflected in the mirrors were the sort of faces one feels one ought to know by sight; the cabaret was 'Artistic'.

'What's he to Hecuba?'

Mrs Viveash murmured the response, almost piously, as though she were worshipping almighty and omnipresent Nil. 'I adore this tune,' she said, 'this divine tune.' It filled up a space, it moved, it jigged, it set things twitching in you, it occupied time, it gave you a sense of being alive. 'Divine tune, divine tune,' she repeated with emphasis, and she shut her eyes, trying to abandon herself, trying to float, trying to give Nil the slip.

'Ravishing little Toreador, that,' said Gumbril, who had been following the black-breeched travesty with affectionate interest.

Mrs Viveash opened her eyes. Nil was unescapable. 'With Piers Cotton, you mean? Your tastes are a little common, my dear Theodore.'

'Green-eyed monster!'

Mrs Viveash laughed. 'When I was being "finished" in Paris,' she said, 'Mademoiselle always used to urge me to take fencing lessons. *C'est un exercice très gracieux. Et puis,*' Mrs Viveash mimicked a passionate earnestness, "*et puis, ça dévelope le bassin.* Your Toreador, Gumbril, looks as though she must be a champion with the foils. *Quel bassin!*'

'Hush,' said Gumbril. They were abreast of the Toreador and her partner. Piers Cotton turned his long greyhound's nose in their direction.

'How are you?' he asked across the music.

They nodded. 'And you?'

'Ah, writing such a book,' cried Piers Cotton, 'such a brilliant, brilliant, flashing book.' The dance was carrying them apart. 'Like a smile of false teeth,' he shouted across the widening gulf, and disappeared in the crowd.

'What's he to Hecuba?' Lachrymosely, the hilarious blacka-moors chanted their question, mournfully pregnant with its foreknown reply.

Nil, omnipresent nil, world-soul, spiritual informer of all matter. Nil in the shape of a black-breeched moon-basined Toreador. Nil, the man with the greyhound's nose. Nil, as four blackamoors. Nil in the form of a divine tune. Nil, the faces, the faces one ought to know by sight, reflected in the mirrors of the hall. Nil this Gumbril whose arm is round one's waist, whose feet step in and out among one's own. Nothing at all.

That's why there'll be no wedding. No wedding at St George's, Hanover Square, – oh, desperate experiment! – with Nil Viveash, that charming boy, that charming nothing at all, engaged at the moment in hunting elephants, hunting fever and carnivores among the Tikki-tikki pygmies. That's why there'll be no wedding on Wednesday week. For Lycidas is dead, dead ere his prime. For the light strawy hair (not a lock left), the brown face, the red-brown hands and the smooth boy's body, milk-white, milk-warm, are nothing at all, nothing, now, at all – nil these five years – and the shining blue eyes as much nil as the rest.

'Always the same people,' complained Mrs Viveash, looking round the room. 'The old familiar faces. Never any one new. Where's the younger generation, Gumbril? We're old, Theo-dore. There are millions younger than we are. Where are they?'

'I'm not responsible for them,' said Gumbril. 'I'm not even responsible for myself.' He imagined a cottagey room, under a roof, with a window near the floor and a sloping ceiling where you were always bumping your head; and in the candle-light Emily's candid eyes, her grave and happy mouth; in the darkness, the curve, under his fingers, of her firm body.

'Why don't they come and sing for their supper?' Mrs Viveash went on petulantly. 'It's their business to amuse us.'

'They're probably thinking of amusing themselves,' Gumbril suggested.

'Well, then, they should do it where we can see them.'

'What's he to Hecuba?'

'Nothing at all,' Gumbril clownishly sang. The room, in the cottage, had nothing to do with him. He breathed Mrs Viveash's memories of Italian jasmines, laid his cheek for a moment against her smooth hair. 'Nothing at all.' Happy clown!

Way down in old Bengal, under the green Paradisiac palms, among the ecstatic mystagogues and the saints who scream beneath the divine caresses, the music came to an end. The four negroes wiped their glistening faces. The couples fell apart. Gumbril and Mrs Viveash sat down and smoked a cigarette.

CHAPTER XVI

The blackamoors had left the platform at the end of the hall. The curtains looped up at either side had slid down, cutting it off from the rest of the room – 'making two worlds,' Gumbril elegantly and allusively put it, 'where only one grew before – and one of them a better world,' he added too philosophically, 'because unreal.' There was the theatrical silence, the suspense. The curtains parted again.

On a narrow bed – on a bier perhaps – the corpse of a woman. The husband kneels beside it. At the foot stands the doctor, putting away his instruments. In a beribboned pink cradle reposes a monstrous baby.

The Husband: Margaret! Margaret!

The Doctor: She is dead.

The Husband: Margaret!

The Doctor: Of septicæmia, I tell you.

The Husband: I wish that I too were dead!

The Doctor: But you won't to-morrow.

The Husband: To-morrow! But I don't want to live to see to-morrow.

The Doctor: You will to-morrow.

The Husband: Margaret! Margaret! Wait for me there; I shall not fail to meet you in that hollow vale.

The Doctor: You will not be slow to survive her.

The Husband: Christ have mercy upon us!

The Doctor: You would do better to think of the child.

The Husband (*rising and standing menacingly over the cradle*): Is that the monster?

The Doctor: No worse than others.

The Husband: Begotten in a night of immaculate pleasure, monster, may you live loveless, in dirt and impurity!

The Doctor: Conceived in lust and darkness, may your own impurity always seem heavenly, monster, in your own eyes!

400

THE HUSBAND: Murderer, slowly die all your life long!

THE DOCTOR: The child must be fed.

THE HUSBAND: Fed? With what?

THE DOCTOR: With milk.

THE HUSBAND: Her milk is cold in her breasts.

THE DOCTOR: There are still cows.

THE HUSBAND: Tubercular shorthorns. (*Calling.*) Let Short-i'-the-horn be brought!

VOICES (*off*): Short-i'-the-horn! Short-i'-the-horn! (*Fadingly.*) Short-i'-the ...

THE DOCTOR: In nineteen hundred and twenty-one, twenty-seven thousand nine hundred and thirteen women died in childbirth.

THE HUSBAND: But none of them belonged to my harem.

THE DOCTOR: Each of them was somebody's wife.

THE HUSBAND: Doubtless. But the people we don't know are only characters in the human comedy. We are the tragedians.

THE DOCTOR: Not in the spectator's eyes.

THE HUSBAND: Do I think of the spectators? Ah, Margaret! Margaret! ...

THE DOCTOR: The twenty-seven thousand nine hundred and fourteenth.

THE HUSBAND: The only one!

THE DOCTOR: But here comes the cow.

(*Short-i'-the-horn is led in by a Yokel.*)

THE HUSBAND: Ah, good Short-i'-the-horn! (*He pats the animal.*) She was tested last week, was she not?

THE YOKEL: Ay, sir.

THE HUSBAND: And found tubercular. No?

THE YOKEL: Even in the udders, may it please you.

THE HUSBAND: Excellent! Milk me the cow, sir, into this dirty wash-pot.

THE YOKEL: I will, sir. (*He milks the cow.*)

THE HUSBAND: Her milk – her milk is cold already. All the woman in her chilled and curdled within her breasts. Ah, Jesus! what miraculous galactagogue will make it flow again?

THE YOKEL: The wash-pot is full, sir.

THE HUSBAND: Then take the cow away.

THE YOKEL: Come, Short-i'-the-horn; come up, good Short-i'-the-horn. (*He goes out with the cow.*)

THE HUSBAND (*pouring the milk into a long-tubed feeding-bottle*): Here's for you, monster, to drink your own health in. (*He gives the bottle to the child.*)

CURTAIN.

'A little ponderous, perhaps,' said Gumbril, as the curtain came down.

'But I liked the cow,' Mrs Viveash opened her cigarette-case and found it empty. Gumbril offered her one of his. She shook her head. 'I don't want it in the least,' she said.

'Yes, the cow was in the best pantomime tradition,' Gumbril agreed. Ah! but it was a long time since he had been to a Christmas pantomime. Not since Dan Leno's days. All the little cousins, the uncles and aunts on both sides of the family, dozens and dozens of them – every year they filled the best part of a row in the dress circle at Drury Lane. And buns were stickily passed from hand to hand, chocolates circulated; the grown-ups drank tea. And the pantomime went on and on, glory after glory, under the shining arch of the stage. Hours and hours; and the grown-ups always wanted to go away before the harlequinade. And the children felt sick from eating too much chocolate, or wanted with such extreme urgency to go to the w.c. that they had to be led out, trampling and stumbling over everybody else's feet – and every stumble making the need more agonizingly great – in the middle of the transformation scene. And there was Dan Leno, inimitable Dan Leno, dead now as poor Yorick, no more than a mere skull like anybody else's skull. And his mother, he remembered, used to laugh at him sometimes till the tears ran down her cheeks. She used to enjoy things thoroughly, with a whole heart.

'I wish they'd hurry up with the second scene,' said Mrs Viveash. 'If there's anything that bores me, it's *entra'ctes*.'

'Most of one's life is an *entr'acte*,' said Gumbril, whose present mood of hilarious depression seemed favourable to the enunciation of apophthegms.

'None of your cracker mottoes, please,' protested Mrs Viveash. All the same, she reflected, what was she doing now but waiting for the curtain to go up again, waiting, with what unspeakable weariness of spirit, for the curtain that had rung down, ten centuries ago, on those blue eyes, that bright strawy hair and the weathered face?

'Thank God,' she said with an expiring earnestness, 'here's the second scene!'

The curtain went up. In a bald room stood the Monster, grown now from an infant into a frail and bent young man with bandy legs. At the back of the stage a large window giving on to a street along which people pass.

THE MONSTER [*solus*]: The young girls of Sparta, they say, used to wrestle naked with naked Spartan boys. The sun caressed their skins till they were brown and transparent like amber or a flask of olive oil. Their breasts were hard, their bellies flat. They were pure with the chastity of beautiful animals. Their thoughts were clear, their minds cool and untroubled. I spit blood into my handkerchief and sometimes I feel in my mouth something slimy, soft and disgusting, like a slug – and I have coughed up a shred of my lung. The rickets from which I suffered in childhood have bent my bones and made them old and brittle. All my life I have lived in this huge town, whose domes and spires are wrapped in a cloud of stink that hides the sun. The slug-dank tatters of lung that I spit out are black with the soot I have been breathing all these years. I am now come of age. Long-expected one-and-twenty has made me a fully privileged citizen of this great realm of which the owners of the *Daily Mirror*, the *News of the World* and the *Daily Express* are noble peers. Somewhere, I must logically infer, there must be other cities, built by men for men to live in. Somewhere, in the past, in the future, a very long way off. ... But perhaps the only street improvement schemes that ever really improve the streets are schemes in the minds of those who live in them: schemes of love mostly. Ah! here she comes.

[*The* YOUNG LADY *enters. She stands outside the window, in the street, paying no attention to the* MONSTER; *she seems to be waiting for somebody.*]

403

She is like a pear tree in flower. When she smiles, it is as though there were stars. Her hair is like the harvest in an eclogue, her cheeks are all the fruits of summer. Her arms and thighs are as beautiful as the soul of St Catherine of Siena. And her eyes, her eyes are plumbless with thought and limpidly pure like the water of the mountains.

THE YOUNG LADY: If I wait till the summer sale, the *crêpe de Chine* will be reduced by at least two shillings a yard, and on six camisoles that will mean a lot of money. But the question is: can I go from May till the end of July with the under-clothing I have now?

THE MONSTER: If I knew her, I should know the universe!

THE YOUNG LADY: My present ones are so dreadfully middle-class. And if Roger should ... by any chance. ...

THE MONSTER: Or, rather, I should be able to ignore it, having a private universe of my own.

THE YOUNG LADY: If – if he did – well, it might be rather humiliating with these I have ... like a servant's almost. ...

THE MONSTER: Love makes you accept the world; it puts an end to criticism.

THE YOUNG LADY: His hand already ...

THE MONSTER: Dare I, dare I tell her how beautiful she is?

THE YOUNG LADY: On the whole, I think I'd better get it now, though it will cost more.

THE MONSTER [*desperately advancing to the window as though to assault a battery*]: Beautiful! beautiful!

THE YOUNG LADY [*looking at him*]: Ha, ha, ha!

THE MONSTER: But I love you, flowering pear tree; I love you, golden harvest; I love you, fruitage of summer; I love you, body and limbs, with the shape of a saint's thought.

THE YOUNG LADY [*redoubles her laughter*]: Ha, ha, ha!

THE MONSTER [*taking her hand*]: You cannot be cruel! [*He is seized with a violent paroxysm of coughing which doubles him up, which shakes and torments him. The handkerchief he holds to his mouth is spotted with blood.*]

THE YOUNG LADY: You disgust me! [*She draws away her skirts so that they shall not come in contact with him.*]

THE MONSTER: But I swear to you, I love – I – [*He is once more interrupted by his cough.*]

THE YOUNG LADY: Please go away. [*In a different voice.*] Ah, Roger! [*She advances to meet a snub-nosed lubber with curly hair and a face like a groom's, who passes along the street at this moment.*]

ROGER: I've got the motor-bike waiting at the corner.

THE YOUNG LADY: Let's go, then.

ROGER [*pointing to the* MONSTER]: What's that?

THE YOUNG LADY: Oh, it's nothing in particular.

[*Both roar with laughter.* ROGER *escorts her out, patting her familiarly on the back as they walk along.*]

THE MONSTER [*looking after her*]: There is a wound under my left pap. She has deflowered all women. I cannot ...

'Lord!' whispered Mrs Viveash, 'how this young man bores me!'

'I confess,' replied Gumbril, 'I have rather a taste for moralities. There is a pleasant uplifting vagueness about these symbolical generalized figures which pleases me.'

'You were always charmingly simple-minded,' said Mrs Viveash. 'But who's this? As long as the young man isn't left alone on the stage, I don't mind.'

Another female figure has appeared in the street beyond the window. It is the Prostitute. Her face, painted in two tones of red, white, green, blue and black, is the most tasteful of *nature-mortes*.

THE PROSTITUTE: Hullo, duckie!

THE MONSTER: Hullo!

THE PROSTITUTE: Are you lonely?

THE MONSTER: Yes.

THE PROSTITUTE: Would you like me to come in to see you?

THE MONSTER: Very well.

THE PROSTITUTE: Shall we say thirty bob?

THE MONSTER: As you like.

THE PROSTITUTE: Come along then.

[*She climbs through the window and they go off together through the door on the left of the stage. The curtains descend for a moment, then rise again. The* MONSTER *and the* PROSTITUTE *are seen issuing from the door at which they went out.*]

THE MONSTER [*taking out a cheque-book and a fountain-pen*]: Thirty shillings ...

THE PROSTITUTE: Thank you. Not a cheque. I don't want any cheques. How do I know it isn't a dud one that they'll refuse payment for at the bank? Ready money for me, thanks.

THE MONSTER: But I haven't got any cash on me at the moment.

THE PROSTITUTE: Well, I won't take a cheque. Once bitten, twice shy, I can tell you.

THE MONSTER: But I tell you I haven't got any cash.

THE PROSTITUTE: Well, all I can say is, here I stay till I get it. And, what's more, if I don't get it quick, I'll make a row.

THE MONSTER: But this is absurd. I offer you a perfectly good cheque ...

THE PROSTITUTE: And I won't take it. So there!

THE MONSTER: Well then, take my watch. It's worth more than thirty bob. [*He pulls out his gold half-hunter.*]

THE PROSTITUTE: Thank you, and get myself arrested as soon I take it to the pop-shop! No, I want cash, I tell you.

THE MONSTER: But where the devil do you expect me to get it at this time of night?

THE PROSTITUTE: I don't know. But you've got to get it pretty quick.

THE MONSTER: You're unreasonable.

THE PROSTITUTE: Aren't there any servants in this house?

THE MONSTER: Yes.

THE PROSTITUTE: Well, go and borrow it from one of them.

THE MONSTER: But really, that would be too low, too humiliating.

THE PROSTITUTE: All right, I'll begin kicking up a noise. I'll go to the window and yell till all the neighbours are woken up and the police come to see what's up. You can borrow it from the copper then.

406

THE MONSTER: You really won't take my cheque? I swear to you it's perfectly all right. There's plenty of money to meet it.

THE PROSTITUTE: Oh, shut up! No more dilly-dallying. Get me my money at once, or I'll start the row. One, two, three ... [*She opens her mouth wide as if to yell.*]

THE MONSTER: All right. [*He goes out.*]

THE PROSTITUTE: Nice state of things we're coming to, when young rips try and swindle us poor girls out of our money! Mean, stinking skunks! I'd like to slit the throats of some of them.

THE MONSTER [*coming back again*]: Here you are. [*He hands her money.*]

THE PROSTITUTE [*examining it*]: Thank you, dearie. Any other time you're lonely ...

THE MONSTER: No, no!

THE PROSTITUTE: Where did you get it finally?

THE MONSTER: I woke the cook.

THE PROSTITUTE [*goes off into a peal of laughter*]: Well, so long, duckie. [*She goes out.*]

THE MONSTER [*solus*]: Somewhere there must be love like music. Love harmonious and ordered: two spirits, two bodies moving contrapuntally together. Somewhere, the stupid brutish act must be made to make sense, must be enriched, must be made significant. Lust, like Diabelli's waltz, a stupid air, turned by a genius into three-and-thirty fabulous variations. Somewhere ...

'Oh dear!' sighed Mrs Viveash.

'Charming!' Gumbril protested.

... love like sheets of silky flame; like landscapes brilliant in the sunlight against a background of purple thunder; like the solution of a cosmic problem; like faith ...

'Crikey!' said Mrs Viveash.

... Somewhere, somewhere. But in my veins creep the maggots of the pox ...

'Really, really!' Mrs Viveash shook her head. 'Too medical!'

407

... crawling towards the brain, crawling into the mouth, burrowing into the bones. Insatiably.

The Monster threw himself to the ground, and the curtain came down.

'And about time too!' declared Mrs Viveash.

'Charming!' Gumbril stuck to his guns. 'Charming! charming!'

There was a disturbance near the door. Mrs Viveash looked round to see what was happening. 'And now on top of it all,' she said, 'here comes Coleman, raving, with an unknown drunk.'

'Have we missed it?' Coleman was shouting. 'Have we missed all the lovely bloody farce?'

'Lovely bloody!' his companion repeated with drunken raptures, and he went into fits of uncontrollable laughter. He was a very young boy with straight dark hair and a face of Hellenic beauty, now distorted with tipsiness.

Coleman greeted his acquaintances in the hall, shouting a jovial obscenity to each. 'And Bumbril-Gumbril,' he exclaimed, catching sight of him at last in the front row. 'And Hetaira-Myra!' He pushed his way through the crowd, followed unsteadily by his young disciple. 'So you're here,' he said, standing over them and looking down with an enigmatic malice in his bright blue eyes. 'Where's the physiologue?'

'Am I the physiologue's keeper?' asked Gumbril. 'He's with his glands and his hormones, I suppose. Not to mention his wife.' He smiled to himself.

'Where the hormones, there moan I,' said Coleman, skidding off sideways along the slippery word. 'I hear, by the way, that there's a lovely prostitute in this play.'

'You've missed her,' said Mrs Viveash.

'What a misfortune,' said Coleman. 'We've missed the delicious trull,' he said, turning to the young man.

The young man only laughed.

'Let me introduce, by the way,' said Coleman. 'This is Dante,' he pointed to the dark-haired boy; 'and I am Virgil. We're making a round tour – or, rather, a descending spiral tour of hell. But we're only at the first circle so far. These, Alighieri, are two damned souls, though not, as you might suppose, Paolo and Francesca.'

The boy continued to laugh, happily and uncomprehendingly.

'Another of these interminable *entr'actes*,' complained Mrs Viveash. 'I was just saying to Theodore here that if there's one thing I dislike more than another, it's a long *entr'acte*.' Would hers ever come to an end?

'And if there's one thing *I* dislike more than another,' said the boy, breaking silence for the first time, with an air of the greatest earnestness, 'it's ... it's one thing more than another.'

'And you're perfectly right in doing so,' said Coleman. 'Perfectly right.'

'I know,' the boy replied modestly.

When the curtain rose again it was on an aged Monster, with a black patch over the left side of his nose, no hair, no teeth, and sitting harmlessly behind the bars of an asylum.

THE MONSTER: Asses, apes and dogs! Milton called them that; he should have known. Somewhere there must be men, however. The variations on Diabelli prove it. Brunelleschi's dome is more than the magnification of Cléo de Mérode's breast. Somewhere there are men with power, living reasonably. Like our mythical Greeks and Romans. Living cleanly. The images of the gods are their portraits. They walk under their own protection. [*The* MONSTER *climbs on to a chair and stands in the posture of a statue.*] Jupiter, father of gods, a man, I bless myself, I throw bolts at my own disobedience, I answer my own prayers, I pronounce oracles to satisfy the questions I myself propound. I abolish all tetters, poxes, blood-spitting, rotting of bones. With love I recreate the world from within. Europa puts an end to squalor, Leda does away with tyranny, Danae tempers stupidity. After establishing these reforms in the social sewer, I climb, I climb, up through the manhole, out of the manhole, beyond humanity. For the manhole, even the manhole, is dark; though not so dingy as the doghole it was before I altered it. Up through the manhole, towards the air. Up, up! [*And the* MONSTER, *suiting the action to his words, climbs up the runged back of his chair and stands, by a miraculous*

409

feat of acrobacy, on the topmost bar.] I begin to see the stars through other eyes than my own. More than dog already, I become more than man. I begin to have inklings of the shape and sense of things. Upwards, upwards I strain, I peer, I reach aloft. [*The balanced* MONSTER *reaches, strains and peers.*] And I seize, I seize! [*As he shouts these words, the* MONSTER *falls heavily, head foremost, to the floor. He lies there quite still. After a little time the door opens and the* DOCTOR *of the first scene enters with a* WARDER.]

THE WARDER: I heard a crash.

THE DOCTOR [*who has by this time become immensely old and has a beard like Father Thames*]: It looks as though you were right. [*He examines the* MONSTER.]

THE WARDER: He was for ever climbing on to his chair.

THE DOCTOR: Well, he won't any more. His neck's broken.

THE WARDER: You don't say so?

THE DOCTOR: I do.

THE WARDER: Well, I never!

THE DOCTOR: Have it carried down to the dissecting-room.

THE WARDER: I'll send for the porters at once.

[*Exeunt severally, and* CURTAIN.]

'Well,' said Mrs Viveash, 'I'm glad that's over.'

The music struck up again, saxophone and 'cello, with the thin draught of the violin to cool their ecstasies and the thumping piano to remind them of business. Gumbril and Mrs Viveash slid out into the dancing crowd, revolving as though by force of habit.

'These substitutes for the genuine copulative article,' said Coleman to his disciple, 'are beneath the dignity of hell-hounds like you and me.'

Charmed, the young man laughed; he was attentive as though at the feet of Socrates. Coleman had found him in a night club, where he had gone in search of Zoe, found him very drunk in the company of two formidable women fifteen or twenty years his senior, who were looking after him, half maternally out of pure kindness of heart, half professionally; for he seemed to be carrying a good deal of money. He was incapable of looking after himself. Coleman had pounced on him at once, claimed an old friendship which the youth was too tipsy to be able to deny, and carried him off. There was something, he always thought, peculiarly interesting about the spectacle of children tobogganing down into the cesspools.

'I like this place,' said the young man.

'Tastes differ!' Coleman shrugged his shoulders. 'The German professors have catalogued thousands of people whose whole pleasure consists of eating dung.'

The young man smiled and nodded, rather vaguely. 'Is there anything to drink here?' he asked.

'Too respectable,' Coleman answered, shaking his head.

'I think this is a bloody place,' said the young man.

'Ah! but some people like blood. And some like boots. And some like long gloves and corsets. And some like birch-rods. And some like sliding down slopes and can't look at Michelangelo's "Night" on the Medici Tombs without dying the little death, because the statue seems to be sliding. And some ...'

'But I want something to drink,' insisted the young man.

Coleman stamped his feet, waved his arms. '*A boire! à boire!*' he shouted, like the newborn Gargantua. Nobody paid any attention.

The music came to an end. Gumbril and Mrs Viveash reappeared.

'Dante,' said Coleman, 'calls for drink. We must leave the building.'

'Yes. Anything to get out of this,' said Mrs Viveash. 'What's the time?'

Gumbril looked at his watch. 'Half-past one.'

Mrs Viveash sighed. 'Can't possibly go to bed,' she said, 'for another hour at least.'

They walked out into the street. The stars were large and brilliant overhead. There was a little wind that almost seemed to come from the country. Gumbril thought so, at any rate; he thought of the country.

'The question is, where?' said Coleman. 'You can come to my bordello, if you like; but it's a long way off and Zoe hates us all so much, she'll probably set on us with the meat-chopper. If she's back again, that is. Though she may be out all night. *Zoe mou, sas agapo.* Shall we risk it?'

411

'To me it's quite indifferent,' said Mrs Viveash faintly, as though wholly preoccupied with expiring.

'Or there's my place,' Gumbril said abruptly, as though shaking himself awake out of some dream.

'But you live still farther, don't you?' said Coleman. 'With venerable parents, and so forth. One foot in the grave and all that. Shall we mingle hornpipes with funerals?' He began to hum Chopin's 'Funeral March' at three times its proper speed, and seizing the young stranger in his arms, two-stepped two or three turns on the pavement, then released his hold and let him go reeling against the area railings.

'No, I don't mean the family mansion,' said Gumbril. 'I mean my own rooms. They're quite near. In Great Russell Street.'

'I never knew you had any rooms, Theodore,' said Mrs Viveash.

'Nobody did.' Why should they know now? Because the wind seemed almost a country wind? 'There's drink there,' he said.

'Splendid!' cried the young man. They were all splendid people.

'There's some gin,' said Gumbril.

'Capital aphrodisiac!' Coleman commented.

'Some light white wine.'

'Diuretic.'

'And some whisky.'

'The great emetic,' said Coleman. 'Come on.' And he struck up the March of the Fascisti. '*Giovinezza, giovinezza, primavera di bellezza. ...*' The noise went fading down the dark, empty streets.

The gin, the white wine, and even, for the sake of the young stranger, who wanted to sample everything, the emetic whisky, were produced.

'I like your rooms,' said Mrs Viveash, looking round her. 'And I resent your secrecy about them, Theodore.'

'Drink, puppy!' Coleman refilled the boy's glass.

'Here's to secrecy,' Gumbril proposed. Shut it tightly, keep it dark, cover it up. Be silent, prevaricate, lie outright. He laughed and drank. 'Do you remember,' he went on, 'those instructive advertisements of Eno's Fruit Salts they used to have when we were young? There was one little anecdote about a doctor who advised the hypochondriacal patient who had come to consult him, to go and see Grimaldi, the clown; and the patient answered, "I am Grimaldi." Do you remember?'

'No,' said Mrs Viveash. 'And why do you?'

'Oh, I don't know. Or rather, I do know,' Gumbril corrected himself, and laughed again.

The young man suddenly began to boast. 'I lost two hundred pounds yesterday playing *chemin de fer*,' he said, and looked round for applause.

Coleman patted his curly head. 'Delicious child!' he said. 'You're positively Hogarthian.'

Angrily, the boy pushed him away. 'What are you doing?' he shouted; then turned and addressed himself once more to the others. 'I couldn't afford it, you know – not a bloody penny of it. Not my money, either.' He seemed to find it exquisitely humorous. 'And that two hundred wasn't all,' he added, almost expiring with mirth.

'Tell Coleman how you borrowed his beard, Theodore.'

Gumbril was looking intently into his glass, as though he hoped to see in its pale mixture of gin and Sauterne visions, as in a crystal, of the future. Mrs Viveash touched him on the arm and repeated her injunction.

'Oh, that!' said Gumbril rather irritably. 'No. It isn't an interesting story.'

'Oh yes, it is! I insist,' said Mrs Viveash, commanding peremptorily from her death-bed.

Gumbril drank his gin and Sauterne. 'Very well then,' he said reluctantly, and began.

'I don't know what my governor will say,' the young man put in once or twice. But nobody paid any attention to him. He relapsed into a sulky and, it seemed to him, very dignified silence. Under the warm, jolly tipsiness he felt a chill of foreboding. He poured out some more whisky.

Gumbril warmed to his anecdote. Expiringly Mrs Viveash laughed from time to time, or smiled her agonizing smile. Coleman whooped like a Redskin.

'And after the concert to these rooms,' said Gumbril.

Well, let everything go. Into the mud. Leave it there, and let the dogs lift their hind legs over it as they pass.

'Ah! the genuine platonic fumblers,' commented Coleman.

'I am Grimaldi,' Gumbril laughed. Further than this it was difficult to see where the joke could go. There, on the divan, where Mrs Viveash and Coleman were now sitting, she had lain sleeping in his arms.

'Towsing, in Elizabethan,' said Coleman.

Unreal, eternal in the secret darkness. A night that was an eternal parenthesis among the other nights and days.

'I feel I'm going to be sick,' said the young man suddenly. He had wanted to go on silently and haughtily sulking; but his stomach declined to take part in the dignified game.

'Good Lord!' said Gumbril, and jumped up. But before he could do anything effective, the young man had fulfilled his own prophecy.

'The real charm about debauchery,' said Coleman philosophically, 'is its total pointlessness, futility, and above all its incredible tediousness. If it really were all roses and exhilaration as these poor children seem to imagine, it would be no better than going to church or studying the higher mathematics. I should never touch a drop of wine or another harlot again. It would be against my principles. I told you it was emetic,' he called to the young man.

'And what are your principles?' asked Mrs Viveash.

'Oh, strictly ethical,' said Coleman.

'You're responsible for this creature,' said Gumbril, pointing to the young man, who was sitting on the floor near the fireplace, cooling his forehead against the marble of the mantelpiece. 'You must take him away. Really, what a bore!' His nose and mouth were all wrinkled up with disgust.

'I'm sorry,' the young man whispered. He kept his eyes shut and his face was exceedingly pale.

'But with pleasure,' said Coleman. 'What's your name?' he asked the young man, 'and where do you live?'

'My name is Porteous,' murmured the young man.

'Good lord!' cried Gumbril, letting himself fall on to the divan beside Mrs Viveash. 'That's the last straw!'

CHAPTER XVII

THE two o'clock snorted out of Charing Cross, but no healths were drunk, this time, to Viscount Lascelles. A desiccating sobriety made arid the corner of the third-class carriage in which Gumbril was sitting. His thoughts were an interminable desert of sand, with not a palm in sight, not so much as a comforting mirage. Once again he fumbled in his breast-pocket, brought out and unfolded the flimsy paper. Once more he read. How many times had he read it before?

'Your telegram made me very unhappy. Not merely because of the accident – though it made me shudder to think that something terrible might have happened, poor darling – but also, selfishly, my own disappointment. I had looked forward so much. I had made a picture of it all so clearly. I should have met you at the station with the horse and trap from the Chequers, and we'd have driven back to the cottage – and you'd have loved the cottage. We'd have had tea and I'd have made you eat an egg with it after your journey. Then we'd have gone for a walk; through the most heavenly wood I found yesterday to a place where there's a wonderful view – miles and miles of it. And we'd have wandered on and on, and sat down under the trees, and the sun would have set, and the twilight would slowly have come to an end, and we'd have gone home again and found the lamps lighted and supper ready – not very grand, I'm afraid, for Mrs Vole isn't the best of cooks. And then the piano; for there is a piano, and I had the tuner come specially from Hastings yesterday, so that it isn't *so* bad now. And you'd have played; and perhaps I would have made my noises on it. And at last it would have been time for candles and bed. When I heard you were coming, Theodore, I told Mrs Vole a lie about you. I said you were my husband, because she's fearfully respectable, of course; and it would dreadfully disturb her if you weren't. But I told myself that, too. I meant that you should be. You see, I tell you

415

everything. I'm not ashamed. I wanted to give you everything I could, and then we should always be together, loving one another. And I should have been your slave, I should have been your property and lived inside your life. But you would always have had to love me.

'And then, just as I was getting ready to go and call at the Chequers for the horse and trap, your telegram came. I saw the word "accident", and I imagined you all bleeding and smashed – oh, dreadful, dreadful. But then, when you seemed to make rather a joke of it – why did you say "a little indisposed"? that seemed, somehow, so stupid, I thought – and said you were coming to-morrow, it wasn't that which upset me; it was the dreadful, dreadful disappointment. It was like a stab, that disappointment; it hurt so terribly, so unreasonably much. It made me cry and cry, so that I thought I should never be able to stop. And then, gradually, I began to see that the pain of the disappointment wasn't unreasonably great. It wasn't merely a question of your coming being put off for a day; it was a question of its being put off for ever, of my never seeing you again. I saw that that accident had been something really arranged by Providence. It was meant to warn me and show me what I ought to do. I saw how hopelessly impracticable the happiness I had been imagining really was. I saw that you didn't, you couldn't love me in anything like the same way as I loved you. I was only a curious adventure, a new experience, a means to some other end. Mind, I'm not blaming you in the least. I'm only telling you what is true, what I gradually came to realize as true. If you'd come – what then? I'd have given you everything, my body, my mind, my soul, my whole life. I'd have twisted myself into the threads of your life. And then, when in due course you wanted to make an end to this curious little adventure, you would have had to cut the tangle and it would have killed me; it would also have hurt you. At least I think it would. In the end, I thanked God for the accident which had prevented you coming. In this way, Providence lets us off very lightly – you with a bruise or two (for I do hope it really is nothing, my precious darling), and me with a bruise inside, round the heart. But both will get well quite soon. And all our lives, we shall have an afternoon under the trees, an evening of music and in the darkness, a night, an eternity of happiness, to look back on. I shall go away from Robertsbridge at once. Good-bye, Theodore. What a long letter! The last you'll ever get from me. The last – what a dreadful hurting word that is. I shall take it to post at once, for fear, if I leave it, I may be weak enough to change my mind and let you come to-morrow. I shall take it at once, then I shall come home again and pack up and tell some new fib to Mrs Vole. And after that, perhaps I shall allow myself to cry again. Good-bye.'

Aridly, the desert of sand stretched out with not a tree and not even a mirage, except perhaps the vague and desperate hope that he might get there before she started, that she might conceivably have changed her mind. Ah, if only he'd read the letter a little earlier! But he hadn't woken up before eleven, he hadn't been down before half-past. Sitting at the breakfast-table, he had read the letter through.

The eggs and bacon had grown still colder, if that was possible, than they were. He had read it through, he had rushed to the A.B.C. There was no practicable train before the two o'clock.

If he had taken the seven-twenty-seven he would certainly have got there before she started. Ah, if only he had woken up a little earlier! But then he would have had to go to bed a little earlier. And in order to go to bed earlier, he would have had to abandon Mrs Viveash before she had bored herself to that ultimate point of fatigue at which she did at last feel ready for repose. And to abandon Mrs Viveash – ah, that was really impossible, she wouldn't allow herself to be left alone. If only he hadn't gone to the London Library yesterday! A wanton, unnecessary visit it had been. For after all, the journey was short; he didn't need a book for the train. And the *Life of Beckford*, for which he had asked, proved, of course, to be out – and he had been utterly incapable of thinking of any other book, among the two or three hundred thousand on the shelves, that he wanted to read. And, in any case, what the devil did he want with a *Life of Beckford*? Hadn't he his own life, the life of Gumbril, to attend to? Wasn't one life enough, without making superfluous visits

417

to the London Library in search of other lives? And then what a stroke of bad luck to have run into Mrs Viveash at that very moment! What an abject weakness to have let himself be bullied into sending that telegram. 'A little indisposed. ...' Oh, my God! Gumbril shut his eyes and ground his teeth together; he felt himself blushing with a retrospective shame.

And of course it was quite useless taking the train, like this, to Robertsbridge. She'd be gone, of course. Still, there was always the desperate hope. There was the mirage across the desiccated plains, the mirage one knew to be deceptive and which, on a second glance, proved not even to be a mirage, but merely a few livery spots behind the eyes. Still, it was amply worth doing – as a penance, and to satisfy the conscience and to deceive oneself with an illusion of action. And then the fact that he was to have spent the afternoon with Rosie and had put her off – that too was highly satisfying. And not merely put her off, but – ultimate clownery in the worst of deliriously bad taste – played a joke on her. 'Impossible come to you, meet me 213 Sloane Street, second floor, a little indisposed.' He wondered how she'd get on with Mr Mercaptan; for it was to his rococo boudoir and Crébillon-souled sofa that he had on the spur of the clownish moment, as he dashed into the post office on the way to the station, sent her.

Aridly, the desiccated waste extended. Had she been right in her letter? Would it really have lasted no more than a little while and ended as she prophesied, with an agonizing cutting of the tangle? Or could it be that she had held out the one hope of happiness? Wasn't she perhaps the one unique being with whom he might have learned to await in quietness the final coming of that lovely terrible thing, from before the sound of whose secret footsteps more than once and oh! ignobly he had fled? He could not decide, it was impossible to decide until he had seen her again, till he had possessed her, mingled his life with hers. And now she had eluded him; for he knew very well that he would not find her. He sighed and looked out of the window.

The train pulled up at a small suburban station. Suburban, for though London was already some way behind, the little sham half-timbered houses near the station, the newer tile and rough-cast dwellings farther out on the slope of the hill proclaimed with emphasis the presence of the business man, the holder of the season ticket. Gumbril looked at them with a pensive disgust which must have expressed itself on his features; for the gentleman sitting in the corner of the carriage facing his, suddenly leaned forward, tapped him on the knee, and said, 'I see you agree with me, sir, that there are too many people in the world.'

Gumbril, who up till now had merely been aware that somebody was sitting opposite him, now looked with more attention at the stranger. He was a large, square old gentleman of robust and flourishing appearance, with a face of wrinkled brown parchment and a white moustache that merged, in a handsome curve, with a pair of side whiskers, in a manner which reminded one of the photographs of the Emperor Francis Joseph.

'I perfectly agree with you, sir,' Gumbril answered. If he had been wearing his beard, he would have gone on to suggest that loquacious old gentlemen in trains are among the supernumeraries of the planet. As it was, however, he spoke with courtesy, and smiled in his most engaging fashion.

'When I look at all these revolting houses,' the old gentleman continued, shaking his fist at the snuggeries of the season-ticket holders, 'I am filled with indignation. I feel my spleen ready to burst, sir, ready to burst.'

'I can sympathize with you,' said Gumbril. 'The architecture is certainly not very soothing.'

'It's not the architecture I mind so much,' retorted the old gentleman, 'that's merely a question of art, and all nonsense so far as I'm concerned. What disgusts me is the people inside the architecture, the number of them, sir. And the way they breed. Like maggots, sir, like maggots. Millions of them, creeping about the face of the country, spreading blight and dirt wherever they go; ruining everything. It's the people I object to.'

'Ah well,' said Gumbril, 'if you will have sanitary conditions that don't allow plagues to flourish properly; if you will tell mothers how to bring up their children, instead of allowing nature to kill them off in her natural way; if you will import unlimited supplies of corn and meat: what can you expect? Of course the numbers go up.'

The old gentleman waved all this away. 'I don't care what the causes are,' he said. 'That's all one to me. What I do object to, sir, is the effects. Why sir, I am old enough to remember walking through the delicious meadows beyond Swiss Cottage, I remember seeing the cows milked in West Hampstead, sir. And now, what do I see now, when I go there? Hideous red cities pullulating with Jews, sir. Pullulating with prosperous Jews. Am I right in being indignant, sir? Do I do well, like the prophet Jonah, to be angry?'

'You do, sir,' said Gumbril, with growing enthusiasm, 'and the more so since this frightful increase in population is the world's most formidable danger at the present time. With populations that in Europe alone expand by millions every year, no political foresight is possible. A few years of this mere bestial propagation will suffice to make nonsense of the wisest schemes of to-day – or would suffice,' he hastened to correct himself, 'if any wise schemes were being matured at the present.'

'Very possibly, sir,' said the old gentleman, 'but what I object to is seeing good cornland being turned into streets, and meadows, where cows used to graze, covered with houses full of useless and disgusting human beings. I resent seeing the country parcelled out into back gardens.'

'And is there any prospect,' Gumbril earnestly asked, 'of our ever being able in the future to support the whole of our population? Will unemployment ever decrease?'

'I don't know, sir,' the old gentleman replied. 'But the families of the unemployed will certainly increase.'

'You are right, sir,' said Gumbril, 'they will. And the families of the employed and the prosperous will as steadily grow smaller. It is regrettable that birth control should have begun at the wrong end of the scale. There seems to be a level of poverty below which it doesn't seem worth while practising birth control, and a level of education below which birth control is regarded as morally wrong. Strange, how long it has taken for the ideas of love and procreation to dissociate themselves in the human mind. In the majority of minds they are still, even in this so-called twentieth century, indivisibly wedded. Still,' he continued hopefully, 'progress is being made, progress is certainly, though slowly, being made. It is gratifying to find, for example, in the latest statistics, that the clergy, as a class, are now remarkable for the smallness of their families. The old jest is out of date. Is it too much to hope that these gentlemen may bring themselves in time to preach what they already practise?'

'It *is* too much to hope, sir,' the old gentleman answered with decision.

'You are probably right,' said Gumbril.

'If we were all to preach all the things we all practise,' continued the old gentleman, 'the world would soon be a pretty sort of bear-garden, I can tell you. Yes, and a monkey-house. And a wart-hoggery. As it is, sir, it is merely a place where there are too many human beings. Vice must pay its tribute to virtue, or else we are all undone.'

'I admire your wisdom, sir,' said Gumbril.

The old gentleman was delighted. 'And I have been much impressed by your philosophical reflections,' he said. 'Tell me, are you at all interested in old brandy?'

'Well, not philosophically,' said Gumbril. 'As a mere empiric only.'

'As a mere empiric!' The old gentleman laughed. 'Then let me beg you to accept a case. I have a cellar which I shall never drink dry, alas! before I die. My only wish is that what remains of it shall be distributed among those who can really appreciate it. In you, sir, I see a fitting recipient of a case of brandy.'

'You overwhelm me,' said Gumbril. 'You are too kind, and, I may add, too flattering.' The train, which was a mortally slow one, came grinding for what seemed the hundredth time to a halt.

'Not at all,' said the old gentleman. 'If you have a card, sir.'

Gumbril searched his pockets. 'I have come without one.'

'Never mind,' said the old gentleman. 'I think I have a pencil. If you will give me your name and address, I will have the case sent to you at once.'

Leisurely, he hunted for the pencil, he took out a notebook. The train gave a jerk forward.

'Now, sir,' he said.

Gumbril began dictating. 'Theodore,' he said slowly.

'The – o – dore,' the old gentleman repeated, syllable by syllable.

The train crept on, with slowly gathering momentum, through the station. Happening to look out of the window at this moment, Gumbril saw the name of the place painted across a lamp. It was Robertsbridge. He made a loud, inarticulate noise, flung open the door of the compartment, stepped out on to the footboard and jumped. He landed safely on the platform, staggered forward a few paces with his acquired momentum and came at last to a halt. A hand reached out and closed the swinging door of his compartment and, an instant afterwards, through the window, a face that, at a distance, looked more than ever like the face of the Emperor Francis Joseph, looked back towards the receding platform. The mouth opened and shut; no words were audible. Standing on the platform, Gumbril made a complicated pantomime, signifying his regret by shrugging his shoulders and placing his hand on his heart; urging in excuse for his abrupt departure the necessity under which he laboured of alighting at this particular station – which he did by pointing at the name on the boards and lamps, then at himself, then at the village across the fields. The old gentleman waved his hand, which still held, Gumbril noticed, the notebook in which he had been writing. Then the train carried him out of sight. There went the only case of old brandy he was ever likely to possess, thought Gumbril sadly, as he turned away. Suddenly, he remembered Emily again; for a long time he had quite forgotten her.

The cottage, when at last he found it, proved to be fully as picturesque as he had imagined. And Emily, of course, had gone, leaving, as might have been expected, no address. He took the evening train back to London. The aridity was now complete, and even the hope of a mirage had vanished. There was no old gentleman to make a diversion. The size of clergymen's families, even the fate of Europe, seemed unimportant now, were indeed perfectly indifferent to him.

CHAPTER XVIII

Two hundred and thirteen Sloane Street. The address, Rosie reflected, as she vaporized synthetic lilies of the valley over all her sinuous person, was decidedly a good one. It argued a reasonable prosperity, attested a certain distinction. The knowledge of his address confirmed her already high opinion of the bearded stranger who had so surprisingly entered her life, as though in fulfilment of all the fortune-tellers' prophecies that ever were made; had entered, yes, and intimately made himself at home. She had been delighted, when the telegram came that morning, to think that at last she was going to find out something more about this man of mystery. For dark and mysterious he had remained, remote even in the midst of the most intimate contacts. Why, she didn't even know his name. 'Call me Toto,' he had suggested, when she asked him what it was. And Toto she had had to call him, for lack of anything more definite or committal. But to-day he was letting her further into his secret. Rosie was delighted. Her pink underclothing, she decided, as she looked in the long glass, was really ravishing. She examined herself, turning first one way, then the other, looking over her shoulder to see the effect from behind. She pointed a toe, bent and straightened a knee, applauding the length of her legs ('Most women,' Toto had said, 'are like dachshunds'), their slenderness and plump suavity of form. In their white stockings of Milanese silk they looked delicious; and how marvellously, by the way, those Selfridge people had mended those stockings by their new patent process! Absolutely like new, and only charged four shillings. Well, it was time to dress. Good-bye, then, to the pink underclothing and the long white legs. She opened the wardrobe door. The moving glass reflected, as it swung through its half-circle, pink bed, rose-wreathed walls, little friends of her own age, and the dying saint at his last communion. Rosie selected the frock she had bought the other day at one of those little shops in Soho, where they sell such smart things so cheaply

423

to a clientage of minor actresses and cocottes. Toto hadn't seen it yet. She looked extremely distinguished in it. The little hat, with its inch of veil hanging like a mask, unconcealing and in- viting, from the brim, suited her to perfection. One last dab of powder, one last squirt of synthetic liles of the valley, and she was ready. She closed the door behind her. St Jerome was left to communicate in the untenanted pinkness.

Mr Mercaptan sat at his writing-table – an exquisitely amusing affair in papier mâché, inlaid with floral decorations in mother- of-pearl and painted with views of Windsor Castle and Tintern in the romantic manner of Prince Albert's later days – polishing to its final and gem-like perfection one of his middle articles. It was on a splendid subject – the 'Jus Primæ Noctis, or Droit du Seigneur' – 'that delicious *droit*,' wrote Mr Mercaptan, 'on which, one likes to think, the Sovereigns of England insist so firmly in their motto, *Dieu et mon Droit – de Seigneur*.' That was charming, Mr Mercaptan thought, as he read it through. And he liked that bit which began elegaically: 'But, alas! the Right of the First Night belongs to a Middle Age as mythical, albeit happily different, as those dismal epochs invented by Morris or by Chesterton. The Lord's right, as we prettily imagine it, is a fig- ment of the baroque imagination of the seventeenth century. It never existed. Or at least it did exist, but as something deplorably different from what we love to picture it.' And he went on, eruditely, to refer to that Council of Carthage which, in 398, demanded of the faithful that they should be continent on their wedding-night. It was the Lord's right – the *droit* of a heavenly Seigneur. On this text of fact, Mr Mercaptan went on to preach a brilliant sermon on that melancholy sexual perversion known as continence. How much happier we all should be if the real historical *droit du Seigneur* had in fact been the mythical right of our 'pretty prurient imaginations'! He looked forward to a golden age when all should be seigneurs possessing rights that should have broadened down into universal liberty. And so on. Mr Mercaptan read through his creation with a smile of satis- faction on his face. Every here and there he made a careful correction in red ink. Over 'pretty prurient imaginations' his pen hung for a full minute in conscientious hesitation. Wasn't it per-

haps a little too strongly alliterative, a shade, perhaps, cheap? Perhaps 'pretty lascivious' or 'delicate prurient' would be better. He repeated the alternatives several times, rolling the sound of them round his tongue, judicially, like a tea-taster. In the end, he decided that 'pretty prurient' was right. 'Pretty prurient' – they were the *mots justes*, decidedly, without a question.

Mr Mercaptan had just come to this decision and his poised pen was moving farther down the page, when he was disturbed by the sound of arguing voices in the corridor, outside his room.

'What is it, Mrs Goldie?' he called irritably, for it was not difficult to distinguish his housekeeper's loud and querulous tones. He had given orders that he was not to be disturbed. In these critical moments of correction one needed such absolute tranquillity.

But Mr Mercaptan was to have no tranquillity this afternoon. The door of his sacred boudoir was thrown rudely open, and there strode in, like a Goth into the elegant marble vomitorium of Petronius Arbiter, a haggard and dishevelled person whom Mr Mercaptan recognized, with a certain sense of discomfort, as Casimir Lypiatt.

'To what do I owe the *pleasure* of this unexpected ...?' Mr Mercaptan began with an essay in offensive courtesy.

But Lypiatt, who had no feeling for the finer shades, coarsely interrupted him. 'Look here, Mercaptan,' he said. 'I want to have a talk with you.'

'Delighted, I'm sure,' Mr Mercaptan replied. 'And *what*, may I ask, about?' He knew, of course, perfectly well; and the prospect of the talk disturbed him.

'About this,' said Lypiatt; and he held out what looked like a roll of paper.

Mr Mercaptan took the roll and opened it out. It was a copy of the *Weekly World*. 'Ah!' said Mr Mercaptan, in a tone of delighted surprise, 'The *World*. You have read my little article?'

'That was what I wanted to talk to you about,' said Lypiatt.

Mr Mercaptan modestly laughed. 'It hardly deserves it,' he said.

Preserving a calm of expression which was quite unnatural to him, and speaking in a studiedly quiet voice, Lypiatt pronounced with careful deliberation: 'It is a disgusting, malicious, ignoble attack on me,' he said.

'Come, *come*!' protested Mr Mercaptan. 'A critic must be allowed to criticize.'

'But there are limits,' said Lypiatt.

'Oh, I *quite* agree,' Mr Mercaptan eagerly conceded. 'But, after all, Lypiatt, you can't pretend that I have come anywhere near those limits. If I had called you a *mur*derer, or even an *adul*terer – then, I admit, you would have some cause to complain. But I haven't. There's nothing like a personality in the whole thing.'

Lypiatt laughed derisively, and his face went all to pieces, like a pool of water into which a stone is suddenly dropped.

'You've merely said I was insincere, an actor, a mountebank, a quack, raving fustian, spouting mock heroics. That's all.'

Mr Mercaptan put on the expression of one who feels himself injured and misunderstood. He shut his eyes, he flapped deprecatingly with his hand. 'I *merely* suggested,' he said, 'that you protest *too* much. You defeat your own ends; you lose emphasis by trying to be over-emphatic. All this *folie de grandeur*, all this hankering after *terribiltà* –' sagely Mr Mercaptan shook his head, 'it's led so *many* people astray. And, in any case, you can't *really* expect *me* to find it very sympathetic.' Mr Mercaptan uttered a little laugh and looked affectionately round his boudoir, his retired and perfumed poutery within whose walls so much civilization had finely flowered. He looked at his magnificent sofa, gilded and carved, upholstered in white satin, and so deep – for it was a great square piece of furniture, almost as broad as it was long – that when you sat right back, you had of necessity to lift your feet from the floor and recline at length. It was under the white satin that Crébillon's spirit found, in these late degenerate days, a sympathetic home. He looked at his exquisite Condor fans over the mantelpiece; his lovely Marie Laurencin of two young girls, pale-skinned and berry-eyed, walking embraced in a shallow myopic landscape amid a troop of bounding heraldic dogs. He looked at his cabinet of *bibelots* in the corner where the nigger mask and the superb Chinese phallus in sculptured rock crystal contrasted so amusingly with the Chelsea china, the little ivory Madonna, which might be a fake, but in any case was quite as good as any mediæval French original, and the Italian medals. He looked at his comical writing-desk in shining black papier mâché and mother-of-pearl; he looked at his article on the 'Jus Primæ Noctis', black and neat on the page, with the red corrections attesting his tireless search for, and his, he flattered himself, almost invariable discovery of, the inevitable word. No, really, one couldn't expect *him* to find Lypiatt's notions very sympathetic.

'But I don't expect you to,' said Lypiatt, 'and, good God! I don't want you to. But you call me insincere. That's what I can't and won't stand. How dare you do that?' His voice was growing louder.

Once more Mr Mercaptan deprecatingly flapped. 'At the most,' he corrected, 'I said that there was a certain look of insincerity about some of the pictures. Hardly avoidable, indeed, in work of this kind.'

Quite suddenly, Lypiatt lost his self-control. All the accumulated anger and bitterness of the last days burst out. His show had been a hopeless failure. Not a picture sold, a press that was mostly bad, or, when good, that had praised for the wrong, the insulting reasons. 'Bright and effective work.' 'Mr Lypiatt would make an excellent stage designer.' Damn them! damn them! And then, when the dailies had all had their yelp, here was Mercaptan in the *Weekly World* taking him as a text for what was practically an essay on insincerity in art. 'How dare you?' he furiously shouted. 'You – how dare you talk about sincerity? What can you know about sincerity, you disgusting little bug!' And avenging himself on the person of Mr Mercaptan against the world that had neglected him, against the fate that had denied him his rightful share of talent, Lypiatt sprang up and, seizing the author of the 'Jus Primæ Noctis' by the shoulders, he shook him, he bumped him up and down in his chair, he cuffed him over the head. 'How can you have the impudence,' he asked, letting go of his victim, but still standing menacingly over him, 'to touch anything that even attempts to be decent and big?' All these years, these wretched years of poverty and struggle and courageous hope and failure and repeated disappointment; and now this last failure, more complete than all. He was tremblng with anger; at least one forgot unhappiness while one was angry.

Mr Mercaptan had recovered from his first terrified surprise. 'Really, *really*,' he repeated, '*too* barbarous. Scuffling like hobbledehoys.'

'If you knew,' Lypiatt began; but he checked himself. If you knew, he was going to say, what those things had cost me, what they meant, what thought, what passion— But how could Mercaptan understand? And it would sound as though he were appealing to this creature's sympathy. 'Bug!' he shouted instead, 'bug!' And he struck out again with the flat of his hand. Mr Mercaptan put up his hands and ducked away from the slaps, blinking.

'Really,' he protested, '*really. ...*'

Insincere? Perhaps it was half true. Lypiatt seized his man more furiously than before and shook him, shook him. 'And then that vile insult about the vermouth advertisement,' he cried out. That had rankled. Those flaring, vulgar posters! 'You thought you could mock me and spit at me with impunity, did you? I've stood it so long, you thought I'd always stand it? Was that it? But you're mistaken.' He lifted his fist. Mr Mercaptan cowered away, raising his arm to protect his head. 'Vile bug of a coward,' said Lypiatt, 'why don't you defend yourself like a man? You can only be dangerous with words. Very witty and spiteful and cutting about those vermouth posters, wasn't it? But you wouldn't dare to fight me if I challenged you.'

'Well, as a matter of *fact*,' said Mr Mercaptan, peering up from under his defences, 'I didn't invent *that* particular piece of criticism. I borrowed the *apéritif*.' He laughed feebly, more canary than bull.

'You borrowed it, did you?' Lypiatt contemptuously repeated. 'And who from, may I ask?' Not that it interested him in the least to know.

'Well, if you really *want* to know,' said Mr Mercaptan, 'it was from our friend Myra Viveash.'

Lypiatt stood for a moment without speaking, then putting

his menacing hand in his pocket, he turned away. 'Oh!' he said non-committally, and was silent again.

Relieved, Mr Mercaptan sat up in his chair; with the palm of his right hand he smoothed his dishevelled head.

Airily, outside in the sunshine, Rosie walked down Sloane Street, looking at the numbers on the doors of the houses. A hundred and ninety-nine, two hundred, two hundred and one – she was getting near now. Perhaps all the people who passed, strolling so easily and elegantly and disengagedly along, perhaps they all of them carried behind their eyes a secret, as delightful and amusing as hers. Rosie liked to think so; it made life more exciting. How nonchalantly distinguished, Rosie reflected, she herself must look. Would any one who saw her now, sauntering along like this, would any one guess that, ten houses farther down the street, a young poet, or at least very nearly a young poet, was waiting, on the second floor, eagerly for her arrival? Of course they wouldn't and couldn't guess! That was the fun and the enormous excitement of the whole thing. Formidable in her light-hearted detachment, formidable in the passion which at will she could give rein to and check again, the great lady swam beautifully along through the sunlight to satisfy her caprice. Like Diana, she stooped over the shepherd boy. Eagerly the starving young poet waited, waited in his garret. Two hundred and twelve, two hundred and thirteen. Rosie looked at the entrance and was reminded that the garret couldn't after all be very sordid, nor the young poet absolutely starving. She stepped in and, standing in the hall, looked at the board with the names. Ground floor: Mrs Budge. First floor: F. de M. Rowbotham. Second floor: P. Mercaptan.

P. Mercaptan. ... But it was a charming name, a romantic name, a real young poet's name! Mercaptan – she felt more than ever pleased with her selection. The fastidious lady could not have had a happier caprice. Mercaptan ... Mercaptan. ... She wondered what the P. stood for. Peter, Philip, Patrick, Pendennis even? She could hardly have guessed that Mr Mercaptan's father, the eminent bacteriologist, had insisted, thirty-four years ago, on calling his first-born 'Pasteur'.

A little tremulous, under her outward elegant calm, Rosie

mounted the stairs. Twenty-five steps to the first floor – one flight of thirteen, which was rather disagreeably ominous, and one of twelve. Then two flights of eleven, and she was on the second landing, facing a front door, a bell-push like a round eye, a brass name-plate. For a great lady thoroughly accustomed to this sort of thing, she felt her heart beating rather unpleasantly fast. It was those stairs, no doubt. She halted a moment, took two deep breaths, then pushed the bell.

The door was opened by an aged servant of the most forbiddingly respectable appearance.

'Mr Mercaptan at home?'

The person at the door burst at once into a long, rambling, angry complaint, but precisely about what Rosie could not for certain make out. Mr Mercaptan had left orders, she gathered, that he wasn't to be disturbed. But some one had come and disturbed him, 'fairly shoved his way in, so rude and inconsiderate,' all the same. And now he'd been once disturbed, she didn't see why he shouldn't be disturbed again. But she didn't know what things were coming to if people fairly shoved their way in like that. Bolshevism, she called it.

Rosie murmured her sympathies, and was admitted into a dark hall. Still querulously denouncing the Bolsheviks who came shoving in, the person led the way down a corridor and, throwing open a door, announced, in a tone of grievance: 'A lady to see you, Master Paster' – for Mrs Goldie was an old family retainer, and one of the few who knew the secret of Mr Mercaptan's Christian name, one of the fewer still who were privileged to employ it. Then, as soon as Rosie had stepped across the threshold, she cut off her retreat with a bang and went off, muttering all the time, towards her kitchen.

It certainly wasn't a garret. Half a glance, the first whiff of potpourri, the feel of the carpet beneath her feet, had been enough to prove that. But it was not the room which occupied Rosie's attention, it was its occupants. One of them, thin, sharp-featured and, in Rosie's very young eyes, quite old, was standing with an elbow on the mantelpiece. The other, sleeker and more genial in appearance, was sitting in front of a writing-desk near the window. And neither of them – Rosie glanced desperately

430

from one to the other, hoping vainly that she might have over-looked a blond beard – neither of them was Toto.

The sleek man at the writing-desk got up, advanced to meet her.

'An unexpected pleasure,' he said, in a voice that alternately boomed and fluted. '*Too* delightful! But to what do I owe –? *Who*, may I ask –?'

He had held out his hand; automatically Rosie proffered hers. The sleek man shook it with cordiality, almost with tenderness.

'I ... I think I must have made a mistake,' she said. 'Mr Mercaptan ...?'

The sleek man smiled. 'I am Mr Mercaptan.'

'You live on the second floor?'

'I never laid claims to being a mathematician,' said the sleek man, smiling as though to applaud himself, 'but I have always calculated that ...' he hesitated ... '*enfin, que ma demeure se trouve, en effet*, on the second floor. Lypiatt will bear me out, I'm sure.' He turned to the thin man, who had not moved from the fireplace, but had stood all the time motionlessly, his elbow on the mantelpiece, looking gloomily at the ground.

Lypiatt looked up. 'I must be going,' he said abruptly. And he walked towards the door. Like vermouth posters, like vermouth posters! – so that was Myra's piece of mockery! All his anger had sunk like a quenched flame. He was altogether quenched, put out with unhappiness.

Politely Mr Mercaptan hurried across the room and opened the door for him. '*Good*-bye, then,' he said airily.

Lypiatt did not speak, but walked out into the hall. The front door banged behind him.

'Well, *well*,' said Mr Mercaptan, coming back across the room to where Rosie was still irresolutely standing. 'Talk about the *furor poeticus*! But *do* sit down, I beg you. On Crébillon.' He indicated the vast white satin sofa. 'I call it Crébillon,' he explained, 'because the soul of that great writer undoubtedly tenants it, *undoubtedly*. You know his book, of course? You know *Le Sopha*?'

Sinking into Crébillon's soft lap, Rosie had to admit that she didn't know *Le Sopha*. She had begun to recover her self-possession. If this wasn't *the* young poet, it was certainly *a* young poet. And a very peculiar one, too. As a great lady she laughingly accepted the odd situation.

'Not know *Le Sopha*?' exclaimed Mr Mercaptan. 'Oh! but, my dear and mysterious young lady, let me lend you a copy of it at once. *No* education can be called *complete* without a knowledge of that divine book.' He darted to the bookshelf and came back with a small volume bound in white vellum. 'The hero's soul,' he explained, handing her the volume, 'passes, by the laws of metempsychosis, into a sofa. He is doomed to remain a sofa until such time as two persons consummate upon his bosom their reciprocal and equal loves. The book is the record of the poor sofa's hopes and disappointments.'

'Dear me!' said Rosie, looking at the title-page.

'But now,' said Mr Mercaptan, sitting down beside her on the edge of Crébillon, 'won't you please explain? To what happy quiproquo do I owe this sudden and altogether delightful invasion of my privacy?'

'Well,' said Rosie, and hesitated. It was really rather difficult to explain. 'I was to meet a friend of mine.'

'Quite so,' said Mr Mercaptan encouragingly.

'Who sent me a telegram,' Rosie went on.

'He sent you a telegram!' Mr Mercaptan echoed.

'Changing the – the place we had fixed and telling me to meet him at this address.'

'Here?'

Rose nodded. 'On the s–second floor,' she made it more precise.

'But *I* live on the second floor,' said Mr Mercaptan. 'You don't mean to say your friend is also called Mercaptan and lives here too?'

Rosie smiled. 'I don't know what he's called,' she said with a cool ironical carelessness that was genuinely *grande dame*.

'You don't know his name?' Mr Mercaptan gave a roar and a squeal of delighted laughter. 'But that's *too* good,' he said.

'S–second floor, he wrote in the telegram.' Rosie was now perfectly at her ease. 'When I saw your name, I thought it was his name. I must say,' she added, looking sideways at Mr Mercaptan and at once dropping the magnolia petals of her eyelids, 'it seemed to me a very charming name.'

'You overwhelm me,' said Mr Mercaptan, smiling all over his cheerful, snouty face. 'As for *your* name – I am too discreet a *galantuomo* to ask. And, in any case, what *does* it matter? A rose by any other name ...'

'But, as a matter of fact,' she said, raising and lowering once again her smooth, white lids, 'my name does happen to be Rose; or, at any rate, Rosie.'

'So you are sweet by right!' exclaimed Mr Mercaptan, with a pretty gallantry which he was the first to appreciate. 'Let's order tea on the strength of it.' He jumped up and rang the bell. 'How I congratulate myself on this astonishing piece of good fortune!'

Rosie said nothing. This Mr Mercaptan, she thought, seemed to be even more a man of the great artistic world than Toto.

'What puzzles me,' he went on, 'is why your anonymous friend should have chosen my address out of all the millions of others. He must know me, or, at any rate, know about me.'

'I should imagine,' said Rosie, 'that you have a lot of friends.'

Mr Mercaptan laughed – the whole orchestra, from bassoon to piccolo. '*Des amis, des amies* – with and without the mute "e",' he declared.

The aged and forbidding servant appeared at the door.

'Tea for two, Mrs Goldie.'

Mrs Goldie looked round the room suspiciously. 'The other gentleman's gone, has he?' she asked. And having assured herself of his absence, she renewed her complaint. 'Shoving in like that,' she said. 'Bolshevism, that's what I –'

'All right, all right, Mrs Goldie. Let's have our tea as quickly as possible.' Mr Mercaptan held up his hand, authoritatively, with the gesture of a policeman controlling the traffic.

'Very well, Master Paster.' Mrs Goldie spoke with resignation and departed.

'But tell me,' Mr Mercaptan went on, 'if it *isn't* indiscreet – what does your friend look like?'

'W–well,' Rosie answered, 'he's fair, and though he's quite young he wears a beard.' With her two hands she indicated on her own unemphatic bosom the contours of Toto's broad blond fan.

'A beard! But, good heavens,' Mr Mercaptan slapped his thigh, 'it's Coleman, it's obviously and undoubtedly Coleman!'

'Well, whoever it was,' said Rosie severely, 'he played a very stupid sort of joke.'

'For which I thank him. *De tout mon cœur.*'

Rosie smiled and looked sideways. 'All the same,' she said, 'I shall give him a piece of my mind.'

Poor Aunt Aggie! Oh, poor Aunt Aggie, indeed! In the light of Mr Mercaptan's boudoir her hammered copper and her leadless glaze certainly did look a bit comical.

After tea Mr Mercaptan played cicerone in a tour of inspection round the room. They visited the papier mâché writing-desk, the Condor fans, the Marie Laurencin, the 1914 edition of *Du Côté de chez Swann*, the Madonna that probably was a fake, the nigger mask, the Chelsea figures, the Chinese object of art in sculptured crystal, the scale model of Queen Victoria in wax under a glass bell. Toto, it became clear, had been no more than a forerunner; the definitive revelation was Mr Mercaptan's. Yes, poor Aunt Aggie! And indeed, when Mr Mercaptan began to read her his little middle on the 'Droit du Seigneur', it was poor everybody. Poor mother, with her absurd, old-fashioned, prudish views; poor, earnest father, with his Unitarianism, his *Hibbert Journal*, his letters to the papers about the necessity for a spiritual regeneration.

'Bravo!' she cried from the depths of Crébillon. She was leaning back in one corner, languid, serpentine, and at ease, her feet in their mottled snake's leather tucked up under her. 'Bravo!' she cried as Mr Mercaptan finished his reading and looked up for his applause.

Mr Mercaptan bowed.

'You express so exquisitely what we –' and waving her hand in a comprehensive gesture, she pictured to herself all the other fastidious ladies, all the marchionesses of fable, reclining, as she herself at this moment reclined, on upholstery of white satin, 'what we all only feel and aren't clever enough to say.'

Mr Mercaptan was charmed. He got up from before his writing-desk, crossed the room and sat down beside her on Crébillon. 'Feeling,' he said, 'is the important thing."

Rosie remembered that her father had once remarked, in blank verse: 'The things that matter happen in the heart.'

'I quite agree,' she said.

Like movable raisins in the suet of his snouty face, Mr Mercaptan's brown little eyes rolled amorous avowals. He took Rosie's hand and kissed it. Crébillon creaked discreetly as he moved a little nearer.

It was on the evening of the same day. Rosie lay on her sofa – a poor, hire-purchase thing indeed, compared with Mr Mercaptan's grand affair in white satin and carved and gilded wood, but still a sofa – lay with her feet on the arm of it and her long suave legs exposed, by the slipping of the kimono, to the top of her stretched stockings. She was reading the little vellum-jacketed volume of Crébillon, which Mr Mercaptan had given her when he said 'good-bye' (or rather, '*À bientôt, mon amie*'); given, not lent, as he had less generously offered at the beginning of their afternoon; given with the most graceful of allusive dedications inscribed on the fly-leaf:

To

BY-NO-OTHER-NAME-AS-SWEET,

With Gratitude,

from

CRÉBILLON DELIVERED.

À bientôt – she had promised to come again very soon. She thought of the essay on the 'Jus Primæ Noctis' – ah! what we've all been feeling and none of us clever enough to say. We on the sofas, ruthless, lovely and fastidious. ...

'I am proud to constitute myself' – Mr Mercaptan had said of it – '*l'esprit d'escalier des dames galantes.*'

Rosie was not quite sure what he meant; but it certainly sounded very witty indeed.

She read the book slowly. Her French, indeed, wasn't good enough to permit her to read it anyhow else. She wished it were better. Perhaps if it were better she wouldn't be yawning like this. It was disgraceful: she pulled herself together. Mr Mercaptan had said that it was a masterpiece.

435

In his study, Shearwater was trying to write his paper on the regulative functions of the kidneys. He was not succeeding.

Why wouldn't she see me yesterday? he kept wondering. With anguish he suspected other lovers; desired her, in consequence, the more. Gumbril had said something, he remembered, that night they had met her by the coffee-stall. What was it? He wished now that he had listened more attentively.

She's bored with me. Already. It was obvious.

Perhaps he was too rustic for her. Shearwater looked at his hands. Yes, the nails *were* dirty. He took an orange stick out of his waistcoat pocket and began to clean them. He had bought a whole packet of orange sticks that morning.

Determinedly he took up his pen. 'The hydrogen ion concentration in the blood ...' he began a new paragraph. But he got no further than the first seven words.

If, he began thinking with a frightful confusion, if – if – if – Past conditionals, hopelessly past. He might have been brought up more elegantly; his father, for example, might have been a barrister instead of a barrister's clerk. He mightn't have had to work so hard when he was young; might have been about more, danced more, seen more young women. If he had met her years ago – during the war, should one say, dressed in the uniform of a lieutenant in the Guards. ...

He had pretended that he wasn't interested in women; that they had no effect on him; that, in fact, he was above that sort of thing. Imbecile! He might as well have said that he was above having a pair of kidneys. He had only consented to admit, graciously, that they were a physiological necessity.

O God, what a fool he had been!

And then, what about Rosie? What sort of a life had she been having while he was being above that sort of thing? Now he came to think of it, he really knew nothing about her, except that she had been quite incapable of learning correctly, even by heart, the simplest facts about the physiology of frogs. Having found that out, he had really given up exploring further. How could he have been so stupid?

Rosie had been in love with him, he supposed. Had he been in love with her? No. He had taken care not to be. On principle. He had married her as a measure of intimate hygiene; out of protective affection, too, certainly out of affection; and a little for amusement, as one might buy a puppy.

Mrs Viveash had opened his eyes; seeing her, he had also begun to notice Rosie. It seemed to him that he had been a loutish cad as well as an imbecile.

What should he do about it? He sat for a long time wondering.

In the end he decided that the best thing would be to go and tell Rosie all about it, all about everything.

About Mrs Viveash too? Yes, about Mrs Viveash too. He would get over Mrs Viveash more easily and more rapidly if he did. And he would begin to try and find out about Rosie. He would explore her. He would discover all the other things besides an incapacity to learn physiology that were in her. He would discover her, he would quicken his affection for her into something livelier and more urgent. And they would begin again; more satisfactorily this time; with knowledge and understanding; wise from their experience.

Shearwater got up from his chair before the writing-table, lurched pensively towards the door, bumping into the revolving bookcase and the arm-chair as he went, and walked down the passage to the drawing-room. Rosie did not turn her head as he came in, but went on reading without changing her position, her slippered feet still higher than her head, her legs still charmingly avowing themselves.

Shearwater came to a halt in front of the empty fireplace. He stood there with his back to it, as though warming himself before an imaginary flame. It was, he felt, the safest, the most strategic point from which to talk.

'What are you reading?' he asked.

'*Le Sopha*,' said Rosie.

'What's that?'

'What's that?' Rosie scornfully echoed. 'Why, it's one of the great French classics.'

'Who by?'

'Crébillon the younger.'

'Never heard of him,' said Shearwater.

437

There was a silence. Rosie went on reading.

'It just occurred to me,' Shearwater began again in his rather ponderous, infelicitous way, 'that you mightn't be very happy, Rosie.'

Rosie looked up at him and laughed. 'What put that into your head?' she asked. '*I*'m perfectly happy.'

Shearwater was left a little at a loss. 'Well, I'm very glad to hear it,' he said. 'I only thought ... that perhaps *you* might think ... that *I* rather neglected you.'

Rosie laughed again. 'What is all this about?' she said.

'I have it rather on my conscience,' said Shearwater. 'I begin to see ... something has made me see ... that I've not. ... I don't treat you very well ...'

'But I don't n—notice it, I assure you,' put in Rosie, still smiling.

'I leave you out too much,' Shearwater went on with a kind of desperation, running his fingers through his thick black hair. 'We don't share enough together. You're too much outside my life.'

'But after all,' said Rosie, 'we are a civ—vilized couple. We don't want to live in one another's pockets, do we?'

'No, but we're really no more than strangers,' said Shear- water. 'That isn't right. And it's my fault. I've never tried to get into touch with your life. But you did your best to understand mine ... at the beginning of our marriage.'

'Oh, *then—n*!' said Rosie, laughing. 'You found out what a little idiot I was.'

'Don't make a joke of it,' said Shearwater. 'It isn't a joke. It's very serious. I tell you, I've come to see how stupid and in- considerate and un-understanding I've been with you. I've come to see quite suddenly. The fact is,' he went on with a rush, like an uncorked fountain, 'I've been seeing a woman recently whom I like very much, and who doesn't like me.' Speaking of Mrs Vive- ash, unconsciously he spoke her language. For Mrs Viveash people always euphemistically 'liked' one another rather a lot, even when it was a case of the most frightful and excruciating passion, the most complete abandonments. 'And somehow that's made me see a lot of things which I'd been blind to before – blind deliberately, I suppose. It's made me see, among other things, that I've really been to blame towards you, Rosie.'

Rosie listened with an astonishment which she perfectly disguised. So James was embarking on his little affairs, was he? It seemed incredible, and also, as she looked at her husband's face – the face, behind its bristlingly manly mask, of a harassed baby – also rather pathetically absurd. She wondered who it could be. But she displayed no curiosity. She would find out soon enough.

'I'm sorry you should have been unhappy about it,' she said.

'It's finished now.' Shearwater made a decided little gesture.

'Ah, no!' said Rosie. 'You should persevere.' She looked at him, smiling.

Shearwater was taken aback by this display of easy detachment. He had imagined the conversation so very differently, as something so serious, so painful and, at the same time, so healing and soothing, that he did not know how to go on. 'But I thought,' he said hesitatingly, 'that you ... that we ... after this experience ... I would try to get closer to you ...' (Oh, it sounded ridiculous!) ... 'We might start again, from a different place, so to speak.'

'But, *cher ami,*' protested Rosie, with the inflection and in the preferred tongue of Mr Mercaptan, 'you can't seriously expect us to do the Darby and Joan business, can you? You're distressing yourself quite unnecessarily on my account. I don't find you neglect me or anything like it. You have your life – naturally. And I have mine. We don't get in one another's way.'

'But do you think that's the ideal sort of married life?' asked Shearwater.

'It's obviously the most civ–vilized,' Rosie answered, laughing.

Confronted by Rosie's civilization, Shearwater felt helpless. 'Well, if you don't want,' he said. 'I'd hoped ... I'd thought ...'

He went back to his study to think things over. The more he thought them over, the more he blamed himself. And incessantly the memory of Mrs Viveash tormented him.

CHAPTER XIX

AFTER leaving Mr Mercaptan, Lypiatt had gone straight home. The bright day seemed to deride him. With its shining red omni-buses, its parasols, its muslin girls, its young-leaved trees, its bands at the street corners, it was too much of a garden party to be tolerable. He wanted to be alone. He took a cab back to the studio. He couldn't afford it, of course; but what did that matter, what did that matter now?

The cab drove slowly and as though with reluctance down the dirty mews. He paid it off, opened his little door between the wide stable doors, climbed the steep ladder of his stairs and was at home. He sat down and tried to think.

'Death, death, death, death,' he kept repeating to himself, moving his lips as though he were praying. If he said the word often enough, if he accustomed himself completely to the idea, death would come almost by itself; he would know it already, while he was still alive, he would pass almost without noticing out of life into death. Into death, he thought, into death. Death like a well. The stone falls, falls, second after second; and at last there is a sound, a far-off, horrible sound of death and then nothing more. The well at Carisbrooke, with a donkey to wind the wheel that pulls up the bucket of water, of icy water ... He thought for a long time of the well of death.

Outside in the mews a barrel-organ struck up the tune of 'Where do flies go in the winter-time?' Lypiatt lifted his head to listen. He smiled to himself. 'Where *do* flies go?' The question asked itself with a dramatic, a tragical appositeness. At the end of everything – the last ludicrous touch. He saw it all from out-side. He pictured himself sitting there alone, broken. He looked at his hand lying limp on the table in front of him. It needed only the stigma of the nail to make it the hand of a dead Christ.

There, he was making literature of it again. Even now. He buried his face in his hands. His mind was full of twisted darkness, of an unspeakable, painful confusion. It was too difficult, too difficult.

The inkpot, he found when he wanted to begin writing, contained nothing but a parched black sediment. He had been meaning for days past to get some more ink; and he had always forgotten. He would have to write in pencil.

'Do you remember,' he wrote, 'do you remember, Myra, that time we went down into the country – you remember – under the Hog's Back at that little inn they were trying to make pretentious? "Hotel Bull" – do you remember? How we laughed over the Hotel Bull! And how we liked the country outside its doors! All the world in a few square miles. Chalk-pits and blue butterflies on the Hog's Back. And at the foot of the hill, suddenly, the sand; the hard, yellow sand with those queer caves, dug when and by what remote villains at the edge of the Pilgrims' Way? the fine grey sand on which the heather of Puttenham Common grows. And the flagstaff and the inscription marking the place where Queen Victoria stood to look at the view. And the enormous sloping meadows round Compton and the thick, dark woods. And the lakes, the heaths, the Scotch firs at Cutt Mill. The forests of Shackleford. There was everything. Do you remember how we enjoyed it all? I did, in any case. I was happy during those three days. And I loved you, Myra. And I thought you might, you might perhaps, some day, love me. You didn't. And my love has only brought me unhappiness. Perhaps it has been my fault. Perhaps I ought to have known how to make you give me happiness. You remember that wonderful sonnet of Michelangelo's, where he says that the loved woman is like a block of marble from which the artist knows how to cut the perfect statue of his dreams. If the statue turns out a bad one, if it's death instead of love that the lover gets – why, the fault lies in the artist and in the lover, not in the marble, not in the beloved.

> Amor dunque non ha, nè tua beltate,
> O fortuna, o durezza, o gran disdegno,
> Del mio mal colpa, o mio destino, o sorte,
>
> Se dentro del tuo cor morte è pietate
> Porti in un tempo, e ch'l mio basso ingegno
> Non sappia ardendo trarne altro che morte.

441

Yes, it was my *basso ingegno*: my low genius which did not know how to draw love from you, nor beauty from the materials of which art is made. Ah, now you'll smile to yourself and say: Poor Casimir, he has come to admit that at last? Yes, yes, I have come to admit everything. That I couldn't paint, I couldn't write, I couldn't make music. That I was a charlatan and a quack. That I was a ridiculous actor of heroic parts who deserved to be laughed at – and *was* laughed at. But then every man is ludicrous if you look at him from outside, without taking into account what's going on in his heart and mind. You could turn Hamlet into an epigrammatic farce with an inimitable scene when he takes his adored mother in adultery. You could make the wittiest Guy de Maupassant short story out of the life of Christ, by contrasting the mad rabbi's pretensions with his abject fate. It's a question of the point of view. Every one's a walking farce and a walking tragedy at the same time. The man who slips on a banana-skin and fractures his skull describes against the sky, as he falls, the most richly comical arabesque. And you, Myra – what do you suppose the unsympathetic gossips say of you? What sort of a farce of the Boulevards is your life in their eyes? For me, Myra, you seem to move all the time through some nameless and incomprehensible tragedy. For them you are what? Merely any sort of a wanton, with amusing adventures. And what am I? A charlatan, a quack, a pretentious, boasting, rhodomontading imbecile, incapable of painting anything but vermouth posters. (Why did that hurt so terribly? I don't know. There was no reason why you shouldn't think so if you wanted to.) I was all that – and grotesquely laughable. And very likely your laughter was justified, your judgment was true. I don't know. I can't tell. Perhaps I am a charlatan. Perhaps I'm insincere; boasting to others, deceiving myself. I don't know, I tell you. Everything is confusion in my mind now. The whole fabric seems to have tumbled to pieces; it lies in a horrible chaos. I can make no order within myself. Have I lied to myself? have I acted and postured the Great Man to persuade myself that I am one? have I something in me, or nothing? have I ever achieved anything of worth, anything that rhymed with my conceptions, my dreams (for those were fine; of that, I *am* certain)? I look into the

442

chaos that is my soul and, I tell you, I don't know, I don't know. But what I do know is that I've spent nearly twenty years now playing the charlatan at whom you all laugh. That I've suffered, in mind and in body too – almost from hunger, sometimes – in order to play it. That I've struggled, that I've exultantly climbed to the attack, that I've been thrown down – ah, many times! – that I've picked myself up and started again. Well, I suppose all that's ludicrous, if you like to think of it that way. It is ludicrous that a man should put himself to prolonged inconvenience for the sake of something which doesn't really exist at all. It's exquisitely comic, I can see. I can see it in the abstract, so to speak. But in this particular case, you must remember I'm not a dispassionate observer. And if I am overcome now, it is not with laughter. It is with an indescribable unhappinèss, with the bitter-ness of death itself. Death, death, death. I repeat the word to myself, again and again. I think of death, I try to imagine it, I hang over it, looking down, where the stones fall and fall and there is one horrible noise, and then silence again; looking down into the well of death. It is so deep that there is no glittering eye of water to be seen at the bottom. I have no candle to send down. It is horrible, but I do not want to go on living. Living would be worse than ...'

Lypiatt was reaching out for another sheet of paper when he was startled to hear the sound of feet on the stairs. He turned towards the door. His heart beat with violence. He was filled with a strange sense of apprehension. In terror he awaited the approach of some unknown and terrible being. The feet of the angel of death were on the stairs. Up, up, up. Lypiatt felt himself trembling as the sound came nearer. He knew for certain that in a few seconds he was going to die. The hangmen had already pinioned him; the soldiers of the firing squad had already raised their rifles. One, two, ... he thought of Mrs Viveash standing, bare-headed, the wind blowing in her hair, at the foot of the flagstaff from the site of which Queen Victoria had admired the distant view of Selborne; he thought of her dolorously smiling; he remembered that once she had taken his head between her two hands and kissed him: 'Because you're such a golden ass,' she had said, laughing. Three ... There was a little tap at the door. Lypiatt pressed his hand over his heart. The door opened.

A small, bird-like man with a long, sharp nose and eyes as round and black and shining as buttons stepped into the room.

'Mr Lydgate, I presume?' he began. Then looked at a card on which a name and address were evidently written. 'Lypiatt, I mean. A thousand pardons. Mr Lypiatt, I presume?'

Lypiatt leaned back in his chair and shut his eyes. His face was as white as paper. He breathed hard and his temples were wet with sweat, as though he had been running.

'I found the door down below open, so I came straight up. I hope you'll excuse ...' The stranger smiled apologetically.

'Who are you?' Lypiatt asked, reopening his eyes. His heart was still beating hard; after the storm it calmed itself slowly. He drew back from the brink of the fearful well; the time had not yet come to plunge.

'My name,' said the stranger, 'is Boldero, Herbert Boldero. Our mutual friend Mr Gumbril, Mr Theodore Gumbril, junior,' he made it more precise, 'suggested that I might come and see you about a little matter in which he and I are interested and in which perhaps you, too, might be interested.'

Lypiatt nodded, without saying anything.

Mr Boldero, meanwhile, was turning his bright, bird-like eyes about the studio. Mrs Viveash's portrait, all but finished now, was clamped to the easel. He approached it, a connoisseur.

'It reminds me very much,' he said, 'of Bacosso. Very much indeed, if I may say so. Also a little of ...' he hesitated, trying to think of the name of that other fellow Gumbril had talked about. But being unable to remember the unimpressive syllables of Derain he played for safety and said – 'of Orpen.' Mr Boldero looked inquiringly at Lypiatt to see if that was right.

Lypiatt still spoke no word and seemed, indeed, not to have heard what had been said.

Mr Boldero saw that it wasn't much good talking about modern art. This chap, he thought, looked as though something were wrong with him. He hoped he hadn't got influenza. There was a lot of the disease about. 'This little affair I was speaking of,' he pursued, in another tone, 'is a little business proposition that Mr Gumbril and I have gone into together. A matter of pneumatic trousers,' he waved his hand airily.

Lypiatt suddenly burst out laughing, an embittered Titan. Where do flies go? Where do souls go? The barrel-organ, and now pneumatic trousers! Then, as suddenly, he was silent again. More literature? Another piece of acting? 'Go on,' he said, 'I'm sorry.'

'Not at all, not at all,' said Mr Boldero indulgently. 'I know the idea does seem a little humorous, if I may say so, at first. But I assure you, there's money in it, Mr Lydgate – Mr Lypiatt. Money!' Mr Boldero paused a moment dramatically. 'Well,' he went on, 'our idea was to launch the new product with a good swingeing publicity campaign. Spend a few thousands in the papers and then get it good and strong into the Underground and on the hoardings, along with Owbridge's and John Bull and the Golden Ballot. Now, for that, Mr Lypiatt, we shall need, as you can well imagine, a few good striking pictures. Mr Gumbril mentioned your name and suggested I should come and see you to find out if you would perhaps be agreeable to lending us your talent for this work. And I may add, Mr Lypiatt,' he spoke with real warmth, 'that having seen this example of your work' – he pointed to the portrait of Mrs Viveash – "I feel that you would be eminently capable of ...'

He did not finish the sentence; for at this moment Lypiatt leapt up from his chair and, making a shrill, inarticulate, animal noise, rushed on the financier, seized him with both hands by the throat, shook him, threw him to the floor, then picked him up again by the coat collar and pushed him towards the door, kicking him as he went. A final kick sent Mr Boldero tobogganing down the steep stairs. Lypiatt ran down after him; but Mr Boldero had picked himself up, had opened the front door, slipped out, slammed it behind him, and was running up the mews before Lypiatt could get to the bottom of the stairs.

Lypiatt opened the door and looked out. Mr Boldero was already far away, almost at the Piranesian arch. He watched him till he was out of sight, then went upstairs again and threw himself face downwards on his bed.

CHAPTER XX

ZOE ended the discussion by driving half an inch of penknife into Coleman's left arm and running out of the flat, slamming the door behind her. Coleman was used to this sort of thing; this sort of thing, indeed, was what he was there for. Carefully he pulled out the penknife which had remained sticking in his arm. He looked at the blade and was relieved to see that it wasn't so dirty as might have been expected. He found some cotton wool, mopped up the blood as it oozed out, and dabbed the wound with iodine. Then he set himself to bandage it up. But to tie a bandage round one's own left arm is not easy. Coleman found it impossible to keep the lint in place, impossible to get the bandage tight enough. At the end of a quarter of an hour he had only succeeded in smearing himself very copiously with blood, and the wound was still unbound. He gave up the attempt and contented himself with swabbing up the blood as it came out.

'And forthwith came there out blood and water,' he said aloud, and looked at the red stain on the cotton wool. He repeated the words again and again, and at the fiftieth repetition burst out laughing.

The bell in the kitchen suddenly buzzed. Who could it be? He went to the front door and opened it. On the landing outside stood a tall slender young woman with slanting Chinese eyes and a wide mouth, elegantly dressed in a black frock piped with white. Keeping the cotton wool still pressed to his bleeding arm, Coleman bowed as gracefully as he could.

'Do come in,' he said. 'You are just in the nick of time. I am on the point of bleeding to death. And forthwith came there out blood and water. Enter, enter,' he added, seeing the young woman still standing irresolutely on the threshold.

'But I wanted to see Mr Coleman,' she said, stammering a little and showing her embarrassment by blushing.

'I am Mr Coleman.' He took the cotton wool for a moment from his arm and looked with the air of a connoisseur at the

446

blood on it. 'But I shall very soon cease to be that individual unless you come and tie up my wounds.'

'But you're not the Mr Coleman I thought you were,' said the young lady, still more embarrassed. 'You have a beard, it is true; but ...'

'Then I must resign myself to quit this life, must I?' He made a gesture of despair, throwing out both hands. 'Out, out, brief Coleman. Out, damned spot,' and he made as though to close the door.

The young lady checked him. 'If you really need tying up,' she said, 'I'll do it, of course. I passed my First-Aid Exam in the war.'

Coleman reopened the door. 'Saved!' he said. 'Come in.'

It had been Rosie's original intention yesterday to go straight on from Mr Mercaptan's to Toto's. She would see him at once, she would ask him what he meant by playing that stupid trick on her. She would give him a good talking to. She would even tell him that she would never see him again. But, of course, if he showed himself sufficiently contrite and reasonably explanatory, she would consent – oh, very reluctantly – to take him back into favour. In the free, unprejudiced circles in which she now moved, this sort of joke, she imagined, was a mere trifle. It would be absurd to quarrel seriously about it. But still, she was determined to give Toto a lesson.

When, however, she did finally leave Mr Mercaptan's delicious boudoir, it was too late to think of going all the way to Pimlico, to the address which Mr Mercaptan had given her. She decided to put it off till the next day.

And so the next day, duly, she had set out for Pimlico – to Pimlico, and to see a man called Coleman! It seemed rather dull and second-rate after Sloane Street and Mr Mercaptan. Poor Toto! – the sparkle of Mr Mercaptan had made him look rather tarnished. That essay on the 'Jus Primæ Noctis' – ah! Walking through the unsavoury mazes of Pimlico, she thought of it, and, thinking of it, smiled. Poor Toto! And also, she mustn't forget, stupid, malicious, idiotic Toto! She had made up her mind exactly what she should say to him; she had even made up her mind what Toto would say to her. And when the scene was over

447

they would go and dine at the Café Royal – upstairs, where she had never been. And she would make him rather jealous by telling him how much she had liked Mr Mercaptan; but not too jealous. Silence is golden, as her father used to say when she used to fly into tempers and wanted to say nasty things to everybody within range. Silence, about some things, is certainly golden.

In the rather gloomy little turning off Lupus Street to which she had been directed, Rosie found the number, found, in the row of bells and cards, the name. Quickly and decidedly she mounted the stairs.

'Well,' she was going to say as soon as she saw him, 'I thought you were a civilized being.' Mr Mercaptan had dropped a hint that Coleman wasn't really civilized; a hint was enough for Rosie. 'But I see,' she would go on, 'that I was mistaken. I don't like to associate with boors.' The fastidious lady had selected him as a young poet, not as a ploughboy.

Well rehearsed, Rosie rang the bell. And then the door had opened on this huge bearded Cossack of a man, who smiled, who looked at her with bright, dangerous eyes, who quoted the Bible and who was bleeding like a pig. There was blood on his shirt, blood on his trousers, blood on his hands, bloody fingermarks on his face; even the blond fringe of his beard, she noticed, was dabbled here and there with blood. It was too much, at first, even for her aristocratic equanimity.

In the end, however, she followed him across a little vestibule into a bright, whitewashed room empty of all furniture but a table, a few chairs and a large box-spring and mattress, which stood like an island in the middle of the floor and served as bed or sofa as occasion required. Over the mantelpiece was pinned a large photographic reproduction of Leonardo's study of the anatomy of love. There were no other pictures on the walls.

'All the apparatus is here,' said Coleman, and he pointed to the table. 'Lint, bandages, cotton wool, iodine, gauze, oiled silk. I have them all ready in preparation for these little accidents.'

'But do you often manage to cut yourself in the arm?' asked Rosie. She took off her gloves and began to undo a fresh packet of lint.

'One gets cut,' Coleman explained. 'Little differences of opinion, you know. If your eye offend you, pluck it out; love your neighbour as yourself. Argal: if his eye offend you – you see? We live on Christian principles here.'

'But who are "we"?' asked Rosie, giving the cut a last dressing of iodine and laying a big square of lint over it.

'Merely myself and – how shall I put it? – my helpmate,' Coleman answered. 'Ah! you're wonderfully skilful at this business,' he went on. 'You're the real hospital-nurse type; all maternal instincts. When pain and anguish wring the brow, an interesting mangle thou, as we used to say in the good old days when the pun and the Spoonerismus were in fashion.'

Rosie laughed. 'Oh, I don't spend all my time tying up wounds,' she said, and turned her eyes for an instant from the bandage. After the first surprise she was feeling her cool self again.

'Brava!' cried Coleman. 'You make them too, do you? Make them first and cure them afterwards in the grand old homœopathic way. Delightful! You see what Leonardo has to say about it.' With his free hand he pointed to the photograph over the mantelpiece.

Rosie, who had noticed the picture when she came into the room, preferred not to look at it too closely a second time. 'I think it's rather revolting,' she said, and was very busy with the bandage.

'Ah! but that's the point, that's the whole point,' said Coleman, and his clear blue eyes were alive with dancing lights. 'That's the beauty of the grand passion. It *is* revolting. You read what the Fathers of the Church have to say about love. They're the men. It was Odo of Cluny, wasn't it, who called woman a *saccus stercoris*, a bag of muck. *Si quis enim considerat quæ intra nares et quæ intra fauces et quæ intra ventrem lateant, sordes ubique reperiet.*' The Latin rumbled like eloquent thunder in Coleman's mouth. '*Et si nec extremis digitis flegma vel stercus tangere patimur, quomodo ipsum stercoris saccum amplecti desideramus.*' He smacked his lips. 'Magnificent!' he said.

'I don't understand Latin,' said Rosie, 'and I'm glad of it. And your bandage is finished. Look.'

449

'Interesting mangle!' Coleman smiled his thanks. 'But Bishop Odo, I fear, wouldn't even have spared you; not even for your good works. Still less for your good looks, which would only have provoked him to dwell with the more insistency on the visceral secrets which they conceal.'

'Really,' Rosie protested. She would have liked to get up and go away, but the Cossack's blue eyes glittered at her with such a strange expression and he smiled so enigmatically, that she found herself still sitting where she was, listening with a disgusted pleasure to his quick talk, his screams of deliberate and appalling laughter.

'Ah!' he exclaimed, throwing up his hands, 'what sensualists these old fellows were! What a real voluptuous feeling they had for dirt and gloom and sordidness and boredom, and all the horrors of vice. They pretended they were trying to dissuade people from vice by enumerating its horrors. But they were really only making it more spicy by telling the truth about it. *O esca vermium, O massa pulveris!* What nauseating embracements! To conjugate the copulative verb, boringly, with a sack of tripes – what could be more exquisitely and piercingly and deliriously vile?' And he threw back his head and laughed; the blood-dabbled tips of his blond beard shook. Rosie looked at them, fascinated with disgust.

'There's blood on your beard,' she felt compelled to say.

'What of it? Why shouldn't there be?' Coleman asked.

Confused, Rosie felt herself blushing. 'Only because it's rather unpl–leasant. I don't know why. But it is.'

'What a reason for immediately falling into my arms!' said Coleman. 'To be kissed by a beard is bad enough at any time. But by a bloody beard – imagine!'

Rosie shuddered.

'After all,' he said, 'what interest or amusement is there in doing the ordinary things in the obvious way? Life *au naturel*.' He shook his head. 'You must have garlic and saffron. Do you believe in God?'

'Not m–much,' said Rosie, smiling.

'I pity you. You must find existence dreadfully dull. As soon as you do, everything becomes a thousand times life-size. Phallic

450

symbols five hundred feet high,' he lifted his hand. 'A row of grinning teeth you could run the hundred yards on.' He grinned at her through his beard. 'Wounds big enough to let a coach-and-six drive into their purulent recesses. Every slightest act eternally significant. It's only when you believe in God, and especially in hell, that you can really begin enjoying life. For instance, when in a few moments you surrender yourself to the importunities of my bloody beard, how prodigiously much more you'd enjoy it if you could believe you were committing the sin against the Holy Ghost – if you kept thinking calmly and dispassionately all the time the affair was going on: All this is not only a horrible sin, it is also ugly, grotesque, a mere defecation, a –'

Rosie held up her hand. 'You're really horrible,' she said. Coleman smiled at her. Still, she did not go.

'He who is not with me is against me,' said Coleman. 'If you can't make up your mind to be with, it's surely better to be positively against than merely negatively indifferent.'

'Nonsense!' exclaimed Rosie feebly.

'When I call my lover a nymphomaniacal dog, she runs the penknife into my arm.'

'Well, do you enjoy it?' asked Rosie.

'Piercingly,' he answered. 'It is at once sordid to the last and lowest degree and infinitely and eternally significant.'

Coleman was silent and Rosie too said nothing. Futilely she wished it *had* been Toto instead of this horrible, dangerous Cossack. Mr Mercaptan ought to have warned her. But then, of course, he supposed that she already knew the creature. She looked up at him and found his bright eyes fixed upon her; he was silently laughing.

'Don't you want to know who I am?' she asked. 'And how I got here?'

Coleman blandly shook his head. 'Not in the very least,' he said.

Rosie felt more helpless, somehow, than ever. 'Why not?' she asked as bravely and impertinently as she could.

Coleman answered with another question. 'Why should I?'

'It would be natural curiosity.'

451

'But I know all I want to know,' he said. 'You are a woman, or, at any rate, you have all the female stigmata. Not too sumptuously well-developed, let me add. You have no wooden legs. You have eyelids that flutter up and down over your eyes like a moving shutter in front of a signalling lamp, spelling out in a familiar code the letters: A.M.O.R., and not, unless I am very much mistaken, those others: C.A.S.T.I.T.A.S. You have a mouth that looks as though it knew how to taste and how to bite. You ...'

Rosie jumped up. 'I'm going away,' she said.

Coleman leaned back in his chair and hallooed with laughter. 'Bite, bite, bite,' he said. 'Thirty-two times.' And he opened and shut his mouth as fast as he could, so that his teeth clicked against one another with a little dry, bony noise. 'Every mouthful thirty-two times. That's what Mr Gladstone said. And surely Mr Gladstone' – he rattled his sharp, white teeth again – 'surely Mr Gladstone should know.'

'Good-bye,' said Rosie from the door.

'Good-bye,' Coleman called back; and immediately afterwards jumped to his feet and made a dash across the room towards her.

Rosie uttered a cry, slipped through the door and, slamming it behind her, ran across the vestibule and began fumbling with the latches of the outer door. It wouldn't open, it wouldn't open. She was trembling; fear made her feel sick. There was a rattling at the door behind her. There was a whoop of laughter, and then the Cossack's hands were on her arms, his face came peering over her shoulder, and the blond beard dabbled with blood prickled against her neck and face.

'Oh, don't, don't, don't!' she implored, turning away her head. Then all at once she began violently crying.

'Tears!' exclaimed Coleman in rapture, 'genuine tears!' He bent eagerly forward to kiss them away, to drink them as they fell. 'What an intoxication,' he said, looking up to the ceiling like a chicken that has taken a sip of water; he smacked his lips.

Sobbing uncontrollably, Rosie had never in all her life felt less like a great, fastidious lady.

CHAPTER XXI

'WELL,' said Gumbril, 'here I am again.'

'Already?' Mrs Viveash had been reduced, by the violence of her headache, to coming home after her luncheon with Piers Cotton for a rest. She had fed her hungry pain on Pyramidon and now she was lying down on the Dufy-upholstered sofa at the foot of her full-length portrait by Jacques-Emile Blanche. Her head was not much better, but she was bored. When the maid had announced Gumbril, she had given word that he was to be let in. 'I'm very ill,' she went on expiringly. 'Look at me,' she pointed to herself, 'and me again.' She waved her hand towards the sizzling brilliance of the portrait. 'Before and after. Like the advertisements, you know. Every picture tells a story.' She laughed faintly, then made a little grimace and, sucking in the breath between her lips, she put her hand to her forehead.

'My poor Myra.' Gumbril pulled up a chair to the sofa and sat there like a doctor at his patient's bedside. 'But before and after what?' he asked, almost professionally.

Mrs Viveash gave an all but imperceptible shrug. 'I don't know,' she said.

'Not influenza, I hope?'

'No, I don't think so.'

'Not love, by any chance?'

Mrs Viveash did not venture another laugh; she contented herself with smiling agonizingly.

'That would have been a just retribution,' Gumbril went on, 'after what you've done to me.'

'What have I done to you?' Mrs Viveash asked, opening wide her pale-blue eyes.

'Merely wrecked my existence.'

'But you're being childish, Theodore. Say what you mean without these grand, silly phrases.' The dying voice spoke with impatience.

'Well, what I mean,' said Gumbril, 'is merely this. You pre-

453

vented me from going to see the only person I ever really wanted to see in my life. And yesterday, when I tried to see her, she was gone. Vanished. And here am I left in the vacuum.'

Mrs Viveash shut her eyes. 'We're all in the vacuum,' she said. 'You'll still have plenty of company, you know.' She was silent for a moment. 'Still, I'm sorry,' she added. 'Why didn't you tell me? And why didn't you just pay no attention to me and go all the same?'

'I didn't tell you,' Gumbril answered, 'because, then, I didn't know. And I didn't go because I didn't want to quarrel with you.'

'Thank you,' said Mrs Viveash, and patted his hand. 'But what are you going to do about it now? Not quarrelling with me is only a rather negative satisfaction, I'm afraid.'

'I propose to leave the country to-morrow morning,' said Gumbril.

'Ah, the classical remedy ... But not to shoot big game, I hope?' She thought of Viveash among the Tikki-tikkis and the tsetses. He was a charming creature; charming, but ... but what?

'Good heavens!' exclaimed Gumbril. 'What do you take me for? Big game!' He leaned back in his chair and began to laugh, heartily, for the first time since he had returned from Robertsbridge, yesterday evening. He had felt then as though he would never laugh again. 'Do you see me in a pith helmet, with an elephant gun?'

Mrs Viveash put her hand to her forehead. 'I see you, Theodore,' she said, 'but I try to think you would look quite normal; because of my head.'

'I go to Paris first,' said Gumbril. 'After that, I don't know. I shall go wherever I think people will buy pneumatic trousers. I'm travelling on business.'

This time, in spite of her head, Mrs Viveash laughed.

'I thought of giving myself a farewell banquet,' Gumbril went on. 'We'll go round before dinner, if you're feeling well enough, that is, and collect a few friends. Then, in profoundest gloom, we'll eat and drink. And in the morning, unshaved, exhausted and filled with disgust, I shall take the train from Victoria, feeling thankful to get out of England.'

454

'We'll do it,' said Mrs Viveash faintly and indomitably from the sofa that was almost genuinely a death-bed. 'And, meanwhile, we'll have a second brew of tea and you shall talk to me.'

The tannin was brought in. Gumbril settled down to talk and Mrs Viveash to listen – to listen and from time to time to dab her brows with eau-de-Cologne, to take a sniff of hartshorn.

Gumbril talked. He talked of the marriage ceremonies of octopuses, of the rites intricately consummated in the submarine green grottos of the Indian Ocean. Given a total of sixteen arms, how many permutations and combinations of caresses? And in the middle of each bunch of arms a mouth like the beak of a macaw.

On the backside of the moon, his friend Umbilikoff, the mystic, used to assure him, the souls of the dead in the form of little bladders – like so much swelled sago – are piled up and piled up till they squash and squeeze one another with an excruciating and ever-growing pressure. In the exoteric world this squeezing on the moon's backside is known, erroneously, as hell. And as for the constellation, Scorpio – he was the first of all constellations to have a proper sort of backbone. For by an effort of the will he ingurgitated his external armour, he compressed and rebuilt it within his body and so became the first vertebrate. This, you may well believe, was a notable day in cosmic history.

The rents in these new buildings in Regent Street and Piccadilly run to as much as three or four pounds a square foot. Meanwhile, all the beauty imagined by Nash has departed, and chaos and barbarism once more reign supreme, even in Regent Street. The ghost of Gumbril Senior stalked across the room.

Who lives longer: the man who takes heroin for two years and dies, or the man who lives on roast beef, water and potatoes till ninety-five? One passes his twenty-four months in eternity. All the years of the beef-eater are lived only in time. 'I can tell you all about heroin,' said Mrs Viveash.

Lady Capricorn, he understood, was still keeping open bed. How Rubens would have admired those silk cushions, those gigantic cabbage roses, those round pink pearls of hers, vaster than those that Captain Nemo discovered in the immemorial

455

oyster! And the warm dry rustle of flesh over flesh as she walks, moving first one leg, then advancing the other.

Talking of octopuses, the swim-bladders of deep-sea fishes are filled with almost absolutely pure oxygen. *C'est la vie* – Gumbril shrugged his shoulders.

In Alpine pastures the grasshoppers start their flight, whizzing like clockwork grasshoppers. And these brown invisible ones reveal themselves suddenly as they skim above the flowers – a streak of blue lightning, a trailing curve of scarlet. Then the overwing shuts down over the coloured wing below and they are once more invisible fiddlers rubbing their thighs, like Lady Capricorn, at the foot of the towering flowers.

Forgers give patina to their mediæval ivories by lending them to stout young Jewesses to wear for a few months hanging, like an amulet, between their breasts.

In Italian cemeteries the family vaults are made of glass and iron, like greenhouses.

Sir Henry Griddle has finally married the hog-faced gentlewoman.

Piero della Francesca's fresco of the Resurrection at San Sepolcro is the most beautiful picture in the world, and the hotel there is far from bad. Scriabine = *le* Tschaikovsky *de nos jours*. The dullest landscape painter is Marchand. The best poet ...

'You bore me,' said Mrs Viveash.

'Must I talk of love, then?' asked Gumbril.

'It looks like it,' Mrs Viveash answered, and closed her eyes.

Gumbril told the anecdote about Jo Peters, Connie Asticot and Jim Baum. The anecdote of Lola Knopf and the Baroness Gnomon. Of Margherita Radicofani, himself, and the Pastor Meyer. Of Lord Cavey and little Toby Nobes. When he had finished these, he saw that Mrs Viveash had gone to sleep.

He was not flattered. But a little sleep would do her headache, he reflected, a world of good. And knowing that if he ceased to speak, she would probably be woken by the sudden blankness of the silence, he went on quietly talking to himself.

'When I'm abroad this time,' he soliloquized, 'I shall really begin writing my autobiography. There's nothing like a hotel bedroom to work in.' He scratched his head thoughtfully and

456

even picked his nose, which was one of his bad habits, when he was alone. 'People who know me,' he went on, 'will think that what I write about the governess cart and my mother and the flowers and so on is written merely because I know in here,' he scratched his head a little harder to show himself that he referred to his brain, 'that that's the sort of thing one ought to write about. They'll think I'm a sort of dingy Romain Rolland, hopelessly trying to pretend that I feel the emotions and have the great spiritual experiences, which the really important people do feel and have. And perhaps they'll be right. Perhaps the Life of Gumbril will be as manifestly an *ersatz* as the Life of Beethoven. On the other hand, they may be astonished to find that it's the genuine article. We shall see.' Gumbril nodded his head slowly, while he transferred two pennies from his right-hand trouser pocket to his left-hand trouser pocket. He was somewhat distressed to find that these coppers had been trespassing among the silver. Silver was for the right-hand, copper for the left. It was one of the laws which it was extremely unlucky to infringe. 'I have a premonition,' he went on, 'that one of these days I may become a saint. An unsuccessful flickering sort of saint, like a candle beginning to go out. As for love – m'yes, m'yes. And as for the people I have met – I shall point out that I have known most of the eminent men in Europe, and that I have said of all of them what I said after my first love affair: Is that all?'

'Did you really say that about your first love affair?' asked Mrs Viveash, who had woken up again.

'Didn't you?'

'No. I said: This *is* all – everything, the universe. In love, it's either all or nothing at all.' She shut her eyes and almost immediately went to sleep again.

Gumbril continued his lullaby-soliloquy.

' "This charming little book." ... *The Scotsman.* "This farrago of obscenity, slander and false psychology." ... *Darlington Echo.* "Mr Gumbril's first cousin is St Francis Xavier, his second cousin is the Earl of Rochester, his third cousin is the Man of Feeling, his fourth cousin is David Hume." ... *Court Journal.*' Gumbril was already tired of this joke. 'When I consider how my light is spent,' he went on, 'when I consider! ... Herr Jesu, as

Fraulein Nimmernein used to exclaim at the critical moment. Consider, dear cow, consider. This is not the time of year for grass to grow. Consider, dear cow, consider, consider.' He got up from his chair and tiptoed across the room to the writing-table. An Indian dagger lay next to the blotting-pad; Mrs Viveash used it as a paper-knife. Gumbril picked it up, executed several passes with it. 'Thumb on the blade,' he said, 'and strike upwards. On guard. Lunge. To the hilt it penetrates. Poniard at the tip' – he ran the blade between his fingers – 'caress by the time it reaches the hilt. Z–zip.' He put down the knife and stopping for a moment to make a grimace at himself in the mirror over the mantelpiece, he went back to his chair.

At seven o'clock Mrs Viveash woke up. She shook her head to feel if the pain were still rolling about loose inside her skull.

'I really believe I'm all right,' she said. She jumped up. 'Come on,' she cried. 'I feel ready for anything.'

'And I feel like so much food for worms,' said Gumbril. 'Still, *Versiam*' *a taẓẓa piena il generoso umor.*' He hummed the Drinking Song out of *Robert the Devil*, and to that ingenuously jolly melody they left the house.

Their taxi that evening cost them several pounds. They made the man drive back and forth, like a shuttle, from one end of London to the other. Every time they passed through Piccadilly Circus Mrs Viveash leant out of the window to look at the sky signs dancing their unceasing St Vitus's dance above the monument to the Earl of Shaftesbury.

'How I adore them!' she said the first time they passed them. 'Those wheels that whizz round till the sparks fly out from under them: that rushing motor, and that lovely bottle of port filling the glass and then disappearing and reappearing and filling it again. Too lovely.'

'Too revolting,' Gumbril corrected her. 'These things are the epileptic symbol of all that's most bestial and idiotic in contemporary life. Look at those beastly things and then look at that.' He pointed to the County Fire Office on the northern side of the Circus. 'There stands decency, dignity, beauty, repose. And there flickers, there gibbers and twitches – what? Restlessness, distraction, refusal to think, anything for an unquiet life ...'

'What a delicious pedant you are!' She turned away from the window, put her hands on his shoulders and looked at him. 'Too exquisitely ridiculous!' And she kissed him.

'You won't force me to change my opinion.' Gumbril smiled at her. '*Eppur' si muove* – I stick to my guns like Galileo. They move and they're horrible.'

'They're me,' said Mrs Viveash emphatically. 'Those things are me.'

They drove first to Lypiatt's mews. Under the Piranesian arch. The clothes-lines looped from window to window across the street might have been those ropes which form so essential and so mysterious a part of the furniture of the Prisons. The place smelt, the children were shouting; the hyena-like laughter of the flappers reverberated between the close-set walls. All Gumbril's sense of social responsibility was aroused in a moment.

Shut up in his room all day, Lypiatt had been writing – writing his whole life, all his ideas and ideals, all for Myra. The pile of scribbled sheets grew higher and higher. Towards evening he made an end; he had written all that he wanted to write. He ate the remains of yesterday's loaf of bread and drank some water; for he realized suddenly that he had been fasting the whole day. Then he composed himself to think; he stretched himself out on the brink of the well and looked down into the eyeless darkness.

He still had his Service revolver. Taking it out of the drawer in which it was kept, he loaded it, he laid it on the packing-case which served him as a table at his bed's head, and stretched himself out on the bed. He lay quite still, his muscles all relaxed, hardly breathing. He imagined himself dead. Derision! there was still the plunge into the well.

He picked up the pistol, looked down the barrel. Black and deep as the well. The muzzle against his forehead was a cold mouth.

There was nothing new to be thought about death. There was not even the possibility of a new thought. Only the old thoughts, the horrible old questions returned.

The cold mouth to his forehead, his finger pressing on the trigger. Already he would be falling, falling. And the annihilating crash would be the same as the far-away sound of death at the bottom of the well. And after that, in the silence? The old question was still the same.

After that, he would lie bleeding. The flies would drink his blood as though it were red honey. In the end the people would come and fetch him away, and the coroner's jury would look at him in the mortuary and pronounce him temporarily insane. Then he would be buried in a black hole, would be buried and decay.

And meanwhile, would there be anything else? There was nothing new to be thought or asked. And there was still no answer.

In the room it began to grow dark; colours vanished, forms ran together. The easel and Myra's portrait were now a single black silhouette against the window. Near and far were fused, become one and continuous in the darkness, became a part of the darkness. Outside the window the pale twilight grew more sombre. The children shouted shrilly, playing their games under the green gas lamps. The mirthless, ferocious laughter of young girls mocked and invited. Lypiatt stretched out his hand and fingered the pistol.

Down below, at his door, he heard a sharp knocking. He lifted his head and listened, caught the sound of two voices, a man's and a woman's. Myra's voice he recognized at once; the other, he supposed, was Gumbril's.

'Hideous to think that people actually live in places like this,' Gumbril was saying. 'Look at those children. It ought to be punishable by law to produce children in this street.'

'They always take me for the Pied Piper,' said Mrs Viveash. Lypiatt got up and crept to the window. He could hear all they said.

'I wonder if Lypiatt's in. I don't see any sign of a light.'

'But he has heavy curtains,' said Mrs Viveash, 'and I know for a fact that he always composes his poetry in the dark. He may be composing poetry.'

Gumbril laughed.

'Knock again,' said Mrs Viveash. 'Poets are always absorbed, you know. And Casimir's always the poet.'

'*Il Poeta* – capital P. Like d'Annunzio in the Italian papers,' said Gumbril. 'Did you know that d'Annunzio has books printed on mackintosh for his bath?' He rapped again at the door. 'I saw it in the *Corriere della Sera* the other day at the club. He reads the *Little Flowers of St Francis* by preference in his bath. And he has a fountain-pen with waterproof ink in the soap-dish, so that he can add a few Fioretti of his own whenever he feels like it. We might suggest that to Casimir.'

Lypiatt stood with folded arms by the window, listening. How lightly they threw his life, his heart, from hand to hand, as though it were a ball and they were playing a game! He thought suddenly of all the times he had spoken lightly and maliciously of other people. His own person had always seemed, on those occasions, sacred. One knew in theory very well that others spoke of one contemptuously – as one spoke of them. In practice – it was hard to believe.

'Poor Casimir!' said Mrs Viveash. 'I'm afraid his show was a failure.'

'I know it was,' said Gumbril. 'Complete and absolute. I told my tame capitalist that he ought to employ Lypiatt for our advertisements. He'd be excellent for those. And it would mean some genuine money in his pocket.'

'But the worst of it is,' said Mrs Viveash, 'that he'll only feel insulted by the suggestion.' She looked up at the window.

'I don't know why,' she went on, 'this house looks most horribly dead. I hope nothing's happened to poor Casimir. I have a most disagreeable feeling that it may have.'

'Ah, this famous feminine intuition,' laughed Gumbril. He knocked again.

'I can't help feeling that he may be lying there dead, or delirious, or something.'

'And I can't help feeling that he must have gone out to dinner. We shall have to give him up, I'm afraid. It's a pity. He's so good with Mercaptan. Like bear and mastiff. Or rather, like bear and poodle, bear and King Charles's spaniel – or whatever those little dogs are that you see ladies in eighteenth-century French engravings taking to bed with them. Let's go.'

'Just knock once again,' said Mrs Viveash. 'He might really be

461

preoccupied, or asleep, or ill.' Gumbril knocked. 'Now listen. Hush.'

They were silent; the children still went on hallooing in the distance. There was a great clop-clopping of horse's feet as a van was backed into a stable door near by. Lypiatt stood motionless, his arms still crossed, his chin on his breast. The seconds passed.

'Not a sound,' said Gumbril. 'He must have gone out.'

'I suppose so,' said Mrs Viveash.

'Come on, then. We'll go and look for Mercaptan.'

He heard their steps in the street below, heard the slamming of the taxi door. The engine was started up. Loud on the first gear, less loud on the second, whisperingly on the third, it moved away, gathering speed. The noise of it was merged with the general noise of the town. They were gone.

Lypiatt walked slowly back to his bed. He wished suddenly that he had gone down to answer the last knock. These voices – at the well's edge he had turned to listen to them; at the well's extreme verge. He lay quite still in the darkness; and it seemed to him at last that he had floated away from the earth, that he was alone, no longer in a narrow dark room, but in an illimitable darkness outside and beyond. His mind grew calmer; he began to think of himself, of all that he had known, remotely, as though from a great way off.

'Adorable lights!' said Mrs Viveash, as they drove once more through Piccadilly Circus.

Gumbril said nothing. He had said all that he had to say last time.

'And there's another,' exclaimed Mrs Viveash, as they passed, near Burlington House, a fountain of Sandeman's port. 'If only they had an automatic jazz band attached to the same mechanism!' she said regretfully.

The Green Park remained solitary and remote under the moon. 'Wasted on us,' said Gumbril, as they passed. 'One should be happily in love to enjoy a summer night under the trees.' He wondered where Emily could be now. They sat in silence; the cab drove on.

Mr Mercaptan, it seemed, had left London. His housekeeper had a long story to tell. A regular Bolshevik had come yesterday, pushing in. And she had heard him shouting at Mr Mercaptan in his own room. And then, luckily, a lady had come and the Bolshevik had gone away again. And this morning Mr Mercaptan had decided, quite sudden like, to go away for two or three days. And it wouldn't surprise her at all if it had something to do with that horrible Bolshevik fellow. Though of course Master Paster hadn't said anything about it. Still, as she'd known him when he was so high and seen him grow up like, she thought she could say she knew him well enough to guess why he did things. It was only brutally that they contrived to tear themselves away.

Secure, meanwhile, behind a whole troop of butlers and footmen, Mr Mercaptan was dining comfortably at Oxhanger with the most faithful of his friends and admirers, Mrs Speegle. It was to Mrs Speegle that he had dedicated his coruscating little 'Loves of the Pachyderms'; for Mrs Speegle it was who had suggested, casually one day at luncheon, that the human race ought to be classified in two main species – the pachyderms, and those whose skin, like her own, like Mr Mercaptan's and a few others, was fine and 'responsive,' as Mr Mercaptan himself put it, 'to all caresses, including those of pure reason.' Mr Mercaptan had taken the casual hint and had developed it, richly. The barbarous pachyderms he divided up into a number of subspecies: steatocephali, acephali, theolaters, industrious Judæorhynci – busy, compact and hard as dung-beetles – Peabodies, Russians and so on. It was all very witty and delicately savage. Mr Mercaptan had a standing invitation at Oxhanger. With dangerous pachyderms like Lypiatt ranging loose about the town, he thought it best to avail himself of it. Mrs Speegle, he knew, would be delighted to see him. And indeed she was. He arrived just at lunch-time. Mrs Speegle and Maisie Furlonger were already at the fish.

'Mercaptan!' Mrs Speegle's soul seemed to be in the name. 'Sit down,' she went on, cooing as she talked, like a ring-dove. There seemed to be singing in every word she spoke. She pointed to a chair next to hers. 'N'you're n'just in time to tell us all about *n'your* Lesbian experiences.'

And Mercaptan, giving vent to his fully orchestrated laugh – squeal and roar together – had sat down and, speaking in French

partly, he nodded towards the butler and the footman, '*à cause
des valets*,' and partly because the language lent itself more
deliciously to this kind of confidences, he had begun there and
then, interrupted and spurred on by the cooing of Mrs Speegle
and the happy shrieks of Maisie Furlonger, to recount at length
and with all the wit in the world his experience among the Isles of
Greece. How delicious it was, he said to himself, to be with really
civilized people! In this happy house it seemed scarcely possible
to believe that such a thing as a pachyderm existed.

But Lypiatt still lay, face upwards, on his bed, floating, it
seemed to himself, far out into the dark emptinesses between the
stars. From those distant abstract spaces he seemed to be looking
impersonally down upon his own body stretched out by the
brink of the hideous well; to be looking back over his own
history. Everything, even his own unhappiness, seemed very
small and beautiful; every frightful convulsion had become no
more than a ripple, and only the fine musical ghost of sound
came up to him from all the shouting.

'We have no luck,' said Gumbril, as they climbed once more
into the cab.

'I'm not sure,' said Mrs Viveash, 'that we haven't really had a
great deal. Did you genuinely want very much to see Mercaptan?'

'Not in the least,' said Gumbril. 'But do you genuinely want
to see me?'

Mrs Viveash drew the corners of her mouth down into a painful smile and did not answer. 'Aren't we going to pass through
Piccadilly Circus again?' she asked. 'I should like to see the
lights again. They give one temporarily the illusion of being
cheerful.'

'No, no,' said Gumbril, 'we are going straight to Victoria.'

'We couldn't tell the driver to ...?'

'Certainly not.'

'Ah, well,' said Mrs Viveash. 'Perhaps one's better without
stimulants. I remember when I was very young, when I first
began to go about at all, how proud I was of having discovered
champagne. It seemed to me wonderful to get rather tipsy.
Something to be exceedingly proud of. And, at the same time,

how much I really disliked wine! Loathed the taste of it. Sometimes, when Calliope and I used to dine quietly together, *tête-à-
tête*, with no awful men about, and no appearances to keep up, we
used to treat ourselves to the luxury of a large lemon-squash, or
even raspberry syrup and soda. Ah, I wish I could recapture the
deliciousness of raspberry syrup.'

Coleman was at home. After a brief delay he appeared himself
at the door. He was wearing pyjamas, and his face was covered
with red-brown smears, the tips of his beard were clotted with
the same dried pigment.

'What have you been doing to yourself?' asked Mrs Viveash.

'Merely washing in the blood of the Lamb,' Coleman
answered, smiling, and his eyes sparkling blue fire, like an electric
machine.

The door on the opposite side of the little vestibule was open.
Looking over Coleman's shoulder, Gumbril could see through
the opening a brightly lighted room and, in the middle of it, like
a large rectangular island, a wide divan. Reclining on the divan
an odalisque by Ingres – but slimmer, more serpentine, more like
a lithe pink length of boa – presented her back. That big, brown
mole on the right shoulder was surely familiar. But when,
startled by the loudness of the voices behind her, the odalisque
turned round – to see in a horribly embarrassing instant that the
Cossack had left the door open and that people could look in,
were looking in, indeed – the slanting eyes beneath their heavy
white lids, the fine aquiline nose, the wide, full-lipped mouth,
though they presented themselves for only the fraction of a
second, were still more recognizable and familiar. For only the
fraction of a second did the odalisque reveal herself definitely
as Rosie. Then a hand pulled feverishly at the counterpane,
the section of buff-coloured boa wriggled and rolled; and,
in a moment, where an odalisque had been, lay only a long
packet under a white sheet, like a jockey with a fractured skull
when they carry him from the course.

Well, really ... Gumbril felt positively indignant, not jealous,
but astonished and righteously indignant.

'Well, when you've finished bathing,' said Mrs Viveash, 'I
hope you'll come and have dinner with us. Coleman was stand-

ing between her and the farther door; Mrs Viveash had seen nothing in the room beyond the vestibule.

'I'm busy,' said Coleman.

'So I see.' Gumbril spoke as sarcastically as he could.

'Do you see?' asked Coleman, and looked round. 'So you do!' He stepped back and closed the door.

'It's Theodore's last dinner,' pleaded Mrs Viveash.

'Not even if it were his last supper,' said Coleman, enchanted to have been given the opportunity to blaspheme a little. 'Is he going to be crucified? Or what?'

'Merely going abroad,' said Gumbril.

'He has a broken heart,' Mrs Viveash explained.

'Ah, the genuine platonic towsers?' Coleman uttered his artificial demon's laugh.

'That's just about it,' said Gumbril, grimly.

Relieved by the shutting of the door from her immediate embarrassment, Rosie threw back a corner of the counterpane and extruded her head, one arm and the shoulder with the mole on it. She looked about her, opening her slanting eyes as wide as she could. She listened with parted lips to the voices that came, muffled now, through the door. It seemed to her as though she were waking up; as though now, for the first time, she were hearing that shattering laugh, were looking now for the first time on these blank, white walls and the one lovely and horrifying picture. Where was she? What did it all mean? Rosie put her hand to her forehead, tried to think. Her thinking was always a series of pictures; one after another the pictures swam up before her eyes, melted again in an instant.

Her mother taking off her pince-nez to wipe them – and at once her eyes were tremulous and vague and helpless. 'You should always let the gentleman get over the stile first,' she said, and put on her glasses again. Behind the glasses her eyes immediately became clear, piercing, steady and efficient. Rather formidable eyes. They had seen Rosie getting over the stile in front of Willie Hoskyns, and there was too much leg.

James reading at his desk; his heavy, round head propped on his hand. She came up behind him and threw her arms round his neck. Very gently, and without turning his eyes from the page, he undid her embrace and, with a little push that was no more than a hint, an implication, signified that he didn't want her. She had gone to her pink room, and cried.

Another time James shook his head and smiled patiently under his moustache. 'You'll never learn,' he said. She had gone to her room and cried that time too.

Another time they were lying in bed together, in the pink bed; only you couldn't see it was pink because there was no light. They were lying very quietly. Warm and happy and remote she felt. Sometimes as it were the physical memory of pleasure plucked at her nerves, making her start, making her suddenly shiver. James was breathing as though he were asleep. All at once he stirred. He patted her shoulder two or three times in a kindly and business-like way. 'I know what that means,' she said, 'when you pat me like that.' And she patted him – pat-pat-pat, very quickly. 'It means you're going to bed.' 'How do you know?' he asked. 'Do you think I don't know you after all this time? I know that pat by heart.' And suddenly all her warm, quiet happiness evaporated; it was all gone. 'I'm only a machine for going to bed with,' she said. 'That's all I am for you.' She felt she would like to cry. But James only laughed and said, 'Nonsense!' and pulled his arm clumsily from underneath her. 'You go to sleep,' he said, and kissed her on the forehead. Then he got out of bed, and she heard him bumping clumsily about in the darkness. 'Damn!' he said once. Then he found the door, opened, and was gone.

She thought of those long stories she used to make up when she went shopping. The fastidious lady; the poets; all the adventures.

Toto's hands were wonderful.

She saw, she heard Mr Mercaptan reading his essay. Poor father, reading aloud from the *Hibbert Journal*!

And now the Cossack, covered with blood. He, too, might read aloud from the *Hibbert Journal* – only backwards, so to speak. She had a bruise on her arm. 'You think there's nothing inherently wrong and disgusting in it?' he had asked. 'There is, I tell you.' He had laughed and kissed her and stripped off her clothes and caressed her. And she had cried, she had struggled, she had tried to turn away; and in the end she had been over-come by a pleasure more piercing and agonizing than anything she had ever felt before. And all the time Coleman had hung over her, with his blood-stained beard, smiling into her face, and whispering, 'Horrible, horrible, infamous and shameful.' She lay in a kind of stupor. Then, suddenly there had been that ringing. The Cossack had left her. And now she was awake again, and it was horrible, it was shameful. She shuddered; she jumped out of bed and began as quickly as she could to put on her clothes.

'Really, really, won't you come?' Mrs Viveash was insisting. She was not used to people saying no when she asked, when she insisted. She didn't like it.

'No.' Coleman shook his head. 'You may be having the last supper. But I have a date here with the Magdalen.'

'Oh, a woman,' said Viveash. 'But why didn't you say so before?'

'Well, as I'd left the door open,' said Coleman, 'I thought it was unnecessary.'

'Fie,' said Mrs Viveash. 'I find this very repulsive. Let's go away.' She plucked Gumbril by the sleeve.

'Good-bye,' said Coleman, politely. He shut the door after them and turned back across the little hall.

'What! Not thinking of going?' he exclaimed, as he came in. Rosie was sitting down on the edge of the bed pulling on her shoes.

'Go away,' she said. 'You disgust me.'

'But that's splendid,' Coleman declared. 'That's all as it should be, all as I intended.' He sat down beside her on the divan. 'Really,' he said, admiringly, 'what exquisite legs!'

Rosie would have given anything in the world to be back again in Bloxam Gardens. Even if James did live in his books all the time ... Anything in the world.

'This time,' said Mrs Viveash, 'we simply must go through Piccadilly Circus.'

'It'll only be about two miles farther.'

'Well, that isn't much.'

Gumbril leaned out and gave the word to the driver.

'And besides, I like driving about like this,' said Mrs Viveash.

468

'I like driving for driving's sake. It's like the Last Ride Together. Dear Theodore!' She laid her hand on his.

'Thank you,' said Gumbril, and kissed it.

The little cab buzzed along down the empty Mall. They were silent. Through the thick air one could see the brightest of the stars. It was one of those evenings when men feel that truth, goodness and beauty are one. In the morning, when they commit their discovery to paper, when others read it written there, it looks wholly ridiculous. It was one of those evenings when love is once more invented for the first time. That, too, seems a little ridiculous, sometimes, in the morning.

'Here are the lights again,' said Mrs Viveash. 'Hop, twitch, flick – yes, genuinely an illusion of jollity, Theodore. Genuinely.'

Gumbril stopped the cab. 'It's after half-past eight,' he said. 'At this rate we shall never get anything to eat. Wait a minute.'

He ran into Appenrodt's, and came back in a moment with a packet of smoked salmon sandwiches, a bottle of white wine and a glass.

'We have a long way to go,' he explained, as he got into the taxi.

They ate their sandwiches, they drank their wine. The taxi drove on and on.

'This is positively exhilarating,' said Mrs Viveash, as they turned into the Edgware Road.

Polished by the wheels and shining like an old and precious bronze, the road stretched before them, reflecting the lamps. It had the inviting air of a road which goes on for ever.

'They used to have such good peep-shows in this street,' Gumbril tenderly remembered: 'Little back shops where you paid twopence to see the genuine mermaid, which turned out to be a stuffed walrus, and the tattooed lady, and the dwarf, and the living statuary, which one always hoped, as a boy, was really going to be rather naked and thrilling, but which was always the most pathetic of unemployed barmaids, dressed in the thickest of pink Jaeger.'

'Do you think there'd be any of those now?' asked Mrs Viveash.

Gumbril shook his head. 'They've moved on with the march

of civilization. But where?' He spread out his hands interrogatively. 'I don't know which direction civilization marches –
whether north towards Kilburn and Golders Green, or over the
river to the Elephant, to Clapham and Sydenham and all those
other mysterious places. But, in any case, high rents have marched
up here; there are no more genuine mermaids in the Edgware
Road. What stories we shall be able to tell our children!'

'Do you think we shall ever have any?' Mrs Viveash asked.

'One can never tell.'

'I should have thought one could,' said Mrs Viveash. Children
– that would be the most desperate experiment of all. The most
desperate, and perhaps the only one having any chance of being
successful. History recorded cases ... On the other hand, it recorded other cases that proved the opposite. She had often
thought of this experiment. There were so many obvious reasons
for not making it. But some day, perhaps – she always put it off,
like that.

The cab had turned off the main road into quieter and darker
streets.

'Where are we now?' asked Mrs Viveash.

'Penetrating into Maida Vale. We shall soon be there. Poor
old Shearwater!' He laughed. Other people in love were always
absurd.

'Shall we find him in, I wonder?' It would be fun to see Shearwater again. She liked to hear him talking, learnedly, and like a
child. But when the child is six feet high and three feet wide and
two feet thick, when it tries to plunge head first into your life –
then, really, no ... 'But what did you want with me?' he had
asked. 'Just to look at you,' she answered. Just to look; that was
all. Music hall, not boudoir.

'Here we are.' Gumbril got out and rang the second floor
bell.

The door was opened by an impertinent-looking little maid.

'Mr Shearwater's at the lavatory,' she said, in answer to Gumbril's question.

'Laboratory?' he suggested.

'At the 'ospital.' That made it clear.

'And is Mrs Shearwater at home?' he asked maliciously.

The little maid shook her head. 'I expected 'er, but she didn't come back to dinner.'

'Would you mind giving her a message when she does come in,' said Gumbril. 'Tell her that Mr Toto was very sorry he hadn't time to speak to her when he saw her this evening in Pimlico.'

'Mr who?'

'Mr Toto.'

'Mr Toto is sorry 'e 'adn't the time to speak to Mrs Shearwater when 'e saw 'er in Pimlico this evening. Very well, sir.'

'You won't forget?' said Gumbril.

'No, I won't forget.'

He went back to the cab and explained that they had drawn blank once more.

'I'm rather glad,' said Mrs Viveash. 'If we ever did find anybody, it would mean the end of this Last-Ride-Together feeling. And that would be sad. And it's a lovely night. And really, for the moment, I feel I can do without my lights. Suppose we just drove for a bit now.'

But Gumbril would not allow that. 'We haven't had enough to eat yet,' he said, and he gave the cabman Gumbril Senior's address.

Gumbril Senior was sitting on his little iron balcony among the dried-out pots that had once held geraniums, smoking his pipe and looking earnestly out into the darkness in front of him. Clustered in the fourteen plane-trees of the square, the starlings were already asleep. There was no sound but the rustling of the leaves. But sometimes, every hour or so, the birds would wake up. Something – perhaps it might be a stronger gust of wind, perhaps some happy dream of worms, some nightmare of cats simultaneously dreamed by all the flock together – would suddenly rouse them. And then they would all start to talk at once, at the tops of their shrill voices – for perhaps half a minute. Then in an instant they all went to sleep again and there was once more no sound but the rustling of the shaken leaves. At these moments Mr Gumbril would lean forward, would strain his eyes and his ears in the hope of seeing, of hearing something – something significant, explanatory, satisfying. He never did, of course; but that in no way diminished his happiness.

Mr Gumbril received them on his balcony with courtesy.

'I was just thinking of going in to work,' he said. 'And now you come and give me a good excuse for sitting out here a little longer. I'm delighted.'

Gumbril Junior went downstairs to see what he could find in the way of food. While he was gone, his father explained to Mrs Viveash the secrets of the birds. Enthusiastically, his light floss of grey hair floating up and falling again about his head as he pointed and gesticulated, he told her; the great flocks assembled – goodness only knew where! – they flew across the golden sky, detaching here a little troop, there a whole legion, they flew until at last all had found their appointed resting-places and there were no more to fly. He made this nightly flight sound epical, as though it were a migration of peoples, a passage of armies.

'And it's my firm belief,' said Gumbril Senior, adding notes to his epic, 'that they make use of some sort of telepathy, some kind of direct mind-to-mind communication between themselves. You can't watch them without coming to that conclusion.'

'A charming conclusion,' said Mrs Viveash.

'It's a faculty,' Gumbril Senior went on, 'we all possess, I believe. All we animals.' He made a gesture which included himself, Mrs Viveash and the invisible birds among the plane-trees. 'Why don't we use it more? You may well ask. For the simple reason, my dear young lady, that half our existence is spent in dealing with things that have no mind – things with which it is impossible to hold telepathic communication. Hence the development of the five senses. I have eyes that preserve me from running into the lamp-post, ears that warn me I'm in the neighbourhood of Niagara. And having made these instruments very efficient, I use them in holding converse with other beings having a mind. I let my telepathic faculty lie idle, preferring to employ an elaborate and cumbrous arrangement of symbols in order to make my thought known to you through your senses. In certain individuals, however, the faculty is naturally so well-developed – like the musical, or the mathematical, or the chess-playing faculties in other people – that they cannot help entering into direct communication with other minds, whether they want to or not. If we knew a good method of educating and drawing out the latent faculty, most of us could make ourselves moderately efficient telepaths; just as most of us can make ourselves into moderate musicians, chess players and mathematicians. There would also be a few, no doubt, who could never communicate directly. Just as there are a few who cannot recognize "Rule Britannia" or Bach's Concerto in D minor for two violins, and a few who cannot comprehend the nature of an algebraical symbol. Look at the general development of the mathematical and musical faculties only within the last two hundred years. By the twenty-first century, I believe, we shall all be telepaths. Meanwhile, these delightful birds have forestalled us. Not having the wit to invent a language or an expressive pantomime, they contrive to communicate such simple thoughts as they have, directly and instantaneously. They all go to sleep at once, wake at once, say the same thing at once; they turn all at once when they're flying. Without a leader, without a word of command, they do everything together, in complete unison. Sitting here in the evenings, I sometimes fancy I can feel their thoughts striking against my own. It has happened to me once or twice: that I have known a second before it actually happened, that the birds were going to wake up and begin their half-minute of chatter in the dark. Wait! Hush.' Gumbril Senior threw back his head, pressed his hand over his mouth, as though by commanding silence on himself he could command it on the whole world. 'I believe they're going to wake now. I feel it.'

He was silent. Mrs Viveash looked towards the dark trees and listened. A full minute passed. Then the old gentleman burst out happily laughing.

'Completely wrong!' he said. 'They've never been more soundly asleep.' Mrs Viveash laughed too. 'Perhaps they all changed their minds, just as they were waking up,' she suggested.

Gumbril Junior reappeared; glasses clinked as he walked, and there was a little rattle of crockery. He was carrying a tray.

'Cold beef,' he said, 'and salad and a bit of a cold apple-pie. It might be worse.'

They drew up chairs to Gumbril Senior's work-table, and

473

there, among the letters and the unpaid bills and the sketchy elevations of archiducal palaces, they ate the beef and the apple-pie, and drank the one-and-ninepenny *vin ordinaire* of the house. Gumbril Senior, who had already supped, looked on at them from the balcony.

'Did I tell you,' said Gumbril Junior, 'that we saw Mr Porteous's son the other evening – very drunk?'

Gumbril Senior threw up his hands. 'If you knew the calamities that young imbecile has been the cause of!'

'What's he done?'

'Gambled away I don't know how much borrowed money. And poor Porteous can't afford anything – even now.' Mr Gumbril shook his head and clutched and combed his beard. 'It's a fearful blow, but of course, Porteous is very steadfast and serene and ... There!' Gumbril Senior interrupted himself, holding up his hand. 'Listen!'

In the fourteen plane-trees the starlings had suddenly woken up.

There was a wild outburst, like a stormy sitting in the Italian Parliament. Then all was silent. Gumbril Senior listened, enchanted. His face, as he turned back towards the light, revealed itself all smiles. His hair seemed to have blown loose of its own accord, from within, so to speak; he pushed it into place.

'You heard them?' he asked Mrs Viveash. 'What can they have to say to one another, I wonder, at this time of night?'

'And did you feel they were going to wake up?' Mrs Viveash inquired.

'No,' said Gumbril Senior with candour.

'When we've finished,' Gumbril Junior spoke with his mouth full, 'you must show Myra your model of London. She'd adore it – except that it has no electric sky-signs.'

His father looked all of a sudden very much embarrassed. 'I don't think it would interest Mrs Viveash much,' he said.

'Oh, yes it would. Really,' she declared.

'Well, as a matter of fact it isn't here.' Gumbril Senior pulled with fury at his beard.

'Not here? But what's happened to it?'

Gumbril Senior wouldn't explain. He just ignored his son's

474

question and began to talk once more about the starlings. Later on, however, when Gumbril and Mrs Viveash were preparing to go, the old man drew him apart into a corner and began to whisper the explanation.

'I didn't want to blare it about in front of strangers,' he said, as though it were a question of the housemaid's illegitimate baby or a repair to the water-closet. 'But the fact is, I've sold it. The Victoria and Albert had wind that I was making it; they've been wanting it all the time. And I've let them have it.'

'But why?' Gumbril Junior asked in a tone of astonishment. He knew with what a paternal affection – no, more than paternal; for he was sure that his father was more whole-heartedly attached to his models than his son – with what pride he regarded these children of his spirit.

Gumbril Senior sighed. 'It's all that young imbecile,' he said.

'What young imbecile?'

'Porteous's son, of course. You see, poor Porteous has had to sell his library, among other things. You don't know what that means to him. All these precious books. And collected at the price of such hardships. I thought I'd like to buy a few of the best ones back for him. They gave me quite a good price at the Museum.' He came out of his corner and hurried across the room to help Mrs Viveash with her cloak. 'Allow me, allow me,' he said.

Slowly and pensively Gumbril Junior followed him. Beyond good and evil? Below good and evil? The name of earwig ... The tubby pony trotted. The wild columbines suspended, among the shadows of the hazel copse, hooked spurs, helmets of aerial purple. The Twelfth Sonata of Mozart was insecticide; no earwigs could crawl through that music. Emily's breasts were firm and pointed and she had slept at last without a tremor. In the starlight, good, true and beautiful became one. Write the discovery in books – in books *quos*, in the morning, *legimus cacantes*. They descended the stairs. The cab was waiting outside.

'The Last Ride again,' said Mrs Viveash.

'Golgotha Hospital, Southwark,' said Gumbril to the driver and followed her into the cab.

'Drive, drive, drive,' repeated Mrs Viveash. 'I like your

father, Theodore. One of these days he'll fly away with the birds. And how nice it is of those starlings to wake themselves up like that in the middle of the night, merely to amuse him. Considering how unpleasant it is to be woken in the night. Where are we going?'

'We're going to look at Shearwater in his laboratory.'

'Is that a long way away?'

'Immensely,' said Gumbril.

'Thank God for that,' Mrs Viveash piously and expiringly breathed.

CHAPTER XXII

SHEARWATER sat on his stationary bicycle, pedalling unceasingly like a man in a nightmare. The pedals were geared to a little wheel under the saddle and the rim of the wheel rubbed, as it revolved, against a brake, carefully adjusted to make the work of the pedaller hard, but not impossibly hard. From a pipe which came up through the floor issued a little jet of water which played on the brake and kept it cool. But no jet of water played on Shearwater. It was his business to get hot. He did get hot.

From time to time his dog-faced young friend, Lancing, came and looked through the window of the experimenting chamber to see how he was getting on. Inside that little wooden house, which might have reminded Lancing, if he had had a literary turn of mind, of the Box in which Gulliver left Brobdingnag, the scenes of intimate life were the same every time he looked in. Shearwater was always at his post on the saddle of the nightmare bicycle, pedalling, pedalling. The water trickled over the brake. And Shearwater sweated. Great drops of sweat came oozing out from under his hair, ran down over his forehead, hung beaded on his eyebrows, ran into his eyes, down his nose, along his cheeks, fell like raindrops. His thick bull-neck was wet; his whole naked body, his arms and legs streamed and shone. The sweat poured off him and was caught as it rained down in a waterproof sheet, to trickle down its sloping folds into a large glass receptacle which stood under a hole in the centre of the sheet at the focal point where all its slopes converged. The automatically controlled heating apparatus in the basement kept the temperature in the box high and steady. Peering through the damp-dimmed panes of the window, Lancing noticed with satisfaction that the mercury stood unchangingly at twenty-seven point five Centigrade. The ventilators at the side and top of the box were open; Shearwater had air enough. Another time, Lancing reflected, they'd make the box air-tight and see the effect of a little carbon dioxide poisoning on top of excessive sweating. It

477

might be very interesting, but to-day they were concerned with sweating only. After seeing that the thermometer was steady, that the ventilators were properly open, the water was still trickling over the brake, Lancing would tap at the window. And Shearwater, who kept his eyes fixed straight before him, as he pedalled slowly and unremittingly along his nightmare road, would turn his head at the sound.

'All right?' Lancing's lips moved and his eyebrows went up inquiringly.

Shearwater would nod his big, round head, and the sweat-drops, suspended on his eyebrows and his moustache, would fall like little liquid fruits shaken suddenly by the wind.

'Good,' and Lancing would go back to his thick German book under the reading-lamp at the other end of the laboratory.

Constant as the thermometer Shearwater pedalled steadily and slowly on. With a few brief halts for food and rest, he had been pedalling ever since lunch-time. At eleven he would go to bed on a shake-down in the laboratory and at nine to-morrow morning he would re-enter the box and start pedalling again. He would go on all to-morrow and the day after; and after that, as long as he could stand it. One, two, three, four. Pedal, pedal, pedal ... He must have travelled the equivalent of sixty or seventy miles this afternoon. He would be getting on for Swindon. He would be nearly at Portsmouth. He would be past Cambridge, past Oxford. He would be nearly at Harwich, pedalling through the green and golden valleys where Constable used to paint. He would be at Winchester by the bright stream. He would have ridden through the beech woods of Arundel out into the sea ...

In any case he was far away, he was escaping. And Mrs Viveash followed, walking swayingly along on feet that seemed to tread between two abysses, at her leisure. Pedal, pedal. The hydrogen ion concentration in the blood ... Formidably, calmly, her eyes regarded. The lids cut off an arc of those pale circles. When she smiled, it was a crucifixion. The coils of her hair were copper serpents. Her small gestures loosened enormous fragments of the universe and at the faint dying sound of her voice they had fallen in ruins about him. His world was no longer safe,

478

it had ceased to stand on its foundations. Mrs Viveash walked among his ruins and did not even notice them. He must build up again. Pedal, pedal. He was not merely escaping; he was working a building machine. It must be built with proportion; with proportion, the old man had said. The old man appeared in the middle of the nightmare road in front of him, clutching his beard. Proportion, proportion. There were first a lot of dirty rocks lying about; then there was St Paul's. These bits of his life had to be built up proportionably.

There was work. And there was talk about work and ideas. And there were men who could talk about work and ideas. But so far as he had been concerned that was about all they could do. He would have to find out what else they did; it was interesting. And he would have to find out what other men did; men who couldn't talk about work and not much about ideas. They had as good kidneys as any one else.

And then there were women.

On the nightmare road he remained stationary. The pedals went round and round under his driving feet; the sweat ran off him. He was escaping, and yet he was also drawing nearer. He would have to draw nearer. 'Woman, what have I to do with you?' Not enough; too much.

Not enough – he was building her in, a great pillar next to the pillar of work.

Too much – he was escaping. If he had not caged himself here in this hot box, he would have run out after her, to throw himself – all in fragments, all dissipated and useless – in front of her. And she wanted none of him. But perhaps it would be worse, perhaps it would be far, far worse if she did.

The old man stood in the road before him, clutching his beard, crying out, 'Proportion, proportion.' He trod and trod at his building machine, working up the pieces of his life, steadily, unremittingly working them into a proportionable whole, into a dome that should hang, light, spacious and high, as though by a miracle, on the empty air. He trod and trod, escaping, mile after mile into fatigue, into wisdom. He was at Dover now, pedalling across the Channel. He was crossing a dividing gulf and there would be safety on the other side; the cliffs of Dover were already behind him. He turned his head as though to look back at them; the drops of sweat were shaken from his eyebrows, from the shaggy fringes of his moustache. He turned his head from the blank wooden wall in front of him over his left shoulder. A face was looking through the observation window behind him – a woman's face.

It was the face of Mrs Viveash.

Shearwater uttered a cry and at once turned back again. He redoubled his pedalling. One, two, three, four – furiously he rushed along the nightmare road. She was haunting him now in hallucinations. She was pursuing and she was gaining on him. Will, wisdom, resolution and understanding were of no avail, then? But there was always fatigue. The sweat poured down his face, streamed down the indented runnel of his spine, along the seam at the meeting-place of the ribs. His loin-cloth was wringing wet. The drops pattered continuously on the waterproof sheet. His calves and the muscles of his thighs ached with pedalling. One, two, three, four – he trod round a hundred times with either foot. After that he ventured to turn his head once more. He was relieved, and at the same time he was disappointed, to see that there was now no face at the window. He had exorcised the hallucination. He settled down to a more leisurely pedalling.

In the annexe of the laboratory the animals devoted to the service of physiology were woken by the sudden opening of the door, the sudden irruption of light. The albino guinea-pigs peered through the meshes of their hutch and their red eyes were like the rear-lights of bicycles. The pregnant she-rabbits lolloped out and shook their ears and pointed their tremulous noses towards the door. The cock into which Shearwater had engrafted an ovary came out, not knowing whether to crow or cluck.

'When he's with hens,' Lancing explained to his visitors, 'he thinks he's a cock. When he's with a cock, he's convinced he's a pullet.'

The rats who were being fed on milk from a London dairy came tumbling from their nest with an anxious hungry squeaking. They were getting thinner and thinner every day; in a few days they would be dead. But the old rat, whose diet was Grade A milk from the country, hardly took the trouble to move. He was as fat and sleek as a brown furry fruit, ripe to bursting. No skim and chalky water, no dried dung and tubercle bacilli for him. He was in clover. Next week, however, the fates were plotting to give him diabetes artificially.

In their glass pagoda the little black axolotls crawled, the heraldry of Mexico, among a scanty herbage. The beetles, who had had their heads cut off and replaced by the heads of other beetles, darted uncertainly about, some obeying their heads, some their genital organs. A fifteen-year-old monkey, rejuvenated by the Steinach process, was discovered by the light of Lancing's electric torch, shaking the bars that separated him from the green-furred, bald-rumped, bearded young beauty in the next cage. He was gnashing his teeth with thwarted passion.

Lancing expounded to the visitors all the secrets. The vast, unbelievable, fantastic world opened out as he spoke. There were tropics, there were cold seas busy with living beings, there were forests full of horrible trees, silence and darkness. There were ferments and infinitesimal poisons floating in the air. There were leviathans suckling their young, there were flies and worms, there were men, living in cities, thinking, knowing good and evil. And all were changing continuously, moment by moment, and each remained all the time itself by virtue of some unimaginable enchantment. They were all alive. And on the other side of the courtyard beyond the shed in which the animals slept or uneasily stirred, in the huge hospital that went up sheer like a windowed cliff into the air, men and women were ceasing to be themselves, or were struggling to remain themselves. They were dying, they were struggling to live. The other windows looked on to the river. The lights of London Bridge were on the right, of Blackfriars to the left. On the opposite shore, St Paul's floated up as though self-supported in the moonlight. Like time the river flowed, silent and black. Gumbril and Mrs Viveash leaned their elbows on the sill and looked out. Like time the river flowed, stanchlessly, as though from a wound in the world's side. For a long time they were silent. They looked out, without speaking, across the flow of time, at the stars, at the human symbol hanging miraculously in the moonlight. Lancing had gone back to his German book; he had no time to waste looking out of windows.

'To-morrow,' said Gumbril at last, meditatively.

'To-morrow,' Mrs Viveash interrupted him, 'will be as awful as to-day.' She breathed it like a truth from beyond the grave prematurely revealed, expiringly from her death-bed within.

'Come, come,' protested Gumbril.

In his hot box Shearwater sweated and pedalled. He was across the Channel now; he felt himself safe. Still he trod on; he would be at Amiens by midnight if he went on at this rate. He was escaping, he had escaped. He was building up his strong light dome of life. Proportion, cried the old man, proportion! And it hung there, proportioned and beautiful in the dark, confused horror of his desires, solid and strong and durable among his broken thoughts. Time flowed darkly past.

'And now,' said Mrs Viveash, straightening herself up, and giving herself a little shake, 'now we'll drive to Hampstead and have a look at Piers Cotton.'